Persevere

A troubled man, a woman's promise

Pearlie D.

Copyright © 2022 **Pearlie D. Publishing**

All rights reserved. No part of this publication may be reproduced, distributed, or transmitted in any form or by any means, including photocopying, recording, or other electronic or mechanical methods, without the prior written permission of the publisher, except in the case of brief quotations embodied in critical reviews and certain other noncommercial uses permitted by copyright law. For permission requests, write to the publisher, addressed "Attention: Book Rights and Permission," at the address below.

Published in the United States of America

ISBN 978-1-958518-21-2 (SC)
ISBN 978-1-959173-03-8 (HC)
ISBN 978-1-958518-22-9 (Ebook)

Pearlie D. Publishing
222 West 6th Street
Suite 400, San Pedro, CA, 90731
www.stellarliterary.com

Order Information and Rights Permission:

Quantity sales. Special discounts might be available on quantity purchases by corporations, associations, and others. For details, contact the publisher at the address above.

For Book Rights Adaptation and other Rights Permission. Call us at toll-free 1-888-945-8513 or send us an email at admin@stellarliterary.com.

Contents

Acknowledgments

Chapter 1

Chapter 2

Chapter 3

Chapter 4

Chapter 5

Chapter 6

Chapter 7

Chapter 8

Chapter 9

Chapter 10

Chapter 11

Chapter 12

Chapter 13

Chapter 14

Chapter 15

Chapter 16

Chapter 17

Chapter 18

Chapter 19

Chapter 20

Chapter 21

Chapter 22

Chapter 23

Chapter 25

Chapter 26

Chapter 27

Chapter 28

Chapter 29

Chapter 30

Chapter 31

Chapter 32

Chapter 33

Thank you to my family, friends, and readers I dedicate Persevere to you. There is not a person alive today that has not been through something. Preserving is a way of life for most. Just know that you are not alone in your journey, no two people manage struggles the same. Always remember, to trust God because troubles don't last always. Remember that God lives within you, and you have the energy to co-create your lives. I challenge you to take your eyes off man and keep them steadfast on God. Stand strong, keep your head up with Love and Respect Persevere.

Acknowledgments

First and foremost, I want to recognize God, my father, my comforter, and my strength, for keeping me and allowing me to share the energy of the Universe. God has provided strength and has given me the wisdom to endure the path that he has set for me. Without him, nothing is possible; but with him, all things are certanly possible. My God is my Lord and Savior. He has helped me through some trying times, and he is indeed my Alpha and Omega.

To Keith Dunford, an amazing man. I thank God for you every day, You will always be my best friend. You have seen me at my strongest and supported me at my weakest. I am so thankful that God has allowed you to be in my life. There will always be a place in my heart for you. I will always be there for you. I mean that.

To my beautiful daughter, Hannah Dunford, the girl I love the most. You will always be Mommy's little woman and Daddy's little girl. You are a mother's dream come true. As you venture into the world know that I will always be with you one way or the other because you my sweet girl are worth it. There is never a mountain too high that I can't reach you know that.

To my wonderful son and friend, Brandon Flack, you have always been my superman. I hope that I am all you expect a mother to be and more. Let God's will be done in your life and know that I love you more than you can imagine. You have been in my life the longest and have had to stand tall while I Persevered thank you for understanding and supporting me.

To all my readers, thank you for allowing me to step into your lives to show you how love and God can overcome any struggles you may experience. I hope you enjoy the strength as well as the courage that Victoria must share through her trials in her life. Understand that God has a path for everyone. Allow God to fight your battles. He loves all of us; nothing catches him by surprise. He was, he is, and he always will be your beginning, as well as the ending. Nothing is ever over until God says it's over. Let him have his way. All battles can be won if God is kept first. Persevere.

Chapter 1

"I'll just wait here, Victoria," my father said in a mellow voice. I took the last box from my hope chest out of the back of the truck while he sat there on the tailgate cleaning his fingernails with his pocketknife.

"Tell your mother I am ready when she is," he said, looking down at the pocketknife. When my father brought out his handy-dandy pocketknife to clean his already-clean fingernails, that always told me that he had something on his mind.

What could I say to him at that point? I saw my dad as being as strong as an ox, but I knew when it came to me, especially now that I was leaving home, he was as weak as a kitten. In his mind, he was losing his little girl. In my mind, I was a young woman starting my life's journey. Without saying a word, I just put down the box, reached over, gave him our infamous snug-bug hug, and whispered, "I love you, Daddy." Choking back tears of my own, I picked up the box and headed into my apartment. As I reached the doorway, he called out to me and said, "The doors are always open if you ever want to come back, you know." Giving him an understanding nod, I headed inside.

Daddy didn't talk as much as he joked around, but he loved his family. He was a man who only talked when he had something that needed to be said. Daddy was a simple man. He worked hard at a manufacturing plant, and he was a devoted father and husband. He spent most of his time in his little shed at the house, stealing a little nip as he would call it, to relax himself. He spent other free time working in his garden or cutting firewood for the winter months. I knew I was once his little girl, but I had now blossomed into a young woman. I was finally moving out of my parents' home and on my own, preparing to start the life that was dealt to me.

"That's it," I said to my mother, trying to sound cheerful as I entered the doorway to my tiny one-bedroom apartment. "That's the last of the boxes."

Mother turned to look at me with tearful eyes. She said, "Please let me stay and help you get these things in order."

"Now, Mother, you and Daddy have helped me enough. I can finish on my own," I said, trying not to hurt her feelings. "If I run into a snag, you will be the first one I call. Now go," I protested in a teasing manner. "Daddy's waiting."

Although she was obviously hesitant, Mother did as I asked. She too looked at me as being her little girl. I had big plans for my life's journey, and I had to make my parents let go in order for me to put those plans in action. I walked her out to the truck, where Daddy sat waiting.

It was a bittersweet moment, but I was anxious to set my life's wheels in motion. We were a close family, a family that had shared a lot of joy. Momma was a God-fearing woman who believed that without God in your life, there was no purpose. She was a firm believer that God had a purpose for everyone, and if it was in his will, then it would always work out for the good.

She went to church faithfully every Sunday. She was a well-respected Sunday schoolteacher who was devoted to God and the church as well as to being a mother and a wife. That is the reason Daddy felt he had to steal a nip; he didn't want to disrespect Momma or her beliefs. Even though I was raised on Momma's God-fearing beliefs, I didn't go to church as often as I should have. I only went from time to time, not as much as my mother would have wanted but enough to pacify her. I spent most of my spare time writing in my journal at the willow tree. I sometimes wished I had a brother or a sister, yet I was content with the way our family was.

I knew my parents were optimistic for my future. I was their only hope for success; there was not another child to pick up the pieces. In my heart I knew that if I failed at life's challenges, they would think they had failed as parents. Even though Momma didn't force me to go to church, she would sometimes come in my room with her Bible, and we would discuss some of the scriptures that she would read. The trivial things that we did together is what made us so close. If it was up to my parents, I would probably never have left their home.

Daddy interrupted my thoughts by starting up the truck, which prompted me to look at their sad faces. "It's hard for me too, guys," I said, looking at the two and knowing that they were dreading this day, "but it's time. Nothing will change. I will still be there to help prepare for Sunday dinner," I said, looking at Momma, "and I will still move the dirt over the holes after you and I plant the garden," I said to my father. At least those were my intentions. "In time it will be like I never left." Trying to reassure them that this was the right decision, I added, "You raised me well. You are still my parents, but now is the time that we can also be friends."

Momma chimed in, "Just promise me, Victoria, no matter what your choices are, you promise me that you will keep God in the midst of it all."

"I promise," I said, looking at her tearstained face. Thinking again those are my intentions. "Well, I better get inside. There is a lot to do." By the way they were acting, one would have thought that I was moving across the universe, but I was only a few blocks away.

Daddy put the truck in reverse and slowly backed out of my driveway, almost as if he wanted me to change my mind and hop on the back of the truck. I hurried back inside so I wouldn't start tears of my own. Not tears from wanting to change my mind, but tears from seeing the hurt in their faces. Yet I was glad that I was finally an adult, able to make my own choices, able to do whatever without the fear of disappointing them, without the fear of not being good enough. I was sure I was going to make mistakes, but now I had the opportunity to fix my mistakes without the fear of them finding out, without the fear of letting them down.

Looking around my apartment, I suddenly felt a sense of sadness. The dejection that came over me took my mind long enough for me to end up in front of my mirror. I was at the tender age of nineteen. I hadn't dated nor had a boyfriend since him. Up until now, I didn't have a desire to. My life started with him, and before I ventured in another direction, I wanted to wait to see if our paths would ever cross again, giving us a chance to finish what we started. My heart had not yet healed from that terrible day that our love was suddenly taken from us, the day that it was ended by something beyond our control. It had been two years since I saw him, and I was now ready to venture into this life's journey to find the perfect one to share my hopes and dreams. My only hope was that God would grant us the opportunity at least to find out where the love we once shared could have led us.

I stood there staring at my semi-curvy shape. I guess I wanted to see what he—or any man, for that matter—would see if he was looking at me. Not bad, Victoria, I thought. I weighed in about 140, shoulder-length light brown hair, hazel eyes. I stood five foot four—unless I was standing on my tippy toes, and then I could push five foot five. I had curves in all the right places. I still got it, I thought, but I need to keep it. It was time I tried to find a man to call my own. Even though I wanted him, I didn't know where he was or how I could ever find him. Trying to get him off my mind, I decided to tear into the living room full of boxes and unpack everything I needed to make my apartment at least livable. I would have plenty of time later to put on the finishing touches.

Already tired, I managed to hang a clock in my living room and put out a few of my whatnots from my hope chest, and then I settled on the floor by my couch to go through some of my boxes so that I could place treasures in their home spot. I must have slept on my floor because that is where I was when the birds woke me up by singing their early-morning songs, calling out to the other birds that this would be their last few songs before they headed south.

It was an early fall morning in October 1981. I got up off the floor, my body hurting from the awkward position in which I slept through the night. I looked at the clock that I had placed on the wall the night before; the time was seven-thirty. I managed to get to the kitchen and put on a pot of tea. Sunday, I thought to myself, this is a day of rest. I've taken Monday off for my move, so I might as well rest today. Tomorrow will be soon enough to finish my apartment. I sat at my window watching the birds playing their last game of tag before they headed south for the winter. While drinking my tea, I thought about how I would spend my day.

After fully waking up, I took my shower. While in the shower, I thought of the willow tree. It would be a wonderful day to spend time at the willow tree writing in my journal. After the shower, I threw on a pair of sweats and an old T-shirt, picked up the apple off my counter that was screaming for attention, and went into my bedroom to get my journal off the nightstand. Before I grabbed my jacket, I called Momma, whom I was sure was sitting by the phone waiting on my call. When she answered the phone on the first ring, that gave me confirmation that I was correct in my thinking.

"Good morning," she said in a raspy voice that let me know either she hadn't had any sleep, or she had just woken up.

I didn't want her worrying, so in the most cheerful voice that I could pull from the pit of my stomach, I replied, "Good morning to you."

"Did you sleep well?" she asked.

"Not wanting her to know that my body was aching from sleeping in my slumped over position I replied "I did, did you?"

"I did on and off. Without you being here, I am sure it's going to take some getting used to. Well," she said, trying to change the subject, "how much did you get done?"

"Some—but not as much as I would have liked to; I fell asleep. I guess I am only tired from all the moving we did yesterday. I decided I would take a break today and visit my willow tree. I can work on it some more tomorrow."

As if Momma approved of my break, she said, "You don't want to overdo it. Moving into a new place takes time. Take a break today, and if you like, I can come help you tomorrow."

I knew that Momma wanted to be a part of my transition every step of the way, so I gave in and agreed to her coming over the next day to help.

"What's Daddy doing?" I asked, wanting to check on him before I hung up the phone.

"He's in his shed. He's been there all morning piddling around; you know your father," she said.

I smiled to myself because I did know my father all too well; I had hoped he wasn't in the shed taking a little nip this early in the morning. I told her to tell him I said hello and I was fine. We said our good-byes and hung up the phone.

I grabbed my jacket, wrapped it around my waist, took a bottle of water from the fridge, and headed to my favorite place. As I walked to the park, I noticed that the frost had blanketed the flowers through the night. My weeping willow was calling my name. I wouldn't be able to visit much more this year. The almanac called for a bad winter, and the way I felt with the air crushing my bones with every blast, it was right.

As I walked to that old tree, I could hear music as cars drove down the somewhat busy street around me. Playing in the background was a song that caught my attention. This song kept saying a phrase that he would always say to me. After all these years, in 1981 they finally made a song that captured his words in a way that neither he nor I could ever have imagined. It was a song from Diana Ross and Lionel Richie, "Endless Love." That song and the memories of him took complete control of my attention. He was my endless love, a love that abruptly found its ending.

I felt myself going into a trance remembering him as I made it to my willow tree. Although my willow tree didn't show the magic it had shown throughout the spring and summer months—the once-blooming beautifully branches were now naked, no blooms or flowers—it still served its purpose. I sat down in my familiar spot under my tree and watched the children playing on the slightly dew-moistened grass with their families. My mind went back to my desires of the teenage boy I once knew and the young man that I felt I would never know. I sat there wondering if I made the right decision to move out and wondering where my life was about to take me. Although moving out on my own was a big step, it was just a stepping-stone to where I really wanted to be in my life.

A few hours into my day, the park became full of children playing dodgeball, while teenage kids sat laughing in their little groups of friends under the other trees in the park. It all faded out as my memories took control. The reminiscing of my life's song began playing in my mind. The countryside, a picket fence, a five-bedroom house, children, the pitter-patter of little feet rushing across the floor, and a country boy by the name of James Andrews—that would have been all it would have taken to make my life complete. James called me Vicky. I met James when I was in ninth grade.

I had just turned fifteen in February when Daddy gave us the heartbreaking news that we were going to move to Virginia. It was my father's job that transferred us to this tiny town called Pocahontas. I remember the day we moved here. It was in April, spring of 1977. We had just hit this town's city limits. While riding down the street, I sat in the backseat in my own little world as we passed the town's park. My mother said, "Victoria," pointing to a brick building with lots of windows across the street, "that is your new school." It wasn't the school that caught my eye, but what sat across from it on the other side of the street mesmerized me.

It was the most beautiful tree I had ever seen. This tree had a certain uniqueness. I remember it was the only tree in the park that was almost in full bloom; it seemed magical. The rest of the trees looked naked compared to that tree. It shaded the grass from the sun that was peeking through the clouds, branches almost touching the ground, gently dancing to the faint wind's beat. It seemed like a safe place, a place that hid secrets. Of course, the only secret I had in my life at that time was that I really didn't want to be in Virginia. I was already missing my friends and the place that I used to call home. The tree itself had a distinct shape about it; its branches were so heavy that they parted in the middle, bending down, causing it to look like a bunch of arms with beautiful flowers gathering at the branches' ends. This gave me the impression of hands inviting me to come join them. "Look at the beautiful weeping cherry tree. Some people call them cherry willow or just weeping willows" "I haven't seen one that beautiful in years" he said interrupting my thoughts. I knew one thing for sure that tree was incredibly beautiful.

The root of the tree had come out of the ground just enough to make it obvious that this was an old tree. There was something special about that old willow tree, and through the years, it would prove how special it really was. I felt a sense of closeness to that old tree, and my curiosity was at its peak. I had to get a closer look at what was drawing me in. I was pleased to discover that we would be moving into a three-bedroom house just a couple of blocks from that old willow tree. After the unpacking was done, I decided to take a walk to the willow tree. Considering it was just a few blocks away, my parents didn't mind me venturing to the park alone.

As I approached the tree, I felt my heart beating faster. It was as if the tree was speaking to me. I felt in the pounding of my heart that I was supposed to be near this tree. The closer view proved to be more rewarding than the view from the road. Its blooms were a dark shade of pink. I had never seen a tree with this type of bloom, and it was clear that this tree held a mystery that I was too young to understand. As time passed, I would come to know my purpose for being at this tree and the mystery that it held within. As I took a seat under that old tree, I felt a sense of comfort; I was almost invisible from the park's eye. As the branches swayed to the cool breeze, I felt pleased with my discovery and settled in for some private time with my thoughts and my journal.

I began spending evenings at this old tree with the journal that I had been keeping ever since I was able to put words into sentences and writing my two best friends whom I had left in Colorado. After a month or so, the letters I wrote them, as well as the letters they wrote me, dwindled away. Phone calls were few because of the distance and it was too painful to write. It just wasn't the same if we couldn't see or talk; we would just have to pick up where we left off once we got old enough to make our own decisions. I had spent the biggest part of my young life with my friends from back home and I didn't know if Daddy would have to move again, so I decided that I wouldn't get attached to anyone else for fear we would have to pick up and move and my heart would be broken all over again. I decided to run solo until I was big enough to decide where I wanted to live, and it would be then that I would make my friends.

I spent hours on end expressing what I was feeling while sitting under this tree. It was magical. Families were there with their children trampling on the grass around this tree. I would peek out from the branches every so often to get a feel of my surroundings. Even though families were interacting around me, I felt that I was alone in the park. The tree made me feel invisible. It was as though I could see them, but they couldn't see me. The evenings would be reaching for the shade of darkness before I would leave that tree, and that was the start of my life's song, a song that would play on for decades to come.

My new school also had its rewards because that was the same school that James was attending. I remember my first attraction to him. It was when I was in the ninth grade in gym the last day of school. I was playing on the tumble bars during recess. I had flipped off, twisting my ankle. I was a loner so I hung out alone, I tried to be the tough girl, not wanting to show my embarrassment for fear I would be made fun of, but the pain was so severe that it brought tears to my eyes and without thinking, I started to cry. James suddenly appeared out of nowhere, rushing to my side. He sat there holding my hand while the gym teacher put the infamous ice pack on my ankle. At every little throb of pain, I brushed away a tear. At first, I was surprised by his actions, but when he grabbed my hand, I forgot about the pain that I was feeling, and my tears went away. James never spoke a word that day, and he didn't have to—his actions and show of concern were clearer than anything he could have thought to say; he just sat there holding my hand until my tears dried up, and then he was off back to wherever he had come from.

Although my focus was the pain that seemed to be thriving from my fall. I managed to feel a bit uncomfortable with his presence, but I loved the way he made me feel while he was holding my hand. He made me feel special, and I knew at that instant, at that moment, that somehow, someway, we would one day be friends. I didn't realize just how good of friends we would become. The encounter with James, as well as my hurting ankle, didn't seem that important as the days went on compared to spending the summer at my willow tree. It was about four days after my ankle injury that I was able to go to my tree. Every child in that small town was in the park that day, which gave the clear indication that school was out. Even though seventies' tunes were blasting from the eight-tracks within the cars, once I sat under my tree, that all faded away.

I could feel the warm breeze blowing through the branches of that tree, letting me know that summer had hit its peak. The sun was blazing down on the crumpled grass, while the girls in the park were greased up with suntan lotion trying to distract the sun so that it would give them its full attention. I just sat there in the protection of the willow tree's shade, with my journal in hand and thoughts of my friends flashing through my mind. I found myself thinking of our good times and wondered what they were doing and even if they reminisced about me at all. Don't get me wrong I wanted friends I wanted that growing up bond that was created as the years past. Making new friends was easy that wasn't the problem. My dad's job had moved him four times since my birth and each time I had to let go of my long-lasting friendships. There weren't any guarantees that we would be in Pocahontas until I could make my own decisions. I think it would be best if I just spent my time focusing on my dreams, my journal and graduating so I could be ready to embrace my life's journey. I had to prepare myself to make good life decisions messing up wasn't a choice. I was my parents only shot to have a successful child and I was going to give it my best. Making them proud was at the top of my list maybe not first but it was at the top. Snapping back to the present I found myself sitting Indian style journal and pen in hand. I had sat there probably an hour or so when I noticed through the tree's branches that someone was approaching me. I could tell by the way this figure was walking that it was a boy, but I couldn't make out who he was until he was a few feet in front of me.

"How's the ankle?" he said. It wasn't until the breeze from the wind parted the branches that I could see who was speaking to me. To the surprise of my heart, I saw it was James. He speaks, I thought. "Better," I heard my voice say, "thanks for asking." He just stood there; I guess he was waiting for me to say something, but what? Although I was a bit smitten by him, I wasn't sure I wanted him to share my space under my tree. Becoming friends was one thing but sharing my space under my willow was another; besides, I didn't feel that a one-time encounter could classify him as being special enough to share my tree. I never invited him to join me. I just continued with my writing like he wasn't there, hoping he would just get the hint and leave. Instead, he decided to strike up an unwanted conversation. Looking down at my journal, with a smile on his face, he asked, "What are you writing? School is out."

"Just things," I said, never directly looking at him, all the while thinking it's really none of your business and I think I liked you better when you didn't talk. Without giving him the opportunity to continue the conversation, I looked down at my watch and said, "Will you look at the time! I had better get going. It's after noon, and I was supposed to go to the store with my mother." I was lying, of course, but I was hoping that after I left, he would do the same and I could return to the privacy of my willow tree. As I tried to get up, my ankle, still a little weak from my earlier fall, made me stumble, and he caught me. Feeling a little annoyed and embarrassed, I turned to just say thank you, but his eyes drew me in. They were so dark they were like a never-ending tunnel; they too showed mystery. I didn't want to stare, but the deep brown, big marbles reminded me of a tunnel of darkness, a tunnel that possibly led to his soul.

It was James who broke my trance by saying, "Your name is Vicky; my name is James Andrews, just in case you were wondering." His words, pulling me out of my trance, brought back the annoyance, which made me a little angry. "I wasn't wondering," I said, the annoyance showing in my voice. Not only did he invade my tree; he just automatically thought I wanted to know his name. Some nerve he's got, I thought. Pulling away from his grasp, I picked up my journal and headed to my house. Before I got out of the park, I heard him shout, "See you around, Vicky." Not stopping to respond, I continued on my journey home.

Momma was fixing lunch when I approached her in the kitchen. "Are you back from the tree so soon?" she said, barely looking up.

"Um-hum," I said, not wanting to tell her the real reason why I had left my tree so early in the day. I said, "I am going to lie down in my room. The park is too crowded with school being out, and the sun is way too hot. I will go back later."

In my room while lying on my bed, I couldn't get his eyes out of my mind. They were gorgeous, if the truth be told, and so was he. He was around five foot nine. His eye color matched his hair color—dark brown, almost black. He wore a short haircut, spiked on top, short on the sides. He weighed in around 150. A mustache was just beginning to faintly show around his lips. I lay in my bed picturing him until I fell asleep. I was awakened by the smell of Momma's pork chops frying in the skillet.

It wasn't until after dinner that I decided to return to my tree. By now the summer day was winding down, so I thought most of the kids would be home or at least sitting in their cars in the parking lot listening to music. Not surrounding my tree like they had earlier. I called out to my parents that I was heading back out to the tree, and I was on my way, with my journal in hand. As I was leaving, I heard my father say, "Be home before it becomes too dark."

I was right about one thing: the parking lot was full of teenagers blasting music from their cars. They won't bother me, I thought as I quickly moved past them toward my tree. I can drown the music out once I'm under my tree. As I got closer to my tree, I could see that someone was under it. Someone was crowding my space. I had been at that tree for months and no one was ever there, but now someone was under my tree. Anger welled up inside of me to the point that even though I wasn't a fighter, but I was willing to fight, if necessary, for my tree, my space. Not fully using my brain, I pushed back its branches—and there he sat.

Before I could protest, he started to speak. "What took you so long? What store did you have to go to?" he said teasingly. "I have been waiting here for hours."

I stood there speechless, not knowing what to say. Although I was angry, I felt a sense of calm when he spoke to me. "What are you still doing here?" I said, still wanting to defend my space.

"I have a right to be here; this is my tree," he said.

"A right? Your tree?" I said, with the anger returning. "What makes this your tree, and who gave you the right to this tree?"

"I have had claims on it for years," he said, pointing to the carving in the tree that read, "The Andrews tree of love." "My last name is Andrews. I even have a bigger secret than that old carving, and one day I might even share the secret with you. I knew you were coming here, and I didn't have the heart to tell you. So, I decided out of the kindness of my heart that we could share."

"Share!" I spoke. "I don't want to share."

"Well," he said, with a chuckle that showed off his beautiful straight teeth and seeing that I was angry while he was enjoying every minute of it, "that is the only choice you have."

"Choice!" I yelled back at him. "What kind of choice is that? Fine," I said, too angry to argue, "keep your old dumb tree. I will find me another one." His nerve, I thought as I headed out of the park. Share my tree with him? Never. Just because there is a stupid carving on that tree, which I hadn't noticed until he pointed it out, doesn't make it his tree. Anybody could have put that carving there. As for the dumb secret, anybody can make up secrets. But I'm not going to argue over a dumb old tree. I am sure there are more trees that I can call my own. How dare he take my tree from me? What a summer this is going to be.

I managed to sneak into the house and into my room without disturbing my parents. I didn't want to have to explain why I wasn't at my willow tree. Sleep didn't come easily for me that night; I was too angry to sleep. The anger of having to share my tree made me restless. I didn't want to share, but I knew I would miss that tree if I didn't decide to share with James. At that point, my mind was made up. I wasn't going to share my tree, and I didn't care what that old carving read or what secrets he made up. I needed something more than an old carving or a dumb secret to give up my tree. The purpose of me going there was to have my space and privacy. How dare he give me a choice? Not wanting to face the thought of not having my tree, I faded off to sleep, only waking to the thoughts of having to share my tree. Was it big enough to share? Could I not sit at the opposite side of him? Could I not pretend that he wasn't there? My choice was either to give in to him or lose my tree—some choice that was.

I looked at the clock on my nightstand. It shouted in big bold red numbers 3:15. I closed my eyes and thought I had fallen asleep, but I turned to the clock, and it shouted 4:15, then 5:15. Finally 6:10 and the birds were beginning to chirp, letting me know a new day had begun. I lay in my bed and wrote in my journal about James and my tree until I saw the sun slowly peak out from the clouds. What would this day hold for me? I wondered. I must return to my willow tree. I can't just let it go.

Chapter 2

I didn't know what to expect that morning as I took the walk to the tree. Would he still be sitting there waiting to taunt me, or was his fun over and he decided to give up and let me have my tree back? It was a quiet walk to the park. The sun had come out, and the birds were chirping louder now. There was almost no traffic, which told me most people were still at home in their beds or at least at home planning out their day. I couldn't tell from the road if someone was under my tree, but it was waving its branches as though telling me to come join it. Walking to my tree, I realized that there were other trees I could sit at, but none like my willow tree. I would be foolish to give up my tree, especially to someone who claimed it just because of a carving that was put there long ago.

As I approached my tree, there was no sign of anybody there, but a piece of paper that was pinned to the tree caught my eye. I took the piece of paper out of the tree. It read, "I knew you would come back. If it means that much to you, then you can have the tree. The secret will remain just that, a secret. One day, if you discover the secret, you will better understand. Until then, enjoy the tree. I am patient; I can wait. James." How thoughtful, I thought. He is willing to give this tree up to me. I guess I am being a little selfish. I don't guess it would hurt to share the tree sometimes. After all, I am sure he wouldn't be here all the time. As far as the secret, I guess I already know the peace and the magic that this tree holds; but I won't tell him that because, if he knew that I knew, then he might make me share. My mind was racing back and forth from him to my tree, wondering when he would show up or if he had just let it go. I was thinking that he must have thought that I was a selfish soul, not wanting to share. I continued to watch as the park filled up with families playing and music thumping, and I continued to write in my journal. James never showed.

Three days passed, and things were back to normal. I was under my willow tree, and the families were gathered at the park. It was on a Saturday around noon. The sun had reached its peak for the day, blazing down on the blades of grass. I was sitting under my willow tree reading thoughts that I had written months before. Resting my eyes and taking a break, I decided to step from underneath its branches to get a full view of my surroundings.

At a short distance away in the park sat James. He was just sitting on a bench watching the families play with their children, speaking not a word to the passers-by. There was this one girl that went to our school that went to the bench where James was sitting. I couldn't hear the conversation but within minutes she was sitting next to him. He didn't pay her a lot of mind but that was to be expected she wasn't very pretty rather a plain Jane. Every now and again I could see him wipe beads of sweat off his brow, which gave the sign that the sun was doing what it set out to do. She didn't seem to care about the rays of sun she just sat there as if she was sitting under shade. One could tell that she liked James, but he didn't seem to share the interest. He kept kicking his rocks and after about 20 minutes I think she got the hint because she got up and went back over to the group of girls that were watching.

Sitting there reliving our argument I felt kind of bad that he had to sit out in that hot sun, but I feared if I invited him under my tree, he would never leave. My heart got the best of me, so I walked over to him as I approached it was like every girl including the one that left him on the bench was on guard waiting to see what was going to happen from our encounter. Conversations stopped as I could feel all eyes on me. For a quick moment I felt empowered. Yet my mind quickly turned to thinking about him totally ignoring me like he did the other girls. Maybe the on lookers would take some of my empowerment if he treated me the same. They weren't my friends, so it really doesn't matter what they thought. One way or the other I wanted to make things right. James was sitting on the park bench kicking little pebbles of rocks when I approached. "There is more shade under the tree."

"Yeah, I know," was all he said while looking straight ahead. He never turned to look at me he just kept kicking the little pebbles. I felt a little stupid but under the circumstances I was determined to have him join me if not but for a few minutes. Although I didn't care what the other girls thought of me. He was handsome enough and if I could capture his attention, I am sure I would be the envy of all the other girls.

"Want to come over? I feel like sharing today."

"Today?" he replied.

"It's just an offer," I said, becoming annoyed. I could feel my forehead crinkle and frustration was rising quickly. "I just thought I would ask." His uncaring tone was getting the best of me and at that point I didn't care what the other girls thought handsome or not my patience was running thin and if the truth be known. I didn't want to share my tree with anybody especially him since he claimed he owned it. Without another word, I turned and walked back to my shaded spot under the tree. As I passed the other girls my eyes caught theirs. I guess feeling a little embarrassed for me they quickly lost eye contact and pretended not to notice what just happened. My first thought was to ask them if they were satisfied but feeling a little rejected, I decided to keep my thoughts to myself. They weren't close enough to hear our little conversation, so they didn't know what was said or why I suddenly walked away. It wasn't that serious anyways once I made it back to my tree, I decided to watch him from the distance. He was handsome enough. He squinted his eyes, trying to shelter his pupils from the sun. Girls repeatedly passed by him as if they wanted him to notice them. He didn't even acknowledge them with a simple hello. He just kept kicking the little pebbles and every now and again he would look over to the tree but then he would go back to the pebble kicking.

A crashing sound took my attention off him; it sounded like a car in the street behind me hit something. People were racing to the street to see just what the thundering sound was. Not really caring, I turned my attention back to where James was sitting—only he wasn't sitting there any longer. He must have wanted to know what all the excitement was about. So, I scooted back from the limbs and continued to read my journal. Minutes after that, I heard him speak from around the tree.

"It was too hot out there," he said. "It is more shaded in here."

"Is it?" I replied. "Well, my offer no longer stands!"

"What?" he said. "Oh yes, it does," and before I could go for round two, he was sitting beside me under my willow tree extending his hand. "Truce," he said.

I hesitated, but his eyes made my lips respond, "Truce." One could say that my curiosity got the best of me that prompted me to look in between the branches at the girls that was sunbathing. I had to wonder what was on their mind now.

"I saw you watching me," he said, catching me off guard.

"No," I said, trying to get past the fact that I was caught. I for whatever reason just started to giggle. Then I said, "I wasn't watching you silly I was watching everybody including the girl that sat down with you."

"Who April?" he said, "naaaa she is just a girl that I have went to school with since kindergarten."

"What are you jealous?"

"Jealous------me-----just for noticing why should I be jealous?." "It makes no difference to me who sits with you or who you sit with for that matter I am just here to enjoy my tree nothing more nothing less."

"Sure" he said with a sly grin that complimented his face. "I know you want me too he said it's just a matter of time."

"Matter of time, ---matter of time for what. The only reason I came and got you is because it was hot out there. I am not heartless we can share this tree isn't that want friends do?"

"Are we friends now?" he asked awaiting my answer

"Maybe, maybe not we shall see because time will tell I am not sure I don't know you that well all I know is that you wanted to steal my tree and that isn't a good way to start a friendship." With those words James gently gave me a few pokes in my side that made me giggle. I mean, isn't that what girls do when they don't have anything to say? We had small talk that day, and that was the beginning of a friendship that would blossom into something more, something that at the age of fifteen, I didn't begin to understand.

From then to the beginning of school, James and I would meet at that willow tree daily. We began to talk and became friends and sharing my willow tree with him didn't seem that bad. As a matter of fact, my feeling was that he belonged there too. The tree was now showing its magic. Its blooms were fully colored a light shade of pink, and the parted branches continued to dance with each breeze. Even though the magic of the tree was obvious, my attention was more on James instead of the willow tree. My journal didn't seem that important to me any longer. I didn't have to write my feelings down; I could just tell James. James, on the other hand, didn't talk much about his feelings; he seemed more interested in mine.

When I would talk about my mom and dad, he would sit there as if he was in deep thought; and when I spoke about his family, he would always change the subject.

When it was time to go home, he would get up, and then help me to my feet. We would verbally say our good-byes like normal people would, but his eyes held me in that standing position like he was searching, wanting to say something. Then he would just stop his searching and say, "See you tomorrow, Vicky. Same time, same place." We would then part ways, my mind still on him and the conversations we shared, only to meet at the same time in the same spot the very next day and start all over again. We did this all summer and hated the last day because we didn't know what the new school year would bring. We were starting the tenth grade. We knew things would be different, and the pressure of growing up was fast approaching.

He never mentioned the secret again, and neither did I. I just figured one day we would have secrets of our own about this tree. The day before school started, we were sitting under the willow tree and talking about how great our summer had been. It was getting late, and although I didn't want to leave, I knew it was time to go. James didn't say anything. This time he just stood up, cupped his hands, and pulled me up, this time a little closer to him than usual. We stood there for moments that quietly passed by, and then he said, "It doesn't have to end," as if he had read my mind. "Want to meet here in the morning and walk to school together?"

My heart was beating so fast at that moment; I thought he was going to kiss me. I felt the beating of my heart was so loud that whatever I said would be drowned out.

James thought I was thinking about it, so he said, "Well, if not, I guess we could see each other after we get there."

Not wanting to let go of the moment, I managed to speak maybe even a little to fast. "I will meet you here at seven thirty," knowing we didn't have to be at school until eight o'clock. I wanted a few extra minutes with him before we became separated. "Then seven thirty it is" he said with a smile that let me know he liked spending time with me just as much as I liked spending time with him.

My walk home was something short of a skip. I was walking on sunshine. My thoughts were on James, the willow tree and whatever was next in this blossoming friendship. I didn't want the evening to end but since it did, I couldn't wait for morning to get here. Virginia isn't such a bad state after all.

Chapter 3

I didn't sleep a wink last night. I felt I had just closed my eyes when my alarm blared its signal for me to get up. Bleep Bleep Bleep Bleep. When I got my wits about me enough to wake up, I remembered that I set my alarm ahead an hour. I wanted to have time enough to look my best today. For James and the other girls because I know that all eyes will definitely be on me again especially when we arrive together. I thought it would be a nice added touch to add a little mascara, a light spray of perfume and lip gloss. I went in the kitchen and momma was already fixing breakfast. I didn't have an appetite and I knew she expected me to eat something. Not wanting her to question my added touches I quickly turned around and went back to my room. Sitting on the bed I was trying to figure out how I could get out of not only eating but out the door without her seeing my additions. Momma with her Christian views would disapprove. She calls makeup devils paint, and she thinks that all women have a natural beauty. I don't need a lecture this morning. Looking in the mirror, I decided to take off the lip gloss until I was well out of sight. The mascara wouldn't be that noticeable, if she asks, I will just tell her that I put it on last night just playing around and I thought I had it all off.

"Victoria" I heard mom yell across the house. "Come eat something before you go to school. You need your strength and food for thought today." Here goes it's showtime I thought. "Lord please don't let her notice the mascara. "Coming" I yelled back. Looking into the mirror one last time before I made my grand entrance. Victoria, you got this, take a deep breath you got this.

I put on my best smile added a little pep in my step and walked into the kitchen bright eyed, and bushy tailed. "Good morning, Mommy dearest" I said with a little giggle kissing her gently on her cheek. I was glad that I took off the lip gloss fearing that she would have felt it from my kiss. Still not trying to make contact I stood next to her looking at the breakfast she prepared. Feeling nauseated knowing that my nerves wouldn't allow food to enter my stomach I said, "momma I don't think I can eat anything this morning with it being the first day of the tenth grade." I will grab something from the cafeteria later if that is ok." Not looking up she started to fix daddy a plate she said, "very well Victoria I kind of figured you wouldn't have an appetite, just promise that you will eat a bite at school." "I promise" I replied as I looked across the room to see daddy entering the kitchen. "Good morning how are my beautiful ladies doing this morning" he said before giving momma her morning kiss. He turned to walk toward me, as he got closer, he stopped with an added grin and right after he gave me a kiss he said, "somebody sure smells pretty today momma you shouldn't have put on perfume this early for me." Momma gave me a quick glance and said "well, I am glad you noticed honey it does smell awfully pretty but it's not me." The blood in my body rushed down my frame and gathered at the tips of my feet and I suddenly felt faint. Before losing my balance, I grabbed hold of the chair. I thought a minute before I stammered out my words that I knew was a lie. "Oh, can you still smell it, It's my shower gel. I used it last night when I took my shower, remember momma you bought it for me last Christmas I used the lotion too." I immediately looked around the room to see if they bought what I was saying or was I caught in my attempt to please James. Momma laid daddy's plate down on the table before saying "Yes Victoria I remember. I had been wondering when you were going to use it. I am glad you like it." It was daddy that proved I needed to practice more on my lying skills because he looked at me rubbed his eyes as if to notice my mascara and said with a chuckle, "Oh I see, that is some kind of shower gel because it sure did leave a trace. Something good for the eyes I mean nose to smell. Not a bad thing though it smells pretty." I looked at my dad and playfully rolled my eyes. I know that daddy wouldn't say anything that would upset our morning. My mouth suddenly became dry, it felt like I had a mouth full of flour, without drinking something I wouldn't be able to speak words. I'm sure it was just nerves, but I needed something to drink before I left to meet James. Reaching for my glass of orange juice I drank it down rather quickly then got another before I excused myself and headed to the park. "Have a wonderful day Victoria" momma said as I was leaving. "Try not to sweat out all the pretty smell during recess" daddy said with a wink as I headed for the door. I couldn't leave fast enough and all I could think of on my walk to meet James is what was my parents saying about me? I wondered if they knew what I was really doing. I reached in my pocket and readded my lip gloss. It was quick for them to notice my change I wondered if James would follow suit and if he did would my actions speak louder than my words.

When I got to the willow tree, he was already there, waiting patiently. As soon as I was by his side, he looked at me as if he was thinking on something and said, "you look and smell pretty today Vicky." "Thank you" was all I could bring myself to say. He approved that was enough for me. It seemed like we were walking our last walk together. We both walked in silence, not knowing what this day would bring. A hint of cool wind began to blow letting me know that fall was traveling our way. The summer months were fighting their last fight to stay a little longer. My vote was for the summer months because winter would prove hard for me and James to meet at my tree. I thought without being able to see James at the tree would prove to be a long, lonely winter.

As we approached the school, children were scurrying around trying to make it to the gym to see where their names were on the board and who would be their teachers for that year. We had more than enough stares and whispering. I saw girls nudge other girls as they looked our way.

April walked up to us not even acknowledging my presence and told James they had three classes together. He just said "ok" then he looked at me and said, "let's go see how many classes we have together Vicky." I tried not to gloat or show my victory in a way that I would seem snobbish, but I silently wished that James would grab my hand but instead James and I just walked to the board and searched for our names. Secretly I didn't want to know, for fear that I would be separated from James throughout the day. It was by the grace of God that we were only separated during one of our classes. I for my personal satisfaction scanned Aprils name so I could see which three classes she had with James. Turns out she had every class with me.

When I was away from James, she wasn't with him either. James and I decided that when we had the time, we would write to each other during our class, letting the other one know what we were experiencing during our time away. After class, we would hand each other our little note and then spend the other classes together writing little notes trying to rush the day away.

There was a romance blooming, and it would be a romance that I hoped would last forever. After school, I would go home long enough to pacify my parents, telling them about my day, and then I would go meet James at the willow tree until the sun moved out and let the moon close the day.

It was the beginning of November. Fall was moving out and winter was settling in, and I was helping Mother set the table. My mind was on James and what we would talk about once I made it to the willow tree. We sat down for dinner, and it was then that daddy decided to ask the most dreadful questions that a girl my age could ever imagine. "Victoria, what's his name? When are you going to bring him home to meet your mom and me?"

My dad was a man who never judged or commented unless he was sure of himself, so trying to lie to him wasn't easy and convincing him of a lie was almost impossible. He was a jokester and my fifteen years on this earth allowed me to understand when he was joking and when he was serious. This particular time he was dead serious. I had wished at that moment in time that I had planned and prepared for that dreadful question. It was too late now, and they were going to meet James so without protesting, praying, or even thinking I said, "His name is James Andrews, and we are just friends for now," I said, hoping he couldn't see through my emotions to know that my heart felt more. "He's just a boy that goes to my school." Trying to take the heat off me I decided a different approach. Before Daddy had time to think of another dreadful question I continued "I decided since our last move I didn't want to have girlfriends I thought guy friends would soften the blow if I had to say goodbye. I met him last year and we hang out together. Nothing to it" I added hoping they will have compassion for me because I had to leave my friends and so that the questions would stop or so that was my goal.

Momma chimed in with "Does he go to church? Have you met his parents?"

"We never talk about church, Momma, but I will ask him if he would like to go with us sometime."

"We don't really talk about family when we are together so that has never been a discussion, but I am sure I will one day." I thought that was the best answer to stop the questions so I could choke down the rest of my dinner and head to the park. I was hoping for a quieter dinner and not at my expense and praying that the food I was able to chomp down would safely settle in the pits of my stomach instead of coming back up displaying the fact that I barely chewed any of it, but my father felt the need to continue.

"It would be nice to know what kind of young man my daughter is giving her time to," my daddy said, dipping his biscuit into his gravy. "Maybe its high time that we meet this mystery fellow."

"I will tell him when we meet this evening, and he will come," I said, half sure of myself. Daddy's request wouldn't allow me to chomp down my last bite of food, I cleared away my dishes, ask momma if I could go to the park before I washed the dishes since they were still eating after her approval, I asked to be excused so I could rush to the tree and meet James. I didn't want to spring my family on him, but I knew that if they didn't meet him, one day they would just show up at the tree. To me, that would be much more humiliating than just bringing him to the house.

"Be sure you dress warm, Victoria," my momma said as I was about to leave. Warm to Momma was winter coat, scarf, hat, and gloves. I didn't want James to see me dressed like an Eskimo, as soon as I was out of sight of my house, I took off the hat and gloves and placed them in my jacket pocket.

My mind was in overdrive on my way to the park walking through the November wind, trying to figure out how I would ask James to meet my parents. Did he want to keep our relationship just between me, him, and the willow tree? Would asking him to meet my parents make him think I was pushing myself on him? Would he not want to meet my parents? Meeting family was never in our conversation, so I feared the outcome that our visit held for the evening.

When I arrived at the tree, James was already there. He had on his winter jacket. Seeing him without a hat and gloves made me think how glad I was for taking mine off and putting them in my pocket. Our visits at the old tree were becoming shorter and shorter. The tree had shed its beautiful blossoms that it had throughout the spring and summer months; now it was just bare branches hanging from the tree, which didn't provide much heat for the winter months.

James had been sitting under the willow tree waiting patiently for my arrival. I sat down, and James must have seen the tension on my face because he said, "What's wrong with you? No words of wisdom to share?"

I barely heard those words. My mind was overcome with how I would spring my parents on him. "James," I started—better now than never— "I know that you are not my boyfriend or anything like that, but my parents are wondering who I am spending all my time with." Looking up at him for a reaction made me a little nervous. I didn't know what his thoughts were, and despite the cold that came with November, I could feel myself beginning to sweat as I waited for him to say something before, I continued. He just sat there as if he was pondering on what to say. It was as if the tree knew I was nervous, so to cover up my perspiration, it parted its wooden branches with just a little breeze, sending a sense of calm.

It was only seconds—though it seemed like hours—before James spoke. "Well, I should go meet them," he said in a playful tone. "The only thing is," he said in an unsure sort of way, "I thought we were dating." This time it was James who was looking for some type of reaction.

Feeling that perspiration returning, praying that the tree would blow another breeze, hoping that this was the start of something beautiful, I quickly found the strength to say, "I didn't know, James. You never asked me."

James turned to me after my last response and looked into my eyes before he spoke. My anticipation was getting the best of me, but I sat there as he searched my eyes. It was as though he wanted my eyes to give him the answer. I was a little startled when he grabbed my hands, which had started sweating the moment I sat down. I don't think he even noticed if he did, he didn't say but what he did say proved to be music to my ears. "Well," he said with a half grin, "Vicky, will you be my girl?"

Whether it was nerves or the air turning cold, I felt my hands turning numb as he held them. I felt like the world had stopped so I could savor the moment. It had been five months, and I was finally James's girl. I started to ask him if we should get April's approval, but I didn't need to bring up another girl, especially one that wasn't really any competition. Getting lost in the moment and his eyes I just sat there like the bumbling teenager I was. I must have lost track of the time and the question because it was the look on James face that brought me to the present time. He went from wondering and smiling to having a worried look and the grin was erased. I felt that he felt he was about to be rejected.

"Is it a yes or a no, Vicky?" he said, as the show of nervousness switched from me to him.

Trying to contain my laughter I thought it was a good time to test his playful skills. "Well since you asked now it's safe to tell you that I can't be your girl until you get my daddy's approval you must ask him first. That is why they want to meet you so you can ask them properly." He quickly brought his hands up to rest on his head, as he bent his head down, he said "I thought that was only to get married not to date." I quickly chimed in, "Not my dad he's real strict, I am his only child you see so he must have strict rules so I can be a success. Is that a problem" I said trying to sound concerned? He sat there for a minute or two then with the sweetest look on his face he said, "suppose he doesn't like me, and he says no, then what? "Well, I guess he will have the final say." Not being able to keep up the joke because I could see that he was worried I leaned toward him touched him on the side of his face and said, "I'm only teasing James, you and my dad will get along just fine, you don't have to ask him to date me." As I witness relief take over his expression, and not trying to sound too excited I said "Yes, James," I said, "I will be your girl." As far as meeting my parents, "Sunday after church," was all I could manage to say. I decided to throw church in because I knew it was only a matter of time before he heard it from my mother. After I saw the way, he took my little joke I thought I should tell him all that he needed to know so he wouldn't be caught off guard.

I didn't want to invite him to church; I felt that would be a bit much for his first meeting with my parents. Excitement welled up in me like a bolt of thunder grasping my heart. I was excited about being his girl, and I was also excited that he was willing to meet my parents. When James let go of my hand, we just sat there. I knew that sleep would not be easy for me that night. I just hoped that the bags that no sleep would produce wouldn't show just how hard it had been.

James and I just sat at that old tree, not saying a word. The cold had returned, and darkness was filling the sky, so it was I who ended the night. "Good night, James. I better head home," I said, not wanting the night to end. I still must wash dishes and get prepared for school tomorrow. That was only part of it the other part is that I didn't want our night to end but I also didn't want my parents to get suspicious or have any added concerns before they met James. We each had our own thoughts about moving forward because James surprised me with what he said next.

"I think I should walk you home tonight," he said as we got up to leave. "That way I will know where you live, and besides, I can't let my girl walk home alone now, can I?"

I thought that was a great idea; that way we would have a few more moments to share. We walked hand in hand through the calmness of the evening. The wind had slowed down as if to be sure we didn't get cold on our walk to my house. Once we were in front of my house, as he turned to leave, something happened that night that would change my life forever. James turned to me, and after looking into my eyes, he pulled me close and gently kissed my lips. My knees started trembling, and my breath faded away for a moment. I was glad that there was no dogs to bark because I didn't want momma and daddy to be prompted to look out the window. I thought I was going to pass out, wishing he had done that under the willow tree so it could give me that calming breeze that I so desperately needed at that moment. I was beside myself and even though I was in a moment I didn't care at that point if they saw him kiss me or not. Well--- no--- maybe I was glad that they didn't see him I don't need the questions or concerns. It was just living in the moment that made my brain stop and all ration and reality was gone out the window. In time not now but in time. That was the first kiss of my life, and so far, that was the best night of my life.

After my first kiss we stood there for just a moment probably wondering what each other was thinking. I know I was, but I pulled back in for a hug, whispered good night then headed in the house. I tried to be as quiet as a church mouse because I couldn't conversate with my parents or answer any more questions. I was glad momma done the dishes. It took everything in me to walk in the house and into my safe haven. As I sat on the corner of my bed, I relived the events that transpired at my tree and decided anything else just wasn't important except for sleep but I knew that wasn't going to happen tonight. Even though my body would demand it my mind wasn't going to do its part. James will keep my mind occupied once my body settled in and I guess that was just part of it. No matter how hard I tried I know that sleep wasn't in my near future because James had taken over my thoughts.

Chapter 4

I met James at the tree the next morning. I was right; sleep hadn't come easy for me. I tried hard to fight it, but I tossed and turned; and when I thought I had finally gone to sleep for a few hours, I woke up and looked at the clock to find out that it was only minutes that had passed. James, on the other hand, was full of energy. His first words to me that morning was, "How does it feel to know that you are now taken?" "Did you sleep well"? "Did you tell your parents I'm coming to visit?"

I knew James had concerns. I am sure he didn't sleep either. I'm sure he was nervous about meeting my parents I would feel the same way if it was me. He never asked me to meet his parents and I am not going to offer one hurdle at a time was about all I could have. "Hmm," I said in a playful sort of way, trying to shake the edge off. "It feels, it feels like we have been together for over five months now." I wanted to shout at the top of my lungs that I was the happiest girl alive, but he didn't need to know that. I tried to be as calm as I could, even though I was indeed the happiest girl alive. James stole my thoughts with his actions.

As we entered the school, he took hold of my hand, as if he wanted to let the other boys know that I was his girl. I was fine with that because it put the girls on notice too. With those actions, my heart began to beat hard, so hard that I heard it and I thought he did too. If he did, he never said a word. He just kept walking as though we had been walking this way all along.

When we got to the class where we had to separate, James repeated his actions from the night before. He gently kissed my lips as he squeezed my hand. I couldn't think of a thing in class that hour and a half except James. I was so happy and excited that James and I were finally together.

After school, James and I walked to the park. We sat there talking about the families that were playing with their children, our desires in life, and what our future held. James kissed me again. This time he backed up enough to whisper, "Does this feel like a love that is endless?" I focused hard on his words, "a love that is endless." Was James trying to tell me he was in love with me? I wanted so badly to whisper the words that I loved him, but I thought that in time, I would not even have to think about it. Those words would just come just as naturally as our conversations. I knew that I had to be experiencing love because nothing in my life thus far had made me feel the way I did when I was with him. Even before we decided to become a couple, I had the feeling that our love would be truly endless. I know for sure. I am in for the long haul.

The next evening at the dinner table, I told my parents that James would be coming to dinner on Sunday after church. It was as if my mother read my mind because she quickly replied, "So you are going to church Sunday."

Just to clarify, I said, "Church, not Sunday school." I wouldn't miss it for the world because I needed God to be there when James met my parents. I just nodded my head, and Momma said, "Then I need to call my Sunday school replacement. I will take what I can get. If you just want to go to church, then we will just go to church this Sunday. I think I am beginning to like this James boy already. If he can get you to come to church, then I think I have already made my decision," she said, smiling and winking at the same time.

I had to speak about the "embarrassing thing" because I knew my father, and knowing him the way I did, I knew he would try to embarrass me on purpose. "Daddy, now you are not going to embarrass me or James, right?"

With a chuckle, Daddy answered, "Now why would I do a thing like that?"

Ok I thought daddy is going to show off and bring embarrassment with it. His words let me know that he was going to do just that. My daddy loved to play and cut up and I knew that he and James would get along great, but the initial meeting would be a little uneasy for me. James was more laid-back and quieter. I just didn't want my father to overdo his playing to the point that it made James nervous.

The week flew by, and before I could catch my breath, it was Sunday. I got up way before my parents. I wanted God to know that I was anxious to go to his house. I wanted him to feel the same when James came to mine. Mother preferred coffee and I preferred tea, but today coffee was the drink of choice, I thought as I started breakfast. I wanted my parents to wake up in a good mood.

I was almost done with breakfast before my mother joined me in the kitchen. "Well, well, I think we should have asked James to come over way before now. Aren't you the little domestic goddess this morning? What gets you up early this morning? Couldn't sleep," my mother said teasingly, "thinking about your exciting day? Needing the Lord to intervene to make this day perfect?" she continued, with laughter that followed.

"I just thought I would start this day off early," I teased back. "I already know that it's going to be a wonderful day."

"Sure, sure," Momma said as she left the kitchen. "It's funny how God isn't thought about until we need him."

Right again, I thought. I never even thought about God until James had to come meet my parents. I decided it might just be a good idea to offer a thanksgiving and a little prayer. Quietly to myself I said I am grateful and thankful for all you do and for letting me meet James. Forgive me, Lord. I need you to be with me every step of the way today to make this day as perfect as it can be. At least that was what I was hoping as I took the store-bought biscuits out of the oven. These were not the usual Sunday-morning biscuits that Momma usually prepared. She made hers from scratch, but these would have to do. I was only fifteen. What do they expect? I thought as I got the jam out of the refrigerator.

"It smells like somebody is cooking up something good," my daddy said as he entered the kitchen. "Good morning, princess," he said as he sat at the table.

"Good morning, Daddy," I said as I was giving the sausage the last flip in the pan before sending them to their final destination. "Did you sleep well?"

"I did," he said, almost laughing. "The question is, did you sleep well? I can't remember the last time you got up on your own. Usually, your mother has to pry you from the pillow and sheets."

I looked up at Mother, who was laughing as she joined him at the table. "Now, honey, be easy on her," she said. "You remember how you felt when you met my parents for the first time. I am sure you had a sleepless night. She's just a little anxious, that's all. I'm sure that sleep will come back to her sometime-----next week." They joined each other in laughter. Although I became a little annoyed, I continued with my breakfast preparations like nothing had been said.

It was Mother who broke the ice again. "Okay, honey, we will leave you alone. We know that you are a little unnerved this morning. Let's eat this feast that you have so carefully prepared and get off to the Lord's house. I'm sure he's waiting for us to come." That was the extent of that conversation for the rest of our time at breakfast; we just sat eating quietly. Glancing up a time or two, I could see my parents smiling at each other, but my mind was totally focused on James.

Chapter 5

I entered the church doors with my mind on God and my heart on James. I walked in silence, and Mother walked in praising the Lord. At times that was somewhat embarrassing, but today it was acceptable. The church was in sequence with my mother. She said, "Praise the Lord, everybody," and they joined in and said, "Praise the Lord." Then she said, "God is good all the time," and they said, "All the time, God is good." I was glad on that day that my mother had a good relationship with God because, even though I didn't know him like my mother did, I was in need of his presence today and by me being her daughter, I felt he would look after me too. The congregation read the devotions, and then the pastor entered his podium.

I secretly said to myself, "Please don't let him notice me, please don't let him notice me," because if he did, he would ask if I had anything I wanted to say. Needless to say, I didn't. I just wanted him to say what the Lord wanted him to say so that I could get this day over with.

"Let us pray," he said, and everyone in the church bowed their heads. Whew, I thought he didn't notice me. While they were praying, I was looking around to see who was praying and who was just watching. Momma must have felt my movement because it was her nudge that told me that my head should be bowed too. I acknowledged her nudge and said a quick prayer. "Lord, please let this day be a good day for me and James. Amen." Then I just stood there in silence while the preacher finished his prayer with "In Jesus name," followed by amen.

"Please be seated," he said. I sat through his sermon feeling numb. I had my thoughts elsewhere, and although I felt a little guilty, I knew God knew what I was thinking so I couldn't fool him.

After church, everybody gathered around talking about how great the sermon was, and I was sorry that I had missed it. I was only there in body; my mind was with James.

"The Lord is definitely in this house," one of the ladies said as she hugged Momma. "It is so good to see you too, Victoria," she added as she moved on through the crowd of people.

As we started to leave, the pastor called out to us, "It's so good to see you back in the house of the Lord, Victoria. You are not here by chance, but by divine invitation."

"Okay," I said, not knowing or even caring what he was talking about.

"Don't be a stranger in the house of the Lord. Even though you may not see it now, young lady, one day he will be the one you seek for answers and guidance." His words caused chills to run through my body. I tugged on Momma's dress jacket as if to say, "Can we go now?"

She gave me an annoyed look, but then said, "That sermon was another great message from God, Pastor. I will see you on Tuesday for Bible study." As we were walking to the car, Momma asked, "Did you get anything out of the sermon today, Victoria?"

Not wanting to disappoint her, I said, "Yes, Momma, a little bit."

She talked all the way home, but I never heard a word she was saying. I just saw her lips moving, and occasionally I would nod, trying to make her think I was listening. All the while, I was just praying that James had not arrived at our house yet.

Turning into the driveway, I saw Daddy walking from his shed. That assured me that James wasn't there yet. "How was church?" he yelled down as we shut the car doors.

"You wouldn't have to ask if you had gone with us," Momma shot back in a playful sort of way, but she meant her words. "Wonderful message," she said as she passed him on her way into the house.

"Well, Victoria, no sign of the mystery man yet," he said, grinning. "I got my shotgun loaded waiting for him to show up." He belted out laughter that caused me to laugh with him.

"Daddy," I said once the laughter passed, "be nice, please."

"I will," he said. "I will only shoot him once."

I slapped him softly on his back and headed in to change. James had never seen me in a dress, so my first thought was to just leave the dress on until he saw me. Thinking further, I decided to change into something more comfortable; we would probably go to the tree after dinner. Reaching into my drawers to find something comfortable, I heard Mother yelling up the steps, "Victoria, you have company." So much for changing. I figured I had better get downstairs before they ran him off.

I tiptoed down the steps to see how everything was going before I made my entrance. I heard nothing. Then out of nowhere, I heard my daddy laughing. Heart pounding, it was time I made my entrance; it was hard to tell what my daddy was doing. "James," I said as I made it into the living room where they were sitting, "I see you have met my father."

"And your mother," he said, smiling. Momma had gone back to the kitchen to finish dinner.

I knew he approved of them by his smile. I was just wondering if they felt the same.

"I like the dress," he said as if noticing it for the first time. I only wore a dress because momma refused to let me wear pants to church in her eyes it was disrespecting the lord. It was a different touch I guess the upside is James could see what I look like when I present myself as a lady.

"Thank you" was all I could think to say.

Daddy looked at me as if a joke was forming in his mind, and I gave him a look as if to say, "Don't you dare." Instead, he invited James to go sit with him for a chat.

Daddy and James seemed to hit it off very well. Once I saw they were making small talk, I felt comfortable to leave him and help Mother in the kitchen. I was sure that she would let me know her thoughts, and I would find out Daddy's later. In the kitchen, Mother was kneading her dough for the fresh bread she was preparing to make. "He is quiet and handsome," Mother said in between her kneading.

"Yes" was all I could think to say.

"He seems to like you a lot, Victoria." My heart was beginning to beat faster because I knew the next question. "Are you sure you are just friends?"

"Maybe a little more," I said, hoping she couldn't see the love I had for him.

"Hmm," she said, "have you kissed him?"

I couldn't lie, but I didn't want to tell her because I knew what was coming next. "He is a gentleman, Momma," I said, trying to kill all the birds that were gathering.

"I see," she said. "Has he kissed you?"

"Mother," I scoffed, "is this really the time for the birds-and-bees talk?" Mother laughed. "You are right. We can talk about it after he leaves. Your father seems to like him, and that is a good sign." Mommas' words began to fade out as her question "has he kissed you?" played in my mind that kiss with many to follow has been the highlight of my life and I couldn't stop thinking or reliving it, but I couldn't tell momma that. My momma and I had a great relationship. She was easy to talk to and a great listener but kissing a boy, falling in love, discussing possibilities, or giving her details wasn't on my mind right now that would be later not now during his first visit. I don't need anything I mean nothing including bonding with momma to interfere with this visit. When my mind returned to the present time momma was putting her rolls in the oven. "Let's join the boys in the living room," she said, wiping the flour on her apron.

After that little conversation that Mom and I had in the kitchen, I didn't sit beside James for fear they would have known it was much more than a friendship; instead, I chose the chair.

"James and I were just talking," Daddy said. "He someday, not now of course," he said smiling at James, "wants a family of his own." Oh God, I thought, what has Daddy said to him? "Honey," he said looking at Momma, "did you know that they have been dating for over five months?" I didn't know if it was because of the heat that Momma kept at ninety degrees we were experiencing or my father's words that started my skin producing moisture, but whatever it was, I was wishing it would stop.

"Really?" Momma said, looking at me.

"No, no," I said before the conversation got any deeper, trying not to make too much eye contact with James, "we have been friends for over five months but only have been dating for a week."

Daddy looked at Momma, and they both started smiling.

James looked at me as if he had said something wrong. I smiled at him to let him know things were okay.

"Do you like to hunt, fish? Other than spending time with Victoria, James, what do you like to do?"

"Umm," James said, trying to think of the best answer, "I like gardening."

Ding, ding, ding, I thought to myself. That was the correct answer; you have been forwarded to round two. In one of our past conversations, I told James that my father liked gardening.

"Never hunted," James continued, "and fishing is just a little too boring for me."

"I see," Daddy said, repeating his words. "So, what do you do with your extra time besides spend it with Victoria? Gardening only takes up two seasons. What do you do the rest of the year?"

"Just spending time with Victoria," James said in a nervous kind of way.

"Um hum," Daddy said, bringing on the tension.

As though Daddy was extending an invitation, James added, "What did you have in mind, sir?"

"Oh, nothing," Daddy said, "just trying to get to know you, that's all."

Momma sat patiently waiting for her turn to grill him. "Let's go in and set the table," she said, getting up from her seat beside Daddy. "The boys must be starved."

I didn't want to leave James for fear Daddy would ask questions that he couldn't answer or that would make him uncomfortable, but I did as Momma asked, thinking the quicker dinner is over, the faster we can leave and be by ourselves.

The table was set, and dinner was on the table. As we sat down to eat momma said "Let us say grace and thank the good Lord for the food he blessed us with. James," she asked, "do you want to say grace?" putting him on notice that her sermon was about to take form.

James looked at Momma, but before he could speak, I said, "God is good, God is great. Let us thank him for our food. Bow our head as we are fed. Give us, Lord, our daily bread. Amen."

Momma could do nothing at that point but smile. James looked at me with thankful eyes. Daddy, on the other hand, wasn't so silent. He let out a laugh, asking for forgiveness after he finished. Momma gave him her famous disapproving look.

"So, James," she said, spreading butter on her roll. Here it comes, I thought to myself, round two. "Does your mother go to church?"

"Um, no, ma'am," he said. "I wish she did."

"I see. Grandmother?"

"She used to," he said, "but her health has caused her not to go."

"What does your father do for a living?" I heard my father ask.

"Um, I don't really know my father," James said, looking down at his plate.

Change the subject time, I thought, so he can get through dinner without heartburn. I knew James didn't like talking about his family, so I said, "Maybe one day, James, you could come to church with Momma, me, and Daddy," hoping the tension would turn more on Daddy than James.

"That is a lovely idea," Momma said.

Daddy, on the other hand, went silent.

"I would like that," James said.

"You like school?" Momma asked.

"It's okay," James replied.

"What do you want to do after high school, James?" my mother continued.

"I would like to get a good job so one day I, too, can take care of my family."

"No college?" Momma said.

"I think that was a good enough answer," Daddy said, looking at James. "College is too overrated nowadays. I never went to college, and I take good care of my family."

As if James was thinking of the best answer, he sat there for a minute laid down his fork looked back up at momma and said, "I haven't really thought about college, I may go to college if I can't find a good job, but I would need a break first."

To take the spotlight off James and since I knew daddy was on James side, I said, "I feel the same way. I don't really want to go to college straight out of high school." That was no secret to my parents.

James then said, "Maybe I can find a good company and work my way to the top."

"I am beginning to like this kid already," Daddy said as he took a drink of his water to wash down his food.

The rest of the dinner was semi-silent. Every now and then a question would be asked, but nothing that could hurt the relationship that James and I shared. After dinner Momma and I cleared away the dishes while James and Daddy went back into the living room for some Sunday football.

"Well," I said after about fifteen minutes of silence, "what do you think, Momma?" I asked, curiosity burning at my insides.

"I like him," Momma said. "He has a certain type of honesty. He doesn't seem to want to talk much about his family, though. Maybe there is a hidden message within him," she said. "Have you met his parents?"

"Not yet," I replied, "but I am sure I will. Besides, I am dating him, not his family."

"Yeah, but it is good to know the family as well."

"In time, Momma," I said, "in time."

After the dishes were done, I raced upstairs to change so James and I could take a quick walk to our tree. After the handshakes and the good-byes, we were off to be alone. My ears instantly started burning once we were out of their sight. "Are your ears burning?" I asked James as he reached for my hand.

"All the way to my brain," he said, and then we just laughed. We knew we were the topic of my parents' conversation.

"Soo," I asked, wanting to know how he felt about my parents, "what do you think?"

"I like them, Victoria. They seem to be good people. They care a lot about you, and I like that."

That statement caught me by surprise. Why would he care so much about them caring for me? I always thought that parents caring about their children was a given.

"I will meet your momma if you want me to," I said.

"Not now, Victoria. She is nothing like your mother. I would much rather you meet my grandmother, but she is going through something right now and it is not the time. You will, though. I promise you will." I wanted to pry a little more, but I felt he would tell me all about them when he was ready.

Chapter 6

James was now spending time at my house. Fall was finishing its final chapter for the 1977 season, and winter was settling in. James would help Daddy cut and gather firewood; other times we would just spend time alone. Daddy didn't have a son and enjoyed James being around.

The week of Thanksgiving, Momma invited James to church and Thanksgiving dinner. James attended church with us Thanksgiving Day. The whole time he seemed distant; he did walk to the altar during altar call, and he prayed when the pastor told us to, but he had something on his mind in church that day. I just marked it off as he was bored, but as time pressed on, I wondered what those thoughts were.

During Thanksgiving dinner by tradition, Daddy carved the turkey. This time James offered to say grace. I am sure he made it up as he went along. It lasted only a few seconds, but Momma was pleased that he even offered. If he was giving thanks, that was all that mattered.

By tradition, on Thanksgiving Day after blessing the food, we each told what we were thankful for. Momma led the thanksgiving this year. "I am thankful for my family, a loving husband, and a wonderful daughter. I am thankful for God granting me another day to prove faithful. I am also thankful that Victoria has found such a special friend in James. Victoria," she said, her eyes moving around the table, "what are you thankful for?"

"I am thankful for my family, and I am thankful for having James in my life." I then turned to James and said, "James, what are you thankful for?"

He looked at me for a moment, and then he said, "I am thankful for you, Victoria, and I am thankful for my grandma. I am also thankful for your family, which shares so much love. I am thankful for being invited to such a good dinner."

"Here, here," Daddy interrupted.

"Mr. Adams," James said, "it's your turn."

"I am thankful," my father said, "for a beautiful wife of eighteen years, a loving daughter of fifteen years, good food, and a good job to take care of my family. Also, for my health, and you, James, for saying grace so I didn't have to." Laughter filled the table. Leave it to Daddy to give the grand finale.

After dinner, Daddy and James watched the traditional football game and then put out the Christmas lights while Momma and I decorated the tree. After they were done with the outside and before Daddy put the angel on the tree, we all sat down for Momma's traditional hot cocoa. Gathering up the cups, Momma said, "It's time to top the tree." Daddy reached into the little box that Mother so carefully wrapped the angel in, and Daddy placed it on the tree. He turned on the lights, and that was truly the prettiest Christmas tree we ever had. James and I sat on the couch and watched the tree glimmer until way after eleven o'clock that night before he went home.

Christmas was another tradition at our house. I worked hard around the house doing extra chores to buy James a present; my parents didn't believe in getting something for free. I shoveled snow, I washed clothes, and I cleaned and cleaned just so I could raise enough money to buy him a special gift. James never talked about anything that he wanted for Christmas. When I asked, he just said that if we were together, that would be the best Christmas present that he could have. On that note, I felt that we were one and the same. I always looked forward to tearing open gifts for Christmas, but this year was different. I had gotten my present earlier than expected, and that present was James.

On Christmas Eve, James and I spent the whole day together. We watched the all-day Christmas marathon, and every now and then I would step away from him to help my mother in the kitchen. When I returned one time, Daddy was sitting in my place, and he and James were engulfed in the Christmas show that was playing. James was watching them as if he was seeing them for the first time. His eyes were glued to the set, and when I would say something to him, I would have to repeat what I had said because he was so interested in what he was watching.

Christmas night, James stayed until midnight. After Momma and Daddy went to bed, James and I sat watching the glimmer of the tree. We became lost in our thoughts as the tree shone on. I got up to get us both some eggnog, and when I got back, James was standing under the mistletoe waiting for his Christmas kiss. I was happy to oblige him. He kissed my lips oh so gently, and I returned the favor. I wanted James to stay the night, but I knew my parents wouldn't accept the idea, so I didn't bother to ask.

After he left, I lay in my bed thanking God for what he had blessed me with. This had been by far the best year of my life.

James came early Christmas morning, and he had gifts with him. He brought me a picture of a willow tree, and in big bold letters at the bottom of the tree, it read the Andrews Willow Tree. I thought that was a nice gesture and I thought he was secretly trying to tell me something. I never asked him, but I felt that in that portrait he was telling me that one day we would have our own tree and we could engrave it like the people before us had engraved their name in the tree where we spent most of our time. That was the best Christmas present I could have imagined. That tree said all the things that James had not said to me, and that was that he loved me. He gave my momma a new Bible and my daddy gardening tools. I bought James a key that hung on a chain. That was my secret way of letting him know that he held the key to my heart. After we ate our dinner and sat around watching it snow, I felt in my heart that life was turning out surprisingly good and there was nothing on this old green earth that could separate us. So, I thought …

Chapter 7

The year 1978 started out rather quiet. I turned sixteen in February. I didn't want the "sweet sixteen big deal" all I wanted was to spend time with James and that is what I did. That was the first time and the only time I was allowed to skip school. James arrived at my house early that morning and we watched movies all day long. Other than making us lunch momma didn't bother us. It was like we were alone just sharing time, making memories.

That day ended to soon the next day we were back in school and going through our same routines. It was still too cold to go to that old willow tree, so James just spent time at my house. Winter dried up, came, and went, and we were hoping for spring to come and go just as fast so we could be set to finish tenth grade. At this time, James and I were closer than any couple could be without being married. The only thing we weren't doing at this stage in our relationship was having sex. He never asked and I never offered. I was satisfied with just the togetherness and sex would come in time. We were just enjoying our teenage years together. There wasn't any rush for anything we had our whole lives ahead of us in time we would completely seal the bond preferably after marriage when we were both ready. But for now, `we continued to hang out at the willow tree; we had invitations to share time with other teenagers, but we chose to hang out alone. We kind of preferred it that way. I don't think either of us wanted to share our space with anyone else. There were other teenagers that we associated with, but that was only on school grounds. They tried to get in our space, but it was too full we only had room for us. Besides I knew some of the girls as well as boys had ill intentions April for instance was at the forefront of my mind. James was good looking and at times I could tell a few of the guys was sweet on me but even though we noticed the extra attention it wasn't a bother. We knew we were a desired couple, envied even yet we only saw each other. Our bond was so tight nothing or no one could enter in, nor could it be broken. When we left school, we never had time for anyone else. We were so absorbed in each other, nobody else really mattered.

The summer of 1978 was right before us- that is when things started to change. We were sitting under the willow tree when from a distance, we saw this woman wondering into the park. She appeared drunk and a little disoriented. I saw her first, and when I pointed her out to James, horror stretched across his face. "Oh God no" I heard James say. Maybe we should help her; I said, feeling as though James knew this woman. "No" he said, standing up. "I will help her. I will have to see you later. Are you going to be all right?" He said as he hurried away. He was approaching the woman before I had a chance to answer his question. "Yes," I said, trying to figure out what had just happened. "I will be fine." I watched James guide that woman, and I sat under that tree for the rest of the evening hoping that James would return, but he never did.

The next day James was there waiting at the tree like nothing ever happened. I asked about the woman that he helped out of the park the day before. He just said, "She is kin to me, with her comes many troubles

Vicky," and he left it at that, and I did too. I felt that if he wanted me to know more, he would tell me in his own time, but I couldn't help but feel that woman that he helped that day was one of the reasons he always daydreamed.

We still went to the willow tree or to my house, but his time with me became shorter and shorter. Although we met like we always had, I felt that James was only there in body; his mind was somewhere else. He started daydreaming and was short with his words when he spoke. It bothered me so much that I had to find out what was happening.

It was the fourth of July when it all started to change. We were sitting under the willow tree waiting for the fireworks to start when James asked, "Could you imagine life without your mom and dad, Vicky?"

"No," I replied, "but why do you ask?" I just felt he was ready to talk about his parents.

"No reason," he said, looking at the families who had gathered for the fireworks. Then he said, "If one of them had to leave you, would you trust that one day they would return for you?"

Again, feeling a little concerned for him, I answered yes and asked why.

He never answered. It was like he didn't hear me; he just kept looking into the crowd. Then he said, "If one or both of them left you, how long do you think it would take for you to get over the fact that they were gone?"

"Never," I answered, now feeling stress jump into my body. "Is someone leaving you, James?" I asked, wanting to take the look of pain from his face.

"They already have, Vicky, but I guess sometimes things happen, and even though you try, you just can't control them." After a pause, he continued, "If you felt that you had only one person left that really cared about you and you felt that they were about to give up and leave you, would you try everything in you to try and stop them?"

"Yes," I replied again. "Do you feel something like that is about to happen, James?" I asked, again not wanting to know the answer.

He just said, "I feel like something like that is about to happen."

I never even saw the fireworks that night. I wasn't looking at them because I was in my own little world. I wished I knew what was about to happen so I could find some way of stopping it, but I had no way of knowing and I felt whatever it was, it was way beyond my control. Through the weeks that passed, James and I were together only in body. I think we were both waiting for that something to happen; instead of building what we had, we were just waiting for it to all tumble down.

It wasn't until the fall before we were to start the eleventh grade that James began to completely withdraw. One autumn night, the sun had shut its eyes and the moon had awakened. James didn't meet me at the willow tree, nor did he come to my house that day. I knew in my heart that something had to be terribly wrong. I was lying in my bed not being able to sleep, it was somewhere around two thirty in the morning. I heard something hitting my window. As I got up to look further, I could see a figure standing below. As I got a closer look, I could see that figure was James. Although I was glad to see him it was the timing that allowed fear to come in. I raised up my window acknowledging his presence. "James" I said in my best whispering voice so I wouldn't wake my parents "what's wrong", what are you doing here? He didn't answer me instead he had an unusual request.

"Vicky," he said in a troubled voice, "will you come with me?" Even though my parents loved James, I knew that if my mother or father had the least bit of a notion that I was leaving the house at that hour, I would have been grounded for life, yet I did as he asked. I felt something was wrong; I felt that James needed me.

As James and I walked to the park that night, I felt my breath trying to leave me. It was as if we were walking the trail to the willow tree for the last time. James was silent and the night was still, and the willow tree's limbs were barely moving to the wind's beat. It was as if something was about to die; death was in the air. When we got to the willow tree, we just sat there, never speaking a word. It wasn't I who grabbed hold of his hand, but it was James who took hold of mine. It wasn't the fact that he held my hand, but it was the way he held it that startled me. It was like a grip, sort of like he was afraid that I was going to leave him. Yet it wasn't I who was leaving.

I decided to bring the attention back to his words. "Is our love still endless, James?" I managed to whisper, trying to make him snap out of the trance that he was in. When he didn't reply, I heard myself asking, "What is wrong? Talk to me. I am sure we could work it out."

He just sat there for moments on end, and then he said, "Sometimes this life can be unfair, Vicky. Sometimes the cards that are dealt for some probably should have been given to the ones that were much stronger. It just doesn't seem fair for troubles to be handed down to someone that is doing all he can to get to the point where he can make his own decisions. Or have you ever wondered how God decides which parents get which children? Or if there was a way……to……. switch without involving social……service." I could tell he wasn't really looking for answers he was just freely speaking because after he said all that his voice just trailed off and he just had a blank stare on his face.

Not knowing what he meant, my heart skipped several beats, letting me know whatever he was saying or about to say would change our lives forever.

"Vicky," he said as his voice trembled in a way that I had not known before, "this has been the happiest year that I can remember." He then turned to look at me, and his eyes caught mine before he spoke again. "You have shown me what love is all about. I love spending time with you, and I love the way my days feel when we are together. I love the way I feel when I am with your family. I just knew the day that you said that you would be my girl, that our love would be endless. That is why telling you what I am about to say saddens me; I feel my world is about to crumble. I must leave. Things are happening in my life right now, and I must leave."

I was thinking that he meant that he had to get back home because it was so late, so I replied, "I understand, James. We probably should get back we can talk more tomorrow."

It was his next statement that drained all the color from my face and numbed my body to the point that I felt paralyzed with fear. "Tomorrow is what I am talking about. I must go…...away. We won't be able to see each other for a while until things get straightened out. I have troubles, Vicky, unspeakable troubles, which are just too complicated to talk about. My family isn't like your family; I would do anything to have a family like yours. If I did, my troubles wouldn't seem that bad. I would be able to have a good life, a life without the troubles that I am faced with. The only family that I have been able to depend on needs me now. It's not my mother or my father, because they are not around, but it's my grandma. I am the only one that she can depend on. I can't let her down."

I was sitting there in a state of numbness, I was hearing him, but I was hoping that I wasn't hearing him as he continued "She went to the doctor today, and they found cancer. I have nobody else to help her through this tough time, and I can't leave her by herself. My mother and father, well they have troubles of their own and they won't make the time to help her. My father left months ago, and my mother is leaving tomorrow, to both my mother and my father I am now just a forgotten memory. They don't want me he said with tears forming in his eyes I don't think they ever did. It will be just me and my grandmother now. We are left to fend for ourselves. The last thing she needs is to have me turn my back on her. I have to move in with my grandmother. Staying with her now and then or making short visits doesn't seem enough right now. She needs me, and even though I need you right now, she needs me more. Since my father left us, my mother has found troubles of her own, she blames my grandmother for my dad leaving and she just don't want to have a child right now. He paused for a minute then said, "there isn't enough room in her life--- for me."

"Ever since my dad and mothers' troubles started my grandmother has been both mother and father to me. Without my grandmother I was going to be awarded to the state. I would have been placed in a foster home with who knows who, living who knows where. When I needed her, she was there. Now it's her that needs me, and I must be there for her. I must make sure she is taking care of. Without me, I fear she won't fight to live." He then turned to look into my teary eyes. "Without her, I fear I will lose my will to …" he paused for a moment and then said "live." He continued as the tears stung my face with wetness, while my mind was trying to grasp on to the fact that this conversation was the beginning of our ending. "I don't expect you to wait for me he continued, for over a year, our heartbeats were as one. I guess I fell in love with us, and I just feel my heart will stop beating until our paths cross again." As James kept talking my mind trailed off to his last statement, "Heartbeats were as one, I guess I fell in love with us." Oh no James loved me too and now he was leaving. How unfair was that. He didn't deserve this, we didn't deserve this, I didn't deserve this. My mind was all over the place, yet I tried to focus in on James's word because I just knew somewhere in his sadness there must be an April fools. I honed back into his words trying to grasp what was happening and patiently waiting for the punch line that never came as he continued with his words. "This decision came yesterday, and I wanted to tell you before I left. That is the reason I didn't meet up with you. Social workers were at my mom's house, and they were trying to take me, but my grandmother stopped them. Now I will live with her, and my mother can now be free. I don't expect you to understand; I just hope that you do.." I didn't feel right just up and leaving. I had to at least explain what was happening."

Words would not release from my lips. His words "fell in love with us" were bittersweet. I longed to hear them, but the last thing I ever expected was for him to say those words to me in the same sentence that said that he was leaving me. Somehow the two just didn't seem to go together in my eyes—tear-filled eyes at that. I was not expecting anything that he was saying. I just felt numb. I felt as though life was about to take a vacation, never to return. I wanted to curse the pain that was about to take him away from me. I had to say something; I had to make myself speak. "We can still see each other, James. We can still be—"

He cut my words off by saying, "It's just too complicated right now. I care about you too much to drag you into the troubles I have."

"My parents will bring me to see you," I said, grasping at every option I could. I just didn't want James to leave me. My voice carried a load of its own. "Please, James," I said, pleading. "Don't leave me. We can work through this together." I just didn't want him to go.

When James turned so the moon shone on his face, it was then that I saw that he had been crying. The tears that had stained his face let my heart and soul know this is real. No April fools, or surprise I was only joking the pain we were experiencing at that moment was real. I had never seen that side of him before, so I couldn't think of a thing to say. I would curse that moment for months; I wished I had changed that situation in some way so I could have made a difference that he could remember. Instead, I sat quietly beside him, hoping that the night would never end. I was afraid in my heart that this was the end of me, and words finally left the both of us. It was as though we couldn't speak... we sat under that old tree for what seemed like hours, time had passed before James spoke the words that I didn't want to hear.

"I had better walk you back before it gets daylight" He grabbed my hand to help me on my feet, he pulled me close, looked into my eyes and said "You are my first love Vicky and ending this isn't an option. I will always remember US... I will do whatever it takes to find you again Vicky, I can only hope that you continue with life with the understanding that I love you and I never meant for this to happen. One day hopefully we will prove that our love is truly endless. I am not leaving us." He now had my face cupped in his hands. I noticed a tear creep out of his eye as he finished. "I'm just forced to leave you. I will be back that I promise" .... As if he was either unsure or trying to convince me he repeated himself. "I will be back I promise." As bad as I wanted to say the words, I love you I just couldn't bring myself to it. As the words danced in my head that is as far as they got before the tears started free falling and my voice dried up.

"Please don't cry Vicky this is hard for both of us. As soon as I find out how to help my grandmother and get her the helps, she needs I will be back I promise." His words seemed to be sincere, but I felt a certain emptiness, it was a feeling that I couldn't explain. I couldn't stop my tears from falling and I felt that it was just my new norm. He wiped my tears with his fingers. No need for that I thought to myself they aren't going anywhere. He grabbed my hand with a little tug letting me know it was time to leave. I felt there was so much to say I just didn't know what. We walked hand and hand back to my house.

Thinking that was our last meeting under the tree, I; wished I had of told him how I truly felt. I knew I love you was only spoken when there is a future, and I felt that our future was now our past. If I told him how I really felt would he find a way to stay, was I being selfish? As bad as I wanted to tell him that he was my everything, that I didn't want to live without him in my life, I just couldn't bring myself to tell him, and I don't think that is what he needed to hear at this time. I guess the only thing I could do at this point was let him go and try to figure it out. I could only hope that it wouldn't take too long or that he realized that he couldn't be without me either and one day when I returned to my tree, he would be sitting there waiting like he had so many times before.

When we arrived at my house, James pulled me close one last time. The salty taste on his lips I am sure matched mine. We both had our waterworks, and I am sure for the same reasons. When his lips touched mine, I felt my body melt in with his for a moment causing us to be one. We stood there as if we were stuck together. That was the longest kiss he ever gave me. With that kiss I knew that our paths would cross again one day….someday……at least that was my prayer.

James spoke it but I am going to be sure of it. I would not let somebody else's troubles stop our love. I didn't know how, when or where but I was determined that even though we were forced to be separated. Like my momma said troubles don't last always and as far as we are concerned neither will our separation. I vowed as I walked away from James that night. We will be together again and that willow tree wont weep for long.

James watched as I climbed back through the window. He stood there with some things that were never said. He then just turned and walked away. As I stood in my window watching him walk into the darkness, I made a promise that one day I would take that hurt away. I would make him my own, and he would never have to experience this kind of hurt and whatever his hurt was that night, he would never experience it again. A burst of anger came over me as I remembered leaving my friends In Colorado. Vowing I would never get close to anyone again. Leaving my friends didn't compare to the pain I was feeling of losing James. It wasn't my father that took me away it was his grandmother. I knew I shouldn't have allowed myself to bond again. It just goes to show that no matter how much you want to stay there is always something or someone who has the final say. So far in my life it hasn't been in my favor.

Days passed, and I found myself going into a deep depression. My appetite had left, and my mind only wanted to think of James and the time we shared. I went to school only because I didn't want to change my routine fearing that would only cause my mom and dad to worry about me, besides going to school helped to pass the time away. I knew there were thoughts and conversations scurrying around about James's sudden disappearance, but I knew no one would dare ask. It wasn't until I was standing at my locker that April found the need to approach me. I didn't see her at first when I closed my locker there, she was.

"Victoria right" she said as she extended her hand, "I'm April, I noticed James hasn't been in school is everything ok. Is his parents at it again?" Even though her words startled me I didn't feel the need to share with her the pain I was feeling.

I just replied with "yeah everything is fine April, he just has somethings that he needs to work through, but we are ok." I decided to throw that in just in case she wanted to become the school reporter, she wouldn't hear about our breakup from me.

"Whew "she said that's good to hear, I was just worried that something bad happened because of well I am sure you know the way his parents treat him?"

No, I thought I don't know April and I don't want you to add salt to my injuries I don't need to worry any more than I already do, and I don't need you spreading rumors, so I said "It doesn't have anything to do with his parents. He needs to help out a relative." That's enough information I thought I need to end this conversation. I won't be a part of spreading lies about James.

Even though she acted as if she knew a lot, but I didn't feel the need to entertain her. I didn't feel much like talking about it and as far as I knew she was the school reporter. She could have been trying to be nice so she could go tell everybody that he left me. That would give them something to talk about. I had to get rid of her without sounding like I was feeling. "April thank you, but I am fine. James has somethings to take care of. We are still together we just see each other after school now that he is attending another school." Ok Victoria my subconscious mind took control. You have said enough rather she believes you or not it doesn't matter you have said enough. "Thank you for your concern, April but I'm fine." As I tried to walk past her, she followed me. "Well, I am here if you need someone she continued. I don't have a lot of friends, so I am a good listener if you need one." I was never happier to reach my class, but I turned to her one last time and said, "thank you I will keep that in mind, but I am fine." With that I entered my class, and she was gone. During class I couldn't help but feel like I wasn't fair to April she seemed nice enough, but I didn't want a girlfriend I wanted James.

I would spend my days daydreaming about him and pretending that after class he would be outside waiting for me. After school I would go to the willow tree, hoping that James would return and we could forget the night that ended our relationship, but he never came. It wasn't until about a week later that Daddy asked the question that made me come to the realization that James wasn't coming back. It was the usual dinner time, and we were sitting at the table. I didn't have an appetite but tried to force down some mashed potatoes so my parents couldn't see my sadness. About ten minutes into dinner, daddy asked about James. "How is James doing? Is he coming over this weekend?" he said as he took a sip of water. "We got some leaves that could use a good raking", my thoughts of James made tears begin to form in my eyes. Not wanting my parents to see them, I asked to be excused from the table. I didn't give them time to answer because I knew if I stayed at the table another second, I wouldn't be able to keep the tears from falling. I hurried to my room, shut the door, and cried into my pillow.

A few minutes later, Daddy knocked on my door. Pushing the door open, he asked, "Can I come in for a minute?" He came into my room carrying both mine and his dinner plate. Really not wanting to be bothered, I sat up in my bed.

Daddy came over to sit on the edge of the bed, as he carefully laid my dinner plate in my lap he said "Victoria, honey these past few days you haven't been eating if you're not careful you will waste away and your old dad won't have his little girl." Trying to force a smile and seeing the hurt in his face I took hold to my fork and looked down at my plate a meal that was once one of my favorites now looked like a plate of mush causing me to lay my fork back down, I could feel my eyes watering back up and the sadness of losing James was taken back over. Before my dad could say anything else I was giving him the whole spill about James leaving.

"He's gone, Daddy," James is gone was all I could force myself to say before the tears started sliding down my face.

"What, where did he go? Is he coming back?" daddy ask with curiosity in his voice. "He has to go take care of his grandmother, his mom and dad left and now he had to leave too. "Oh, Victoria, I am so sorry; don't cry. One day he will come back. Some things we can't control." With concern in his voice, he added, "But you can't make yourself sick over it. It's just not healthy. If he doesn't come back, there will be other James's in your life. I hate that he had to go, but things happen, honey, things we don't understand. We will miss him too."

I was trying to listen to Daddy, but the last conversation that James and I had kept playing in my head.

Daddy continued, "I am here if you want to talk, honey. I am here if you need me." With that he got up and left the room.

An hour or so passed. I was sure Daddy and Momma were discussing James leaving.

Then Momma came into my room. "Honey," she said, "your father told me what happened. I am so sorry. I know you cared for him, but you can't let it get you down. You are way too young to let this get to you like this. Pray, Victoria. Only God knows what the outcome will be. I wish he could have stayed around. He was a lovely boy, but I don't like what this is doing to you. Do you know where he went or how to find him? Maybe one day we could go for a visit?"

"No, Momma. I said he's just gone. I wish he would come back, Momma. I wish that he never had to leave." My heart was broken and looking at Momma's heart breaking made things worse.

She said, "What can I do, Victoria? What can I do to help you through this? All I know to do is pray. I don't like to see you hurting. I don't like to see you going through this at such a young age. Please pray, Victoria. There will be other young boys to capture your heart. This is just the beginning."

Beginning momma, I have lost relationships all my life first daddy moving with his job now James. I love him momma. I know you think I don't know what love is, but I know I do I love him. "I don't want other boys, Momma. I want James. We were close; we were best friends and I know he loved me too. It's all so unfair. I know he is hurting. I know that he needs me, and there isn't anything that I can do, Momma—nothing."

Momma took me in her arms and said, "In time, Victoria, it will become easier for you in time. Just trust in God. If it's meant to be, he will come back. If it's not meant to be, then consider it a blessing. You may not see it now, but the Lord sees everything. He took him away for a reason; and if he sees fit, he will bring him back, but in the meantime, you must continue to live, honey. Please don't cry."

I knew she meant well, but her words meant nothing to me. I wanted James back. That was the only thing to make me feel better, the only thing to dry my tears. Since that wasn't going to happen, what else was there.

I just went through the motions during my junior year in high school. Every now and then I would eat lunch in a group setting and the boys would flirt with me but If I couldn't have James, I didn't want anybody and furthermore, I was done with the dating game. Nobody ever brought

James up and neither did I. Despite my hurt and pain, I still went faithfully to the willow tree. There were times that Momma and Daddy would come around to give me a pep talk, but all in all, I was still missing James and still wanting to know if he had stayed, where we would be right now.

Momma's sadness turned to anger, even though she was a Christian woman. I knew she was mad, maybe not at James, but at the situation.

Right before my senior year daddy got another promotion. The extra money that he was making allowed them to buy some land and build them their dream house. I would still only be a few blocks from my willow tree. Momma thought it would be a good time to get my learners and start driving. I know she knew I had concerns about moving and even though it wasn't a person this time my fear was that I would be too far from my willow tree to walk. Daddy helped me get my driver's license and I knew he thought that one of the main reasons I wanted them was to hopefully somewhere some way run into James. That was the main reason that sparked my desire to drive but I didn't know where or how to find him. We only met at the willow tree and my house so finding him even in this small town is like a needle in a haystack. I used their second vehicle when I wanted to drive which was only to school and back. I didn't need a car of my own because I wasn't a social butterfly, and I could walk to my tree after all.

My senior year came and went with little meaning. I was just trying to race through school so I could find out just where my life was going to take me. Upon graduating my momma and daddy presented me with a brand-new

Jeep. They were more excited than I was. In the back of my mind, I was glad that it was brand new because if and when I decided to find James, I wanted something dependable. I knew in my heart that I would have a chance to find James if that was what was in store for me. I didn't care how or where I just wanted my second chance. I just felt that in a matter of time, if nothing else, James would find me. He said that he would return once he got her help and taken care of, but I was thinking weeks not years. I often wondered if his grandmother had passed or was still living, with him helping her to hold on to what life she had left. There was no way of knowing what he was going through. I was just hoping that God watched after him—and his grandmother for that matter. I didn't know what would happen to James considering he thought she was all he had. I could only hope that if she had past that he was in the process of looking for me. Then the willow tree would creep up and my memories would remind me that I wasn't hard to find if he was looking for me, I could be found underneath the willow tree. Maybe he had a change of heart, maybe I was now a memory. Maybe he didn't want to find me and just maybe he didn't want to be found.

Momma and daddy was right about one thing though in time it did become easier, even though I still thought about him and wished that we could cross paths. I was more accepting to the fact that it was indeed a lost love and one day if God saw fit, we would cross paths again in the meantime I would have to continue with only the memories of what we had and the thoughts of what could have or would have been.

Chapter 8

The smaaaaack was the sound of a dodgeball hitting me across the face, bringing me back to reality. The fall wind seemed cooler now. Fall had finally set in, as had the reality of my life. Just about every tree, including my old faithful willow tree, had lost its fall foliage. They looked dried-up, naked to the eye, with just a leaf or two hanging on for the final breeze of the season. My tree was barely holding onto the hope that summer was not over, barely fighting for the protection it had once given me.

The fall months were rather chilly in Virginia. Summer had finally shut its eyes to yet another season, and fall was making its mark. I was sitting under my familiar willow tree at our city park, thermos of tea by my side, with my journal in hand, visions of the children playing with their families for the last time in the park before Mr. Winter decided to come for a stay. It sent me into my trance and memories of James, and it was the slap of the dodgeball that brought me back. I picked up the ball and rolled it back to a little blond-headed girl with curly locks who couldn't have been more than five years old.

"I'm sorry," she said, anxious to get her ball back.

"That's okay, it didn't hurt," I said smiling. At the same time, the side of my face was burning. I had to laugh, watching her running back to her circle of little friends, screaming, and giggling along the way. I wrote about the little girl, and from time to time couldn't help but watch her, picturing what my little girl would look like.

It would be my third-year anniversary at the local drugstore in a few days. I started that job straight out of high school. I ended up getting an associate degree to assist the pharmacist. I knew it was a dead-end job, but in Virginia you had to get what you could when it was available. My mother would say, "Victoria, try going to school to be a teacher. You would be good with kids." I always felt when I moved out my mother would have the empty nest syndrome; becoming a schoolteacher with kids screaming at me all day was not in my plans. If I was going to look after kids, they would have to be my own.

Even though my job was depressing, it paid my rent for the apartment that I had, and it kept me from being dependent on my parents. It was a rather depressing job, a job that allowed you to watch life dwindle right before your eyes. One day, you would see someone pick up a prescription; and months later, you would hardly recognize the same patient because the illness that they were faced with had taken over their body.

Working at the pharmacy had its perks and although I had my share of hateful customers for instance Mr. Boots, who never had a kind word to say to anyone. His name was Mr. Wilson but, we nick-named him Mr. Boots because our pharmacist said he would like to take his boots and give him a swift kick of kindness. He was in his late fifty's, retired early and now was spending his last days on earth making everybody feel his misery every chance he could get. He had a permanent frown that aligned with a scar that added disfigurement to his face. I thought he probably got the scar in his younger years during a fight that not only went wrong but it was evident that he lost. In reality it came from a bad car accident that almost cost him his life and the only thing else I know about the accident is that it landed him a lot of money. I'm sure that his grumpiness wasn't a new trend he's probably been miserable all his life. Rumor had it that he was one of the richest men in Pocahontas and although once married with a family he now lives alone and entertains the corners finest. I guess people would do anything for money but dealing with him for it would be a deal breaker. He grumbled about everything, nothing was good enough and he hated everybody equally. We all hated the days he came into the pharmacy. You could hear his presence a block away. He started his bickering as soon as he encountered an able body that would give him a few minutes of their time and it would only be a minute or two I have never seen that man continue a conversation longer than that. No one wanted to hear how unhappy he was about his life but that never stopped him from trying to share his misery.

I also had pleasant customers too. My favorite customer was this little old lady named Mrs. Andrews. She never had a cruel word for anyone, and even though life had a difficult plan for her—a plan that showed with every step she took—she was still the humblest customer of all. She was a lady with a caring heart, and a lady who treated life as it ought to be treated. She was a woman who was glad that she was granted another breath to spend another moment in this old world. She wanted to live but was destined to die too soon. She was seventy-five years old, and it showed with her every stride.

I would watch her wobble into the pharmacy, pick up her prescription, and walk around the store with her cane guiding her every move. When she made her way to the register, although pain and suffering were in her face, she would still smile and say, "Victoria, how are you dear? You're such a lovely young girl. I hope you never have to deal with the troubles that life sometimes offers when you get old like me." I would then tell her that even in her old age, she was beautiful, and she was blessed.

I would tease her and tell her that I was going to find her a boyfriend. She would just chuckle and say, "Lord, child, the only man I have ever loved has gone to meet his maker, and unless you can bring him back, it will only be a waste of time. There's not a man alive who could fill his shoes even if they tried. If they managed to put those shoes on, their feet would hurt for days. My husband was a one-of-a-kind man, and he was my first and my only love." Her eyes would glisten when she spoke of him. Even though he had been dead for years, she still kept their love alive. She held on to a love that most people only dreamed of. We would stand at the counter and talk for longer than what was generally allowed, but I was drawn to her, her kindness, and her wisdom. She was a joy to be around, and she was one reason I didn't leave that old depressing place.

While I watched her leave the store, I would find myself wondering if she had family close by to take care of her. Did she catch a taxi to and from her destinations? When she was out of my sight, I would feel that she had a battle that she didn't want to accept, and I couldn't help wanting to take that battle away from her so she could conduct her years without the pain that she was facing. Her crippled hands told me that in years gone by, she had used her hands a lot, probably a gentle squeeze here and there to bring comfort to someone who was hurting. Her stumbling walk helped me to understand that she was up in her years, probably had walked miles, probably carrying on her shoulders a load that belonged to someone else in her life span, and the wrinkles in her face showed me that she had carried her heart on her sleeve while carrying other peoples' burdens. Although I didn't want to end up like her, I wanted to know more about what she went through in her life that brought her to this point. I wanted to know more about her. What made her so humble even though she now carried her own pain? What made her still smile and want to carry on?

After work, I would go to the park to sit under the willow tree with my journal, writing about my days at the park, things I wanted in my life, things that I needed in my life, things that were missing. I would think about how my life was slowing dwindling while I watched families playing with their children and picnicking in the grass. My life continued to haunt me when I had turned twenty-one. My mom being the momma that she was, gave me the missing the best years of my life pep talk. We were sitting on her porch one evening after I had gotten off work, daddy was in the shed piddling around and that is when it started. "Victoria you are twenty-one and you don't go out, you don't date all you do is work and stay under that old tree writing about what you want to do in your life. When are you going to quit writing and start doing those things you write about? These are the best years of your life, and you are wasting them away. It would be nice if you come to church, there are single men that go to church you know. You can find one to just hang out with. This is the time in your life that you should be out living, dating, and enjoying your young years. Before you know it, these years will be gone, and you will look back and wish you could do it all over again. It's time for you to start living life."

I knew she was right I didn't do anything that girls my age considered to be fun. I'd often thought about spinning the dating wheel to see what could happen, but even though it was a teenage love affair that was unfinished and had haunted me for all these years, I still wasn't sure that I wanted another relationship. I still hadn't gotten over James and the way our relationship suddenly had to end. I was becoming lonely, and I longed to become a mother with kids of my own, but I feared dating. What happened between me, and James would creep into my mind, and it would rule out my desires for a family. I didn't want to take the chance of being hurt again. I wouldn't give anyone the chance to hurt my heart again, intentionally, or non-intentionally. It just wasn't going to happen. And then something happened that I would never have dreamed of.

Chapter 9

It's true that time waits for no one. When I was twenty-two years old and still sitting under the willow tree on the eve of Valentine's Day, I hadn't seen Mrs. Andrews at the pharmacy in a while as I was seated under my tree, I noticed a woman being wheeled through the park. A closer look proved that it was Mrs. Andrews. The sun was beaming down, making the air warm enough to enjoy the day. The snow had melted, and if I didn't know better, I could have mistaken that day as a pre-spring day. As she passed by, I threw my hand up to acknowledge her. I didn't want to intrude, and I thought speaking would be sufficient. A young man was with her, even though he looked familiar, I didn't know him—how could I? He looked to be around my age. As he pushed Mrs. Andrews on the walking path, I could tell he was gentle, and his focus was her safety. I didn't say anything to him; my focus was on Mrs. Andrews. I just waved as he wheeled her through the park. I watched as he stopped along the way to pull her blanket back up around her chest. It wasn't until the second time that they passed that she noticed me.

"Victoria," she said, "how are you, dear?"

"I'm good, Mrs. Andrews, how are you feeling today?"

"Pretty good, dear, considering. Just glad to be aboveground," she said with a little chuckle. "Victoria, I want you to meet my grandson, James."

James, I thought, as I got a closer look. Surely it couldn't be my James. The James that I had missed all these years, the James that was once my best friend, the James that I had written of so many times in my book, the James that stole my heart and walked off into the night. The love that left my life, the memory that should have been forgotten by now. That James couldn't possibly be my James and that sweet woman Mrs. Andrews couldn't be the reason my heart was broken years ago. My mind was racing trying to grasp the moment when she continued to speak.

"James," she said, "this is Victoria. She works at the drugstore where I—"

Cutting her off, James looked up at me as if he was noticing me for the first time.

"Vicky Adams," he said, and once I saw that familiar searching, I knew it was the James that I lost more than four years earlier. He wasn't the young teenager that I knew back in school; he was now a man, still the good-looking boy that I remembered, yet his features had matured. He now wore a goatee. He still had the same hair cut short on the sides and spiked on top. He was a good-looking man. He actually looked like he had stepped out of a GQ magazine. His shoulders were broader, and he looked stronger, as though his leisure time was used for working out. He was still a caring man, and Mrs. Andrews was his grandmother. It was no wonder she had a familiar face. Funny how I never put the two last names together. James only told me his last name a few times and since I called him James his last name didn't matter much. He must remember my last name because of my parents Mr. and Mrs. Adams. Besides, it's been years and even though

I thought of him often. His last name never seemed that important until now.

I could barely speak; I felt the beads of sweat pop out on my forehead like bee stings. I just stood there, practically staring at this man, James. I couldn't believe how this boy, my best friend, the little boy that I once knew, the one that had held my heart captive all these years, was now a man, all grown-up and standing before me with those same deep, dark brown eyes that held the same mystery that they had back then in high school, a boy who had grown up to be a handsome man—and I couldn't believe the mess I looked. Here I stood, a twenty-two-year-old single woman, hair in a ponytail, wearing baggy jogging pants and an oversize shirt. The man whom I had waited for over five years was standing before me, looking at me, searching, and wanting me to say something. Fear had gripped me, and I was standing there afraid to talk, fearing that I would drool all over the place and make a fool of myself. I just stood there, hoping he would say something else, so I could maintain my composure and join in the conversation like the adult I had become.

"I see you still come to the willow tree, Vicky," James said. "I miss this old tree."

"Isn't she lovely?" Mrs. Andrews said. I thought she was talking about me, but instead she was talking about the willow tree; it was James who was talking about me. Mrs. Andrews continued on about the willow tree as James stood there staring at me neither of us noticing Mrs. Andrews presence.

Tuning Mrs. Andrews back in James said, "Yes Grandma, she is," he said, "as lovely as she was years ago."

"How have you been, James?" I said, struggling to get the words to come out.

"I'm pretty good, just trying to take care of my girl here," he said, rubbing Mrs. Andrews's shoulders.

"It sure is a little world we live in," said Mrs. Andrews. "Who would have thought you two knew each other?" So, I thought this is the woman that stole James from me years ago. This is his grandmother, and she is still alive. So maybe he hadn't tried to find me. Maybe he was still taking care of her like he said he would. I know her medication is for cancer patients, maybe she has had it all these years. I couldn't help but think that the weight of the world had to be on his shoulders the night he left me. He had a dedication to her and now I better understand.

James, looking at me, said to his grandma, "Back then, her name was Vicky. She's the little girl I used to talk about. We were good friends, weren't we, Vicky? We were a little more than friends, right, Vicky?" he said teasingly. I could only nod my head to his question, and he continued, "But now she is all grown-up. I guess Victoria is her grown-up name." While he took his focus to the carving that was still engraved in the tree, he said, "And we had our first and only argument right under this very tree, didn't we, Vicky?" Not giving me time to answer, he continued, "as well as long nights and good talks." With those words, he looked up at me, searching my eyes as if he wanted to know my feelings were still there. At that point, time stopped and rewound in leaps that took us both back to our teenage years.

I had to get back to reality; I struggled for words to say to bring us back to the present. "Vicky was my teenage name. Victoria is my adult name," I said, letting him know I wasn't the teenager that I used to be but a young woman now, whose expectations of a man were a lot higher than sitting under a tree dreaming about the future. I wanted him to see that I was now a responsible woman and not the giddy teenager who wore a broken heart for years after he left.

Not acknowledging my statement, he asked, "You still live at the same place?"

"No, I have an apartment now right down the street. Right before my senior year, Daddy got a promotion and he always wanted some land of his very own, so they bought out the old Dunne farm and built themselves a house," I said, curious why he wanted to know.

He must have been reading my mind because he said, "I drove by several times when I graduated from high school, but there were children playing on the outside, so I never stopped."

All I could think to say was, "Oh." I would have a talk with myself later about my sudden language disorder. I must admit my heart skipped a few beats when he said he had been looking for me. I just don't understand why he didn't look here, under the willow tree.

"After I left, I never came back to the willow tree he said. I just figured you wouldn't come back, and I had too much going on to relive that night. I just tried to stay focused on my ole girl here."

"Oh" I have got to think of better words I feel like a silly teenager. I hope he didn't notice but I was glad that it still bothered him to come to the tree. Me on the other hand it helped me to feel closer to him, but he didn't need to know that maybe in time. He broke my thoughts with his question.

"You come to the tree often?" he asked.

"Every chance I get," I said, just so he would know where he could find me if he was interested.

"Well," he said, looking down at his grandma, "we must get back. The air is getting a little chilly."

"It was great seeing you again, Vicky, I mean Victoria," he said with a wink. "Maybe we can meet up again sometime." He turned to start the walk back. Before he left the park, he stopped, looked back to where I was standing, gave a quick wave, I watched him as he wheeled her out of sight. He would stop from time to time and pull her quilt up around her to keep her warm. I wondered where he had been. Where had he lived? How long would he stay if something happens to Mrs. Andrews? These were questions I should have asked him if my mouth hadn't frozen up. With that thought, I continued writing in my journal. This time I added James.

Even though I knew I had to work the next day, my mind was consumed with seeing James again and wondering if it was God's will for him to be in my life. I remember Momma speaking about God's will, and her words wouldn't leave my mind. Maybe God had put James back in my life for a reason. Maybe we would meet back up and finish what we had started. With those thoughts, I found myself thinking about James and wondering where life had taken him, feeling glad that his grandmother hadn't passed away. Wondering just how bad her cancer had gotten. If she knew of a time if it was fatal and just how long she had. Then my attention turned to James, how handsome he was still. Hoping that memories of us still laid upon him mind, wishing that he wanted to pick up where we left off to see where that road long ago would have taken us. I can't even imagine what's on his mind now that we have had a long overdue encounter.

It was late when I found my way back to my apartment. I found myself searching for the journal that I had tucked away in the box underneath my bed. I spent the biggest part of my night rewinding my life as I read some of the history that we shared. I tried to picture what we were doing that caused me to write in my journal. I was taken back to a particular day when the troubles seemed to surface. On the page were the words "weeping willows weep." James and I were sitting under the willow tree, and out of the blue, he asked the question, "Why do they call some willow trees, weeping willows?" With a sense of sadness in his eyes, he turned to me, searching for an answer. "That is just a myth," I said, trying to change the mood. "There is sadness here," I remember him saying at that time, not realizing that the sadness belonged to him, not the tree. I told him the tree had brought us joy, not sadness. Besides, I added trying to take the sadness that was forming away, this is a cherry willow tree not a weeping willow.

He answered, "weeping willow or cherry willow they all come from the same family of trees and I'm afraid the joy that this tree has brought us will not be permitted always. It seems joy only lasts for a short time, and then comes the pain that seems to last for eternity." At that point, James was trying to tell me something, something that I should have seen and now wished I had known. It wasn't long after that his words rang true. The joy was erased, and the pain set in for the years to come. This brought back memories of the same little boy I remembered, and now the young man I wanted to know. I lay in my bed reading my journals until I fell asleep.

I was at work the next morning; it was Valentine's Day. I had not had any sleep the night before, and at every turn, my body was reminding me that it was tired. That was erased quickly when the young man arrived, he couldn't have been more than eighteen, but his age wasn't the issue. It was what he was carrying that made every woman in the store excited yet a little nervous. He carried a large bouquet of flowers. Curiosity was in the air, and every woman secretly wished they were for her, including myself, and yet I knew better—I didn't have a man or a secret admirer. The flowers were so beautiful. It was a bouquet filled with red roses. Walking into the room full of overly excited woman made this young boy a little nervous. His face flushed red as the women gathered around him to see just who the lucky girl was that someone thought was special enough to send flowers to. I handed the young man a five-dollar bill, and I took the flowers from him and moved away, hoping the flock of women would turn their drooling elsewhere. The strangest thing was, the flowers were not directed to any one person, and the sender's name was unknown. The card read, "Meet me at the place where our memories first started."

Every girl in the store that day watched the door for the mysterious flower sender, hoping that the flowers were for her. The flowers made a couple of girls a little nervous because they didn't know if the bouquet was from their husband or their lover. Those flowers set up a mass of confusion that the store had never seen before.

Once I got off work, I was off to the park. No one took the flowers home because of their own little secret fears, so we just made them the centerpiece of the store; they were so beautiful that we were all pleased with the decision.

It wasn't until that evening at the park that I knew the flowers had been for me. James came walking through the park gates with the exact same rose in his hand.

James sat down on the grass beside me. At first, he didn't hand me the flower; he just asked if I liked roses. When I asked why he didn't leave a name, he said that he thought if he did, I wouldn't show up. I didn't want to tell him that I didn't know that the flowers were from him and that I came to the tree by chance, not because he asked me to. He then handed me the other rose, and then he started talking about what he had gone through when he had left years ago and how hard it was for him. He spoke about the pressures he was under while helping his grandmother overcome her cancer. He talked about how hard it was while he had to watch her suffer, and how hard the chemo had been on her and him for that matter.

There were many times he said that he felt like giving up and putting her in a nursing home just so he wouldn't have to watch her suffer but when he thought about all she had done for him that gave him the will and strength to keep striving though all the hurt and pain he was going through.

What hurt my heart the most was when he said "Vicky my mother and father forgot about me, it seemed easy enough for them just to forget I was ever their child. I can't tell you how many times I wanted to just put her in that nursing home and forget that she ever existed. Hoping it would be as easy for me as it was for them, but she was there when I didn't have no-one. She comforted me as a child when I would lie in my bed and cry for my mother or father. Taking care of her has showed me a lot, how could they just leave me like I was nothing to them, not knowing where I would end up or even why they put the burden of raising me on my grandmother knowing she wasn't well. I think of how easy it was for them to leave me and forget. They haven't called or visited me I am just a memory."

I could see his forehead wrinkle when he spoke of his momma and daddy, but he continued. I never interrupted because I thought he needed to get things off his chest, and he probably didn't have anybody to share his pain for all those years. "It was hard growing up with a father who didn't choose you and a mother who didn't care." I could still see the pain and anger in his eyes, but when he looked at me, his gaze turned from anger to just deep thought. His forehead crinkled as he sat there searching. I took hold of his hand like I had so many times before, and I told him that was the past, that he had to move forward and forget what should have been and focus on what could be. I wanted to tell him of my desires, but I really didn't know him like I did years earlier, so I took it just as slow as he did, not wanting to throw off the wrong signal. I knew he had something to say and something he wanted me to say, but until I was sure of him, I would keep my thoughts to myself. We sat under that tree until after midnight. I invited him to my apartment, but he declined; he had to get back to Mrs. Andrews. I wondered why he never invited me there. I just thought he wanted to keep his time with her all to himself, by himself. I knew his time with her was sacred, so I didn't want to interfere with that; I felt if she had cancer years ago, he wouldn't have her much longer.

After James and I left the park that night I couldn't help but hurt for him. The only good part of his childhood seemed to be our time together he was forced to grow up faster than his time. It seemed that he didn't have any good memories only the ones that we shared but those were the ones that he didn't speak on. I never spoke about "us", and he didn't either. I just didn't want to put any more pressure on him than what he was faced with We were together again for whatever reason and at that time that is really all that mattered.

The next day at work, I never let on about the flowers; I just let the girls at work wonder, even though I guess I should have told them. It was fun watching their curiosity and hearing the buzz about the mystery man.

James continued to come to the park, and we picked up where we had left off. We talked about the family that we once desired; we talked about the seasons that the willow tree and the park brought us; we sat there wanting to share everything we had in us with each other. It was like we were trying to catch up the years that we should have never lost. Yet at the same time, each of us was afraid that the other wasn't ready for the inevitable. My heart began to fill with the way things used to be and the way that I desired them to start right at this moment. With each word he spoke, I hung on, with my heartbeat joining in sync to catch every breath that he was breathing. I wished that he would touch me the way he used to, holding onto the fact that something beautiful was about to happen. The willow tree must have known my emotion, because even though March had shown its face to let us know that spring was in full bloom, the air was still a little cool—but not under the willow tree. It let off a slight warm breeze, and I could feel that love was yet again blowing in. I didn't want to go home when it was time to leave, but I wouldn't dare push things because I didn't know if he would have to leave again.

It was almost two months of meeting under the tree and talking that James put his hands on my face. While searching my eyes, he kissed me. It was a nervous kiss, sort of like his lips were about to be rejected, but I returned the kiss to let him know it was okay. I was glad he had kissed me. Before he left it was as if the kiss was his way of securing his place until we met again because before he left me that day, he told me that his grandmother was getting worse, and that the hospital had suggested that hospice come in. He said that he didn't know when he would be back to the tree and for me not to give up hope on him that he would wrong his right it was going to take a little time. After saying those words, he said "here's my number Vicky I mean Victoria. If you want to call and check on her, you can. I may need you because I am not sure what lies ahead but I will try to do it on my own."

James, I said, "you don't have to do anything alone anymore I am here. I will call to check on the both of you and if you need me don't hesitate to ask and I will be there." I gave him my number as well and before I knew it, I was back at my apartment reflecting on our conversation.

James didn't come back the next day; it would be another week before I would see him again. I was wondering what had gone wrong. Had she past? Was he to overwhelmed with what he was about to face? Even though he told me what was going on my mind wanted to add fire to my pain of not seeing him. My thoughts switched from the main reason to what else could be wrong. Should I have not returned his kiss? Is he having second thoughts and had I pushed him away? Wasn't he ready to venture out and explore the possibilities of the love we once shared? I wanted to know what was on his mind. What could he have been thinking that he didn't return? Was I wrong in what I was feeling, and had his thoughts of me changed? I didn't know what her dying would do to James. I silently cursed his parents for being hurtful and unfit. I wish they would show up and explain their wrongdoing and beg him to be a part of their lives. I just couldn't imagine all that he was feeling and going through. All I knew at this point was if he allowed me to, I would be there to share his pain every step of the way.

Chapter 10

It was the following Thursday afternoon that James and I had shared that kiss under the willow tree when I saw Mrs. Andrews being wheeled into the store. This time she had James with her. He walked behind her, guiding her wheelchair carefully between the aisles. We stole glances at each other every chance we got.

"Hello, Mrs. Andrews," I managed to say, looking at her while she reached for her money to pay for her prescription. "How are you today?" I managed to steal a glance at James without knowing he was staring at me when I looked in his direction, he gave me a little wink. That sort of eased my mind a bit so I continued to focus on Mrs. Andrews.

"Fine, dear, just fine. How are you?"

"I'm good. Are you feeling okay today?"

"As well as expected, I'm just glad I'm aboveground. My fear is my illness is once again taking control. But I hate to stay in the house in that dreadful bed. I still want to take memories with me. Even though the doctor is against me having outings James and I decided a little while shouldn't hurt, right" she asked as if she was getting a second opinion. I nodded my head letting her know that I approved before I said, "You can do whatever you feel like doing." With a weak smile she asked, "Have you been to the park lately?."

"I hope to go this evening. It all depends on what time I leave from here," I said, looking at James, hoping for some type of reaction. He just stood there watching me as if he had something on his mind.

"I see that willow tree is at its old tricks again," she said. "Well, that was to be expected. There is a story behind that willow tree, and one day before it's too late I hope to share it with you. If the weather and my health don't permit me visiting the tree, when you can get away, you must come to our home for a visit. I feel my days are numbered, so don't be long," she said with a hint of a smile on her face.

"Yes, I must," I said, still looking at James.

He finally spoke and said, "Why don't we meet her there this evening, Grandma, and then she can follow us back to the house?"

I wasn't sure how to read James and for whatever stupid reason I replied "I can't make any promises tonight. I may have to work late," I said, lying, while goose bumps formed over my skin. "We should make it another time." The look on James's face wasn't angry, but he appeared concerned for a moment. He even looked a little disappointed. I marked my words up as my guardian angel protecting my heart because I wanted to see James and learn about the tree. I had a few reserves when it came to James and my heart but playing games with him and considering what he was going through wasn't a good idea. If we were going to rekindle despite what happen years ago this is what I had been waiting for and I didn't need my conscious, subconscious, or guardian angel to screw it up. I needed to find a way to clear my words up a bit. Before I could think of something to fix my lie, I heard Mrs. Andrews say.

"Ah, what a shame, dear; maybe some other time." She then grabbed her prescription off the counter told James that they needed to get going and then without another word they were headed for the door. I couldn't move or speak I just stood there and watched them leave. Confusion and thoughts of them entertained my brain for the rest of the day.

I knew I wanted James, but I wasn't completely sure of his plans for his future. I believed he wanted to rekindle but just how far was he wanting to go. I couldn't help but keep thinking what losing Mrs. Andrews would do to him. I didn't know if he just wanted a friendship. Adult love is probably a lot different from teenage love. Was he expecting something different from me? Should I change my approach to the situation? I didn't know what to do I wanted to be there for him, and I wanted to take away some of his pain, but I didn't know how. I didn't want to be to forward and get my feelings all tangled up again just to find out we are on separate paths. If James wasn't sure of us returning to the love we once shared, then neither was I. If our love was still somewhere on the back burner, then I needed to pump my brakes and listen more and not add any more to his plate. I would wait until I knew he was sure before I continued on. I went home and wrote about him in my journal, hoping he was thinking of me because I knew I would regret not visiting under the willow tree.

It wasn't until around 8:00 o'clock that I had a strange feeling the fact that I lied about working was toying with my mind. As I was thinking about

James and Mrs. Andrews a strange feeling emerged. No matter how hard I tried I couldn't shake the feeling I was encountering. Sitting on the edge of my bed I decided to call James. With butterflies gathering at the pit of my stomach I dialed his number. To my surprise he answered on the second ring.

"Hello" He said

"Hey James, its Vicky I mean Victoria." As I tried not to stammer my words I said, "I'm off work and I was just wondering how you guys were doing."

"Oh, Hey Vicky" he said were ok. Did you work later?

Not wanting to lie again I said, "No I left at my normal time" Think Victoria I thought think and speak. I didn't know if Mrs. Andrews was well enough to come to the park this evening that is why I said that I didn't want to put any pressure on her. I didn't want her to come on my account.

"Oh, I see" he said, "I thought you maybe didn't want to see me."

"Not at all" I replied, "Of course I want to see you James I just don't want to add to your stress."

"I appreciate that" he said, "but my grandma really wants to share her story about the tree, and I really want her to tell you." With a chuckle he said, "because that really is my tree, I inherited it."

I couldn't help but giggle because he knew as well as I did that it was my tree and to keep the joke going, I said. "What tree are you referring to the one that I shared with you?"

He hesitated for a moment then said "ok, ok well you need to hear the story and you will better understand but we can continue to share and one day I promise I will plant your very own tree. Just let history repeat itself" he said laughing again.

Now I am curious I replied. "I really want to hear the story because I have a few stories of my own." With those words James got silent, and I thought he had hung up.

"James, I said are you still there?

"Yes", was all he said and instantly I thought he thinks you want to tell the story about the night he left you. I had to find a way to clean that up, so I said. "I'm sure everybody has great stories about that old tree besides that tree has been good for us, right?"

As if he approved, he said "Right"

With nerves building and goosebumps flaring up I decided to move forward with a plan. "So shall we meet at the tree tomorrow or would you prefer that I come over to your house."

"I know she wants to go back to the tree let's see if she is up to it this week first and I will let you know which is best." But he continued "you should know, you're welcome to come over anytime you want, you heard the invitation today, not that u needed one you are always welcome."

I thought before I spoke. I wanted to say your grandmother invited me James not you, but I wasn't going to open that box up instead I just said "Yes, she did, and I will come for a visit when she is up to company. You just let me know and I will be there."

"Ok" he said, "I will call you tomorrow and let you know how she's feeling ok?"

"Ok tell her I called" I managed to say before I hung ok.

"I sure will, that will do her heart good. I'll talk to you tomorrow" and with that the phone went dead.

The next day I decided not to go to the park despite the warm air and sun shining bright I decided against it. I didn't want to miss James's call. As I left work when I passed my willow tree, I noticed that the season had finally caught up with my willow tree, and the flowers were now blooming beautifully. The birds were singing love songs. The children had returned in full force, tramping on the grass, and screaming with pleasure as they ran in circles chasing one another. I was in my own little world, wondering if James would call me.

I had just stepped into the shower when my phone rang. Thinking it was James I sprinted to the phone. "Hello, Hello" I said thinking I was too late to get the call.

"How was your day at work" the old familiar voice said.

"Hey momma" I said trying to catch my breath while trying not to show disappointment in my voice. My momma was way to canny to not notice.

"What's wrong with you, you sound out of breath." She asked

I giggled to assure her I was fine then I said. "I was actually getting into the shower when you called, and I ran to get the phone."

"Oh, are you expecting a call from someone?" She asked

I laughed again because I didn't want to tell her not right now, but I didn't want to lie to her either.

"I just wanted to get the call before I started my shower." I said half telling the truth and not lying at all. If I didn't get it whoever it was would have probably called back when I was in the shower." That sounded good and I was so glad that it wasn't daddy who I was talking to because he would have seen straight through my hidden tendency's.

"Ok well I was just checking on you, I am sure you want to get your shower and relax after work I'll give you a call later or tomorrow and don't forget we don't live that far from you. I know gas is going up but if that is what is keeping you from visiting, I am sure we can get you some gas." Even though she was teasing I know she was serious. I hadn't been over as much since James showed back up, I didn't go because until I knew what we were doing I didn't want to discuss it.

"Fair enough mother I have just been busy I will be over one day this week I promise."

"That would be lovely Victoria now go get your shower. I love you."

"Love you too momma and tell daddy I love him to." That ended our conversation and as soon as we hung up, I thought I hope he didn't try to call while I was on the phone with momma.

I erased that thought quickly and looked at it another way. I kind of wished he called, and the phone was busy that could make him think "Who could she be talking to" I could only hope.

I took my shower with one ear to the curtain still no call. I went into the kitchen started me a pot of tea and decided to pull out my old journals. That will be how I spent my evening if he doesn't call, I will just reminisce. About ten minutes into my reminiscing session the phone rang. I stood there and picked it up on the third ring. I didn't want to seem too anxious.

"Hello" I said

"Vicky hey its James how are you doing?"

"I am good James how are you?" and Mrs. Andrews.

"She's resting more today she doesn't have a lot of strength left. I figured I would keep her in and let her rest today and tomorrow and we can go to the tree on Wednesday. I was trying to wait until she had more strength because she is determined to go to the tree, and I am not sure how much time she has. How does that sound to you?"

"That's fine James she needs to keep her strength up. I'll meet you there after work Wednesday, let me know if anything changes."

"Will do" he said, and the conversation was over.

At least he called was all I could think to myself. What is so important about my tree. Maybe all my questions will be answered once I meet them there on Wednesday.

Before I could catch my breath, Wednesday morning had arrived. I knew I wouldn't be worth a dime all day. I got up early enough to have a cup of tea and collect my thoughts before I started my day. I couldn't help but laugh at myself remembering the day James and I were to meet at the willow tree before school. I am always running late for work but since James has reappeared, I find myself now a days with little sleep and always on time. I didn't know what our visit meant for me all I knew at that point was I was going to meet them at the tree, and I guess from that point on I will play it by ear.

On the way to the pharmacy, I said a little prayer as I past my tree. Its branches were slowly moving to the faint winds beat. Let this be a good meeting I said please lord make sure I say what I need to say, please and thank you. I knew that the few times in the past that I ran into James I wasn't prepared. I needed to request Gods presence in advance because I knew once that man was in front of me, I would forget to call on God, I would even forget….my name.

Everything was going well. Time was a little slower than usual but I was hoping that it would stop just for a little while so I could at least plan what I would say this evening. While on lunch I decided to just jot down a few questions that I wanted to ask. If I didn't choke on my words and remember that I wrote them down I could leave the page open in my journal and pretend that I was looking at something on my page. Then I would ask a prepared question. Sometimes when my brain works, I surprise myself. After lunch, time seemed to be speeding up and nerves was beginning to overtake me.

The clock struck 3 o'clock, then 4 o'clock the 4:45, fifteen minutes I thought looking up at the clock one last time 15 minutes and I am on my way to my tree. I went in the back to get bags to put at the registers. Right before I was to return to the front, I heard the most horrifying sound that almost took my breath away. Please no I thought please not before my meeting. I peeked around the doorway and there he was the one person who could change the moods of angels, Mr. Boots. His voice and the mood behind it was the last thing I needed before I went to my tree. Taking into consideration that it was just me and the pharmacist left at the store for the day the chore fell on me.

God please I know this want be short and sweet, but can we agree on short. I don't need this man ruining my day. "Don't anybody ever stay home anymore" Here we go I thought. "Every time I leave my house, everybody decides to leave theirs too. You go to a store to get one thing and you must stand in a line for hours. I am going to figure out a way that I never have to encounter the human race. It's the worst thing that God could have thought to create. You can't go out and enjoy a day when you got people everywhere standing around in your way."

I watched him move about the store talking to himself grunting at other customers as he past. If a customer would even glance his way, he would say "what are you looking at I got a right to shop here too. You don't own the place." I absolutely hated what I had to do next, but time was running out. I had to make the announcement that we were closing. That was not going to come across good with old Mr. Boots. 5, 4 ,3 ,2,1 Deep Breath Victoria go, and I said,

"Attention Pharmacy Customers please make you way to the counter with your items the pharmacy is closing in 5 minutes. And as always thank you for shopping with us."

I went back to the counter to wait for the stragglers to check out and as they made their way up to my register, I tried not to look at the clock. My mind was racing all over the place I wanted to get there before they did and now my heart was sinking two minutes before I was to leave a long line was forming. You spoke it Victoria this is what you created because you told Mrs. Andrews that sometimes you got off late so here you go and as an added bonus you get to check out Mr. Boots. I guess a lie is a lie and I spoke it now I am paying for it. I hoped my customers didn't see that I wasn't my normal talkative self. I hope they understand that the pharmacy was closing, and it wasn't time for chatter. I glanced up to see how many people I had left and there he was next to the last peering over his glasses just waiting for the chance to stall me with his undesirable chatter. I kept going at a fast pace hoping he would see me and get the hint that we were running out of time.

"It's a shame old people can't shop when they need too. I heard him grumble. Theres's things I need to get, and I don't have time to even look for what I need before they are forcing me out" Now I got to take another day to come back out and get what I can't get today. It ought to be a law. If you serve the people that is just what you need to do when they need you then you should accommodate them not push them out."

He laid his few items on the counter before he continued. "I know ya'll are in cahoots with the Doctors. I don't even need my blood pressure medicine until I leave the house. I'm not sick it's the corrupt"— "128.43" I said ignoring him the best I could to get him out of the store out of my space.

"What 128.43 for what I only have five things you got to be kidding me. You jack these prices up every time I come in here and I am going to report you to have you shut down. This is utterly ridiculous. 128.43 for what." "For your items and prescriptions sir" He just stood there as if he thought his words would make his items cheaper. "128.43 sir" I said "that is the price either you want them, or you don't. The store is closing."

As he reached in his pocket to get the money he kept on. "I need to find out how to make my own medicine. This world has gone to hell in a hand basket, the prices are too high, and the elected officials are living like fat hogs at my expense. You will never get away with it. I have better things to do with my money besides hand it to you every month. God don't like ugly." What do you know about God I thought your Satan's best friend. As I handed him his bag and receipt I couldn't resist saying "God Bless you sir, come back and see us." He snatched the receipt from my hand and said "if it wasn't for a little bit, I would buy you out and shut you down. Then I would shop when I wanted to." He turned to the little old lady that was behind him and said, "move don't stand in my way I want out of here." He mumbled all the way out the door. I had to giggle when the old lady made her way to the counter looking over the rims of her glasses and said "that man needs a woman not me of course but a woman. Then she said, "I take that back he needs a sheep no woman can tolerate that." I didn't quite understand what she meant but it was funny. He took away my good mood and she brought it back. I hurried up locked the door and counted my draw 20 minutes later I was headed to the park.

When I arrived at the park it was full kids and families were everywhere. As I went to sit under my tree, I heard a familiar voice say "Victoria", as I turned to look, I saw this woman, at first glance I didn't recognize her, I guess she could tell by the look on my face that I was a bit confused, so she said "It's me April from high school. "Oh My God", I didn't recognize you and the reason is that she was the total opposite of what I remembered in school. She couldn't have been more than a size 5 her blond hair flowed down her back the cleavage shirt complemented her breast she had curves in all the right places, and you could tell she tanned faithfully. She wore glasses in school but now she didn't so her green eyes popped out beautifully she look like she could have been a movie star and standing next to her I was the plain Jane managing a smile and hoping she would leave before James got there I said, "How are you girl I haven't seen you in years." She leaned in to give me a hug "April", I said almost in shock that she looked that good. I returned her hugs and said, "I am good how are you?" "Are you still here I haven't seen you since school?" "I just got back after college I decided to do a little traveling and now, I just got back a couple of weeks ago. I start my new position next week she said. I am still not sure if Pocahontas will be my final destination. There would have to be a good reason to stay. I favor the city over a small town, but we will see one never knows until they really know." "Wow" you look really good was all I could think to say because she looked beautiful. I never imagined that age would complement her like that. She continued "Well, you still are as beautiful as you were in school life must be treating you well. Are you married yet, kids? What ever happen with you and James are ya'll still together." Before I could answer her, I heard James say, "not yet but were working on it." We both turned simultaneously and looked at James. I felt the goosebumps take attention on my arms and back as he parked Mrs. Andrews. I couldn't help but see her stare at James. Perfect timing, I thought perfect timing.

April turned to me with a wink and said, "Well that answers that. I could see why Victoria would want to try to work things out. You are as Handsome as ever. You been doing ok." James barely looked up and said, "just taking care of my ole girl here." Silence then filled the air because we were waiting for April to leave so we could continue on with our meeting. She must have felt it because as if to excuse herself she then said "well I will leave you to it. I hope to see you around" and me thinking it was time for her to go before I said something I would regret especially if me and James didn't reunite. She looked at me then glanced at James. He wasn't paying attention because he was focused on Mrs. Andrews but at that point, I was feeling a little annoyed by her. She was talking to me why did she have to look at James. I secretly hoped that she would decide not to live in Pocahontas, I didn't need the competition with someone as pretty as she turned out to be and I already knew if James would show any interest, she would be all in. "Ok" I said not entertaining her stares at James. Knowing I never wanted to see her again I said, "Take care of yourself, it was good seeing you." Before she left, she said it was good seeing the both of you again hope we can all hang out some day." James was fair game he wasn't mine yet, but I don't think that "WE" or "HE" will ever hang out with her as long as my willow tree is standing. James never looked up when she passed him "Goodbye" she said-----"See ya" I replied I wanted to add I see ya looking at my man get over yourself it will never happen." Considering Mrs. Andrews was present I didn't want her to see the angry side of me, so I left it at that and sat down beside her wheelchair. Once she seen I was comfortably seated she said "Victoria," Mrs. Andrews said. "Beautiful day, isn't it, dear?"

"Yes," I said, trying not to look at James.

"Have you been here long?" she asked.

"Not very long," I said, "just about 15 minutes."

With that James released the brakes on her wheelchair and sat down beside her opposite me. At first, I had thought that James would want to sit with me. At that point, my heart fell, and I just felt that not going for the visit was the biggest mistake I could have ever made.

"Isn't it funny," Mrs. Andrews said, lifting up her wrinkled hands, "how it takes the sun and the rain to make things beautiful? The rain is so dreary, but then the sun comes, and that old dreary rain is forgotten. Then the dried-up-looking buds turn into such beautiful flowers, such beautiful love. It takes both the sun and the rain to make the flowers strong and beautiful."

I couldn't help but feel that she was talking about me and James, but I didn't comment. I just listened, as he did.

Mrs. Andrews chatted away. She talked about the children playing, and what she said next would cause me to take a second look at my willow tree. "Victoria," she said, looking into my eyes as though she was searching like James had done so many times before. She cleared her throat before she started talking, as if this was the biggest speech of her life. "What do you know about this willow tree?"

Not knowing where she was headed with this question, I responded, "I know that it is beautiful; I know that it makes me feel safe." Looking at James, I said, "I know that it holds memories that are dear to me. Why do you ask?" I said with curiosity getting the best of me.

She turned to James and said, "Do you want to tell her or should I?" With those words, I began to feel a little nervous.

James told her, "It's your story, Grandma. You tell her."

"Very well then," she said, turning her attention back to me. "This willow tree holds memories for a lot of people—secrets too," she started, still searching my face. "Memories that have gone to graves, and some memories that will live on forever. You see, Victoria, it was my husband who planted this very tree. He planted it back on April 11, 1920. I will never forget it because it was our first-year anniversary, and I used to sit in the very spot that you are sitting at right now. Of course, the tree wasn't here then, but I had troubles in my family so I would come to this park. Of course, it wasn't a park then, just a little hillside, but I started coming here when I was just fourteen. This was my crying spot. I was young, and I didn't know where else to go or what else to do to let out my pain. It was a quiet place, and it was, I thought at the time, a secret place."

"This is where I met Mr. Andrews. He was six years older than I was, but one day he heard me crying, so he came up to me. I will never forget his words," she said with a twinkle in her eye. "What's a pretty little thing like you have to cry about?" I immediately wiped my tears, filled with embarrassment. I was also a little annoyed that he had found my spot, so I got up without saying a word and left. The next time I wanted to release my pain, I returned to my hillside again; only this time, Mr. Andrews was sitting in my spot. My anger rose up in me, and I forgot about my troubles, and I blasted him about being in my space." She chuckled. "When he saw the fire in me, he started laughing, and his laugh was so deep it caused me to laugh also. Before I knew it, I was sitting beside this man, and my troubles didn't seem so bad. It was then that we started meeting at this spot, and before I knew it, this man knew everything about me, and I was in love. My tears dried up, and happiness replaced what seemed like at the time the roughest part of my teenage life. We started dating, and a year later, I became Mrs. Andrews right in the spot where you are now resting. In those days, marrying at a young age wasn't uncommon like it is today "On our first anniversary, he promised that I would never have to shed another tear. His words were, 'we will let the tree do that for you.' I didn't know what he was talking about because there wasn't a tree there. That day he brought me down to this little hillside, saying he had something that he had waiting for me. He had come down in the early morning hours and planted this tree, the weeping willow. This became our favorite spot. We would come here and picnic. We would come here and just sit for hours watching this very tree grow, and I never cried again. Now there were times that I wanted to, but when I got to this tree, it was as if the tree knew why I was here, and it took the pain away. We watched this tree grow and grow."

"Oh, you could not imagine the horror I felt when the town spoke of turning this hillside into a park. I just knew that they were going to take down the willow tree. It held so many memories for me and Clarence. We would come here every chance we could and sit under the tree and watch the workers form the park. It was our way of letting them know that cutting down the willow tree was not an option. One day one of the workers told us that they would have to cut down the willow tree. Clarence protested and told him he would tie himself to it and they would have to kill him to cut down this tree. Seeing the sincerity in his voice—and he meant it too—the young man told him he would do what he could to save it. Being a little discouraged and knowing that protesting wouldn't be enough, Clarence told me that we wouldn't return, and he would plant another one at our home. He didn't want to see the hurt that it would bring, so it wasn't until the park was finished that we rode by, knowing that our tree was no more. To our surprise, there she stood just as pretty as you please. They had not cut it down. So again, we claimed it."

"We continued to come here until the time when he got a sickness and passed on, but before he died, he told me that he wanted to be cremated and have his ashes buried right under the willow tree. Cancer had taken over his body and his mind, but he remembered this tree like it was instilled in him from the beginning, almost like it was a part of him. I knew it was a big part of us, and God allowed him even in his darkest hours to remember our tree. We made a pact that day that this was the place where we both should lie once we closed our eyes for the final time. When he died, I rushed out to the funeral home and had two urns made: one for me to keep and one to bury his ashes. Matter of fact, his urn is right under that old carving, where the roots have gathered above the ground."

That must be the secret James was speaking about years ago, I thought. So, this really was the Andrews tree.

Mrs. Andrews continued, "Even though I have an urn at home, I have joy when I come here, knowing that he is still there where our love began and that he is waiting for me. I always knew that one day it would bring someone else as much joy as it had brought us. Sure enough, decades later, she is still standing tall, and she is the oldest tree in this park. The reason I still come here is because I know the history behind it, and I," she continued, with tears welling up in her eyes, "Me, Clarence, and that young man are the only people who have tramped on God's green earth who know the significance of this tree, and yet that young man doesn't know the secret. That is where Clarence is resting. It was the strong hands of my husband that started it all. So why shouldn't it be the place where he rests? When he died, his wish was to be cremated. He wanted a hole dug underneath that carving—right there," she said, pointing to the space beside me, "and then he wanted some of his ashes to be scattered about the willow tree. Those are my wishes also. I wish to stay joined with him here. And that is how it is supposed to be, you know, ashes to ashes and dust to dust. It must remain the same."

By this time, I had tears of my own. I tried to hide them, but nothing could stop them. I silently thanked God that I knew of the tree's existence and that James years ago was willing to allow me to be a part of this memory, this history, and the willow tree, which gave a breeze that dried up my tears. Mrs. Andrews continued on. She talked about her early days coming to this very park, sitting under this very tree. James and I both just listened. She spoke of Mr. Andrews—how he had taken care of her up until his dying days. And now, she said, it was about her time to join him. She spoke of her cancer; she had fought it off in years past, but now it had returned, taking over her body.

With those words, James spoke. "Grandma, you will outlive us all," he said, with pain and uncertainty in his voice. It was his words that made me feel the need to comfort both of them. I agreed with James. I heard myself say, "You will be here for many more years to come." It was her following words that put silence in the air. What she said next, I don't think either James or I expected.

"No, no," she said, "my days are now numbered. My last visit to the doctor, I was told that I don't have many months to share this world with the things I love most. This old illness has finally got the upper hand. It won't be long for me now. My only goal left is to prepare myself to go to my final destination. My only hope is that I can rest beside the one man who has given me the love that I never knew as a child from my own family but came to know of its existence once I became his wife."

To my surprise, James got up and walked away. My first thought was to go comfort him, but I didn't even know him. I knew those words hurt him, but he might not want my company, so I just sat there with Mrs. Andrews, choking back tears of my own.

Even though she saw James walk away, she didn't acknowledge it. She kept talking. "I don't want anyone sad for my departure. I don't desire a funeral or memorial. I don't have anyone but James, and I just want to be put away privately. I am ready, Victoria. Life has been good to me, and I am a bit tired now. My only sadness will be to leave James. He has depended on me for years gone by, but it will be my ashes to comfort him like Clarence's ashes comforted me. Without those ashes, I feel he may feel that he is alone in this world."

"My only hope," she said, with wisdom and sadness both in her eyes, "is that he can find the happiness he needs to continue once I'm gone. I know that James has a friendship in you. My desire is for James to be that man that I need him to be to carry on with.... life. He would make someone a good man, Victoria," she said, looking at me as if she was telling me to grab hold to him. "He has troubles, but it is just a family curse. He can change things, but he needs the right person to help him do so. All he needs is a little understanding and love, and he will be the perfect man."

"I have prayed shame on his mother and father for what they did to that boy. They put their own lives in front of his, living their lives selfishly, and he didn't deserve that. They should have given him the love and support that he needed to prosper as a man before they made their foolish decisions. They are suffering now, but the suffering they put on him is shameful, just wrong, my only hope is that the scars his parents put on him don't last forever. I hope he can get past that and be the man I know he could be. What they did as parents scarred that boy, and I have done everything that I could do to take those scars away; but now it's my time to leave, and I just hope that all the work that I have put into him doesn't go left unnoticed. Whatever God's will is for him, I pray that someday he meet back up with his parents and show them that even though he needed them, and they weren't there, well, he didn't need them after all. It will be them that need him, and I hope that he finds it in his heart to give them the love that they will need and that they will feel shame of what they did to him."

What could I say to her? I had no words to give her the assurance she needed to feel for her grandson. It was at least half an hour and many words later that James returned. I didn't want to stare at him, but it looked as though he had been crying. It was then that I saw a side of him that was beautiful to me. He was a handsome man, and not only that, but he also had a side to him that warmed my heart.

"Are you ready, Grandma?" he said, as he put his hand on her shoulder.

"Yes, son, I am."

His eyes caught mine, and his shyness drew me closer to him to the point I wanted to hug him. That wasn't the proper thing to do, though, so I just sat there.

James looked at me long enough to ask the question, "Are you going to be around later, Vicky?"

"I can be," I said, wanting him to come back. I wanted to take away some of his hurt and pain.

"I hope to see you soon, Victoria," Mrs. Andrews said, and they headed out of the park. James guided the moves of the wheelchair while she snuggled under the little knitted throw that covered her fragile body. I watched them as they stopped only long enough to pull the blanket up around her body. My eyes followed their every move until they had disappeared, and I just sat there reliving and trying to picture each word of her story. This tree was magical, and it held something more, something that had matured through the years that it was maturing. It indeed had secrets, secrets that were filled with love.

My mind went back to the first day that I saw this old tree and the magic I had felt. I thought of how I was offended, just like Mrs. Andrews had been when Mr. Andrews first invaded her space—only then it was just a new planting on a hillside, but now it was a beautiful tree. My focus turned from the willow tree back to James. I couldn't help but think of James this evening and the pain he must have felt. It was evident that he loved his grandma, and it was also evident that he was hurting because her days were numbered.

I spent the evening thinking about James and the look he had when he heard the most difficult words that anybody could hear when it came to their loved ones. The way he ran away when she started talking about her last days told me that he couldn't deal with pain. The way he returned told me that he didn't really want to leave her, but it would be her that was leaving him. Dark was crowning the day, and I began to leave the park. I felt that James wouldn't return. Hurt must have overcome him.

I made it to my car before I heard him call after me. "You leaving?" he asked.

"It's getting dark," I said.

"Dark never stopped you before," he called back, and that was so: we had sat under the stars many nights, so why not tonight?

I shut my door and headed back to our tree.

I couldn't stop myself before I asked the question, "Why did you stop coming back to the park, James?"

"My grandma is really sick; Vicky, I'm afraid I won't have her long. The day I left you was the day she found out that she had the cancer. I couldn't be away from her knowing that she had the fear and pain to bear alone. When my grandpa had cancer, it took his life fast I was afraid that her cancer would be the same way. I knew she was scared and when I was scared as a child, she was always there for me. When my parents left me, she was the only one that I had to take away the fear and the pain. I couldn't leave her alone. Even since the cancer has returned, there are times when I don't want to leave her because I fear that when I return, she will be gone." Pain showed in his face, and I wanted to ask him exactly what his parents did to him, but I didn't want to violate Mrs. Andrews's trust.

I listened as he continued, "This is not how I want to start a relationship with you. This is so hard for me, and I don't want to push you away, but my priority lies with her. I don't know where I would have been without her in my past years; and now with her days being only weeks or months before she leaves, I really don't know where that will leave me. I don't know how to get in touch with my dad, and the last time Grandma and my mother spoke, they had words. Even though I am a man now and my troubles have stopped, in reality are they not just beginning? The only family I have ever known is about to leave me and I will be all alone in this world."

At the time his words helped me to understand the reasons that he stayed away. I felt foolish and selfish. I felt that he was glad that darkness surrounded us it was like he didn't want me to see his pain. "You still have me and my family, James," I said, hoping that my family would be accepting of him after the pain he caused me.

"I miss your dad," he said. "I would like to see him again."

"You will," I said. "Let's just get past this. I am sure Daddy would love to see you again," I added, saying those words I could only hope. I knew my parents knew the pain that James had caused me, but surely, they would understand now that he was losing the only family he had ever known.

From that moment on, we just sat like we used to and didn't say a word until it was time to leave.

James and I sat there what seemed like hours then he said, "I must get back to my ole girl. I do want to see you again, and your family too, Vicky," he said. "I'm just going through something right now. Please don't give up on me. I remember our talks, and I will come around as much as I can. But right now, my grandma," he paused long enough to take a breath before continuing, "who has been there for me, well, I just feel that it's her time now."

Even though I wanted to spend every moment with him, I had no choice but to understand. That would be the last time I saw them at the park together.

Night had fallen, and the willow tree had closed its eyes for the night. The air was still, and there we stood, just looking into each other's eyes, wanting our minds to read each other's, but all I could think about was him leaving me. I couldn't let that happen again. I wouldn't let that happen again. With those thoughts lingering in my head, as if he was reading my mind, he pulled me close and kissed my lips softly and then said, "Don't give up on me, Victoria. Even though it may seem like we are apart, and we may be, we will still be together, and one day it will be forever, I promise. Remember what Grandma said about the sunshine and the rain. Things take time, and we have that now. I had better go now; Grandma may need me. I will see you soon." With those words, he was gone again.

Chapter 11

James called faithfully every day. It wasn't like seeing him, but at least we still had contact. I knew he had a lot on his hands, but I wanted so desperately to be a part of this because I needed him to know that I was there for him. I didn't want him to feel alone in this world once Mrs. Andrews passed.

A few days passed with not a word from James, so I decided to call him one Friday evening. I had the weekend off, and it seemed like the perfect time to pay James and Mrs. Andrews a visit. When I got off work, I went to my apartment. At first, I waited, contemplating my boundaries at that point, but I had to call boundaries or not. I needed to know that they were okay. Neither James nor Mrs. Andrews had come in for her usual prescription the last couple of weeks. I decided I had to do something. I didn't know what to expect, but it didn't matter at this point.

Nervously my fingers began to shake, but I managed to clear my throat and take his number off of my nightstand to dial. It only rang about three times before the voice on the other end spoke.

"Hello," the person said.

"Hello," I said, barely getting my words out. Nerves had taken over my body to the point where I wanted to just hang up. "May I speak to James?"

"Vicky," the voice said, "this is James. Is everything okay?"

With fear still in my voice, I tried to continue on with my purpose for calling. "Yes, I am fine. I was just worried about you and Mrs. Andrews. I hate to pry, but I just wanted to know that the two of you were okay."

"It doesn't look too good for Grandma. They called in hospice. They say that her organs are shutting down. She is resting now, though."

His words gripped my heart. Now the worst was near. Before I could think of what to say next, my voice took control. "Well, do you want me to come over for a little while?" I said, clenching my fist to my heart, fearing what he would say next.

"That would be great, Vicky. I am sure she would want to see you." James explained to me where he lived. I jotted down the directions, took a quick shower, and was on my way across town.

Mrs. Andrews's house was a few miles outside the city limits, a little farther than I had expected. No wonder James left years ago. He really had no choice. This house was in another school district, I thought as I pulled into their driveway. I said a little prayer for the Lord to give me the right words to say as nerves took over my body. As I made it to the porch, I felt a sense of peace come over my body, I knocked lightly on the door because I didn't want to startle Mrs. Andrews.

Moments later, James came to the door. In spite of what he was going through, he managed to smile. His face told me that he had stress in his heart. Without thinking, I reached out and pulled him close to me. I embraced him, and he returned my embrace in a way that I felt he wanted me there. We stood in the doorway for moments before he released me. Then he said, "I am so glad you came, Vicky."

Chills took over my body before I could respond, "I am glad I am here too."

With those words, he grabbed my hand and guided me into the house. The house smelled of sickness. Although Mrs. Andrews kept a clean house, it had a smell as if death was near and there was nothing cooking on the stove. I followed him into the room where Mrs. Andrews was sleeping.

"Grandma," James said, "Victoria is here."

I touched him on his arm and motioned for him to leave her room. "James, let her rest. I will be here when she wakes up."

He then turned without another word and guided me into the living room.

On the mantel, I saw pictures of his grandma and him. There was a man that he pointed out to be Mr. Andrews, but no other pictures of relatives were present. I saw pictures from the time when he was a teenager until his age now. It seemed the family was only the three of them.

"James," a tiny scruffy voice said, coming from Mrs. Andrews's bedroom.

James instantly left my side and went to his grandmother. "Vicky," he called back, "she's awake now."

I went into the room. The first thing I noticed was the urn sitting safely on her nightstand while she lay in a fetal position. She looked thin, as if she had aged since the last time, I saw her.

"Yes, Grandma, I am here," James said.

I walked through the door. Beside her bed on the same nightstand that contained the urn was a hospital pitcher of water. I watched as James carefully poured water from that pitcher into a glass. He then tilted Mrs. Andrews's head forward, and I watched as she took a few sips.

"Easy, ole girl," he said. "Take your time."

My heart was breaking as I watched them interact with each other—he patiently being careful not to hurt her, she is taking her sips of water watching his face. After a few sips of water, he carefully laid her head back down on her pillow.

"Thank you," she said, weak tears rolling down her cheeks.

"Hello, Mrs. Andrews," I said.

"Oh, dear," she said, "what a lovely surprise. I was hoping you would come by to see me."

James turned and left the room.

"Can I get you anything?"

"Not right now," she said, extending her hand.

I took hold of her hand and told her that I missed seeing her come by the store and that I thought of her often.

"My days left here are not long, there is no amount of medicine that can help me now taking pills is just a bother and since it won't help why bother.

Victoria. I hear the trumpets sounding, and they are coming for me. They started off at a distance, but as the days draw near, they become louder and louder, letting me know that it won't be long."

I asked if she needed her pillow turned or fluffed, and she told me she was fine. I just sat there and rubbed her hand as she spoke.

"You're a good girl, Victoria, a pretty little thing. I am so glad James is not alone now," she said as she coughed uncontrollably. Clearing her voice, she continued, "You are a good friend, Victoria—a strong young woman. I was praying that someone would help him through this, and then here you are. My prayers have been answered. Please make sure I am cremated. I don't want no fuss; I just want to be placed beside Clarence. I must rest now," she said, "and prepare for my journey." With those words she closed her eyes, and I released her hands.

I returned to the living room where James was sitting, thinking that I didn't want him to go through this alone. I really didn't know what to do, and I knew he mentioned he didn't know where his father was, and his mother and Mrs. Andrews had had words. I felt a big weight fall on my shoulders. I knew that James had no one to share this pain with, and the sadness returned. It was I who had to be there for him. I needed to bring comfort if nothing else.

I stayed with James until I knew he was ready for bed. The bags that were forming underneath his eyes let me know that he was tired. I knew he needed all the rest that he could get. I told him I would return the next day.

As I rode through the dark streets on my way home, my thoughts drifted back to the night that James left me. I knew Mrs. Andrews was his concern then as she was his concern now. I knew that prayer for James and Mrs. Andrews was needed, so first thing in the morning, I would make a call to Momma. That conversation should be interesting considering that I had not told her that I had been communicating with James again.

When I arrived back to my apartment, I wasn't a bit sleepy. My thoughts were consumed with James and Mrs. Andrews. Knowing what James was about to face, not to mention my conversation with Momma in the morning, with thoughts dancing through my head, I decided to write in my journal until I was tired enough to go to sleep.

The next morning, I was startled by the phone ringing. I must have been in a deep sleep because I didn't notice until I tried to open my eyes that the sun was shining brightly through my window. As I picked up the phone, I said, "Hello."

"Good morning, honey."

"Hey, Momma," I replied.

"Did I wake you?"

"Yeah, but that's okay," I said, still half asleep. Not letting my brain catch up with my mouth, I said, "I've got to get up anyways to check on Mrs. Andrews and James."

"Who are James and Mrs. Andrews?" Momma asked with curiosity in her voice.

"James, Momma, you know, my friend from school."

"Oh," she said, taking a moment to remember.

Not wanting to give her too much to remember about the boy who broke my heart, I said, "Mrs. Andrews is his grandmother and a very good customer at the pharmacy. Recently I just found out that the two were related."

"Well, why do you have to check on them, and wherever did you meet back up with him?"

"Twenty questions, Momma, really," I said, not wanting to get into the whole spill of what was going on. "What time is it anyway?"

"It's eight thirty-five, to be exact," she said.

"Momma, for now can I just ask for you to pray for them? They're really in the need of prayer. Call up your prayer warriors and pray hard, and as soon as I get the chance, I will tell you all about it."

"Okay, Victoria, but all I am going to say is be careful and keep God in the midst of whatever is going on."

"Okay," I responded, "just pray, and pray hard. Love you. Bye."

"Love you too, girl," she said, and then we hung up the phone.

I immediately called James. "Hey," I said when he answered, "good morning."

"Morning," he said.

"Well, how are things this morning? How did the night go?"

"Well, she slept through the night. I am getting ready to see if she will eat something."

"Okay. I just woke up. I will get my shower, grab a bite to eat, and then I will come sit with you. Do you want or need anything?"

"No, we are fine."

"Okay, then I will see you soon."

"Okay," he responded, and that was the end of that conversation and the start of my day.

Within two hours, I was pulling up in Mrs. Andrews's driveway. James had left the door cracked, and I assumed it was to await my arrival, so I just went on in without knocking.

"Hey," I said, trying to sound cheerful, "mmmm, that looks good," I said as I watched as James fix Mrs. Andrews a plate.

"You want some? I made plenty," he said.

"No," I said, "I ate before I came." Then he picked up her plate, and I followed him into her room.

As we entered the room, she opened her eyes. As if noticing me first, she asked, "Victoria, have you been here all day?"

"It's morning, Grandma," James said as if he was reminding her.

"No, ma'am," I said. "I just came this morning."

"Land sakes," she said. "I get the days and nights mixed up now."

As James set down the plate, I watched as he set her up enough so she could eat. "I hope you are hungry," he said, forcing a smile.

"Not too much," she said, "but I will give it a try." As she sat up, she asked, "Victoria, can you run in the bathroom and get me a washcloth so I can at least wash my face and hands?"

I did as she requested. When I went back in the room, I helped her clean up. Since she was too weak to feed herself, I watched as James fed her. When she was done with all she could eat, I heard her say to James, "Thank you, son, I appreciate all that you are doing for me."

My thoughts for whatever reason went to Mr. Boots—my hateful pharmacy customer. Why couldn't he take this sickness and let her be allowed to stay a little longer. I quickly erased those thoughts from my mind as I watched James gather up her plate to take to the kitchen, with the little strength that she had left, she motioned for me to come sit. I sat on the edge of her bed, and she took hold of my hand.

"I'm ready, Victoria. I am ready to meet my maker. I don't want to stay here any longer. Promise me, promise me that I will be cremated, and my ashes will be scattered about the willow tree like Clarence's were. Not all, of course. Dig a hole right under the carving and put some of my dust in there, then scatter me about and let my ashes fly. I know that James will hurt, but I know that he will find the strength to carry on. That has been my prayer through this sickness, that James will find his strength.

"I have asked the Lord to take me then and only then, so if I go, you have to trust, and James has to know that my God has given him strength within to deal with my leaving. I don't want to go until I have that reassurance. Through the years God has proved faithful and he knows my heart, so when I go, know that God has a plan for James, and he will be okay. It's funny how some people can ask the Lord for something, and in his faithfulness, he does it, but that person who asked may be long gone."

She had continued to speak as James entered the room, and she then paused as if she was thinking on what to say next. She looked at James, then back at me, and said "Persevere. Endure. Remember that trouble doesn't last always. It takes both the bad and the good to make things beautiful, sort of like the sun and the rain. Things can't grow nor prosper with only one or the other. I don't know what your future holds, but I can tell you that I have never known my God to make a mistake. Honestly, through all of my years, maybe not in my time, I may not live to see my prayers answered but God has never failed me." Getting weaker in her words, she said, "I must rest now; we will talk more later."

James helped her to lie down, and we left her to rest. It wasn't long before the bacon smell left, and the sickness smell returned. I was helping James straighten the kitchen back up from breakfast when there was a knock on the door. He looked at me and said, "Hospice." He left the kitchen, only to return with a woman by his side.

"Hi," she said, "my name is Judy. I will be Mrs. Andrews's hospice nurse." She extended her hand.

I said, "Hello, I am Victoria."

Before I could get out my last name, she said, "Mrs. Andrews, it's a pleasure to meet you. "Well," she continued as if there was not a moment to lose, "can we go somewhere and chat before I see my patient?"

James never told her that I wasn't Mrs. Andrews and neither did I, although I told her she could call me Victoria. Then we just led her to the living room. As we walked to the living room she said. I will be here for the next few days and then after my supervisor will come for the final stages.

As we settled in the living room for our conversation on what to expect, Judy said, "I will be her nurse until she makes her transition. I will feed her, check her blood pressure, vital signs, clean her up and change her urine bag. I will comfort her in every way possible. I know this is hard for the both of you, but we don't want her to suffer now, do we?" James and I both shook our heads. "If I can get you to fill out the paperwork, I will get started," she said, handing me the stack of papers to sign. She continued once I see a major change my supervisor will come do a final check and give you the timeframe of her homegoing.

I then looked at James and said, "I will take her to Mrs. Andrews, and I will be back to help you."

I got up and led her into Mrs. Andrews's room. As Judy and I approached Mrs. Andrews's bed, Judy said, "I will change her urine bag, and then I will check her over, okay?"

"Okay," I said, and then to give the nurse her privacy, I left the room.

Back in the living room, James said, "I don't even know where to start."

I said, "I will read and explain them, and you can sign." So that is what we did.

We spent the next hour going through all the paperwork, and after that was finished, Judy returned. James handed her the papers, and she sat in the chair opposite us.

"Well, her heartbeat is slowing down, and her urine is weak. When was the last time you changed the urine bag?"

"Yesterday," James said.

"Well, considering it wasn't a lot, which tells me that her kidneys aren't functioning properly. Only give her something when she asks for it; don't force her to eat or drink, okay? At this point, we don't want to gather fluid. What about a bowel movement? Has she had one of those?"

"Not for a few days," James said, adding, "but she hasn't eaten much."

"That is to be expected," Judy said. "I'm sure you understand why I am here, and I want you to know that I am here for the two of you too. I want to make this as painless as possible. Even though it's my job, I take my patients' lives personally. Now if you like, I can offer around-the-clock service, daytime, or evening, whichever you prefer. How about I come back in the morning around seven o'clock and I will stay until five? Then if that doesn't work out, we can change it. My estimation—and this is only an estimation—if things keep going the way they are, then—understand I have been doing this for eighteen years—I say we have only a few days left with her. I want to prepare you," she said. "I don't believe in surprises, so love her, say kind things, and be prepared to let her go. She is a kind woman. She is prepared, and just the little time that I spent with her, I can tell that she loves her grandson," she said, winking at me, "so, yes, this is hard but not impossible. You can make it through this. Are there any questions for me?"

We shook our heads no.

"Well then," she said, "I will go sit with her, and I will leave around seven this evening if that's okay."

"That's fine," James said.

As Judy left us, James was in his own thoughts. I guess the actual fact that he was losing his grandma was weighing on his mind.

Judy stayed as promised until seven, and then she left.

After she was gone, James went in to check on Mrs. Andrews. "She's sleeping," he said as we gathered back in the living room. James continued, "I think Judy is right. I don't think I have very much longer with my ole girl."

Wanting to know his plans once Mrs. Andrews passed, I asked, "James, are you going to stay around here, or are you going to leave?"

"I'm not sure. I don't know what tomorrow holds. Her wishes are for me to rekindle my relationship with my mother and father I don't know that I want to or if they want to or even where to find them."

Fair enough, I thought. It's time to put my feelings on hold; he could be leaving soon.

James didn't offer for me to spend the night and I didn't suggest it, His eyes showed that he was tired and as he yawned, I felt that was my cue to leave so I gathered up my things and headed for the door I told him that I would come back tomorrow. As he walked me to the door, my heart hoping that he would ask me to stay, I said, "James, are you going to be, okay?"

His response was, "I'll be okay."

I felt that was my cue to leave.

When I told him that I would be back the next day, he said, "Vicki, I would like that. I don't think I could get through this without you." He then hugged me good night, and as he pulled back, his eyes met mine and he began searching my face as if he wanted to say something. Instead, moments later, he opened the door for me and walked me to my car.

The streetlights were glaring down on me as I traveled home. Thoughts ran through my mind, rewinding Mrs. Andrews's words with every thought I had of James.

The next day I returned to Mrs. Andrews's house, and the door was open again as if James was expecting me, so I let myself in. I heard Mrs. Andrews in a weaker voice speaking to James.

"She is good," I heard Mrs. Andrews say, "a strong woman, James, not like your mother. Don't look at her as being like your mother all women are not the same. I can tell she was raised good; she is caring, and she has a good head on her shoulders. Don't make a mistake and lose what you have because of the family curse. She can show you the love that you never had, but you have to be strong; you have to be a man to win over a girl like her. Your mother's and father's marriage failed, but it had nothing to do with you. So don't ponder on what happened to them. You need to move on and make the best out of the life that God has dealt for you. She can be that person to make you complete. She seems like she is an understanding person."

"Don't let the past affect your future. Be a man, a good man, like your grandfather, and forget about what your mother and father have done to you. I am leaving, and I need you to tell me that you will move on and give your all in all that you missed as a child growing up. I have prayed for you every day since God sent you to me since the cancer has taken me over, so now it will be up to you. I am ready. I want to go, son. I am tired, I am so tired, and I just need to know that you will give your all after I am gone and know that I will still be watching over you every step of the way. I don't think God will take that privilege from me. Can you promise me that you will at least try?"

"I promise, Grandma," he said, followed by a sniffle.

"If you try, you can't fail, James; the hardest part is the trying. This old world owes you nothing. Your mother and father, well, that is a different story, but my desire is that you find them and continue life with the love that they have missed out on. Don't hate them; just pray for them. God will see you through. I love you, James, and I'm ready, so if you will allow me to go without grief, then God's will won't be prolonged any longer. We can't stop his will, but we can prolong it by our choices."

"It just hurts, Grandma. I will miss you. I love you and I don't want you to go, but if that is what you desire, then I will make myself ready. I promise I will put you with Grandpa, and I will carry on like you desire. I want you happy; that is what you deserve. Tell Grandpa I love him."

A part of me wished I had come sooner so I could have heard the whole conversation. Why did she say I was good. Just more unanswered questions that I needed answered but in time I thought in time. Not wanting them to find out that I was listening, I eased back to the door, wondering if Mrs. Andrews was referring to me when she talked of the woman for James. I rattled my bags so they could stop the conversation if they didn't want me to hear, and I went to her room. James turned to look at me; his face was stained with tears.

Mrs. Andrews said, "Victoria, how are you, dear?"

"I'm okay, considering," I said. "How are you today?"

"Not up to eating," she said, "but I am a willing soul. Just spending a little time with my grandson," she added.

"I see," I said. "Well, I can step out and let you have your time," I said, not wanting them to know I heard the conversation but deep down wanting to hear more.

"No, no," she said. "I'm tired; it's time for me to rest. Go on," she said, looking at James. "Visit with Victoria."

James got up, kissed her on the forehead, and whispered as if he didn't want me to hear, "I'm ready, Grandma. You've spent enough time trying to make me happy. It's your time now; go be with Grandpa. I will put you with grandpa. I will scatter your ashes as you desire."

"Well," I said once we were settled in the living room, "how has your day been?"

"She's getting weaker; her skin is a lot paler now," he said. I think it's time this is the most she has spoken to me. She mostly sleeps but I just feel that she had some things she needed to say before she went, I think the time is getting closer.

Not knowing how to respond, I said, "I stopped and got dinner. Will you eat with me? We need our strength."

Not saying another word, James got up and followed me into the kitchen. We sat at the table and ate. James briefed me on what all was going on with Mrs. Andrews. "A couple more day is all I think I have with her; that is what Judy told me today. She said her supervisor will be here this evening and she will be able to tell us how much time.

As I cleaned up, he went back into Mrs. Andrews's room.

I was sitting with Mrs. Andrews when there was a knock at the door. James left to see who it was, and I sat there silently praying that this transition will be easy for everyone. Moments later James came in with the Supervisor. When I turned to speak to her horror took over my body again. The supervisor was none other than April. Even though she was dressed in her smocks she was still a sexy woman. I wanted to climb up beside Mrs. Andrews and scream that God should take me and leave her. I maintained my composure in spite of the shock that shown on my face that I hoped she didn't notice.

"Hello, April, good to see you again despite the circumstances." I said faking a smile. She looked shocked to see me there.

"Victoria, Hey so, we meet again" she said showing her straight pearly whites. Looking down at Mrs. Andrews she said in a louder than normal voice "Hello Mrs. Andrews I'm April I'm here to make sure that your well taken care of. How are you feeling today." I thought to myself quick hollering she isn't death she can hear just fine. Ms. Andrew tried to clear her throat before she responded. I am good dear. I'm a little cold but I am still above ground." She never said she was cold now I felt a little embarrassed thinking they thought I wasn't looking after her good enough. I just instantly pulled her covers up around her and without a word got another blanket that was at the bottom of her bed and added that one too.

"Is that better Mrs. Andrews I didn't know you were cold" I said just to make it known that I wasn't neglecting her. She nodded her head that it was better and then she said, "I didn't want to bother you Victoria but its better now thank you." April looked at James and said "Let me have a few moments to look her over then I will join you in the other room. As James and I left the room I found myself regretting that I didn't friend her in school because maybe if she considered us friends she wouldn't go after James. I'm sure James had his mind on Mrs. Andrews but needless to say my mind was on, April. With her in the picture I have to step up my game. James and I aren't together so again he's fair game and if looks play a part in the competition she would win hands down. I did have one on her by knowing Mrs. Andrews but now she would be taking care of her. Since James adored his grandmother anybody that helped her would have a spot in James's memory and now that included April.

April stayed in the room with Mrs. Andrews for about thirty minutes before she came in the living room with us. James and I were sitting on the couch, and she came and sat down right beside of him. "Easy girl" I thought to myself you are treading on dangerous ground.

"Ok" she began, well it's about that time. "After examining her I have concluded she has about two days before her transition." James put his head down and before I could grab his hand April had beat me too it. "If you want me to stay here I will-I can do whatever you need me to do." Thinking I've come too far, and I am not going out like this I spoke up and said. "What will she need because I have made preparation to stay here with James and Mrs. Andrews during this time. Is there something she will need that we can't do that we will need help with?"

Looking through her paperwork she looked up to say, "I see that she's doesn't want revived has that changed." James said in a weak sounding voice "no she won't be revised those are her wishes. "Does she choose to pass at home, or would the hospital be a better option I can arrange for an ambulance to pick her up if you like?"

"No, she wants to be here like my grandfather was she doesn't really like hospitals."

"Oh, Ok well Just keep a watch on her and when something changes just call the rescue squad. I can stay and help you through it just in case you need anything" April said.

No no no…. I thought you are not squeezing in on James. I decided to ask a question hoping James would agree with me. That was his grandmother, and I didn't want to seem selfish so I said, "I think we will be ok don't you James" I mean we can call the rescue squad and I know CPR, but she doesn't want that, so I really don't see the need to trouble April do you"? Goose bumps formed all over my body when he didn't answer right away. I felt flush. I am sure my face turned beet red as April and I stood by waiting on James to answer. I knew this was his grandmother, but we definitely didn't need her here. It felt like minutes went by as James sat there as if pondering on the idea of April staying or going then he said "If you think we can manage it then we won't trouble April and you are staying right Vicky" he added. I had to give props "Thank you Jesus" I said to myself before saying "Of course I am" I thought I wouldn't leave you now for nothing in this world and I meant that whole heartedly. I was also glad that James wanted me to stay. She may have me on looks but I got her on time. I will use vacation if I have to, I thought there was no way I was going to allow April to be alone with my man when he is vulnerable. "Then its settled" I said, and I was so glad that it was this is not the time to play mama bear with my man, Mrs. Andrews passing at this moment was more important.

"Ok" April said in a low voice as if she was disappointed and defeated all rolled up in one. I felt that even though she was being professional and since I have never been through any of this before as far as I know she could have genuinely cared but I felt like she was giving him options because I guess she felt she needed to try one more act to get his attention or maybe even a chance for his love because she said "well James I am going to leave my number and if you need me don't hesitate to call me." She wrote down her number and handed it to James who took it and that didn't set well with me, but I could have been overreacting because she wasn't a wild girl in school so maybe she was being real. I had to accept that because I really didn't know her in high school. James and I both knew she had a secret crush on him but surely, she had a boyfriend as pretty as she was there was no way she was single. I just didn't want to take any chances. I wanted to put her on notice that I was his girl whether I was or not she couldn't have him.

Having April's number provided opportunities if James decided he didn't want me and that is just not how things work so in the most respectful tone I said without even looking at April. "James, give me the number and I will hold on to it because if we need her and you're not in your right mind the number could be misplaced so I will take it and hold on to it." I don't know if she realized how loud it was, but I heard April sigh as if she attempted but I stopped her acts. When James handed me the number that told me that I was still other than his grandmother the most important. I was right in my thinking because the look on her face when James handed me the number was priceless. She wanted him to have her number and not for his grandmother either. As she got up to leave James thanked her and she reached in for a hug that I felt was inappropriate, because she didn't reach in to hug me. but I had her number not James and he wasn't going to get it because there was no point.

As if April was begging out of desperation she continued "Going through this can be very difficult I am trained to assist, and it will be no trouble at all I would be glad to help I mean I look at you guys as friends. Seeing how we went to school together, were practically extended family." My mind wandered for a few seconds thinking we didn't even talk in school we don't even know you just because we were in the same place for 4 years doesn't mean that we are family. There was a reason that I didn't become her friends years ago and I must think my subconscious mind when the dust clears. Becoming a little frustrated with her need to help I said "we appreciate that April we truly do but I think we can manage it. If not I-- will definitely call you." The look on her face lead me to believe that she knew what I was doing, and I was hoping she also understood my words because my inner self was screaming them to be loud and clear.

"Ok" she said looking at James "I don't want to impose…. my offer will stand. I hope Mrs. Andrews transition goes well, but I also respect privacy so with that I will leave you to it. Know that I" ----she reached out for James's arm then continued. "I will be praying for you."

"You why not ya'll?" She was also a little too touchy feely with James in a vulnerable state. With that James walked her to the door and I followed. When she was leaving, I had the strangest feeling come over me, she looked back at me and said. "James, I have your number on file I will call you in a few days to see how everything went if that's ok?" James nodded and I cringed then she said, "Victoria you take care now." Then she got in her car and was gone.

Later James and I sat in the living room for the rest of the evening, each taking our turn to go check on Mrs. Andrews. I never brought up April or her offer, I felt it wasn't the right time, as much as I wanted to know how he felt about what all she said or even how she looked but I will wait until we get through all this before I even mention her name, but I was determined to do so just not at that time. As I saw sleep fall on him, I decided it was time to leave. I went into Mrs. Andrews's room to check on her one last time before I left.

James was waiting for standing at the doorway to Mrs. Andrews room. His words to me sort of caught me off guard. "Vicky," he said, "I thought you were going to stay with me. I know that you are working, but I will make sure you get up for work. I just don't know what tomorrow holds."

"Oh James" I said looking at the confusion on his face." "I thought you wanted me here tomorrow I didn't know you wanting me to stay tonight. I'll run home and get some clothes then I will come back I'll work tomorrow but after that I'll be here for the duration I promise.," I said, trying to reassure him. He pulled me close to him, and this time he acted as though he didn't want to let me go. So, before I pulled back, I rested in his arms.

"I will be really quick hour tops. Do you want me to pick up anything?", James shook his head no, I didn't want to leave him at that point because I could see sadness and worry overtake his face, He looked tired and even a few years older. I gave him a quick kiss on his cheek and said "I will help you through this. I won't leave you for long. I'll be back" He nodded his head, and I was out the door

On my way to the house April flooded my mind to a point I felt ashamed of my present feelings. I felt that if I didn't stay April could call to check on James and Mrs. Andrews and he could tell her I wasn't there and I know she would go over there. I just felt it in my gut. I was glad that I took the number and with that thought I rolled my window down and let it fly through the wind. Oh no I thought I lost her number. I fought for my tree so why wouldn't I fight for my man I thought or soon to be man.

When I arrived back at their house James was sitting beside her bed. Not talking just sitting. I went over to him put my hands on his shoulders and as not to disturb Mrs. Andrews whispered, "how is she doing?" He said about the same, but her breathing is lighter listen. As we stood in silence,

I listened for Mrs. Andrews breathing and I barely could hear it. I reached for his hand to lead him out of the room I didn't think that we shouldn't discuss her where she could hear us, it could make her sad. When I was out of the room, so he could better prepare and understand what was happening I told James they gave her two more days, so her body is probably preparing for her transition. We will keep watch over her we will get through this. We took turns through the night watching her making sure she was still breathing.

Sleep didn't come easy for me I tried to check on Mrs. Andrews just as much as James did. James and I both slept sitting up on the couch. At one point I woke up my head was resting on James shoulder, and he had his arm around me. He said I could sleep in his bed, but I didn't want to leave him alone. At that point I was just satisfied with being with him. We didn't talk much at all we were each in our own feelings. Priority must stay on Mrs. Andrews we would have plenty of time to talk once we get through this.

I went to work on less than three hours of sleep. I tried as hard as I could to rush through my day, praying that I would make it there before Mrs. Andrews passed on. Every time the store phone would ring my heart would skip a beat. I feared that James would call in a panic. As if my day wasn't stressful enough, just as I was cleaning off my counter, my least favorite customer entered the store—Mr. Boots. It was time for my break, but considering I was the only associate in the store that could tolerate him and having a bit of misery of my own I decided to stay for one more round of complaining.

"Lovely day isn't it," I said as he approached.

"For whom?" he said. "Not for me. I had to call a cab, only to pay these god-awful prices here at your pharmacy. "Tell me," he said, "just how big of a bonus do you get off of someone like me? I believe I'm the reason you are still in business. Highway robbery. If I was a police officer, I would lock you up, I tell you, and throw away the key. I'm trying to get my medicine to live, and you are trying to kill me. Who is the president anyway? They should have enough in their budget to buy my prescriptions."

Trying my best to ignore him, I said, "Sixty-four seventy-five." Mr. Boo---I mean sir

"What?" he said. "God knows what you're doing, missy, so you may be getting away with it down here but remember you one day will have to face the great throne of judgment. You're going to meet your maker. You can't take it with you."

You will meet your maker too, I thought as he continued, "I won't be back; then what are you going to do then? Don't try to purchase that new car you've been thinking about because it isn't going to happen. I won't be back, and within the next month, you will be at the unemployment office. I hope then you'll think of how bad you have done me."

"Good day," I said. "See you soon."

"Whatever," he said as he left the pharmacy.

Sharon, my coworker, had been standing by and overheard our conversation. She said, "He's enough to turn anybody's stomach, but go to lunch—if you can eat after that conversation. Oh, by the way, during your encounter with Mr. Personality, your momma called. She wants you to call her on your lunch break."

Sharon was great. She was the closest thing to a friend that I had at the pharmacy. She was also the lead person. Even though she and I were close, I hesitated to tell her that I needed the rest of the week off. I will do it after my conversation with Momma, one beast at a time, I thought.

After I grabbed a pack of Nabs, I went to call Momma. It was as if she was waiting by the phone; on the first ring, she answered, "Hello."

"Hey, Momma," I said, "how are you?"

"I'm blessed and highly favored," she said, "but other than that, how are you? I know you don't have much time, but I have been calling you for days. Where have you been?"

"Well, to make a long story short, Momma, I have met back up with James, and now his grandmother is dying from cancer." Trying to allow Momma to get past the hurt she felt for me years ago, I said, "She was the reason that James left me years ago, and now she is dying, not to mention she's my favorite customer here at the pharmacy. They have called in hospice, and I have been spending my evenings trying to help out my friend." As if she only heard that James and I are now friends again, Momma asked, "So, you are not dating him again?"

"No, Momma, we are just friends. I am just kind of giving him support right now."

"Okay," she said, "but pray and be careful. Not to bring up the past but remember the last time how he made you feel. You don't want to experience that again."

Changing the subject, I said, "Well, I do need you, Momma. I need you to call up the prayer warriors and put him and Mrs. Andrews on the prayer list. I will call you soon, but don't worry about me. I'm an adult now, not the teenager that he once knew."

"I know, Victoria." she said, "Just keep God first."

"I will, Momma," I said. "I will."

Hanging up the phone, I thought, that wasn't as bad as I had thought it would be.

I left the phone and went to Sharon. I said, "Sharon, I know that I have the weekends off, but James's grandmother is dying. She only has a day or two to live. Is it possible for me to take a week's vacation starting tomorrow?"

Sharon looked at me at first like she was thinking, and then she said, Oh no why are you here now you should be with him, we haven't been busy I think we can handle it. Just so you know our soon to be new boss lady, Ms. Fable is coming to tour the store. I heard she is pretty rough they say her name speaks for itself she's a sharpshooter and she wants to meet our staff, but I am good at making excuses. She doesn't have to know that your vacation wasn't already planned. We can oversee things until you return. Now go and let me know if there is anything I can do."

Grateful, I just nodded my head. Sharon knew of my desire to be with James, although she had tried to hook me up with a few of her friends, with no hope. I looked at the clock it was 12:53 pm I decided she was right I clocked out and headed to my apartment to get some clothes for a few days and then I was headed to James's.

When I turned the corner on James's street, what I saw first took my breath and I felt weak. Heat rose from my neck to my dome. While weakness turned to anger, Mrs. Andrews gripped my mind and my vision for a moment went blurry. No, I thought please it can't be. Was I too late? It was April's car. I sat there before a moment hoping my face would regain its color before I went in. Knocking wasn't an option because she was in my space, I wasn't in hers. I eased through the kitchen before I made it to Mrs. Andrews bedroom. James was standing behind April by Mrs. Andrews bed and April had taken my seat in Mrs. Andrews's room. I didn't hide the fact I was there; I stood in the doorway so I could be seen. James immediately felt my presence. He turned around and said, "Hey, Vicky."

"Hello," I said as I entered the room. "What's going on?" I'm sure the curiosity in my voice struck some cords.

"She is sleeping," he said. "She has been sleeping all day." James must have noticed the concern on my face. He got up to leave the room as if he didn't want Mrs. Andrews or April for that matter to hear the conversation. I could feel the heat on my face so hot one could have fried an egg. At that point April never acknowledged my presence. As if he felt the need to explain and it was needed regardless of the situation, I wanted to know what made April come here. "Um well I got a little worried because she has not wakened since last night. April called to check on her and once I told her she showed up. She checked her over and we have just been sitting around waiting for her to wake up.

"Oh, was all I could think to say I couldn't put my frustration on James because I saw sincere hurt come across his face. Along with the bags underneath the eyes he had a crinkle that rested on his forehead and to be honest I felt it wasn't his fault he wanted Mrs. Andrews to be ok and how could I take that from him. I couldn't nor would I be the villain after all this plays out so I can hear it for the duration of our lives. I thought that I needed to speak my concerns with April. If it got to the point, I felt her presence was a problem but for now I had to keep in my minds forefront that it wasn't about me and James at this time, but it was about Mrs. Andrews.

I felt disrespected by April because she was a woman and I know she had a crush on James's years ago. Times had changed he didn't want her then and in spite her beauty and charisma I refuse to let her squeeze in on him now.

I just looked at him and told him not to worry I was there now, and I wouldn't leave him again. I gave him a hug and whispered in his ear. We got this……remember her goal is to be with your grandfather now, so we need to let her go. We need to not hold her from her destination. I leaned out from my hug and looked him square in his eyes and said, "Isn't that what she wants didn't we promise her that?" he nodded his head and said, "your right Vicky." That is what she wants, and I told her I would be ok It's just hard, but you are right."

We walked back to Mrs. Andrews room where April was sitting. She wasn't in smocks today she wore a shirt that showed off her cleavage and magnified the color of her eyes and a pair of Jeans that butter would have to be applied to be taken off and everything about her at that moment seemed perfect and I needed to be more observant James and I just found each other again and I wasn't even sure if we would be together. I felt that I was reading too much into it so for now I would just hold my peace. Who knows we probably would never see her again once Mrs. Andrews passed. Besides talking to her at this point could go either way I thought. I didn't want her to think that I was a jealous girl or that her presence bothered me because that could give her the indication that I was insecure, and she had a chance if she wanted it. Deep in the pit of my stomach I felt hopeless because if she continued, she might grab his attention then where would that leave me. After James retook his seat and I knew he was settled for the moment I said to April. "Thank you for coming April. WE really appreciate it. I think we can take it from here I am sure you have other people waiting for you and before I gave her a change to protest. I sternly looked at her in disapproval and gave the hand gesture while saying let me walk you to your car."

As if she knew her actions were wrong, she said "Absolutely" as we were walking out, she looked back at James and noticed he wasn't coming with us and as if she knew what was coming or wanted to take control she then said "I will continue to keep her in my prayers and you too James" I made a point to stand behind her and walk so she would follow suit. Once outside my first impulse was to pull every strand of that blond hair out of her head but instead as she reached for her door she turned to me and as if she knew I knew what she was trying to accomplish she said " Despite what you may think Victoria I am a nurse and I genuinely care about patience and their families, I was only trying to help nothing more, nothing less.

I said "April, I appreciate you coming by to help us, I truly do worse case scenario if something happens that we can't handle we will call the ambulance."

"Well then", she said "I'll leave you to it take care." I stood there as she got in her car and drove away, wondering what exactly she was thinking, or should have I entertained her words and told her what I truly was thinking, but I thought against it because if she tried to justify her position then an ambulance would have been called but not for Mrs. Andrews. but I quickly erased that from my mind and went in to be with James.

As I approached him in Mrs. Andrews room, he turned to look at me and said Vicky did April tell you what she told me. My heart immediately stopped to where I couldn't feel any airflow to my brain almost to the point, I thought I was going to pass out. I regained my composure and asked with fear in my heart "No she didn't tell me anything, why what did she tell you." I asked not really wanting to know, I tried to brace myself because I am sure she told him about the crush she had when we were in school as if he didn't know but I stood there trying not to get defensive and listened while he spoke the words that made me feel ashamed of myself. "That Grandma will be lucky if she makes it through the night."

I could tell by the look on James's face that he had been crying. His pain was surreal, and I felt like a foolish woman, and I wondered what he would do if he found out that I had turned into this jealous bitty of a woman. I had to try to forget April and focus on what was happening at that moment, so I cleared my throat and said, "Well, I will be here. I took the rest of the week off. I won't leave you, James. We'll get through this."

James and I went in the living room. Being away from Mrs. Andrews made him uncomfortable, so we decided to sit by her bed for the rest of the night. We sat there waiting for some type of reaction, but there wasn't any. Once or twice, James put his hand on her chest to make sure that she was still breathing. Around five-thirty in the morning, James didn't feel her heartbeat, and he said to me, "Vicky, something is wrong. We have to get her to a hospital."

I immediately called 911.

He kept saying, "Hold on, Grandma, help is coming. Please hold on. Not yet," he said to his grandmother. "Help is on the way."

Within minutes, the ambulance arrived, and the medics began doing CPR.

"Please don't let her die," I heard James say, "not yet."

They finally got her breathing, and then she was rushed to the emergency room. I knew she didn't want to be revived and James nor myself told that to the medics I knew that the time was rather close and once they got her to the hospital if she didn't continue breathing on her own, they would know by her records that she didn't want to be revived and that would be the…. end.

James's rode in the ambulance, and I drove my car. About a mile from the hospital, the ambulance turned off its lights, and the siren stopped. I wondered if James knew what that meant—the end, I thought to myself. I started praying for peace. I hoped that once inside the hospital, they could do something for her.

Once out of the ambulance, James and I rushed beside the paramedics as they pushed her to the room. James stopped before he got to the room and said, "I can't go in there. I can't."

"I'll go." I said. Continuing with the fast stride, I entered the room.

One of the paramedics told me, "You need to step back."

I stood in the doorway as they tried to revive Mrs. Andrews. It was moments later that I heard someone say, "She's gone." As they left the room, I walked over to her bed, wondering how I would tell James.

Before I left her lying there, I grabbed hold of her hand, which was still warm to the touch, for that final squeeze. I leaned over and kissed her softly on her forehead, just hoping she felt my touch before she crossed over. I got up to leave the room, and something told me to look back at her one last time. Although she looked to be in peace, I still had a sadness. As I left her room, I looked back at her one more time, and it was as if a light had overtaken her body and she had a smile on her face. That was a clear indication that she was where she wanted to be. At that instant, I knew she had crossed over. The happiness I felt for her turned to sadness once I saw James. How could I tell this man that the one that he depended on, the only woman who was always there for him, was now gone?

James was waiting outside the room. Sadness took back its control when I saw him standing there.

"James," I said, fighting back my own hurt and tears, "she's gone. James, she's gone."

Silence filled the air; those words had delivered his confirmation. Thinking that one day James would not forget the final goodbyes and wished he could have seen her one last time. I said, "would you like to go see her one last time." His words to me was "what's the point."

The drive home was a quiet one. For the first time, James asked if he could go to my apartment. He didn't want to go home. I stopped by the store to get us some sodas and I asked James if he needed anything and he said, "yeah alcohol." It was still early in the day, and I didn't feel it was a good idea, but I knew he had to get through this so whatever he had to do to cope…that's just what he had to do. I went in the store bought my sodas and bought a twelve pack of beer. This should be enough I thought, and this is just temporary after its all over we can go back to living our lives. It was as if my mother was right beside me when I bought that beer because her words came pouring into my mind with such a force that they were indeed undeniable (*What you accept will be what you will regret as time goes on Victoria)* Those words even though they were ringing true, I didn't think they meant even if I was trying to help someone cope. Drinking never was a problem before and I was sure that once James got over the hurt and pain things would be back to normal, and the drinking would seize. I pushed those words out of my mind paid for my items and left the store.

The drive to my apartment was a silent one. James and I both had our own thoughts to deal with. I'm sure his thoughts were on Mrs. Andrews, and my thoughts, of course, were of him. How would he deal with the loss of the only person he knew as family? I couldn't imagine being left in this world all alone to deal with life's choices with no one to turn to let alone losing the only person who had help me along the way. How could he get past this hurt, and what could I do to contribute to his moving forward?

Arriving at my apartment, James just sat there, and I did too.

Finally, I said, "Let's go in, James." I wanted to get a nap because sleep hadn't come the night before. My body was screaming for rest, and that is what I needed if I was going to be able to help him decide on the arrangements for Mrs. Andrews. As if James was reading my mind he said almost in a whisper "Vicky," James said, almost whispering, "we need to hurry and get her cremated. There is no time to waste. I fear she won't have rest until she is with Grandpa. She can't be lying there cold and lonely. We have to get her underneath that tree; we have to get her with Grandpa. Those were her wishes," he said with a tear trickling down his cheek.

My body and mind were screaming for rest, but my heart was telling me there would be no rest until we got at least that part taken care of. I put the car in reverse and told James we could go to the Mattox's funeral home to see how fast they could get her cremated.

Rest would have to come later, because James was right: the sooner we got her cremated, the sooner James's mind could grab hold to ease, allowing him to move forward. The sooner I could rest.

I chose the Mattox's funeral home because Mr. Mattox was an old friend of Daddy's. If anybody could get it done quickly, it would be him.

Once inside the funeral home, we were greeted by a woman named Myrtle; she was Mr. Mattox's secretary.

"Can I help you?" she said in a quiet, concerned voice.

I asked her if it was possible for me to see Mr. Mattox.

"Sure," she said. "He's in the back. Let me get him for you."

She quickly left the room, returning with Mr. Mattox following behind her.

"Victoria," he said once he recognized me, "what brings you here?"

"Mr. Mattox," I said, hoping he could help, "my friend's grandmother just passed away this morning, and her desires were to be cremated. We were wondering if you could cremate her right away."

Mr. Mattox looked over the rim of his glasses at James and asked, "What was the cause of death?"

"Natural causes," I said at the same time as James said, "Her organs shut down."

"I see," Mr. Mattox said. "Where is she now?"

"Still at the hospital's morgue," I said.

"Myrtle, can you look at my schedule and tell me what it looks like? Let's see what we can do."

Myrtle did as he asked, and then she said, "Jay, you are rather full. I don't see an opening for several weeks,"

"Several weeks?" James said with tears forming. "No, please, she has to be with Grandpa sooner than several weeks."

I looked at Mr. Mattox, wishing that my daddy was here, and said, "Can't you please fit her in sooner?"

Mr. Mattox had a suspicious look on his face and said, "If you don't mind me asking, what is the big hurry?"

Before I could respond, James said, "Her wish is to be placed underneath the willow tree with my grandfather. I want to get her there as soon as I can so that she can have peace. My grandma has been so good to me, and I really don't want to let her down. Please," he said, fighting back tears, "can you help me? I don't want to let her down."

"What is her name?" Mr. Mattox asked.

"Sabrina Andrews."

"Sabrina Andrews," he repeated out loud as if he was thinking on something. "Ah yes, I remember her; she was a pleasant woman. I also remember the urns that she requested for her husband. She ordered two urns, a miniature one and a regular size one. As a matter of fact, she was just as anxious to get him done as you are about getting her done. I was the one who did his cremation also," he said. "I remember her well. Okay, okay, I understand better now. Give me just a few days. I will send my driver over to the hospital to get her. I will do for her what I did for her husband."

"Do you still have the urns that you used for Mr. Andrews?" I asked.

"As a matter of fact, I do," he said. "I will take good care of her."

"I would like that," James said. I could now see a hint of joy dominating his pain.

"Give me a number that I can reach you when I complete the process," said Mr. Mattox.

I jotted down my number and handed it to him.

"You can just pay for it once it's done," he said.

"Thank you so much," I said.

"Tell your old dad that I am still living in the same place. He can drop by to see me if he can ever make time."

"I will," I said, leaving thankful for Mr. Mattox's help. I could tell that knowing James's grandmother would be taken care of right away put a little joy back into his soul. I knew part of James died that night, and I didn't know if he would ever get it back. I couldn't help but play Mrs. Andrews's words over and over again: "I don't want to leave him until he's ready to deal with this on his own, Victoria; he needs you …" Although I needed James's closeness, this was a time that I felt that he needed time alone the most. James was going through something, and I didn't know how to help.

Once we got in the house James opened a beer, he offered me one and as much as I probably needed one to calm my nerves I declined. Later in the evening, I could tell that the alcohol was taking its effect on James. It was brought to my attention when I asked him about working on the obituary, he seemed much more in tuned and calmer but when he stood up, he lost his balance. I pretended not to notice and as he went into the kitchen to refuel up, I went and got the paper and pencil so we could at least get that part out of the way. James and I worked on her obituary together. He didn't know much about these things, and it was a learning experience for me too, but this was something that needed to be done. We were the only two people around to do it, so I wanted it done right. It took longer to post the obituary than it took to write it and seeing it in the paper for the first time made me realize that it was the saddest I had ever seen. It read:

Ms. Sabrina Andrews, 1905–1984.

Her survivors: James Andrews, grandson.

Preceded in death by Clarence Andrews.

A special friend, Victoria Adams.

She will be sadly missed.

Ms. Sabrina Andrews wished to be cremated There will be no services. Per her request, her urn will go to her grandson James Andrews.

And that was it. No sisters, no children, nothing else.

Chapter 12

I had taken a week off to spend time with James. Two days later, I awakened to find James gone. The only place I knew to look for him was Mrs. Andrews's house. I got up, took my shower, drank my usual morning tea, and waited for James to return. Around noon, I drove by the park. As the limbs parted, I could see a figure underneath the willow tree. James, I thought.

I noticed his car was in the parking lot. I parked my car beside his and headed toward the tree, feeling nervous and not knowing what to expect. I stuck my head through the branches, and there he was, carefully digging a hole to place Mrs. Andrews's urn in. "James," I said, "I thought I would find you here. Are you okay?"

I could tell by his teary eyes that he was saddened by his loss. In his hand, he held a shovel. "I must dig her hole so it can be ready for her," he said. He paused long enough to look at me. "I miss her so much already, and she hasn't been gone but a few days. I am just thinking, Vicky—who do I have left? I don't know where my father is, and that's her son; I don't even know if he knows. As for my mother, the last time that they spoke, they had words, and I don't know if she would even care. Grandma has been my mother and my father, all of my family for that matter, and now she's …" Tears stung his eyes, causing him to blink trying to stop them from coming. I silently prayed for God to give me the words to encourage him.

"She's not suffering, James," I said, hoping that my words would send comfort to him. "You have to be strong. I don't know if she can see you or not, but if she can, she doesn't need to know that you're hurting. She didn't want to leave here knowing that you would hurt. I believe her soul has gone on to heaven now with your grandfather, and that is where she really wanted to be. She knew that her time was up, and she knew that you could carry on. Let's not disappoint her. Let her know that you are the man that she left. You are strong and can carry on. Her love for you was so strong, James, and the last thing she would want is for you to be sad. She told me that she knew you were strong by now."

I had James's full attention now. I continued, "she told me that she didn't want to leave you until she felt that you could go on. I believe you can go on. Evidently, she believed it too, so let's not disappoint her. Be that strong man that she knows you can be. Move on. Hurt is expected, but you need to move on, James. You've got me," I said, trying to make him smile, "and you've got my mom and dad. We will help you, James. She would want you to be glad that she is finally with your grandpa, not sad for her."

"Vicky," he said as if that was the only thing he heard, "do you think she is where she wants to be? Do you think she is finally with Grandpa?" he asked, having soaked in my every word.

"I know she is," I said. "James, she has lived her life. Putting you where you needed to be in this world had to be her will. Even God thinks you are where you need to be, or he would not have taken her. Let's be happy for her. She was ready to go. James, she was looking forward to this journey.

Let her cross over in peace, a peace that only God can give her. You want her here, I know, but don't you remember her suffering, losing her meaning to life? She only slept when she was here. She was ready, James; let her go. She has found her happiness—no more suffering, no more pain. Isn't that what it's all about? We want that for the ones that we love—no more hurt and pain."

"Yes," he said now that his tears had dried up, "I want her happy."

"Then let her go. She can't be truly happy if she knows that you are sad. Remember her, love her, but let her go, okay?"

"Okay," he responded.

"One day when God sees fit, you will meet back up with your mother and father again. This time maybe you can have a relationship; maybe this time there will be love to share." Using Mrs. Andrews's words, I said, "It might even be the relationship that you missed growing up, but for now, you have to find your place in this world. It's your time now. If God didn't think you were strong enough, he wouldn't have taken her."

As if pondering on what he had just heard, James laid down the shovel and sat underneath the tree. James and I sat under our tree for at least another hour in silence, and then he said, "Can I stay with you for a little while, Vicky? I don't want to be by myself."

Without thinking of momma's disapproval and because I was so glad, he asked I responded "Of course, you can, James, for as long as you need."

"Will you go to the house so I can get some clothes? I need to get Grandpa's urn too, so when I get her, they can be together."

"Yes," I said. I hoped that he understood my words and would be able to move forward. I drove to the house and James rode with me; neither one of us had been there since we had taken her to the hospital.

As I pulled up into her driveway, I asked James, "Do you want me to wait for you here or go in with you?"

Without hesitation he said, "Will you go in with me?"

I put the car in park and without another word, opened my car door. James took a deep breath and followed me on the porch. As we entered the house, there was still a faint smell of sickness lingering about.

James went straight into his room and gathered up his clothes. The door to her room was closed, and I was glad for that as we were leaving James stopped long enough to stare at her door, as if he was going to enter in, but he decided against it. "Will you go in and get Grandpa's urn, Vicky? It's beside her bed on the table."

Feeling a little nervous, I agreed. I felt him watching me as I entered her room. I quickly got the urn, which was sitting on the nightstand as he'd said, and I left the room, closing the door behind me. Then we left. We were back in route to my apartment. Silence was the mood for the moment, but I was silently praying that God would intervene somehow and give him the strength that he needed to Move forward with his life.

Once back at my place, progress seemed to come into play. We made lunch together, and we sat and ate with no words of Mrs. Andrews. After we ate, we sat and watched movies, and we talked about our lives while we were apart. I learned a little about his mom and dad, and although that part of our conversation was limited, I sort of got the feel of what he experienced as a child. The latter part of the day proved to be much more rewarding than the beginning.

Around six o'clock, James decided to make a run to the store. "Do you need anything?" he asked as he was putting on his jacket.

"No," I said. "I'm fine. Do you want me to go with you?" I asked.

"No, I won't be long," he said as he headed toward the door. I knew he needed his time, and I didn't want to smother him, so going out alone was a great idea—so I thought. While he was gone, that was a great time for me to call Momma. I hadn't talked to her in a while, so before she started worrying, I thought it was best if I gave her a call. When she answered, I said, "Hello, Momma."

"Well, hello, stranger," she said. "And what do I owe the honor of this call to your forgotten mother?"

"I just called to see how you and Daddy were doing and to let you know that Mrs. Andrews passed away."

"Oh, Victoria, I am sorry to hear that. How's James doing?" she asked.

"He's sad," I said, "but he's better than what I expected him to be."

"Good to hear," she said. "Would you like to come over for dinner tomorrow? I know you both have a lot on your plate."

"I'll see, Momma," I said.

As if she knew my thoughts—I was wondering if I could bring James—she said, "You can bring James. I am sure he needs the closeness of family right now. Victoria now is not the time for my feelings about James. I know how you feel about him. You are my daughter. Please don't think that I would say anything out of the way during a time like this. Even though our love is for you, know that we understand, so bring him. It's okay. We will be on our best behavior."

Feeling a little relieved that she had included James, I said, "I will ask him if he is up to it. I will call you by morning to let you know for sure."

"Okay," she said. "Talk to you soon."

I was glad that she wasn't doubtful, and she included James. I thought dinner at my parents' house might be a welcome change for James. With those thoughts, I went in for my shower and waited for James to return.

By the time I was out of the shower and ready to settle in for a movie, James returned. Although he was in a better mood than when he left, I could smell a faint smell of alcohol—sort of the way Daddy smelled after he took a little nip. James tried to hide the smell by chewing gum, so I didn't let on like I knew. I figured James was out drinking, but I knew he had to deal with Mrs. Andrews's death the best that he knew how. He needed a way to cope, and I had to understand that. I didn't entertain that thought much longer before my movie started.

James settled on the couch with me.

"James," I said, "Momma called and invited us to dinner tomorrow. Do you want to go?"

He sat there for a minute before speaking.

"They would love to see you," I said.

"No shotguns involved?" he said, laughing.

"No shotguns, silly. They miss seeing you. There are no hard feelings there," I said, trying to convince him to go.

He finally said, "If you want to, we can go."

"Good," I said. "I will call her in the morning to let her know how anxious you were to accept," I said, laughing. "It will be fine; you will see."

As we sat and watched the movie, I wanted more than anything to know his thoughts. I supposed he was wondering if they would be as accepting as they were years earlier. Silence and thoughts filled the air, and I don't think either of us watched the movie that was playing.

After the movie when it was time for bed, knowing that sleeping on the couch for the past two nights was probably a bit uncomfortable I invited James to sleep in my bed. "I don't mind sleeping on the couch Victoria" James said, His words catching me off guard I would have thought he would jump at the chance to sleep in my bed. "I don't want to cross the boundaries" he said smiling. "You want cross any boundaries" I said?"

"My bed is big enough for the both of us, but no funny stuff," I added in a playful sort of way.

"I promise," he said as we went into the bedroom. As I laid down, I thought to myself this man is really a mystery.

James had already gotten up and started breakfast. When I walked in the kitchen, he said, "Were you going to sleep the day away?"

Looking at the clock, I said, "it's only seven thirty." I stood there for a moment watching James standing there in a pair of shorts and a T-shirt. "Aren't you the desired one up early fixing breakfast?"

"Just wanting to earn my keep," he said with a smile that showed his beautiful teeth.

By eight o'clock, I was pouring a cup of tea and my phone was ringing.

"Hello," Momma said.

"Good morning," I replied back.

"Is dinner on for this evening?"

I said, "My, aren't we persistent this morning?" as I looked at James. "We will be there for dinner. James is so excited to see you and Daddy again," I said, smiling at James. He returned the smile.

"Around four o'clock if that sounds good," Momma said.

"Do you want us to bring anything? … Okay, well then, we will see you at four.… I will," I said. "Tell Daddy the same."

"I will," she said. "See you then."

"See ya then," I replied as I hung up.

James said, "I'm excited? Try nervous," he said.

"Oh, it will be okay," I said, giving him reassurance. I wondered if Momma knew James was here. I wondered if she thought I had broken my oath and James and I were having sex.

James interrupted my thinking by asking, "Eggs scrambled or fried?"

"None for me, thanks," I said. "I will just have bacon, toast, and tea."

Turning my attention back to him, I thought, he is truly a handsome man. If sexy was a word that I used often, his name would be right beside it.

As we sat and had breakfast, James asked, "Besides having dinner at your parents' house, what do you want to do today?"

"I have nothing in mind," I said. "What about you?"

"Nothing in particular," he said. "I will just have to run out about two, but I shouldn't be gone long."

"Okay," I said. "Then we can just hang out here for the day."

After breakfast, James helped me clear away the dishes and make the bed. After that, he took a shower and I followed suit. Then before I knew it, the time was two o'clock, and James was heading out the door. Although it was strange, I felt like James, and I were just friends. No kissing, no sexual advances. One could say that we were living like roommates. Although I wanted more, I was satisfied with just having him around for the time being. Maybe he was afraid to make advances because of momma beliefs, all kinds of thoughts crossed my mind but, I knew he was going through a lot, so in time, I thought to myself, in time. Patience, like they say, is a virtue.

Within an hour, James had returned. The faint smell of alcohol returned with him, but he went in the bathroom and, as if I didn't know, he brushed his teeth and put on a splash of cologne.

"My, don't we smell good?" I said as he came out of the bathroom.

"Is it too much?" he asked, feeling a bit ashamed.

"No, it's just enough," I said. "You smell good," I said in a teasing sort of way.

"I don't want to make your Daddy jealous," he teased back.

"You won't," I said, "but I am sure Momma will notice how good you smell."

Minutes later we were on our way to my parents'.

Momma and Daddy both were on the porch when we arrived. Momma was sitting there holding a flyswatter, and Daddy was cleaning his nails with his pocketknife.

"Good evening," I said as we approached them. "I smell something good."

"Yeah," Daddy said, "your momma has been slapping pans all day long. It better be something in that kitchen cooking," and then he belted out a laugh.

"Oh, how would you know?" Momma snapped back. "You have been in that shed all afternoon."

With Momma's words, we all laughed, each probably with our own thoughts, but I would bet mine and Daddy's were one and the same.

"How have you been, James?" Momma asked. "So sorry for your loss."

"Thank you," James said. "I've seen better days, but I'm okay."

Daddy then looked up and said, "It's about firewood cutting time, James. Would you like to come by and help? It will take your mind off of things."

"I'd like that," James said, looking back at the garden. "Looks like the old garden has been producing good this year."

"Yeah," Daddy said. "Didn't think she was going to come through with all the rain we have had this year, but she found a way to shine on. She's never let me down thus far," Daddy said, proud of his garden. "I hope Momma here cuts fresh tomatoes and cucumbers with a little onion with those fresh green beans I've smelled all day."

"Oh, you haven't smelled anything," Momma said, smiling. "My food doesn't reach that old shed." Again, her words brought laughter.

"What's the flyswatter for?" I asked Momma. "You been beating my daddy?"

"He needs a good swatting," she replied, "but no, actually it's been for the flies and the bees. They have been terrible this year."

Momma got up to go into the kitchen to check on her rolls, and feeling comfortable with leaving James with Daddy, I followed her. Looking back to the porch, I saw that James had taken her seat.

Once in the kitchen, Momma said, "He sure turned out to be a handsome young man, Victoria, and he smells good too."

"Shhhhh," I said, looking at the window, knowing the only thing that was separating them and us was a screen that was in the window. "He will hear you," I said, whispering to Momma.

Putting her hands up to her mouth, she realized what I said was true. She whispered, "I'm sorry."

As I looked out the doorway, I saw Daddy and James leave the porch and head to the garden. Turning back to Momma, I said, "Yes, he is handsome, but for now we are just friends."

"Um–hum," Momma said. "I figured as much. So where is he staying now that his grandmother has passed?" she said with a smile.

"No, really. He stays with me, but I have values, Momma. Right now, I am just trying to help him get through losing Mrs. Andrews. Then maybe we can see where it heads, but now his mind is clouded. The last thing I want to do is start a relationship with him having a clouded mind," I said.

"I'll agree with that. We don't need no repeats," Momma said. Looking at me as if she had said something wrong, she said, "I'm sorry. Forget I said that."

"Forgotten," I responded.

"I know you didn't come over here for me to drill you. I just want you to be careful, that's all."

"I will, Momma. I will."

As Momma took the rolls out of the oven, I stepped to the door to check on James and Daddy. I thought Oh no as I watched them come from the shed. Without saying a word about that to Momma, I started putting butter on her rolls. By the time the rolls were buttered, Daddy and James had returned to the porch with onions, tomatoes, and cucumbers in my daddy's hand, acting as if they never left the garden.

I went outside, and Daddy said, "I was telling James here that my plant was hiring. I probably could get him on with a good job. The only thing, though, is by him coming in at this time, he is subject to being laid off. He has to put some of his money back for that rainy day."

"That's a wonderful idea," Momma said. "With his age and all, that would be a promising future for him."

"I told James," Daddy continued, "to give me a week, and I will set his interview up."

If getting James, a job at the plant could be done, then it could be done by Daddy. He was well-liked, and he himself was a supervisor.

Dinner was a success. We ate and we talked; it was like James had never left. Even though I knew they were only accepting him back into their lives for the sake of my happiness, I knew that with time, they would love him all over again. I just wanted the past to stay in the past; it was time that we all just moved on.

By seven, James was thanking them for a wonderful dinner, and James and I were headed back to my apartment. Once we were back at my apartment, curiosity got the best of me; I asked James what Daddy had to show him in the shed. His look of surprise at the question almost made me laugh.

James quickly said, "Tools. Um, he had new tools that he used in his garden this year, and he wanted to show them to me."

Letting on like I didn't know the real reason they were in the shed, I said, "Oh, that's nice. We had a good time, didn't we, James?" I said.

"Yes, Vicky," he replied, "I really needed that time with your dad."

Time with my dad and the shed, I thought to myself. "Good," I said. "I'm glad."

"Well, I am about to take a shower. Want to join me?" James said.

I looked up at James, but before I could answer, he said, "Just kidding, Vicky."

Little did he know that as wrong as I knew it would be, I might have considered it. I wondered what he would do or say if I joined him anyway. Would I feel like I had let my parents down—and God for that matter? Would the shower be the end, or would he want to make love to me? Trying to erase those thoughts, I decided I would take that time out to write in my journal.

After about thirty minutes, James joined me on the couch. "You still write in that thing?" he asked.

"I still write, yes, but it's a different journal."

"Do you write anything about me?" he asked.

"Maybe, maybe not," I replied. It was then that his eyes caught mine, and it was as if he was searching, trying to figure out what was on my mind. After a few moments of staring, I felt it was a good time for me to take my shower. "I think I will take my shower now," I said, easing off the couch with my journal in hand, getting up to go to the bathroom. As I turned to see what James was doing, I saw that he was watching me. "Want to join me?" I asked. Before he could answer, I said, "I'm only teasing."

Not being used to locking my bathroom door, ten minutes into my shower, I heard James come in. "James Andrews, don't you dare!" I shouted.

"What?" he said. "Talk?"

Thankful that I had double layered my shower curtain so he couldn't see my body's form, I peeked around the curtain to see what he was doing. He had laid down the commode seat, and he was just sitting there.

"Vicky," he asked, "do you think your parents wonder why I left the way I did?"

I didn't know where this conversation was heading and why it couldn't wait until I was out of the bathroom, but I answered him with, "No, James. Why do you ask?"

"You know I didn't want to leave you, right? I mean, years ago."

"I know you couldn't help it," I said. I wanted to finish my shower in peace, but at the same time, I wondered what was on his mind. All the while, I was hoping that he wouldn't peek beyond the curtains while I was showering.

Trying to hurry up with my shower so that we could finish this conversation in the living room, I said, cutting off the water, "Can you reach me a towel?" In no time, a hand and towel appeared. Then I said after drying off, "Can you reach me my robe?" He repeated his same actions. Moments later I emerged from the shower, with my robe snugged tightly to my body.

I was standing in front of the mirror brushing my wet hair when he said, "You are so beautiful, Vicky." I wiped the fog from the mirror to get a better look at him. He was just sitting there watching me with this look on his face. Not saying a word, I continued to brush my hair. When I was all done, I led him out of the bathroom.

James and I went to take our seats back on the couch. "Victoria," he continued, "did you ever forgive me for leaving the way I did?"

"Yes," I said. "I knew it wasn't your fault. I forgave you." I answered his question with a question: "Did you think about me after you left me?"

"Every day," he said.

I wasn't used to getting out of my shower routine, so my body was screaming for lotion and powders. I told James to hold that thought, hoping that he wouldn't follow me. "I will be right back." I went to my room, layered my body with lotion and powders, put on my pj's, and when I came back into the room, James hadn't moved. Yet he had held his thoughts.

As I took my seat, he continued on. "Did you love me, Vicky? Because you never said."

I wasn't sure how to answer that, so I said, "As much as a sixteen-year-old knew how to love." After a moment of silence, I added, "Who really knows what love is at the age of sixteen?"

"Have you dated since we were together?" he asked.

I shook my head no. "Have you?" I heard myself asking.

"No," he said. "Why didn't you date?" he asked.

Knowing I was about to tell a lie, I said, "I kept pressing on with school and all, helping Mom and Dad around the house. I really didn't have much time for dating." He really didn't need to know the real reason why. The past was just that, the past. The truth was that I didn't date because I desired him.

"You have never kissed or been with another man, you know, I mean like sex?"

"Absolutely not," I said. "I do have morals." Feeling almost offended, I felt it was time to turn the questions on him. "Have you?" I asked. "I mean, been with another woman?"

"No," he said.

"And why not?" I asked.

"After the way I left you, I didn't want to feel that way again. I had too much going on in my life. When Grandma got sick, and as good as she was to me when I was alone, I felt that it was my time to look after her."

"And now?" I said, not wanting to bring up the fact that his grandmother was gone but needing to understand where this conversation was heading.

"Now, well, there is this one girl that I have had on my mind for a long time. She is absolutely amazing."

My heart was sinking hearing James speak of another girl to me. I already knew it had to be April, why wouldn't it be she was a successful nurse and not to mention gorgeous. Here goes I thought I am so glad I didn't make a fool of myself by speaking to her about her advances. Maybe they have been thinking about each other all along. He probably thought we would never get back in touch with me and maybe that is why she went to the house. I felt sick to the point I just knew any moment my food was going to find its place on my carpet. Seeing my facial expression, he said, "We are friends, aren't we, Vicky? I can tell you anything, right?"

"Right," I said, thinking to myself, except that you are in love with someone else. Please don't do that to my heart. Yet I continued to let him speak; at least I would know where I stood in all this.

He now turned his look toward me and said, "I haven't really talked to her about my feelings, and I don't know if she feels the same. That is my fear."

"Well," I said, not wanting to hear anymore, "first get past losing your grandmother, and then let the chips fall where they may. If it is meant to be, then it will happen."

"That's just the thing," he said. "Grandma loved her, and I am not sure how long it will take for me to stop missing Grandma. I need her now more than ever, but I don't want to ever hurt this girl the way I hurt you."

I just sat there paralyzed in thought. Why couldn't It be me. I wanted to ask how long he had been thinking about April, or did we ever have a chance. Instead, I just sat there my conscious mind was whispering how foolish I was, and my subconscious mind was saying just listen to him. I continued to listen, while trying to think of something positive to say from this awful conversation.

James continued, "We should be able to confide in our friends. I mean, that is what friends do, right?"

"Right," I said, but not to a friend who wants you to love her, I thought to myself. At this point, what could I do but hold my composure and listen. I mean, if he had feelings for someone else, who was I to stand in the way? He was still my friend, and he came to me for support. That was just what I was going to give him, no matter who this girl was. Even if it was April.

"I have known her for years yet she's someone that I want to get to know. She is all I could ever want in a woman." Is he ever going to stop, I thought, as he continued, "a girl who I want to bear my children." Now he's about to push my buttons. "Yet I want her to want me the same way, and I don't know how to get that. How can I let her know that she is the one I feel is for me?"

"Just tell her," I said. "Maybe if she knew, that could be a beautiful beginning," I said, now on the verge of tears, my voice starting to tremble. I hope he couldn't see just how bad his words hurt my feelings.

"I don't know how to tell her; that's just it. As my grandma said, this girl has her life together. Look at me. I am twenty-three years old, and I don't even know where to start. His voice trailed off and I sat there regretting that I only completed two years of school to be a pharmacy assistant and April was an RN. As much as I didn't want to, I had to give her props because she was exactly where she wanted to be in her life and all she needed was James. Me on the other hand I was trying to figure out where I was headed with…….or…without…. James. I tried to tune back in, so he continued, she is already several steps ahead of me. Vicky, look at my past. Most of my teenage years I had to deal with my parents crap. My adult years so far has been taking care of my grandma. I don't know what my future holds. I am not even sure where to start. All I know is I can't imagine this girl not being a part of my life, not being a part of me."

"James," I said, about sick of listening about this other girl, "if it is meant to happen, it will. God's will is just that, God's will." It may take some time, but if she is meant for you, it will happen."

As if he wasn't hearing me, he said, "Enough of me, Victoria. Is there anybody you're interested in; anybody you have a desire to be with?"

"Well, James," I said, taking a breath at this point—while he sat there searching, probably reading my thoughts.

"I know that we are friends, Victoria, but is there anybody out there that you desire to have more than a friendship with?"

What do you say when the only man you desire has just told you that he has feelings for someone else? Looking into his eyes made me melt inside, but I knew he wanted an answer. Okay, God, help me through this conversation. Give me the right words so I don't sound stupid.

I guess I was taking too long with my answer because James said, "If you don't want to say, it's okay."

"No, no, there, um, I um…. well" …thinking my language barrier needs a checkup. I tried to continue even though I had to force the words to come out of my mouth. "I know there is someone for everyone James and

I know you have a girl in mind that you would like to explore your life with,, and I can respect that but if I am to be honest" I paused considering he once told me that April had a crush on him would he get with April and he tell her that now I was the one with the crush. It was a small town and rumors from kids were a lot different from rumors from adults and I didn't want anyone laughing after speaking my name. I felt if I didn't tell him then he would never know. Maybe that is best I thought and before I could change the subject my subconscious mind connected with my mouth and I heard myself saying I can't move forward to be with anyone else James because there is still a soft spot in my heart for you," and before he let me finish, he leaned forward and kissed me with a passion that I had never felt before. My body was doing its own thing, and it was a joyful feeling. After I tried to hold back, feeling a little confused, I let go and returned his kiss as passionately as he had given it to me. It took James to clear my thoughts after our kiss.

"Victoria, it's you," he said, kissing me again with the same passion. "It's you that I desire; it's you that I am talking about."

I felt the tears forming, but I couldn't let them come. My mouth was out of control because I heard myself say. "I thought you wanted April"?

"What" he said looking in a state of confusion. "Yes, James, I thought you wanted to be with April. It's clear that she still has the crush on you," now feeling a little foolish I said, "never mind I don't really know what I am saying can you just kiss me again?" Now why did I say that I should never plant a seed about April. Mommas use to always tell me watch what you say Victoria. Always speak good intentions and positive thoughts because when you speak your words can plant unwanted seeds. Seeds that can grow into something unwanted. Always be mindful of your words.

James repeated his actions from the first kiss, and I was glad to submit. We finished our kiss and then he looked at me and said "You're the girl that I am referring to, and your kiss let me know that we still have a chance. Victoria, I wanted to know, I needed to know, that there hasn't been another man because I wanted to be the only one. I want to be the one that makes you happy. I want to be the one that you look forward to after a day's work."

James kissed me again, and I leaned back as if I was submitting myself to him. It was as if Momma came to my mind and said, "Be careful, Victoria." Stopping the kiss, I said, "James, no."

Looking a little confused and disoriented, James said, "What, what's—"

Cutting him off I spoke my words quickly so we both could understand why we shouldn't do what we were about to do. One of us had to snap into reality if we didn't the shotgun wedding that James always teased about would have been spoken into reality. Once I got the first words out the rest of them just flowed quickly. I said, with my face becoming hot and my heart rate skyrocketing, giving off signals that my heart was about to jump out of my chest. "I don't use birth control. James, we're not married. I don't want a shotgun wedding. I want it right; I want it to be perfect. I don't want kids before we're married. We talked about that. All we have is time now; we don't have to rush anything." What am I saying? Am I crazy?

I'm turning down the man I have been waiting for, the man that now desires me, and I am turning him down. Trying to catch my breath and think for a moment before I spoke then I said, "Theres nothing more than I would rather do than to have you make love to me, but it has to be right. I only get one chance to lose my virginity and when I do I want my last name to be changed. You and I have talked about this and right now I think we are running on emotions. I was so nervous at that moment that even though I wasn't mad for him trying my words came off louder and probably stronger than usual.

"Calm down" James said almost laughing. "You're right, Vicky," he said. "We have time. We don't need to rush things. I understand your beliefs."

With that having been said, I said, "But there is nothing wrong with holding me."

With those words, James and I went to bed, and I slept in his arms.

Friday came, and James was in deep thought. I didn't know if his thoughts were on me or Mrs. Andrews. I would occasionally walk by him and touch him on his shoulder or arm just to let him know that I was there for him if he needed me. I put my hand on James's back as tears began streaming down his face. Just then, Myrtle called from the funeral home.

"She's ready," she said. "You can pick her up at your earliest convenience."

"Thank you," I said as I hung up the phone. "James, it's time. She's ready."

We went to the funeral home to pick up the urn. James paid for it and said, "We really appreciate it," as he touched the urn.

We walked out of the funeral home hand in hand. I didn't know how James would react once we buried her, but I was glad that he did feel that she was at peace. We left there and went to the park. James carefully placed her in the hole that he had dug only days earlier. Then he took the two wedding bands out of his pocket and placed them into the hole with the urns. I could see Mr. Andrews's urn shining through the dirt, but I never said a word. I just stood there with tears streaming down my face. "I love you, Grandma," he said. "Now you can rest." Tears were constantly falling from his face into the dirt.

After he was done, we sat under the willow tree and reminisced about the good times they had. He told me that she did everything she could to make sure that he was happy, even when she was getting sick. He told me how his mother would come by begging for money so she could get another drink, and he told me how when his father took on another family, that his grandmother was against it. As far as he knew, they hadn't spoken since.

"Through all of those times, she protected me, Vicky. She was the only one who really loved me. I remember crying when my mother came by the house, and she would be mean to my grandma. I remember the anger I felt toward my mother. She blamed my grandma for my father's faults. When it all happened, Momma and I went to stay with Grandma. At first it was a good time, but then Momma changed. She stopped coming home, and I remember crying myself to sleep. It was Grandma who came into my room to comfort me. I remember getting sick catching colds. When I woke up in the middle of the night, it was Grandma who was by my side. When

I started riding my bike, it was her cheering me on. She is the one who taught me how to drive a car, not my mother nor my father."

She thinks one day they will find me and want to have a relationship with me, but I don't know if I really care now. They didn't want to love me then. Why would they want to love me now?"

James and I talked for what seemed like hours. He had a lot he wanted to say. As the darkness took over, he picked up the urn that held the remainder of Mrs. Andrews's ashes, opened up the top, and poured a small pile of ashes into his hand. As if the tree knew what he was doing, it gave a small breeze, and the ashes flew into the park. "I love you, Grandma," he said yet again, and then we headed back to my apartment.

Over the weekend to take James's mind off of things, we went to Momma's and Daddy's. I had to return to work on Monday, and I wanted James to understand that it was okay for him to visit my momma and daddy without me being with him. James helped Daddy cut firewood, and every now and then, they went to the shed. I knew what they were doing, but I never let on like I knew. My concerns weren't for Daddy, but for James. I never knew him to drink, and I didn't want that to become a habit. I remember Momma telling me, "What you accept, Victoria, is what you will sooner or later regret." I knew Momma never lied to me, but I also knew James had to cope with Mrs. Andrews's death in his own way.

The days that followed were kind of awkward. James never made another sexual advance toward me, and after work when we were alone in my apartment, he was sort of quiet and kept to himself. I had thoughts that one day when I came home from work, he would be gone, but each day that I got off work and pulled up to my apartment, his car was always there. *An idle mind is the devil's workshop*, Momma always said. Every day that I left him to go to work, I had those words playing in my head. I wondered what James was doing while I was at work, and he was alone with the ashes of his grandmother.

A week later James finally got a job at Daddy's plant, and I was happy for that because it would help him keep his mind off of things. That was just what he needed and now maybe we can move forward to see what life holds for us. Yes, my patience is finally paying off.

Chapter 13

Even though I wanted to move past the feelings I had for James, I couldn't. He had taken control over my mind, and I didn't know how to move forward. I tried to think of things to occupy my time and energy, but at the end of my trying, my mind returned to James. I wanted more than just the quaint roommate. He helped with the bills, but he never mentioned anything else about "us." I decided that instead of trying to fight my desires, I would approach him about what our future held—if nothing else for the closure that I so desperately needed and deserved. Every time I would start to bring up us, he would change the subject.

I wrote about my thoughts in my journal. I pictured us as a couple, but as time went on, the memories of us began to fade. He spent a lot of time with my dad, and I felt that he was beginning to look at me as a sister, not his woman. I also felt that he found Mrs. Andrews in my father. I knew at that point that again I had lost him, and I felt I couldn't get that back. I often thought it was a challenge. The type of person that James had turned out to be is what made me want him more and more. I knew about his troubles, but I couldn't see past the love that I felt for this man. I didn't know why, and I didn't understand. I felt in my heart that something more was about to come, that something that I could never expect was about to surface.

In my heart I knew, and I could hear my mother's words: "God always has a plan. If you try to do things yourself, you always mess things up. In order for you to have success in things you set out to do, you must include God. You must step aside and let God fight your battles. When it comes to battles, they do not belong to us, Victoria, but they belong to God. Let go, Victoria, and let God." Mother had faith, and when she spoke about God, she knew what she was talking about. She knew the Bible inside and out, and she would tell me that without God, nothing was possible—but include him, and watch how his power worked. Thinking on the words of my mother, I just felt that maybe God did have a plan for us. Maybe I should just turn this entire thing over to him and see what happened.

Instead of taking the final leap to go to church, considering I hadn't been there in years, I decided to get on my knees and say a prayer on behalf of me and James. If the prayer didn't work, then I would go to church. Momma's words flashed in my head: "God's will." Was it God's will for James and me to reconnect? This time would it be for good, or would I just be a stepping-stone in the middle of God's will for James to help him cope with Mrs. Andrews's death?

That night I got on my knees and started my prayer the way my mother taught me. "Lord, I come to you as humble as I know how. I know that I am not deserving, and I do not give you the time that you truly deserve. I ask that you look past my faults and see my needs. I come to you on behalf of James and myself. If it is meant for us to be together, give me a sign. Let us have a chance of love and live as I know it, not as he knows it. Please show me if this is the man you have for me in my future or give me the strength to get over him. I can't do it by myself. I will give you the honor and the praise in Jesus's name. Amen." I ended my prayer in silence and got off my knees.

I thought just to keep the unspoken love alive, I would sit and read about all the thoughts I had about James when there was a chance for him and me. That is what kept my heart warm and the memories real. Momma always spoke of faith, but I didn't quite understand how things hoped for but evidence of things unseen fit into James's and my relationship, so I was just hoping that my prayer would do the trick. I knew that God knew hearts because that is what Momma told me, so I thought God knew my heart and I offered up a prayer, so that should be enough.

It wasn't long before winter started to settle in; the flowers that were once beautiful and feeding the birds and bees were now dead stems dying from the cold. That was the way I saw James: something that once could have been beautiful was now dead and dying from the cold. My tree showed its last leaves for this year, and it wouldn't be much longer before we would be looking forward to New Year. Nineteen eighty-five was fast approaching. New Year, new beginning. Until the new year came in, James and I both worked all the time, as if we were trying to race the time away. Still, he didn't try to make advances toward me, and I felt that it was becoming a lost cause. I wasn't prepared to live my life with James as my roommate; that was not what I had in mind for us. I had to get my life back. I didn't want to be a sex toy either. I wanted to be married, and I didn't want to come to the understanding that after almost eight years, the man that I loved and that I saw as one day being my husband was now just a roommate, just a friend. This was not what I had waited years of my life for, and to me living this way was unacceptable to my future.

When James was at work or at my parents' house, I took the time to try and focus on what I wanted the new year to bring. I could only hope that somewhere there was a deserving man who would come and sweep me off my feet, making me a well-kept woman while I took care of the children and the house. By the look of things between James and me, he was content the way our lives were. He would work and sometimes we would watch a movie together, but most of his free time was spent with my dad. I knew they had developed a bond, but I was sure Daddy didn't know that it bothered me. I would find a way to let James know of my concerns, and then I would talk to my dad if I needed to.

James wasn't turning out the way my desires had once led me. I was feeling that James was just a roommate and this roommate thing was getting old. I didn't know how long he expected me to be a roommate, but since he was on his feet, my thoughts were that he could move out on his own. If he had no plans on being my husband, then I had no plans on being his roommate. I didn't know how to approach him with my thoughts, but they had to be said.

I decided that I would speak on it after I spent the day with Momma at church. That way, whatever the conversation held for me, God would be in the midst.

We got up that Sunday morning, and I got dressed for church; James got dressed to spend the day with Daddy. Once we arrived at my parents' house, Daddy was on the porch having coffee. Momma was in the house getting ready. I left James on the porch with Daddy, and I went in the house with Momma. I guess she could tell by the look on my face that I had something on my mind.

"What is it, Victoria? What's the matter?" she asked.

Not wanting to share my thoughts with Momma, I just said, "Nothing God can't fix."

"That's good enough for me," she said as she grabbed her purse, and we were on our way to church.

Daddy got up to give Momma her usual kiss good-bye, but James just sat there, my heart burning a hole to my soul. "See ya later," was all he thought to say to me, so I just gave him a wave over my shoulder.

When we got in the car, Momma asked the question, "Did you and James have a falling-out?"

"No, Momma," I said. "We never ever had a falling-in, much less a falling-out."

With tears falling, I gave her the spill on how I was feeling. "Momma, I am tired of being his roommate. James and I are just friends. One would think he was more in love with Daddy than he was me. It's like we are living together but we are living apart, and that is not what I want in my life. I am going to pray about it, but I am going to ask him to move out once we get home this evening. I think I have wasted too many years trying to see what was in store for James and me, but now I am ready to just move on. I am tired of waiting."

"Pray about it, Victoria. Never challenge God. Don't tell him what you want, he knows your heart. Tell him to let his will be done in your life and give you the means to accept it. Be careful what you ask for. Let God have his way."

I heard Momma loud and clear, but I knew that I wanted James to want me in the way that I wanted him. I didn't want to be his friend or his sister; I wanted to be his wife.

Once we got to church, that is exactly what I told God. I didn't follow Momma's guidance. I wanted to be his wife, and that is what I told God. I would accept him just the way he was. Once I talked to him this evening, I would have my answer. I was sure of it.

After we made it back to Momma's, I saw Daddy and James coming from the shed. Daddy waved as we pulled up. "Another wonderful sermon, I suppose," he said as we got out the car.

"If you had of gone, you would know," Momma said as she passed him on the way to the house. "I hope you didn't let dinner burn while you were fiddling around in the shed," she scolded as she went into the house.

"Hey, Vicky," James said.

"Hey" was all I could think to say to him. I came close to saying "Hey, brother," but I thought against it.

Momma and I cleared the table and set the dishes. It was a quiet dinner to say the least. Momma was the only one besides God who knew of my plans once I got to the apartment. The only ones who were having a conversation were Daddy and James. If somebody had looked in the window, they would have thought that Daddy and James were having dinner alone.

Was I being selfish? I knew that Daddy always wanted a son, and I knew that Daddy was replacing Mrs. Andrews. Should I wait to see how things panned out, or should I approach the situation head-on? Since I was a head-on kind of girl, I was surprised I let this go on for as long as I had. I wished that God would just make him say the words that I needed to hear that he loved me, and he couldn't live without me. Yet I didn't see those words coming from him in the near future.

Daddy and James took one more trip to the shed before we headed home. The more I thought about it, the madder I got. I thought James was just using me. I was just a stepping-stone to get him through his loss and my daddy was his replacement for Mrs. Andrews. Even though I still wanted a future with James, I felt that letting him go would be the best thing to do. If I let him go and he didn't come back, then I could take it that he was never mine to begin with; but if he came back, I could count that as being he would be mine forever.

There was no conversation on the way home. If there was, I don't remember it. I never asked a single thing about the shed or anything else; my conversation would be better served at home face-to-face.

Once I parked the car, I took a deep breath. This is it, I thought. Either it is or it's not, and whatever will be, will be. I got out of the car and went into the apartment. James followed.

"What's wrong, Vicky?" he said before I got the chance to collect my thoughts.

Since he caught me off guard, I said, "Wrong? What on earth makes you think that something is wrong?"

"Because you have been quiet for days and you are not yourself."

"Who am I?" I said, almost snapping at him.

"You're Vicky," he said.

"No, James, that is not what I am talking about. Since you have been back in my life again, I feel we have nothing."

"What do you mean?" he said, as if he was slightly confused. "What don't we have?"

"A relationship," I said. "I try to give you time to get over Mrs. Andrews, and you get further and further away from me and closer to my dad, James. Where do I stand?" I asked. "What am I to you?"

"What brought this on?" he asked. "I thought you wanted me to be close to your family."

"I do," I said, feeling ashamed of what I was feeling, not to mention what I had just said. I continued on; I was not going to back down now. "I don't want a roommate, James; I want a man. I don't want a brother; I don't want a friend. I need more than what you are willing to give. I didn't wait eight years to be friends. We were closer when we were young, and I want that closeness back If I can't have that, I am afraid that I don't want anything. I will give you time to figure out what you want to do, but you have to decide quickly. If it's not a relationship that you're seeking with me, then I want you to move out." There, I thought, I said it. A part of me was wishing that he would grab me into his arms and tell me how he couldn't live without me, seeing how upset I was. I was hoping for the words that he loved me, but neither happened.

Instead, he said, "Okay."

Okay? I thought. That's it? After all the time I gave him, after all the love and compassion I showed him, all he can think to say is, okay? That's it. With that, I went into my room and shut the door. I cried and cried and cried until I was asleep. Had I done the right thing? Did I push him away? Was he eventually going to come around and be the man that I needed? Had I gone too far?

James never came into my room that night. When I got up to go to work, he was still on the couch. Without saying a word, I got dressed and went to work. When I got home that evening, James was gone. I didn't know where or if he would be coming back. He had taken his urns and his clothes, and he was gone.

Chapter 14

The summer months had gone, fall was vanishing, and winter was setting in; still I had heard no word from James. I just figured Momma had told Daddy what happened and once again he was without a son. Although I knew he saw James at work, Daddy never mentioned him. Neither did I. I decided to set out and give another man a chance at love. I felt that James was history. I had waited long enough on him to be the man that I needed, the man I deserved; if he didn't want that, then why should I? It was over for James and me—or was it?

It was November 10. Snow covered the ground when I woke up this morning; that was a sure sign of a depressing day. I knew before I started out that the roads would be bad, and the traffic would be slow. Mother gave the usual call when the weather was bad. "Be careful, Victoria, this morning going to work. Daddy said that when he went to work this morning, he saw a lot of accidents. Would you like for me to come get you and take you to work?" The only way I could get her off the phone was to tell her that I would be okay, and I would pray before I left my apartment. I knew she meant well, but I just didn't think she ever wanted me to grow up.

I didn't lie to her. I said my quick prayer and ventured on. Going to work was a chore, and she was right: there were many accidents, and some people were driving like they were on dry ground.

When I got to the pharmacy and saw only one car in the lot versus the usual six, I knew that it was going to be a bad day. Just about everybody called in, and it would only be me there to deal with the angry, complaining customers. It wasn't long after I got there that the one, I dreaded most barreled through the door complaining every step that he took. It was not even nine o'clock, and in the door came Mr. Boots. He was the complete opposite of Mrs. Andrews; he was angry at the world. He always wanted something for nothing, and this day was no different. As he was walking around the store, I decided to go ahead and have his prescription ready. That would limit the time that I would have to hear him complain.

When he wobbled to the counter, before he actually made it in front of me, his grumbling started. "There's six inches of snow out there, and I see the godforsaken weatherman got it wrong again. The weather last night said a 30 percent chance of showers, not a snowstorm. They ought to fire that guy. Hell, I could tell the weather better than him just by looking in the almanac."

"I understand, Sir, I totally under—"

Cutting me off, he continued, "I wonder if he knows that old people need their medicine. I wonder if he even cares. I would have come out yesterday if I had of known all of this was going to happen. I can't even get my prune juice because this pharmacy doesn't sell it, for Christ's sake. What is this world coming to? No wonder all these bad things are happening. These sorry people have made God angry, and the rest of us have to suffer through mistakes that we have no control over."

Before he could continue with another complaint, I quickly handed him his prescription. "That will be sixty-four dollars, sir," I said, dreading what was coming next.

"Sixty-four dollars! You got to be kidding me."

Here it comes, I thought.

"For what? These prices make no human sense to me. You pay to go to the doctor, and then you pay for medicine that you really don't need. You know them ole doctors just give you medicine just to keep you coming back. I am on a fixed income. I can barely afford food. Before long if the government continues to take my benefits, I will have to make the choice, either medicine or food. I won't be able to afford both."

He wanted to continue, but I was glad to see a line forming. All I had to say once he paused for breath was "Would you like for me to cut your meds in half for you? This way they would be cheaper for you." That was all it would take to get him to pay and leave. He didn't trust anyone, and to have his meds cut in half only meant that he would have to come back in here sooner to get the other half. He wasn't going to waste his time or money on doing that.

He turned to look at the customer behind him, who was showing that she was a bit irritated by him. He didn't say what he would usually say to the customer that was unlucky enough to get behind him in line. If she had smiled, he would have said, "What are you looking at? I have just as much right to voice my opinion as you do. Just stand there and wait your turn." But seeing that her forehead was wrinkled, and her mood was probably as ugly if not worse than his, he just snarled a bit, paid for his medicine, and left.

"Have a nice day," I said to him as he wobbled out the door grumbling to himself.

Poor Mr. Boots ... I wasn't the only person too busy in their own emotions to listen to him today. I went through the rest of my customers like a robot. Mr. Boots was an exception to the rule. If it wasn't for him, I would have had a peaceful day.

I continued my winter months in my own little safe haven by myself; I had talked myself into never giving in to another man like I had James. I probably wasn't in love with him, I told myself. It was just the fact that he was a mystery, he was different, and he loved his grandma and that was something that drew me close to him.

Chapter 15

The birds singing on my porch woke me up one morning, and that let me know that spring was finally in the air. Thank God, I said. I didn't think I could stand the cold any longer. The sun was shining bright, and there wasn't a cloud in the sky. I promised myself that 1986 would be the best year ever for me and my journey through this life. This, I thought, was a good day to go to the park. I would even pack a lunch and make it an all-day event. Just me, the air, and my little keepsake journal. I didn't imagine a lot of people would be there, but to my surprise, the park was full. Everybody must have had cabin fever. I thought, why not? The sun was beaming down, it was in the lower seventies, and spring was here.

As I started toward the old willow tree, I realized that it was taken by someone else. For nine straight years, I had claimed that old tree, ever since I was in high school. I had claimed that tree, and for someone else to take it was just wrong. They had spread out a blanket, and it looked as though they were getting ready for a picnic. I felt a little violated, but I wanted to see who this person was that had the nerve to take my tree. I thought of losing every letter that was in the word respect and really letting them have my true thoughts so that I could have my tree back, but I decided against it. I turned around and left the park. Eventually I thought they would be gone, and I would return. It wasn't my tree; I hadn't planted it, I thought, so how could I make claims on it?

I decided to spend my time just going for a ride, just long enough for the people at my tree to have their picnic and leave. While driving through the busy streets, I passed by Mrs. Andrews's old house. There was a for sale sign standing tall in her yard. Hmm, I thought, James must be selling her house. I guess it must still be hard for him. Well, that is his problem. I can't worry about what he is going through. I have my own life to think about. I went to the pharmacy and bought a little flower arrangement of red and white roses. I thought Mrs. Andrews would like them. I will take them and put them at the tree where she lies. That will give whoever decides to go there an indication that something must have happened near the tree, and maybe next time, they will decide against sitting there and having a picnic.

I rode around after I had gotten the flowers and I headed back to the park. There stood my tree, budding out at the spring sun, waiting for me to take my place. The park had settled down. It was just a couple of families there, just enough to please my mind and allow me to fantasize about my little family, who would be there one day playing and making their tracks in the grass like the other families did. Oh, how happy I was that spring was in the air.

As I walked toward the tree, I couldn't get Mrs. Andrews off my mind. I had promised her that I would help James through his tough time. I was wondering if she knew that I hadn't seen James since the day I put him out of my apartment. I felt a special kind of closeness to her, but at the same time, I felt that I had let her down. Looking around, I saw other people who had gathered at the part laughing and playing on the grass. Some were jogging; some just wanted to spend some time. It was a happy place, and I knew that in this happy place underneath this willow tree were two urns of people who had been reunited in love. I was sure that she was in heaven looking down on James, watching over him. I carefully placed my flowers over the place where her urn lay, and then I sat there for an hour or so. I had decided that I wouldn't visit the tree for a while. It was a place where James and I held memories, so as I got up to head for my car, I told Mrs. Andrews that I would be back on Memorial Day and that I would make sure that she had more fresh flowers.

Making my way back to the car, I felt like someone was watching me, but I just figured that I was in a park, and everybody watched everybody. It gave me an eerie feeling that soon dissolved with my thoughts of James. I wondered if he was okay, wondered if he thought of me. I made it back to my apartment. To my happiness, my own safe haven.

Days went by in a hurry, and the spring sun was shining down, feeding the trees and flowers their vitamin C. I missed going to my tree, but I thought that if whoever went there didn't get the hint from my flowers, then maybe the love from that tree was meant for them. I went on with life's song in my heart, writing and thinking and envisioning my sweet little family. I decided I wanted a boy and a girl; that would be all the children that I would bear. I wanted to continue to work at the pharmacy; I wanted to stay independent. I didn't want to find a husband; I wanted a husband to find me. I remember my mother telling me, "Let a man pick you, Victoria. That way you will be his choice, but if you pick a husband, he will be your choice, and if things go wrong, you will have to fight a lot harder to keep him."

I remember sitting on our porch one evening when that conversation arose. I had graduated, and Mother and I were sitting one evening having tea. "Victoria," she said, "when are you going to give a young man a chance to get to know you? All you do is work and sit under that old tree. I know that hurt was what you felt when you and James broke up, but you must move past that. It has been over three years, and you haven't dated anyone since. Life is too short to ponder on what could have been."

Sharon, a friend from work, tried to hook me up with some male friends of hers, but I wasn't interested. I just wanted to enjoy my days with my dreams and visions, and one day my husband would come. I didn't feel I had to look for a man; I felt that when the time was right, God would lead him to me. When the time was right, he and I would both know, so for now I would just spend my time working and under my willow tree. I put in extra hours at the pharmacy, so I really didn't have much time for anything else.

"Victoria," she would say, "you are wasting time. You are letting all the good ones go by. The only ones that will be left are old married men, men who were losers from the start. You really need to date, or just get you some sex so it will open up your desires for men. You don't know what you are missing. Being a virgin at your age is unheard of nowadays. I don't care if your mother is a Sunday school teacher. God understands that our flesh is weak. Just get you some, and then ask for forgiveness. God will understand."

I just laughed at the thought of getting "some." I wanted to be pleasing in God's sight. Even though I was a bit old-fashioned, my mother raised me well. When James would touch me, I felt the desires that she was referring to well up inside of me, but in the back of my mind, I knew that my parents and God would want me to wait. I often thought of James making love to me, but they would be just passing thoughts. I didn't know what all making love consisted of; I just knew what I felt when he touched me. I wonder, in spite of my beliefs and the things I was taught by my parents, what would have happened if James was the type of man who wanted to go all the way? Would I have given in to his desires and forgotten about those wholesome beliefs? I wanted to be married when I so-called got "some." Don't get me wrong. Sharon was persistent; she would bring some of the finest men into the store and practically throw them at my feet. But I, being the woman that I am, just kicked them to the side and kept looking at my future.

Memorial Day came, and I knew the cemetery would be full of families that wanted to spend time with their loved ones with minimum interruption. Since I missed putting flowers down at the tree for Mrs. Andrews, I thought it would be a good time to visit with her at my tree. I knew by now she had told Mr. Andrews all about me, so I thought the day after Memorial Day would be a good day to make good on my promise. I decided to go get some flowers. I would get a bigger arrangement than before—one with bright beautiful colors and a little light for nighttime—

and place it carefully underneath the tree. Not the red and white flowers, because I felt they were a figment of a bond with James, and I knew I would probably never see him again.

I left work and headed toward the willow tree. It was a pretty day, and I wanted to get back to my apartment before it got dark. There weren't many people at the park, and I was glad for that. I went to my willow tree with the flowers in my hand. To my surprise, there were fresh flowers. I rearranged the flowers so I could make room for my arrangement. I sat there and just looked at the writing on the tree. "Andrews's tree of love." I'm sure there was love here at the time of her stories, but all I could think about now was that I really did miss her dearly and I was sure James did too.

Sitting there with my back against the tree, I heard the familiar voice.

"She really liked the white and red flowers that you brought her; those were always her favorite," the voice said. It was James. "She also likes bright-colored flowers; she always said bright flowers made her happy."

Instantly my heart started rushing as I turned to face him. Even though I thought I was over him, that instant I wanted that man so bad. My impulse told me to just get up and walk away, just keep walking and never look back. How dare he, I thought. It's been over a year, and I have heard nothing from him. Then this day he was here wanting to start a conversation as if nothing ever happened. I didn't want to have a man that wasn't sure of what he wanted, one that just agreed with whatever at whatever time and then came back when he felt like it. All kinds of emotions ran through my body, and my mind kept saying, "Run, Victoria, run."

It was his searching that made me forget that he had left me alone for all those months. The worrying I had done seemed minor now that I was facing him. I wanted him.

"I'm glad she likes them, James," I said, feeling like my voice was shaking. He was more handsome than I remembered. He was standing there searching my face for words, and I felt he was trying to read me. His muscular build shone through the tight blue shirt he was wearing. He had trimmed the goatee to where it was only a thin line surrounding his lips and chin. I felt those old desires fizzing up inside of my body, and I wanted him to stop looking and start touching.

"How have you been, James?" I asked, trying to get a conversation going.

"Pretty lonely. I miss her so much, Vicky," he said, looking at the base of the willow tree. "I'm not talking about Grandma. Don't get me wrong," he said, trying to clarify, "I miss her too."

Feeling a little nervous and trying to turn the attention back on Mrs. Andrews, I said, "I know you do, James. I have been wondering if you were okay." I was trying not to let it show that I wasn't just wondering; I was going out of my mind missing him. "I saw the house, is it for sale?" I asked.

"Yes," James said. "I couldn't stay there without her. I've thought of you often too, Vicky. I had to face my fears and find closure that is why I went back to grandma's house the first month was a nightmare, but I kept her door closed and made myself face the reality that she was gone.

But the way I acted when she left me, I thought you wouldn't want to be bothered with me. I was confused Vicky I needed your father and I thought that is what you wanted me to do. I do look up to your father, and I feel that I was trying to fill the void I had for Grandma. It was something that I never want to have to go through again, and I'm still hurt. But hurting you doesn't make things any easier." he said. I didn't care about life because it was hard for me to wrap my head around being in this world completely alone. Through all my hurt and confusion, I realized that I had you and honestly your mom and dad to. I knew I had to make the choice to go on living or just give up. It was easier to give up but then my grandma's words would play in my mind. "Live life James", I heard her say. Don't let what your parents did to you affect the love that others have for you. I wanted to come by your apartment, but I didn't know if you had start dating so I just came to the tree hoping again that it wasn't too late and here we are again."

That old tree seemed to bring back the significance it had in the past. James and I talked until dark sitting under the tree, and I knew she was pleased that we were together again, if only for an hour or two.

I was glad that James had come there that day because it started something beautiful. We would meet at the willow tree, and he would sit there reminiscing about the last words that we both heard Mrs. Andrews say at the tree, the story she told me about Mr. Andrews planting the tree. James would make jokes, saying we were reliving their lives, with the only difference being that the tree was already there. When he spoke of little things like that, he would pause long enough to look into my eyes and then he would kiss me in a way that I would lose myself, forget the world existed. Each time he kissed me, the feelings would get stronger and stronger. It wasn't the normal peck of a kiss that we shared in the past; it was a long passionate kiss that screamed, "I want to be inside of you, Vicky. I want to make love to you." He would sit there holding my hand, and at the end of the night, instead of leaving me at the tree, he would walk me to my car, sometimes even following me home, staying overnight and sometimes just for hours on end.

He was never forward about making love, but I knew he wanted to and so did I, although I was glad that he wasn't forward with the thoughts. I kind of wished he would have taken it to the next level. I wanted James to make love to me. I didn't care about my beliefs; I just wanted him. I wanted to feel what the other girls were talking about. I wanted to tell Sharon that it finally happened, but he was patient and so was I. When he spent the night, he would just hold me. He would sometimes spend what seemed like hours kissing me, and I didn't want it to end. My body felt excitement and there were times I felt I had to pee, but when I went to the bathroom, there was no evidence of what was happening.

When I went to Mother's house, James was with me. They seemed glad that we were together once again. James spent time with Daddy, but his focus was now totally on me. Before too long, James was back into my family like the son they never had, but it was different this time; he was now also the man I desired. He would do little things letting me know that he was once again comfortable with my family, little things like go to the frig like he lived there if he was hungry, and he would ask Mother, "What's for dinner?" All the puzzle pieces were slowly forming together, and we were falling in love. The next few months were filled with me falling in love with James and us spending every waking moment together. In our talks about the future and plans of the children we wanted, we were of the same accord, and it was better than I could have imagined.

James sold Mrs. Andrews's house, and even though it was a sad time, it was also good because that would allow him to move forward. He still worked at the plant with Daddy, and when we went to visit, they would sneak off to the shed, but that was okay. My words came rushing back to me, the words that I had once said to God: "I will take him just the way he was," and I was prepared to do just that—or was I?

On Thanksgiving 1986, James officially reentered my family. It was tradition for Daddy to carve the turkey, but this Thanksgiving was different. After Mother led us in our thanksgiving prayer, Daddy looked at James and said, "Would you do us the honors and carve the turkey this time?" James was both surprised and honored. He told my dad after dinner that was the first time, he had ever felt truly thankful.

Daddy treated him like the son that he never had. I could tell that Momma was pleased too. James enjoyed the comfort of my family. I was beginning to feel that he was finally moving past the death of Mrs. Andrews. He and Daddy basically picked up where they left off. He would go and help

Daddy cut grass and plant the garden. He and my daddy would sit on the porch for hours on end just talking. I was a little jealous at first, but I knew he needed that male figure that he had been lacking in his life, so I let them have their time. I must say, we were spending more time at my parents' home, and the closeness that was showing brought joy to my parents. It was my decision to spend time at my parents' house; James never suggested it. I knew that once we were back at my apartment—or his for that matter—he would be all mine. I would much rather share him with my parents than another woman.

After I moved out of my parents' house and lost James for a second time, I was so consumed with myself that I barely visited my parents. I called, but we all knew it wasn't the same until James came around. Now we were closer than we had ever been before, and things were right where they should be. It did my heart good to feel that James was finally able to deal with losing Mrs. Andrews. Daddy got James a promotion at work; he was now a lead person, not a foreman like my father, but he was slowly moving up in the company. It seemed that the chips were falling into place. It wasn't long before they were riding to work together and doing things that you would see fathers and sons doing together.

At Christmastime, James and Daddy fixed the lights outside; Momma and I decorated the tree. It was a great time. Daddy let James put the angel on the tree. It was like he belonged in our family, and our future was looking brighter and brighter.

James and I had our own little Christmas tree at the apartment. We went together and bought the decorations, and this was the first time in what seemed like forever that we spent time apart. It was like we were in competition on who could buy the most presents for the other. I would wait until James left the house to wrap his presents, and he would come over with mine already wrapped. We decided after we bought all we could think of, we would go out together to get my parents' gifts. Since we were inseparable then, why not buy their gifts together?

On Christmas Eve, we went to my parents' house around noon. Momma had the Christmas music playing, and Daddy brought out his special eggnog. That was the only time Mom would allow alcohol in the house. Daddy called it his Christmas cheer. While Mother and I prepared Christmas dinner, James and Daddy were enjoying some Christmas cheer. Before you could say mistletoe, James was showing evidence of being drunk. He was kissing me more and touching me more. Even though I knew it was the eggnog and my parents did too, that made me a little uncomfortable, especially around Mother.

It took James a minute to catch on that I was becoming annoyed; but when he brought out the mistletoe and just about tumbled over instead of receiving the kiss he was after, he knew it was time to sit down and sober up. Mom, on the other hand, didn't blame James, but she scolded Daddy. James had never been drunk—at least that I knew of—and evidently, he couldn't hold his liquor. The boys finally got the picture and settled in to watch some of the old Christmas programs. They became really quiet when the Christmas Carol came on. It was one of Daddy's favorites, but James again acted like he was seeing it for the first time.

We left around midnight, promising to return around noon the next day. They both stood at the door waving as we pulled off, me driving of course.

James and I didn't speak in the car. I was a little disappointed with him—not mad because it wasn't that serious, but he knew how I was feeling because when we got in the apartment, he said, "This will never happen again. Can we put this behind us and have a great Christmas?" How could I resist the man I loved? I gave him the kiss that he missed out on at my parents', and we went to bed, with him holding me and my feeling content that the new year would be the best year of my life.

The next morning, I woke to James shaking a present at my head. "Hmmm, wonder what this is?" he said teasingly. "If you want to find out, you have to get up." I smelled tea brewing, so he must have been up for a while.

"Tea," he said.

"Yes," I nodded, "I am up, I am up, getting out of bed, heading to the bathroom to wash my face. Merry Christmas, honey," I shouted through the apartment.

"Merry Christmas," he shouted back, "and a happy new year," he added.

Of course, I responded. Tea was waiting on the table beside the tree when I got to the living room. "Here," he said, "open this first." He handed me a box about the size of a shoe box.

"What is it?" I asked.

"Open it," he said. Inside it was the most beautiful sculpture I had ever laid eyes on. It was a willow tree with two figurines, and they looked like me and James. It could have been the tree or the figurines that brought on the waterworks but what really made my heartbeat at a fast pace was what the male figurine was wearing around his neck. It was the key that I had given James years ago at our first Christmas together when we were teenagers. The key to my heart, I didn't know that he had kept it all these years.

Tears came to my eyes as I sat there staring at the sculpture. Focusing on the little heart reminiscing about that first Christmas we shared together. "It's beautiful," was the only thing I could say. That was the best gift I could have gotten from him, other than a ring, but we weren't ready for that—or were we?

"Here," I said, "open this one." When he opened the box, it was a football jersey. I knew James was born in Dallas, Texas, and he secretly loved the Cowboys. My daddy told me that James never mentioned it.

"How did you know?" he said.

"Hmm," I said, "let's just say Santa told me."

He walked over to me, looked me in my eyes, and for the first time since we started dating for, you could say, the third time, he said the words that I longed to hear.

"Vicky," he said, "I love you. I truly love you."

I at first, of course, was speechless. I had thought our actions were louder than any words we could ever say, but when he finally said them to me, it was like nothing I had ever heard before. Tears formed in my eyes again, and I whispered the words back to him: "I love you too, James."

The presents didn't mean much after he spoke those words. He took me into my bedroom, gently laid me down on the bed, and started kissing me in a way that we melted into one. He took his hand and gently grabbed mine and placed it over his manhood. For the first time, I felt him.

"I want to make love to you right now, Vicky," he said.

"No," I said before I could stop myself. "Not on Jesus's birthday. We aren't married, and that would be disrespect." I wanted him to, I really did, but this was the last day I wanted to sin. I just felt that something would go wrong if we did it on this day.

All he said was, "I understand." He continued to kiss me, and I continued to respond, but penetration was not going to happen, not on Jesus's birthday; we had come too far for something to go wrong now.

It was the phone that broke our train of thought. I leaped across the bed and grabbed it from the nightstand. Feeling a little weak, I almost dropped it.

"He-hello," I said.

"Merry Christmas, darling." It was Mother.

"Merry Christmas to you too, Mother."

"What are y'all doing?" she asked.

Not wanting to lie but too ashamed to tell the truth, I said, "Opening up presents."

James lay back on the bed and started rubbing my legs while I was on the phone. I was already about to explode, and the last person I wanted to be talking to was my mother, but it was what it was, and it was Christmas.

I ended the call as quickly as I could, not to finish what we started but to get a cold shower so I could concentrate on my presents, which were waiting for me under the tree. James sat on the edge of the bed when I came out. He never saw me without clothes on, and he never tried to. "Come on," I said, tightening up my robe. "Let's finish opening up our presents, and remember, no touching. We have to get through this so we can go to my parents'." We spent the next two hours going through the presents that were so carefully wrapped. I got everything I could have imagined except a ring, and he did too.

We arrived at my parents' around noon. With their gifts in hand, we entered their house.

"Merry Christmas," James shouted as we opened the door.

"Merry Christmas," they replied back. "We are in the kitchen." I could smell Mother's rolls baking as soon as I got to the doorway. James had put their presents under the tree, and we joined them in the kitchen.

"So, what all did you get?" Mother asked when she looked up from slicing the cucumbers and tomatoes.

"Too much to tell, I got clothes, perfume, several journals, and Mother—to save the best for last—James got me this sculpture of a willow tree. I can't wait for you to see it. The figurines look like me and him. Beautiful," I said, picking up one of her freshly cut cucumbers. "I am starving," I said, picking up another one. "What did you get?" I said, already knowing that every year Daddy got her cooking dishes.

"Well," she said, "I got a beautiful dress this year for church. With the shoes to match she said excitement filling the air. Daddy bought me a new Bible and a mother's ring." She flashed the ring, and it had three stones.

"Why three stones?" I asked, filled with curiosity. "It's just Daddy and me."

"It was just Daddy and you," she said, piquing my curiosity even more. "Now there's James."

"Ahhhh," I said, "what a sweet gesture." I looked over at James to see his expression, and for the first time since Mrs. Andrews's death, it looked like he was trying to tear up. I turned to him long enough to kiss him on his nose.

"Hey," Daddy shouted as he left the kitchen, "I want to open my presents."

"He's like a big kid when it comes to opening gifts. Let's go so we don't keep him waiting—and so he doesn't open up mine," Momma said, laughing.

Mother wiped her hands on her apron, grabbed hold of me and James, and said, "We are off to see the wizard." We joined my father in the living room; he was already under the tree shaking presents.

"To Victoria," he said with a ho-ho–ho, handing me my present. Then he looked further and said to James, "Ho-ho–ho," and handed him his present. "Go on; open them."

James tore into his present first. They had bought him Dallas Cowboy gear. He had the jersey, and now he had the hat, a cup, and a Super Bowl ring to match. Needless to say, he was ecstatic.

My present was a new dinnerware and cookware set. I had to laugh. This used to be the kind of presents that Mother got; now they were passed down to me. Rightfully so, though, because, I still had the same hand-me-downs that she gave me when I left. My present was the best ever.

We got Mother manger figurines and a Last Supper plaque. We got Daddy working boots because his had just about had it, and we threw in an electric saw so he wouldn't have to work so hard cutting his wood.

Everyone loved their presents. Daddy was still fiddling around under the tree when he pulled out a tiny box. "Whose is this?" he asked, looking surprised. "It says to Vicky, but it doesn't say from whom. Well, go on, open it."

Tears as well as nervousness came over me so hard that I felt light-headed. "James?" was all I could say.

He replied back with a little sheepish grin. "It's not exactly what you think."

"Go on," Daddy said, "open it."

I opened the box, and he was right: it wasn't exactly what I thought, but it was the most beautiful key I had ever seen except for Mother's. It was just like the key the one that I had given him long ago.

James gave me a squeeze of my hand, and that gave proof that this relationship was real, that we were in it for the long haul.

After dinner, we cleaned up our mess, and James and I headed back to my apartment. Once inside, I went right to my sculpture. It was too cold to go to our willow tree, so this was the next best thing. I set it on the mantel in my living room.

"Vicky," James said as he watched me carefully place the sculpture on the mantle, "come sit with me." I did as he asked. I knelt down in front of him as he said, "This is by far the best Christmas I have ever had in my life. It only shows me what I have missed in my past, but it is time to move on and start those new beginnings. I meant it earlier when I said that I loved you. I have for what seems like forever. It's just those words never meant that much until I got with you. I maybe should have said them sooner, but I needed to make sure what I was feeling was truly love. I love you, Vicky. I love everything about you, your laugh, your smile. I love how strong you are. I love your values. It makes me nervous to think that after all these years, I am finally experiencing what I have been missing, and it terrifies me. I don't want to ever lose you again; you have been there for me so many times, my biggest fear is letting you down. I want so badly for you to be my wife, but I can't help but remember the marriage my mom and dad had. Then I get around your mom and dad, and it's totally night and day. I don't know what I would do if I ever let you down. I don't know what I would do if I would ever lose you.

"Marriage is so serious to me that I don't want to fail at it. I want to be the best father and husband I can be, but the fear that grips me on the inside and the only past that I have ever known as a family makes me think I too will fail. It is a new year. There are new beginnings coming our way. We just have to take time to understand what all is happening and why. I know that you love me. I feel it when you touch me, but I want you to be sure that I am the man that you think I am. I want you to be sure that when you say, 'I do' that it will be forever, and it will be for always."

While James was talking, he was staring me in my eyes as if he was searching for some type of reaction. I felt as though he wanted me to confirm his fears. I never thought of things the way he just said it. Although I knew I loved him, I also knew that he was quick to slip in and out of my life, and that scared me. I too wanted to marry him more than I wanted to breathe, but he was right about one thing: we had to be sure. All I could say was, "I love you too, and we will take it one day at a time. No one knows what tomorrow will bring, but at this moment, I feel this moment will carry us for always. I will continue to love you and want you in my life. I won't make any promises because of our history, because of my fears, but I do know this: when the time comes and we do get married, if I say, 'I do,' it will be for always. I can promise you that. Regardless James regardless of what life throws at us I promise I will love and support you and our family for as long as I have breath. If it's not right, then we will wait until it is but if it's right, we will know it and we will be as one."

As soon as I said those words, he kissed me, not as passionately as earlier but enough to seal our words.

"I am going to run out and visit with Grandma for a little while he said as he got up and put on his jacket. I will be back later on. If you are asleep, I won't wake you," he said, putting on his jacket.

"I will probably be awake," I said because I knew that I wanted him to stay another night. Although he hadn't moved in, I was getting used to the nights that he was there. That was just another sign that we were headed in the right direction.

As he walked to the door, he pulled me close to him one more time, and said, "New year, new beginnings." He pecked my lips, then in the twinkle of an eye, he was gone.

His words played back in my head. The new year, new beginnings, which sounds nice, I thought as I turned on the Christmas tree and stared at the lights, wondering what the new year would bring.

"10, 9, 8, 7, 6," we heard as we sat with the bubbly in hand, watching the ball drop. In seconds, the calendar would turn over another year. James held me close and kissed me while we heard the crowd of people in New York shout, "Happy New Year."

"Happy New Year, 1987, baby," he whispered. "I hope this year will be ten times better than the last."

"Here, here," I said as I lifted my glass to hear the tink, tink of the glasses bumping together. We continued to watch the TV as people celebrated what I hoped would be the best year ever.

The winter months went just as fast as they had come. Our love was growing stronger than ever. James spent more time at my tiny apartment than he did at his. Even though my parents never asked if he stayed and I never told, I am sure they knew. I was almost twenty-five. I had made good decisions thus far; surely, I wouldn't mess things up now. The snow was melting, and the birds were now singing happy tunes. Spring was in the air, and new beginnings were slowly forming. Nineteen eighty-seven would be even better.

Chapter 16

On Valentine's Eve, the weather still had a little nip, but James suggested a picnic dinner at the willow tree for Valentine's Day. It would be cold, I thought. But when I was around James, I didn't even think about the weather.

"It would be fun," he said. "We would be the first people at the park this year."

It was a date. I was to meet him at the park at four. I left work a little early so that I could prepare for the picnic dinner for my valentine. I got to the park about ten minutes early, and as I approached the tree, sadness filled my heart. That same blanket was there. Someone had once again taken possession of my tree, now mine and James's tree. Not wanting them to ruin my day, I got my nerve up. I decided to approach them and ask them how long they thought they would be using the tree. Holding back the tears and thoughts of the blanket people ruining my day, I went around the tree. It was red and white roses surrounding the blanket that made me realize it was James. It was him all along. He was sitting on the blanket waiting for me. At first, I couldn't speak; I just stood there like some bubbly teenager. I couldn't rid my mind of the thoughts of seeing that blanket months ago and it had been him all along.

I must have been standing for a while because James said teasingly, "Are we going to stand up and have our picnic dinner, or are you going to sit down with me?"

With happiness in the air, I sat beside the man whom I so desperately loved. Even though we had said those words before, I guess since it was Valentine's Day, we each wanted the other one to be the first to say, "I love you." But we knew, and I guess that is all that mattered.

James and I sat there for the entire afternoon. I fixed his plate, and we ate. The food had turned cold, but our hearts were warm and that was all that mattered. We walked the park looking for buds that were slowly forming on the flowers and the trees. Before dark, he suggested that we go get some flowers to bring back to the tree for Mr. and Mrs. Andrews. I knew it would be sad for James, and I didn't want our evening spoiled. But this was something that I wouldn't take away from him. So that is what we did.

I was glad that we went to get flowers. The winter months had killed the flowers that I had placed there months before. I didn't want the tree to be a significance of death, but of life. Looking at her flowers, they were a sad sight to see. I know that made James sad, so after we returned to the tree with the fresh flowers, I immediately started putting the new flowers in the dead flowers' place.

James stood there watching me, and once I was done, he sat down beside me. He put his hands on my face and began searching. He wanted me to say something, or he had something that he wanted to say but he never did. He just looked at me with this look of sincerity. His forehead gathered in the middle, and then he just took my hand with a gentle squeeze. I could tell by his sweaty palms that he was nervous about something he wanted to say. Instead of talking, he just let go of my hands and continued to remove the dead flowers off to the side.

What he did next changed our lives forever. He sat down under the tree where the ashes of his grandparents were, and he started to speak. Even though he was looking out into the park, it wasn't me to whom he was speaking, but to his grandma.

"Grandma, I miss you with everything in me. I miss our talks, our walks in the park. I miss you being here to share my life with me." Tears formed in his eyes while he was talking, as if she was there and he could see her. "I hope that you are where you want to be, that you are seeing Grandpa and you are happy. I hope that all the sickness has left you and you are enjoying your life there. I love you, Grandma, and I never thought I could fill the void that was left the day God took you home. Spring is coming, and we would be making plans to go to the park, and I miss that. Victoria is here too, and she has filled the void, Grandma. I want you to know that I love her."

Those words instantly brought tears to my eyes.

"I was sitting in the living room that night when hints of you leaving filled my breathing space. I was hoping that God would change his mind. Yet I knew your desire was to be with Grandpa. It wasn't a prayer that you said—or was it? You let God know that you were ready. It was only my well-being that was on your mind. The thought of you leaving me gripped your soul. I knew you wanted to be close to Grandpa, but I also knew you had your fears of leaving me after you were gone. The only thing you spoke about was having someone love me, to show me love, and it was all for my happiness. The hurt of losing you, Grandma, was a hurt I will never be able to explain.

"In the hospital, I couldn't tell you the things I had to say that I wanted you to hear from me. You have been my light at the end of this dreadful tunnel called life. I knew you needed me, and I needed you. I would take ten years off my life to have you say five words to me, but that isn't going to happen. Vicky has been showing me a different kind of love, a love that I had never known. How can I keep that? I remember you telling me, 'When you truly find love, you will know it.' Well, Grandma, with Vicky, I know it. And I want to marry her."

He reached in his pocket and pulled out the ring. It wasn't like the key from Christmas; it was actually an engagement ring "This is what I bought her, and I want to ask her in front of you because I remember your desires for me, and she has fulfilled them."

He then turned to me. "Victoria," he said, "I......I love you. I need to know that you will always love me. Can you promise me that?"

I couldn't speak, but I nodded my head.

"I will always love you, and I will take care of you the best I can for the rest of your life. I want to love, honor, and cherish you. I couldn't imagine life without you. I couldn't imagine you ever being hurt or sad. I want to make you happy. I want to be the one you depend on. I don't know a lot about being a part of a family, but I want to be a part of yours. I want to have a family with you. If there ever came a time that I let you down, I promise I am not perfect, but I will make it up to you one way or another.

"I've lost you twice; I don't want to lose you a third time. I have made foolish decisions, but at the end of the day, it's you that I love. It's you that I want to spend the rest of my life with. I can't imagine not having you as part of my team. I can't imagine making my dreams come true with anyone else but you. It's like you have been in my life through everything, and I would be counted a fool if I lost you because of something that could be helped. I already told your momma and daddy of my plan and they approved if you did." He then turned to me put his hands in mind, with tears in his eyes, he asked the question that I had waited on all my adult life.

"Will you take this ring and be my wife? Until death do, we part? Never thinking of divorce, never doubting my love for you?"

I took the ring from his hand, sweaty palms and all, and said, "This time, I promise, James. I promise. I will always love you. I will never doubt you or your love. I will never divorce you. I will always put you and our family first."

James then said, "I will be the best provider that has ever had a family. I will do everything I can to make you as happy as you have made me."

He then got up and pulled me close. I had never felt more loved than right at that moment. I just knew it was right.

I put this day down in my book because it had taken some time of going to the park, talking about our dreams, and making plans for our future before James actually asked me to marry him. All James needed was a family of his own, love from the children that we would bear, and a deserving wife. That would be the life we would have together, a life that would be shared as one forever. How hard could that be. Knowing he loved me as much as he did to speak it in front of his grandma. As long as we had our only little family, we were both working so what's, the worse that could happen?

Chapter 17

We were married August 8, 1987. It was the most beautiful day of my life, and even though it called for rain, there wasn't a cloud in the sky. The ceremony was at the willow tree. Even though there were families there at the park, they looked on from a distance, giving us our space for that special time. The tree still had its blooms. It was as if the blooms had been preserved for that special day. As it gave its warm summer breeze, our unity took place.

Daddy gave me to James that day, and he was also the best man. My momma was the matron of honor, and a few friends from work were my flower girls. It wasn't anything big, but it was big to me. I had wished that James's family could have come, but he didn't mention them and neither did I. I think the only family he thought he had was Mrs. Andrews. I had my wedding flowers be a spread of white and red roses that surrounded the tree. We had a picture of Mrs. Andrews there, and, of course, the urns was still secretly placed under the root of the tree. I felt her presence as if she was in human form and actually at the tree.

James and I honeymooned at the beach, and it was the best five nights I could ever imagine. The first night was the one I feared the most. I knew that would be the night I was supposed to give myself to James. We were to consecrate our marriage and bond for the rest of our lives. I was ready, but nervous at the same time.

James was the perfect gentleman. He was my first, and as far as I knew, I was his. If we made a mistake, we didn't know we did. It felt natural, and it was beautiful. He took his time and caressed and kissed me. At that moment, when he first consecrated our marriage, it was like our bodies molded into one. We were finally connected in more ways than one. It was a connection that I would never let go of and a bond that would never be broken. Once we finished which it lasted about 5 minutes, I remember thinking what all the fuss was about. I kept thinking maybe we had done something wrong. If we had of thought about protection, I think we could have done this way before now. Some of our kisses lasted longer than our love making session. I spoke my vows to God again that night that by him blessing me with James, I would never remarry nor part from him until death. I would carry his word in our marriage, and that is to love, honor, and cherish him for the rest of my life.

Work was good and being married to James gave me something to look forward to besides the willow tree.

James and I decided to look for a house. On my days off, Momma would come by, and we would go look for a house for James and me. Once we found a place, I would wait to look at it with James and seek his approval.

After about three weeks of this and a year's worth of excitement mixed with stress, I saw the perfect place for James and me. I knew it was perfect when I first saw it from the road. It had the picket fence that I always wanted. It wasn't the size of the house or the yard that made me want this house so desperately, but it was what was in that yard; it had a huge flower bed, which would allow me to grow the roses that were a symbol of Mrs. Andrews, and out from the flower bed stood my very own willow tree. It wasn't as mature as the tree in the park; it was still young. I knew that it too had a story behind its growth, and to have my family growing up with what started the love of my family would make this house all the more special. There was even enough room in the front to start our own willow tree, and that would be what we would have to start our own history. It had a porch that encircled the front of the house, and I could picture James and I sitting there watching our children playing in the yard. When I got out of the car and stood under the willow tree, I could feel the same breeze that the one in the park offered. The magic was definitely there.

Behind the house was yet another willow tree. This one was just a little bigger than the one in the front yard. Although it was a willow tree, its blooms were white in color. There was a garden near it that seemed like the perfect place for yet another flower bed. It wasn't just for James and me; it was big enough for us to start our family. It was thirty minutes from Momma and Daddy, but it could be ours and that was excitement within itself. I decided to call the realtor so I could find out about the price and all the details about the house. After explaining the house in detail, she told me that I could either set an appointment to look at it or I could go by and look at the house on my own. I couldn't wait to tell James about my discovery.

When James first saw the house, before he even looked in the windows, he told me that he didn't think that we could afford it. He would have to work a lot of overtime to be able to afford a place like this, but he would try. We discussed the price and I thought about asking Momma and Daddy for their help, but I didn't want James to think I doubted him. I tried to reassure him that with the both of us working, we could afford this house, but he didn't seem as interested in the house as I was. I wanted that house and I wanted to start our lives, but I had to wait for James to make a way, and that he did.

James and Daddy drove to work separately on some days. I knew that was because James was working late to make a way to buy our home. He at times looked tired and drained. I knew he was doing everything he could to keep his promise to me fulfilled. After work, tired or not, I made a way to have a hot dinner ready for him and conversation about his long day at work. Even though it was a bit tiring at times for me, I wanted to keep him as happy as he had made me.

I would drive to the house and look in the windows before or after work, picturing how our lives would be inside that house. But at that time, it was just a dream. I wanted to place a deposit on the house to give James time to come up with the money, but I knew our time was running out. Somebody, somewhere, would soon buy this house, and my dream would have to come to an end.

Sometimes I would sneak and sit on the porch and picture our kids playing in the yard by the willow tree, with us on the porch, but still it was just a dream. James was thinking a lot as the weeks passed by. I could tell because his forehead crinkled when he was in deep thought. I didn't bother him because he was working late and he was tired, even though I desired to relive the night of our consecration. I didn't dare tease him because he needed his strength.

Time was of the essence for us to put a deposit on that house. I knew that somebody somewhere would feel the way I felt about the house and buy it out from under us. I liked the little gifts, the flowers or the cards, that James would surprise me with, but in reality, they meant nothing—material things didn't mean much these days. I just wanted our house; that was what I desired.

It seemed like work was becoming more demanding. Sharon had taken a management position at a farmers market. They had added a store onto the pharmacy; I finally met Ms. Fable. She didn't come around much and as luck would have it the times, she did come in the pharmacy I was off for that day Sharon described her to me, so I knew right away when she entered the store that she was the owner. Sharon was off. It was a surprise visit, and the last thing I needed that day was to meet the owner.

She took an interest in me right way. She was kind enough, yet a bit demanding. I remember her saying to me when we met, "So, you are Victoria Andrews. "I have heard so much about you. She walked through the pharmacy a few times looking at different things writing down her notes every now and then she would ask a question about this or that, but she didn't tarry long, and I was glad about that.; I never understood why she said my whole name; it was as if she knew me or knew my family. Nonetheless, work hours seemed longer, and my energy seemed to fade away.

With my vacation week starting in two days and my energy level now at an all-time low, it was hard trying to focus and get through those last days. I started once to call in and rest for those two days before my vacation so I could focus on finding a house, but I knew James was working hard to get our new home, so I decided to tough it out. What's two days? I thought. I can do it. The last day before my vacation, I had the house that I desired on my mind that whole day. I would go take another look at it, feeling as though one day it would be mine.

The first day of my vacation, it was hard waking up and getting James off to work. My body was screaming for another hour or two of sleep. After he was well on his way, I fought the temptation to return to bed and decided to go take another look at the house. Excitement filled my heart as I turned onto the street and looked at the other houses as I passed by them. This, I thought, would be a great neighborhood for my children to grow up in. It seemed peaceful and clean. The houses were just close enough to get to know the neighbors, yet far enough apart so that each house had its privacy.

My excitement quickly turned to horror as I pulled up into the driveway of the house I so deeply desired. The sign that once sat so neatly in the yard reading for sale had been replaced by another sign that now read SOLD. My heart fell to the pit of my stomach, and the waterworks started. My dream of sharing this house with my family had now ended. Feeling nauseated, I just sat there, hating the fact that this house was now somebody's dream come true—but not mine.

I sat in my car for what seemed like hours. I knew I had to get home, but my heart just didn't want to leave. I just knew that the next time I decided to ride by this house, the family that bought it would probably be moved in. My heart was torn apart. As badly as I wanted to, I didn't dare go sit on the porch like I previously did because that would be trespassing. I felt sick just looking at the sign.

It tore my nerves up so badly that as soon as I got back home, I barely made it to the bathroom before my breakfast came up all over the floor. I stayed in bed for the rest of the afternoon until it was time to prepare dinner for my husband. I didn't tell him about the house, nor did I tell him how upset I was that it was sold because that was the last thing that he needed right now after working all the overtime that he had to get the house for us. The good thing about all this was James didn't seem as interested as I had been about the house, so it wouldn't be as hard for him to focus on getting another house. I would just have to find another home for us. I was sure there was one out there that we could both be pleased with.

James held me extra close that night, but it still didn't stop my tears from secretly flowing.

It took everything in me to see him off to work the next morning. My mind was on the house and my stomach was on the bathroom. My nerves were torn up so badly that I couldn't even eat because if I did, I just knew that I would make myself sick. I felt drained, and all I wanted to do was sleep.

Momma called right after James had left. I decided to give my body a few more moments of rest before I ventured on my house hunting, and she told me that she would be over that afternoon with some realtor books. I was glad she was coming over that afternoon versus right away. I really didn't feel like company. As a matter of fact, I didn't feel like getting out of bed. Even though mentally and physically I didn't want to do anything but sleep, I had to make a way to go look for a house. It was hard because my energy level was down, and my nerves were so bad; it took everything in me just to get out of bed. Marriage is a bit demanding but being in love is worth every moment of its demands. I decided to stay in bed and watch a movie or two to get my mind off of things before Momma arrived.

Noon came sooner than I expected, but I got up and took my shower, got dressed, and grabbed a newspaper. I guessed I could look in the paper, and when Momma came, at least I could be presentable enough to look through her book before James got off work. After he was home, we could look for a house together.

Momma and I were sitting in the kitchen about the time for James to come home.

"Honey," she said, "are you all, right? You don't look so good."

I couldn't help but spill it all out to her about losing the house and how I had wanted it so badly and James didn't know it was sold and how my nerves were gone because of it.

All Momma said was, "If it's the Lord's will, he will make a way, Victoria. God will make a way. Now go get freshened up. James will be home any minute, and I don't want James to think I beat his wife all day."

When I finished refreshing, I came back to the kitchen just in time for James and my daddy to pull into the parking lot. We ate dinner, and then we all sat there after dinner talking about finding a house.

Daddy, as if curious, said, "I thought you already picked out the house that you wanted."

James said, "What's wrong with you? Don't you like the house we picked out, Vicky?"

Through tears I told James and Daddy the story. It just didn't feel right keeping it from them.

"There, there," Daddy said, "where there is a will, there is a way."

I don't think Daddy grasped the whole idea that the house I wanted was now sold.

"We will find a place," I said. "That was my dream home and that was the home that I wanted, but James is my husband, and any old house would be a home to us because our love is just that strong."

When I finished that pronouncement, James kissed me. Momma and Daddy left. James and I watched a little television, each in our own thoughts, and then we went to bed.

I still couldn't sleep even though James was holding me tight. I felt his manhood pressing against my body, so I knew that he wanted me to submit myself to him, and I did. James made love to me just like it was our first time. He needed to be inside of me, and I needed the same. My body was with him, but my mind was stuck on the fact that we had lost our dream home. Even though I wanted him to be satisfied and I did submit myself like a wife should I was glad when he finally turned over and fell asleep.

I guess I overslept the next morning because I didn't see James off to work. I felt bad because it was my second day of vacation and I'd had time to rest so that I could see him off to work that morning. I guess I must have tossed and turned that night, so I guessed he didn't want to wake me. I was too tired to care; I felt drained, I must say, from all the thinking I was doing throughout the night. I wanted to please my husband as much as he wanted to please me, but I was so tired. It wasn't until late morning that I realized that James had left me a card on his pillow; the card read:

It's your vacation, and after today, I start mine too because together we are one and without you, I would be nothing. So, your day is mine and mine is yours, and forever we will be one. With all my love.

James

P.S. When I get off work today, the evening is yours. Plan carefully and make a wish.

With that, I felt I should at least get out of bed. Momma came by and we went shopping. We then had lunch, and she insisted on buying me an outfit for my evening with James. I guess that was her way of cheering me up. We rode around for a bit, and then when we got home, I took a nap just so I could be fresh when my husband got home.

James came in the room and woke me up. I was hoping that I would be ready to go when he got home. He was off for a few days, and the last thing I wanted was to spend that time sleeping. We had a house to find.

I had at least gotten my shower before I went to sleep, and it didn't take much for me to get ready while James took his. James showed me his romantic side. I didn't know he had preplanned us a motel, and we spent the night after dinner, of course, making love. It was well needed, and it was absolutely beautiful. We didn't talk at all. He just touched and rubbed and made love to me all night long. That was the best vacation night I ever had. For that one night since I found out about the house being sold, I didn't think of the house at all.

I was surprised the next morning when I woke up that James was already dressed. I insisted that we keep the room for another night and just stay in bed, but that was not in James's plans. He was all excited about us finding a home, and our sheet-shaking night had just brought those feelings back. We needed to have a home of our own, and I understood that. I got out of bed and got dressed, and we went house hunting. We looked at several houses, and none of them was quite what we were looking for. After becoming discouraged, James decided to take me back to Momma and Daddy's house.

They were waiting on the porch when we pulled up. James told Daddy how we had looked for houses, and Daddy told him he had seen a house and wanted to show it to us all. Daddy told us it had belonged to an old friend of his. We hadn't been riding long when Daddy pulled up in front of a house that looked like the house that I had so desperately wanted. It was the same house! This was the same house with the sold sign in the yard. I heard James tell him no, that we had looked at this house, but it had been sold.

Daddy, being persistent as he always was, totally ignored James's wishes and pulled into the driveway. He then looked over at Momma. She shook her head as if to say, "You are making a mistake; let's leave." But Daddy told James that he just wanted us to look at it. It still had that same familiar sign in the yard, Sold. James told Daddy that the house was sold, but that didn't seem to matter to Daddy. He got out of the car and started looking through the windows. I heard James almost yell at my daddy, telling him it was trespassing, and Daddy told him that he knew the police and it would be all right.

Momma never got out the car until Daddy told her to come get a closer look. I myself had seen it dozens of times, and I didn't need the arrow pushed deeper in my heart, so not wanting to leave my comfortable seat in the back of Daddy's truck, I just sat there until James came to the window and said, "Can we just humor your father for just a moment? We can leave after he looks at it."

Not wanting to, I did as my husband asked and went to look at the house that was now sold, feeling it was a waste of our time, but Daddy was a persistent man, and I knew he wouldn't leave until he was pacified. I managed to go to the window and pretend that I was as excited as he was, but at the same time I felt a bit nauseated at the thought of looking in someone else's window.

Daddy tried to open the door, and James told Daddy that he couldn't open the door without a key. Then James reached into his pocket and pulled out a key and unlocked the door. It was the key to the house, and James had bought it for me. I felt my stomach churning with the excitement, and I just knew I would get sick; but I guess once it sunk in that the house was ours, then nothing else mattered.

Daddy and James had planned the whole thing. I looked at Momma as if she too was in on the surprise, and Daddy spoke for her. "Oh, she didn't know," he said. "I barely kept the secret myself. The last person I was going to tell was your momma. She would have told you and ruined the surprise." I felt it didn't matter who knew. All that mattered was it was now our house, a house that we could now call home and start our family.

Once inside the house, it was everything that I had wanted it to be and even more. It was four bedrooms, just enough for a small family—a boy and a girl and a room for Momma and Daddy when they came for a visit. It had a mantle in the living room above the fireplace, and I was sure that was where James would keep the urns of his grandparents. I felt that this house was made for James and me. Since this house was what I dreamed of, I felt that this house was part of God's will. This house was made for me and James for our family. Tears came easily, and this time it was tears of joy. James and I walked the house, with Momma and Daddy close behind. It was perfect. I wanted to know how James made this possible, but I would keep my questions for later because that was our business and maybe James didn't want my family to know. Right at that moment, I just wanted to soak it all in.

"When can we move in?" I asked James.

"Today," he said, grabbing my face, "right now. It's ours, angel," he said, "and we don't ever have to leave."

I imagined how I wanted the house and our children and all that our future would hold in this house. It was a good vision, a happy life. I would be the best wife and mother that James, my dad, and God wanted me to be. I didn't want to leave, but we had packing to do. We had to get the lights and water turned on so we could start our life, our family.

We all talked on the ride back to my parents'. We had a lot to talk about. We had plans to make and furniture to buy. Momma and Daddy offered us furniture and things, and I thought that would be good for a start; but once we got settled in, I would save enough money to buy what was needed to make our house a home. James had yet another surprise for me: he had started us an account at the Bunk-'N'-Sleep furniture store. I was to go down there and pick out furniture for our home.

Everything in our new lives was going so fast. It seemed like only yesterday we were just starting a new relationship, and now we were married and moving into our new home. I didn't want to move forward; I just wanted to keep reliving what we were experiencing, because at this point in time, I didn't feel that this could get any better. Little did I know that there were greater surprises in store for us. I was just hoping that time would stop so I could relive these moments. We were moving forward in high gear, and I needed to stay focused because I didn't want to miss a thing.

Back at the house, I wanted to go shopping right away to buy curtains and pictures, but energy had drained from my body, and I had to get some rest. I knew the next day would come soon enough and there was a lot to be done. The sooner James and I could move in, the sooner we could really start our lives; I had to stay focused so our future wouldn't be postponed.

I woke up to James looking down at me holding me, smiling. I knew we had a lot to do, but I didn't want to get out of bed. I let James cook breakfast, and it didn't smell good, but I didn't dare tell him. I decided to take my shower, and I thought hopefully by the time I was done, the smell would be gone. I was a little hungry, but I didn't dare eat what James had prepared. I thought maybe if I gave James enough time to eat, I could grab something on the way to the furniture store.

When I entered the kitchen, the smell had faded. Needless to say, James suggested that I eat something. I tried to choke down a piece of toast and orange juice, but that was as far as I got. I felt sick to my stomach because the excitement of looking for furniture was a bit overwhelming. I quickly did the dishes, and then James and I headed for the furniture store.

We searched and searched for what seemed like all day, but it was really only for a couple of hours. Karen was the clerk who helped make all our furniture dreams come true. By the time we left the Bunk-'N'-Sleep store, I was more than a little exhausted. James paid cash for our furniture, and I was wondering where he got the money, but that would come out on our ride home. It wasn't proper for me to discuss our business in front of Karen. Our furniture would be delivered in two days, and that would give me plenty of time to get our utilities on and pack enough stuff to start forming our home.

James wanted to shop for curtains and things, but I wanted to go home and go to sleep. All this excitement was draining me, and I needed to get a grip on things. He was my husband, and I couldn't deprive him of making decisions on the house, so we went to the country store for our curtains and things.

The ride home was full of questions for my husband. I wanted to know where this windfall of money had come from and how we would be able to pay for it. I sat in the seat beside James, my mind racing back and forth, not wanting the mood to change from the news. I didn't want to seem questioning, but I wanted to know. I knew James was excited about having certain responsibilities, but I also knew that we had to save; that was taught to me by my daddy. I was afraid that James had borrowed money from somewhere or somebody and it would take us our lifetime to pay it back. Words from my daddy came rushing to my mind: "Not having money is the first sign of troubles in a marriage. Money is not the most important thing in a marriage, but it will become the most important when you are in debt."

"Honey," I said in the most respectful voice I had, "how did we get the money to pay for all this? I mean the house and the furniture. How did you make that possible?"

"I lived with my grandmother from the time I was sixteen years old until she passed away," James said, "and before she died, she left me her house. This is money from the sale of her house. I saved the money for this very reason: to make a good start for my family. I feel that is what Grandma would have wanted. I put my bid on the house the very next day after you said you wanted it, and when it came through, it was close enough to our vacation time that I thought it would be perfect. I closed the deal on Monday. Our house is paid for, and we have furniture, and all that is left is children and our family will be complete. We do have to go to the bank and get your name on my account, but after that, we should be considered one."

With that said, tears formed in my eyes, and for the first time in our short marriage it was official. I really felt like we were married, not just shacking up.

The next day I called for the utilities and the phone to be turned on at our house. Daddy took the day off to help James move the old furniture out. We donated it to Goodwill because our furniture would be arriving the following day. Momma helped me pack up the rest of the house, and by the end of the day, the apartment was just a shell full of boxes. James and I spent the night with Momma. I planned on returning to the house as he left for work to get started on putting up the boxes and things away to have the house almost ready by the time he came home from work.

I got up the following Wednesday morning just barely in time for James to leave for work. He had only taken a few days off, and he had to return to work. He knew I was tired. I still had the rest of the week off—we had had a fun-filled weekend—but the extra days that James took off to get us ready for our move were over. I still had a few more days off and there was work to be done. Once he was gone, I felt myself getting sick. The excitement of our home was still there, but there was no reason present that I should be sick. I ran to the bathroom just in time to heave. Nothing really came up because there was nothing to come up.

I heard Momma come through the door, and she hollered out, "Victoria!"

"In here," I said. I tried to hurry before Momma saw me, but I continued to heave. Momma heard it, and once the heaving stopped, I was faced with a question that through all the excitement I hadn't realized.

"Victoria," Momma said, "are you pregnant?"

Those words ran through and paralyzed my mind. I didn't speak because I couldn't, but my mind was talking to me loud and clear. That would be the best thing in the world, and it would make James the happiest man walking if I was, but we had only had sex a few times since we were married. The most times were just the other day, the start of our vacation. I saw Momma's lips moving but I couldn't hear her words. My mind had captured my ears, and there was nothing I could do about it.

The cool rag and crackers that Momma had brought to me brought me back to the present.

"Momma, could I be pregnant?"

"Those are the symptoms that you are showing, Victoria."

"How could that be?" I said. "We only had sex a few times and it only lasted for a few minutes, each

I was a little embarrassed by what I was saying, but I needed answers. I needed to know as soon as possible.

Momma stood there looking at me with her face filled with excitement she chuckled at my words then said "It only takes one time, Victoria. How long it took doesn't matter. Have you had your period for this month?"

With all the excitement, I hadn't thought about it until now.

"No," I said, "I haven't. The reason I know is that I would have been embarrassed to sleep with James if I had one."

"Let's run out and get a test to be sure," Momma said with excitement in her voice.

I was still numb with the thought of being a momma. A baby would be right on time. Daddy and Momma would be grandparents, something they had wanted for a long time, and James would finally be a father—a good one, I knew. Nerves filled my stomach and my mind, not leaving room for the crackers I had just devoured, so they came back up and entered the toilet.

I couldn't help but think about being a momma and James being a daddy and making Momma and Daddy's dream come true of being grandparents. Excitement filled the car as we went to the pharmacy for the test. I completely forgot about going to my house to wait for the furniture and finish putting the rest of the boxes away. Having a child for James had taken over my mind.

Back at Momma's house, my nerves returned in full swing. My balance was almost unbalanced as I practically ran to the bathroom, Momma close behind. We read the instructions and then I squatted on the toilet, careful to get all the pee I could on that tiny little pregnancy tester stick. Momma was standing in the door watching that I made no mistakes. The look on her face was funny; she looked as though she was the one concentrating. I couldn't help but laugh, while praying at the same time that God would deem me worthy to give James a child.

Those three minutes seemed to take hours, and Momma hovered over the stick with me. If any other people besides Momma and me had seen the way we were hovering over that stick, we probably would have been ruled crazy. As the line on the stick formed, I felt my legs get weak. It wasn't until the middle line formed that we both simultaneously began to cry. Momma hugged me and I returned that hug, and it was a moment worth writing down.

"I'm going to be a granny!" she yelled. "And my baby girl is going to be a momma! Oh, what joy you have brought this family, Victoria!"

I gave Momma her moment before I took over with mine. It was the happiest moment I had seen for her in a while.

"I can't wait to tell your father," she said.

"How will we tell them?"

"We have to tell them soon. Oh, what joy you have brought to this family!" she repeated.

She was hugging me so tight I was thankful that I wasn't further along than what I was because I would have had the baby right then and there. Still with fear inside as well as happiness, I told her, "I'm sure James will be thrilled."

I couldn't get past the thoughts of a little one calling James Daddy and me Mommy, of cooking for my family and just enjoying life. But at that instant, the thrill went away, and fear gripped my heart. Could I be a good momma? Would I make James proud that I was the mother of his child, or would he think that I wasn't good enough? Would I be good enough? Am I capable of taking care of a baby?

We would be thirty minutes away from Momma and Daddy. If I needed my momma, she would be thirty minutes away. I don't know what had the strongest hold, the fear of parenting or the excitement, but I did know that I had to tell my husband. Then I would be able to relax a little—not a lot, but a little.

Gathering up our thoughts there was still work to do on our home. Through all of the excitement we had to get over to our new home and get things in order before James and daddy got off work. I wanted everything to be perfect with the news that I had.

I drove to our home with the thoughts of being a mother encircling my mind. Momma had big plans for her grandchild of her own. Even though I was in a thought process momma was a woman of many words during the drive to my home. The rest of the afternoon is a bit hazy. The lights, water, and phone were turned on and the furniture had arrived, but we didn't get much work done at our house. Time flew by, and we had only put away the dishes and a few boxes of whatnots and hung curtains. Momma wouldn't let me do too much because she wanted me to put the baby's health first.

I made a pitcher of iced tea just in time for James and Daddy to pull up in the driveway. I had the tea waiting for them, and the test stick was carefully placed in the middle of the glasses. Momma had promised she would let me tell the news, but only if I did it quickly; she didn't think she could hold it much longer. I had decided I would give them cold glasses of tea with the test stick in between the two glasses and watch them figure out who would reach for the tea and discover the stick first. That was a way to kind of prepare them for the news, and if they didn't get that, then I would tell them.

Momma and I were sitting on the porch as Daddy and James approached. Momma was smiling as though she was the one pregnant. Daddy approached Momma with the usual evening kiss, and James did the same to me.

"What have you girls been doing all day?" Daddy asked.

"Oh, not much," Momma said. "We did get the curtains hung, put some dishes away."

Momma was now looking at me, ready to explode.

"Yeah," I chimed in, "and I got the lights, phone, and water turned on. They brought the furniture. Honey," I added, "how was your day?"

"Not bad," he said as he looked down and grabbed his glass of tea. Looking at the test stick and raising it to eye level, he asked, "Honey, what is this?"

"Oh, I almost forgot. We put away some whatnots. I wasn't feeling well, so Momma and I bought a pregnancy test. It was positive, and—"

Cutting me off, James said, "What did you just say?"

"Oh, I put away some whatnots," I said, teasing.

"No, about the pregnancy test?"

"Oh, I bought one, and it was positive."

"Are we going to have a baby, Victoria?"

"Yeah, I do believe we are," I said, trying to sound calm.

Daddy looked at Momma. "Am I going to be a granddaddy, honey?"

Momma nodded her head.

James picked me up and whirled me around.

"Easy, easy," Daddy said. "She is in the motherly way."

"That's right," James said. "Did I hurt you, Vicky?" Tears were now forming in his eyes.

Momma and I looked at each other and laughed.

"Am I really going to be a daddy?" James said.

"I do believe you are," Momma said. "The test stick confirms it, but we will need the doctor's opinion."

"We took a test today," I said, "after I got sick trying to let it all sink in, and that was the result. I will make a doctor's appointment to confirm, but that is the way it seems."

James looked at me with those searching eyes filled with tears.

"You have made me the happiest man alive, Vicky. We are going to have a baby of our very own. This is a cause to celebrate. No fixing dinner tonight. We are eating out on me," James said.

We were looking at Momma and Daddy hugging each other with their own set of tears.

"Hey, you two," I said, "are you going? If you keep crying, you will upset the baby," I said teasingly.

I had never seen Daddy cry. He had always been so strong. These were tears of joy, though, and I guess he didn't mind shedding those tears. Making them happy and seeing their excitement was very pleasing to both James and me.

We had a lot to talk about during dinner, and you would have thought that I was Cinderella and James was the prince himself. All the plans and even thinking of names took place at the dinner table. It was a lot to absorb. You would have thought we were the first family to ever have a child. All of them made sure I ate the full meal. I had vegetables, meat, fruit, and dessert. I kept thinking that I will be humungous by the time this baby comes if I keep this up.

Back at home in our bed, James showed his fear. He had a lot to think about, and he shared his thoughts with me. In only a few months of marriage, we were going to be parents. It wouldn't just be me and him, but another life that would depend on us, someone who would depend on us for love and protection. A life that it would be up to us to love and raise. His words made me look at things in a different manner. I had gone from being single to being married and now a mother-to-be in a matter of months. Was I grown up enough to take on such responsibility? Was I so blinded by loving James and playing house that I didn't have time to think about how real all this was? There was a life, a real life, growing inside me, and it needed real love and real safety. It wasn't my momma and daddy's responsibility, but mine and James's. Were we really ready for this?

James was the one who made all these concerns real to me. He was talking to me about the responsibilities of being a husband and a father and how he too was terrified that he wasn't ready, that we had only months to get fully prepared for this life-changing event.

"Books," he said, "we need books so we can understand exactly what's happening. We can listen to your mom and dad, but we can't depend on them. We have to depend on us, Vicky. This is so real, and it's our future and we can't make any mistakes. Mistakes can have this tiny part of us taken from us forever."

He was talking about the welfare office coming and taking the baby and deeming us unfit. He watched the news a lot, but it was the truth. We wouldn't have Momma and Daddy to lean on. Since we moved, we had to be prepared for our child and take care of our child and we couldn't make any mistakes.

My first visit with Dr. Katezet was very interesting and, needless to say, a little uncomfortable. I felt a little awkward with James and the doctor looking at me. Even though James was my husband and that was my doctor, to have to lie down with my knees pointed up in the air was a little unnerving. Dr. Katezet told me to look at the ceiling and try not to think about what he was doing. Yeah, sure, I thought to myself. I was feeling a little violated, yet there was good news to this embarrassing moment. Dr. Katezet was an older doctor, with a great sense of humor. By the time my first visit was over, we were laughing and joking. I was feeling a lot more comfortable with him than when I first lay down on the table. I found out that I was already two months pregnant. He gave me something for the nausea. He let me know that everything I was experiencing was normal and there was a long road ahead.

Before we left his office, he looked at both James and me, and said, "All right, guys, this is something I always ask early on. Once it is discovered, do you want to know the gender of your child?"

James and I both looked at each other. Although I secretly wanted a girl and he secretly wanted a boy at that point, without a second thought, we decided that we would wait to find out the gender when our baby was born. As long as there were no complications and the baby was healthy, that was really all that mattered to us. Besides, it would be fun guessing and preparing for our surprise. No matter what the gender was, we would love it with everything we had, and at the end of the day, which was all that mattered to us. As if reading each other's minds, we both said we'd wait until our baby was born.

Not knowing what gender, we were having, James and I both fantasized on what the room would look like. We talked about who our baby would most favor, and we spent long evenings trying to decide on names. Our lives were good, and everything was right next to perfect. By the time our four-month visit to the doctor rolled around, James had already picked out the name James Brandon Andrews. I was still pondering between Hannah and Chloe. It was funny to watch James; he was so sure it was going to be a boy, he started addressing our child as Brandon.

Dr. Katezet checked the heartbeat and said, "Hmm ... interesting."

"Is that bad or good?" James asked, hoping that everything was okay with our child. "Is Brandon, okay?"

"Brandon?" Dr. Katezet said, laughing. "So, you think it's a boy."

"Well," James said, feeling a little embarrassed, "Well, it could be either. I just picked out that name just in case."

Dr. Katezet gave a chuckle and said, "Let's take a look at the ultrasound to see how 'Brandon' is doing." Winking at me, he said, "Hmm, just as I expected."

"Is everything okay, Dr. Katezet?" I asked James and my eyes pasted to the doctors expression.

"Oh, everything is fine," he said. "Better than expected," he said with another chuckle. "James," he said, "can you see this?" He pointed to something on the ultrasound.

"Yeah," James said. "I see it, but I don't understand it."

Dr. Katezet laughed again and said, "That is just what I thought. Victoria, do you know what this is?" he said, pointing to the exact same thing.

"Nope, can't say that I do. Is it a leg or arm?"

He gave even a bigger laugh. "Something like that," he said. "Well, are you sure you don't want to know the gender of your child?"

James spoke up and said, "No, because I already know."

"Do you now?" Dr. Katezet said. "Well, since you know, I won't tell you," he said, smiling, enjoying the thought that although James was guessing, we really didn't know.

"By your six-month visit, Victoria, you should lose your ankles," he said in a playful sort of way. "Your child will be growing at a face pace. Try and rest as much as possible, and take your vitamins as prescribed, plenty of fruits and vegetables. I will send the nurse in for blood work, and I will see you two in about two months." He patted James on his back and left the room.

In my sixth month, James and I started fixing up our child's room. It was a little less than being a chore. Although James was with me through it all, it was hard, considering that all I had now was belly. My legs had disappeared along with my reflexes. I couldn't wait for nighttime to hit, because I knew then I could rest, and resting was all my body wanted to do those days.

I continued to work, but only part-time, and in the store part, not the pharmacy. When Ms. Fable came by the store, she would insist that I sit at the counter versus stand. I hadn't seen her in a while when one day when she saw how big I had gotten, she said, "Victoria, your baby is growing fast. If I didn't know better, I would say you were having twins." I knew that was just a thought; if she knew how much I was eating, she would have known it was all one child.

We went back to Dr. Katezet for our six-month checkup, and after checking the heartbeat, he said, "Victoria, have you thought of any names just in case it's a girl?"

"I'm stuck on two," I told him, "Hannah and Chloe."

"Two?" he said.

Before he could ask, James said, "You don't even have to ask. My son's name is going to be James Brandon Andrews."

He said it so proudly that Dr. Katezet said, "I love my job." During the ultrasound, he again pointed to something on the screen and asked the same question that he had previously. "Do you know what this is?" We gave the same answers because we really didn't know what we were looking at, but we did see a face. Dr. Katezet printed out the picture, and then he turned to me. We saw the face again, a little different this time, but still we couldn't tell if it was a girl or a boy. He printed that picture also, and James carefully put them away, so they didn't bend.

"How's the ankles?" he said, looking at how they were swollen. "A lot of pain, huh?" he said as he felt the fluid that had gathered around them. "Keep your feet up, Victoria. This is a crucial time in your pregnancy. We don't like fluid to gather, especially at this stage. Are you still working?"

"Not as much," I said. "I sit most of the time. The hardest part is getting there and getting out of the car."

"Well, for the children's sake, I mean, your child's sake, I think you should stop working and get plenty of rest. You have a big job ahead of you, and we want it to be a complete success without complications." After he said those words, he sent in the nurse for more tests, and then we were on our way home.

We had our lovemaking sheets shaken sessions several times, though not as much as before; our real focus was what was growing inside of me. Motherhood as well as fatherhood had a whole different meaning when it was your own child. James and I started attending church with Momma. That even prompted Daddy to start going. I needed a lot from God—a strong marriage and a healthy child—so giving him one day out of my week didn't seem important considering my requests. I had to mature and become responsible on my own. I couldn't wait for others to tell me be careful, don't do that, or that may not be helpful for the baby. I had to be at the top of my motherhood. I was the one who had to choose my actions, my food, and my life carefully. I wanted this baby to be as healthy as possible; it was all up to me, and I wasn't going to let my child down.

I finally stopped working, after having worked all the way up until my ankles started swelling to where I could barely walk. I remember feeling a little nervous about seeing Ms. Fable and quitting. It was a Friday evening. She had come by for her usual store tour, and I was in the office. I was hoping that I could just quit without her knowing until I was gone, but this was my last day and they had given me a surprise baby shower so the obvious was in the air.

"So, this is your last day, Victoria," she said, looking over her glasses.

"Yes, ma'am," I said, trying not to sound nervous.

"Do you have plans on returning?" she asked.

Not knowing what my future held, I replied, "I'm not sure."

"Well, you have really been good for my store, and if you ever need to come back, the offer will still be good. Good luck to you and your family," and with that, she handed me an envelope and walked out of the office.

At that moment, it felt like our baby was riding a bike inside of me. My belly was moving like it was on a drumroll at a grand exit. Easy boy, I remember thinking, the worst is over. I was glad that Ms. Fable made me the offer.

I decided to wait until I got home to open the envelope, thinking it was a card for the baby. I wanted James to be there when I opened it. In my heart, I felt that I wouldn't be returning right away to work. I wanted to stay home and take care of my son. Yet I was glad Ms. Fable left the decision of returning up to me. Although working was still an option, I didn't think that it would be in my near future.

After I got home, James and I opened Ms. Fable's card. It read: "Congratulations, Victoria. You will be a great momma. Accept this as a token of my appreciation of you, and hope this helps with your Gift from God. Best wishes, Ms. Fable." Inside the card was a crisp one-hundred-dollar bill. How thoughtful was that!

James made the comment that it would buy at least a month's worth of Pampers, and we added it to the collection of gifts that we had from the baby shower and went to sit on the porch for the remainder of the evening.

Momma and Daddy came by for their usual visit.

"I'm so excited, Victoria," Momma said, "I can barely sleep. Now that you're not working, I will come by every day so you can get your rest. I won't take no for an answer. Remember, that is what your doctor said for you to do anyway."

We sat there on the porch, and about two hours into our conversation, I had a strange desire for pizza. That had been the first real craving since I got pregnant. I wanted it loaded down with banana peppers. Daddy went to the corner store for banana peppers and James went to get the pizza. He came back with not two but three pizzas. Of course, I loaded one pizza down with banana peppers.

James watched in amazement as I ate the whole thing, and once I was done, I washed it down with a big glass of tea. He then said, "Tell me that she isn't carrying a boy; there is no way a girl could eat that much. Yes, sir, she is carrying the next greatest football player that will go down in the hall of fame. You wait and see."

His words brought lots of laughter. We were all excited and happy that our bundle of joy would be arriving soon.

James continued to go to my doctor's appointment with me, still not knowing the gender and James still convinced it was a boy. I was now in my seventh month, and the practicing as parents was about over. It was just about time for our fantasy to become a reality. James was a good parent already. He read to the baby, and he bought books galore to teach him while he was still inside me. I still was thinking on names but still couldn't decide between the two that I had chosen.

James never changed Brandon's name. It was still James Brandon Andrews. That was a good name, and James Brandon Andrews it was. James was already calling him Brandon. James was his father's first name and Brandon was my father's first name, so that suited me just fine. It tickled my dad to death.

I was blowing up like a balloon, and the doctor told us Brandon was doing fine. I told James I wanted to have the baby naturally. I paraphrased God's words from the Bible when Adam and Eve were receiving their punishment from God; he told them that man would serve the dust and women would have pain during childbirth. I wanted to keep God's word with us because I wanted God to keep my family safe. James was serving the dust by working every day for pay, so I felt I could take the pain of having our child. My mom had natural childbirth without medications, and I figured it was what I needed to do.

James took the ultrasound pictures to work. He showed them to everyone who would look at them. He passed them on to my dad so he could do the same. By the time Brandon came, he would be a household name. Momma was just as bad when we went out. She would have to everyone, and sometimes it was quite embarrassing; I just hoped that they didn't talk about her, that they understood her joy.

The time was coming close. I was having contractions and false labor almost every day. I was going to the hospital so much that the doctors told me that I could stay if I chose to; I was so close to having Brandon and he was playing tricks on coming so much that the doctor said that the next time might not be a trick. But I wanted to go home. Dr. Katezet told me that our child was doing fine but I needed complete bed rest. He insisted that I stay in the hospital, but as long as our baby was doing fine, I wanted to go home; it would be easier on everyone. Once I made my decision, Dr. Katezet said with seriousness in his voice—not the usual humor—"Complete bed rest, Victoria, do you understand?"

"Yes, I understand."

James also responded, "I do too."

"This is going to be a big boy," Dr. Katezet said, his humor returning somewhat. He looked again at me, and then whispered to James as if not to alarm me. At first, James had a look of concern, and then James and Dr. Katezet looked at me and started laughing. During my pregnancy I had laughed so much at James that it seemed fair that they had turned the tables on me. Only James wouldn't be the one with the last laugh; it would be Dr. Katezet.

Once on our way home, curiosity got the best of me. I asked James what Dr. Katezet had said. Teasingly he said, "You don't want to know."

"Yes, I do," I said. "I need to prepare myself, so tell me." I playfully sucker punched him in his arm.

"Ouch, okay, okay," he said. "If it was a boy, it would weigh about seven-and one-half pounds; and if it was a girl, it would weigh around six and one half to seven pounds."

"Well, then, it must be a boy, because I have picked up forty-two pounds since I first found out that I was pregnant. James," I said, "if I don't lose this weight once our child gets here, do you think your desire for me will change?"

He replied, "Victoria, we've made love all the way up until now. You were forty-two pounds lighter; now you're forty-two pounds heavier. Do you honestly think anything will change? As long as you have that dimple in your chin, I will desire you. When that dimple goes away, then we've got problems."

I had a lot of praying to do and I needed all the rest that I could get because once he was here, Momma said there would be no more resting and no more sleeping.

I wanted to be ready, so I decided I would let him come when he was ready. It was like Brandon knew he had played too many tricks, because the coming days, there were no more false labor pains. It was as peaceful as peaceful could be—which turned out to be the calm before the storm.

On my last visit to the doctor, he told me that Brandon was turning, and it wouldn't be much longer. He saw something in my ultrasound all along and it would be a surprise to everyone, but he said that unless something showed up in the blood work, there was nothing for us to worry about. If there was something to worry about, he would tell us. The blood work turned out fine, so we were just looking forward to when we could actually have our little boy and bring him home. Dr. Katezet told me to take it easy for the next couple of days, and within the next week, we should have our child.

A week to the day after we had our last doctor's visit, James was at work and Momma, and I were sitting on my porch with my leg propped on a stool when a gush of water emerged from my body. My water had broken.

She was just as calm as anyone could have expected. She said, "Victoria, we need to get you to the hospital, because your water has broken and that means it won't be long now."

She called Daddy, who in turn got James, and they beat us there. The hospital admitted me right away, and pain is all I remember from that point on. It was severe pain, unheard-of pain, excruciating pain. My legs felt like they were going to buckle, my back felt like it was about to split in two, and all I could seem to think about was, forgive me, Lord, but I need something to erase this pain. My heart kept telling me, "Brandon is worth the pain. You can do it." I kept playing God's words in my head when I could think. I didn't know how my momma did it, but this might be the last time I would try it without medicine. God would just have to understand.

James held my hand and hollered as loud as I did. Every time a pain struck me, he would squeeze my hand, causing more pain. I would have to tell him later, but not now. I wanted medicine badly. Brandon wasn't in any hurry, and the pain got worse and worse. Finally, I was surrounded by what looked to me like every doctor in the hospital. I heard the doctor tell James that something was wrong. My blood pressure had dropped way below normal, and they had to induce my labor and get Brandon out or we would have real complications.

I could see Daddy leading James out, and fear returned to me. Was I losing Brandon? Was this happy time turning into the worst tragedy possible? I felt myself go in and out of consciousness while the doctors worked on me.

I could feel the pain from Brandon slip away. I could remember wishing that the pain would return because that would let me know that Brandon was all right, but that didn't happen. I didn't feel any more pain as I slipped in and out of consciousness.

It was like I had slept for days. The room was dark, and no one was around. I didn't see our baby, and I had tubes running out of my body. I heard someone say, "She's awake now; you may come in."

Silence got louder as I heard feet come across the room. I tried to focus. I saw James, my momma, and Daddy. They looked like they hadn't had any sleep, and concern was all over the faces that I was seeing. Momma looked so tired, as if she had aged since I last saw her, and Daddy had bags under his eyes, as if worry had taken control.

I couldn't really read James. He seemed nervous, and all too anxious for words. He said, "Hey, princess, how do you feel?"

I was grasping onto his words. The reality was there; there was no Brandon, but I had to hear it. I had to hear someone tell me all those nine months of being careful and the days of pain were in vain. I was searching for words, searching for answers to questions I didn't want to ask.

"You gave us quite a scare." With tears in his eyes, James squeezed my hand.

"Where's Brandon?" I said in a panic. They had forgotten the reason I was there; it was for my baby, and they needed to tell me answers. I didn't care about me. I wanted to see my baby.

"Our child is …" I saw James talking, but I could barely make out his words. My mind had taken me on a spin, and all I could figure out was there was no Brandon.

Moments later, a nurse arrived carrying the little bundle of joy. There was another nurse behind her mumbling something, but I paid her no mind. My vision was blurry, and I could barely make out what I was seeing. I thought I had slipped back into my slumbered sleep and was dreaming of the tiny bundle. Brandon was okay, and that was all that mattered. He was healthy, and fear left my body and joy returned. Why had they seemed so concerned about me? Why hadn't they told me right away that Brandon was, okay? Once I got my wits about me, I would ask those questions, but for now I would sleep. I was glad that Brandon was alive and healthy, but all I wanted to do was sleep. I had forgotten about the other bundle that was lying beside my bed, and the Demerol didn't help. At that point, I wanted everybody to go away and let me sleep. My body was limber, and the sheep were calling me.

I vaguely heard James say, "I don't think she—"

After briefly looking at Brandon, I forgot about my worries, and I fell back into a deep sleep. And with that, I was dreaming of my future.

"Mrs. Andrews, we need to get blood work." The lab tech came in, interrupting my sleep. "Honey, I need you to give me your arm." I looked at her in a drunken stare, but all I wanted to do was sleep.

"Can you take it later and let her rest?" I heard a familiar voice say.

"I would. But doctor's orders, we have to make sure that her organs are working correctly and that the strain of her body doesn't cause a problem. I am so sorry for this, but it's only to help her."

"Victoria," I heard. It was James. "Honey, please give her your arm so she can take some blood. Honey are you awake?" he said.

Awake, I thought, and in pain. How dare she bring that ungodly pain back?

"James, I'm hurting. Please, I need something for pain."

"Can you help her?" James asked the nurse. "Can you give her something for the pain?"

"I can't," the lab tech said. "I'm only privileged to take her blood, but I can call her nurse in; she should be able to assist her."

She pushed the button beside the bed and said, "Can Mrs. Andrews have something for pain?"

"The nurse will be right in," she said. Then she proceeded to poke every vein in my body to get the blood she was after.

"You have moving veins," she said. "There is going to be a stick, honey." She poked and moved that needle in my arm like a rat looking for cheese. Not only was my stomach shoving out pain, but now my arm joined in. I was hoping that the nurse would just come in and cut them both off.

"All done," I heard her say. By then I was at least conscious. My thoughts were on Brandon.

"Where's the baby, James?" I asked. "Where is Brandon?"

"Honey," he said, "they are resting."

"They?"

With tears in his eyes, he told me the story. "It seems as though a baby girl was hiding behind Brandon all this time. That's why Dr. Katezet kept asking us if we were sure we didn't want to know the gender of our child; he knew all along."

With his little secret, the hospital donated a month's supply of pampers to help with the additions we would need for our daughter. He said that we had two children instead of one, and even though I just about lost them both, including myself, he said that the three of us were fine.

In the middle of James telling me what the real deal was, the nurse came in with my medicine, and off to sleep I went again.

My dreams came again. This time I dreamed of angels gathering around my children. One angel asked the other one, "What shall we call her? She is a joy."

The other angel said, "She looks like a Hannah, she will have much favor and grace from God, and she can spell her name backwards too. Let's call her Hannah Maria'."

The first angel said, "That would be pleasing to God."

The other angel responded, "Then that it is."

I slept well into the next day. I awoke with James on one side feeding the little girl and Brandon on the other wailing that he was next. He wanted his father to hurry up with her so he could whet his whistle.

"What are you going to name her?" the nurse said. As she put Brandon into my arms to be fed, me trying to get my wits about me, I said, "Hannah Maria', but spell her middle name M-a-r-i-a'

"Then that is what it will be," she said as she left the room.

It seemed like only hours after, but I was actually in the hospital for days. I coded while I was having the twins, and they thought that I was going to die so they gave me an emergency C-section. The children were fine, but I had been in critical condition for three days. I just about died having them. The doctors couldn't get my blood pressure up. It had dropped, and Hannah had gotten stuck when they tried to deliver her naturally. Everything going on had taken its toll on my body, so they wanted to make sure that I was able to care for the twins before they sent me home.

The twins, born May 24, 1988, had to stay in the hospital with me for three days, but they were released three days before I was. I had to stay a few more days to make sure I was able to go home. Sadness and happiness were the mixed emotions that surrounded my being. I was happy that our children were healthy, but sad because I couldn't take care of them. Breast-feeding was out of the question because they were now used to the bottle. Feeling a little confused as to why I couldn't breast-feed, I asked my doctor, and it seemed that whatever the baby becomes used to is what he or she prefers. Even though my breast was full of milk, they were used to the bottle. I wanted so desperately to breast-feed, but since I had been in a coma, they became used to the bottle. I had to be thankful, because I could have lost them both and James could have lost us all.

I was glad I had Momma to take care of the children until I got home. She and Daddy stayed at our house, and James stayed with me. He wouldn't leave my side, and I was glad about that. I thought at that point that I would return the favor if he ever needed me.

I was able to go home within the week. Momma and Daddy still stayed with us until I was able to take care of my family on my own. I was anxious, but I did as the doctor said. He requested that I get complete bed rest so my body could heal properly. I wanted so badly to take care of my family myself, but I knew that I could wind up in the hospital again and I didn't want that.

When we were alone, James said, "Two babies, what a wonderful thing."

I couldn't believe he didn't want to change the name I gave Hannah. Something told me that the angels wouldn't let him.

"You have made me the happiest man in the universe," James said, "with me still trying to soak in the reality of it all. I am a proud papa, and I will love and take care of my family till my dying days." At that point, I knew that God was pleased too. Even though I didn't keep him first, he was still in the midst. My dreams had come true sooner than I had expected, but it was all good. I wasn't able at that time, but I was ready.

It wasn't until the day that I was to leave the hospital that the doctor came in with life-changing news. James was getting my bags together and ready for the drive home, and I was sitting on the bed, my body weak from all the transitions that it had been taken through the past week. Dr. Katezet came into the room, glasses carefully placed on his nose and my charts in his hand. The look on his face was a troubled look, not the usual cheerful look that James and I had become accustomed to the past nine months.

"Folks," he said, "I have discovered something in the test that we recently ran on Victoria, and I am afraid with all the excitement and enjoyment of your twins, I have some bad news."

James stopped packing long enough to sit on the bed and put his arm on my waist.

Dr. Katezet continued speaking, "No more children."

I couldn't have any more children. If I did, then it would be too much for my body and there was a chance that I would not live through it. James and I had to make a decision that I wasn't prepared to make. The doctor suggested that I get my tubes tied. I could have children, but it wouldn't be in my best interest. I was anemic and a high risk because of the toxemia, and the next time James would probably have to make a decision for either me or the child to live. I was glad that I was sitting on the bed because if I wasn't at the time the doctor gave us the news, I probably would have passed out on the floor. When the news rushed around in my head and weakness took over, I felt the life drain out of me at that point, James noticed and caught me by the arm. His eyes met mine; that was the only way we could communicate at that time. I was hoping that he could hear the pain screeching from my heart. I will take my chances, I thought, hoping he could read my thoughts. Please, please, don't take the opportunity from me.

That wasn't in my plans. I wouldn't give up on my dreams. I thought we wanted a house full of kids, and I knew that the doctor was just a worker through God and that God would be the one that made the final decision. But at the same time, looking into James's eyes, I knew I couldn't put James through that. How could he make the choice of either me or our child? How unfair was that? That was a discussion that I wasn't looking forward to, but I knew that it would come.

To my surprise, James chose me for the first time, and it was without the help of Mrs. Andrews. I knew that he wanted a house full of children. We could take our chances. I argued that God would have the final say, but it was the rest of his words that made me realize that two was enough.

"Victoria," he said, "I want ten more kids, twenty if it's allowed. But having those twenty kids wouldn't be the same if I didn't have you. You are what makes us complete. I couldn't imagine someone else raising our creations. It just wouldn't be the same. I might lose what I want for us. I want to take care of you and our two children. I want to give our children what I didn't have—a mother and a father. I don't want your parents to raise our children. I don't exactly know how I would be if I lost you while you were trying to make my dreams come true. I might not love the child, knowing it was the child that took you from me. Let's just appreciate what we have and move on. We will end our family here, and one day, if I get so mixed up in emotions that I want another one, we will adopt. Let's follow the doctor's orders," he said, "because losing you will cause me to lose me."

With those words, it was settled. Brandon and Hannah, as sad as it sounded, would be the only two children that we would have unless we adopted. Even though I didn't think I could love a child that wasn't his, compared to the love of a child that was, I accepted what he said because I knew that making him happy was what I really wanted to do. So, whatever it took was what I would prepare myself to do.

We told the doctor of our choice and that I would have the tubal ligation. Before I left the hospital, the doctor put me on pills; within the next two months, I would be back in the hospital for the procedure. I didn't realize just how hard the two months would be. Brandon and Hannah were now moving around with ease, and Momma made a mistake in making the comment they were growing so fast, they must be moving out of the way for the next one. There would be no next one. I was grateful for my children, and no one is promised tomorrow. I just couldn't help but think after my family had bedded down that this was all the family I was going to have. No stair-step children; no room for making a mistake and having the opportunity to correct it with the next child; no hand-me-down clothes. I had gripped reality to know that once my empty nest was empty, it was going to be just that, empty. One straight shot.

Either we succeeded as parents or we failed, and the thought of failing our two children was a bit overwhelming to the point that little sleep came. I didn't know if my lack of energy came from taking care of our two children or the lack of sleep—probably a combination of both. I thought something like this was what caused postpartum depression. Even though I didn't see the big picture, I was a little angry with God. I didn't know his plan for me, and that made me a little uneasy. All kinds of thoughts as to why I couldn't have more children raced in my head. I had wanted to start my family in church, but I became too busy.

The surgery was a success, or should I say as successful as it could be. Even though I made it through, the outcome was still bittersweet. Momma and Daddy returned home, and our lives basically started completely over. It was now all on us to become the parents that we needed to be, and with the thoughts of not having any more children running through my head, I felt myself becoming a little overprotective.

I was healing as expected. I managed to get up and see James off to work. Daddy would pick him up and drop Momma off. I would feed, bathe, and cloth Brandon and Hannah, and then went through the day with a new routine, while Momma played with the twins. By three o'clock, I would start dinner; Momma would help sometimes. She would let me do it on my own other times. When Daddy and James arrived, Daddy would spend about an hour playing with the twins, and then he and Momma would head home. Sometimes they would eat, and sometimes they would just take a plate home. Everything was going great, but by the end of James's workweek, I would be exhausted. It was a nonstop cycle, but I didn't mind. I was a woman, a wife, and a mother; life was good.

On the weekends, James and I would sometimes visit with Mom and Dad. Sometimes we would just go to the park and let the twins soak up the sun. James would run around the stroller; the twins would look with curiosity, and when James would disappear, they would look disappointed until they could see him again. Then they would just smile and gurgle, and that made James proud.

I made the choice to start going back to church. I had been so wrapped up in my life's journey that I had forgotten about God. Momma's words raced in my mind: "Keep God in the midst. He must be first, Victoria." I hoped that God would understand when I let go of him in my life's path. In my mind, he gave this family to me. He wanted me to do everything I could to love them, and I did. After the exhaustion from the workweek, I found it difficult to get the children ready and take them to church. James didn't go with me. He and Daddy stayed home to keep the shed company and to watch after the dinner that Momma left simmering on the stove. Momma and the rest of the congregation helped with the children, but instead of my workweek starting on Mondays, I felt that it was starting on Sundays. James didn't get to spend but one whole day with the children, so I took church out of my options so he could spend more time with his family and less time with Daddy and the shed.

Momma missed me in church, and one morning after I had missed about four Sundays in a row, she told me in her motherly way, "Victoria, God gives, and God takes away. Never put anything before God, for he is a jealous god and if you put your family before him, he might take them away."

I nodded at those words, but the reality was I knew God wouldn't take my family away. He wouldn't put any more on me than what I could bear, and if I lost my family, God knew I would die. So, I knew Momma meant well, but I would still pray and read the Bible to the twins, and I knew they didn't understand my readings, I even bought children bible stories because I was just too tired to make it to church. Once I got the hang of things, I would return to church, and God would understand.

James and I would lie in bed at night, and we would talk about how the twins were progressing, each one exploring his or her own identity. They were both crawling now, trying to walk at six months. They would pull themselves up, trying to keep their balance. Most of the time Hannah would wait until Brandon pulled himself up, and then she would grab hold of him so he could help her, only to fall back down, laughing along the way. They were the joy of our lives, and they made our family strong. Daddy and Momma still came over, but not as often as they had in the past. I guess they felt that we were doing okay on our own.

Thanksgiving was coming up, and I wanted to prepare the feast at our home this year. It would be the first real holiday at our home, and I wanted to make it special. Momma and Daddy decided to spend the night. Momma would help me prepare the food, while Daddy and James went out for the Christmas tree. This was our family tradition, and just because we were in our own home, we wouldn't break it.

Daddy and James returned just in time to watch the game. Daddy took the opposing team so he and James could argue the whole game—not really arguing, but Daddy knew how James felt about his team, and he always liked to get him going.

Momma and I finished dinner around halftime, and the boys took time out from the game to eat with us. James cut the turkey, and then Momma led the prayer. James and Daddy forgot about the blessing, because the whole-time during dinner, they argued with each other about which team was cheating who and how the referees favored the winning team. Momma and I just focused on the twins because that was a battle that we wouldn't dare interfere with. After dinner, the boys retook their seats in front of the TV, and Momma and I cleared the dishes away. I was thankful that James's team won the game; if they hadn't, I don't think Momma and I could have stood them. Daddy would have spent the rest of the evening teasing James, and he would have gone to bed early with disappointment. After dinner, we put the children down to bed for the night so we could decorate the tree and grab hold to the Christmas spirit.

We put on Christmas music and sang and danced until we were in the Christmas spirit. We made eggnog, and while Momma and I decorated the tree, Daddy and James decorated the outside. After the tree was decorated, James put the angel on top and plugged in the tree. We sat around the tree and watched it glistening and shining. Too soon, Daddy decided it was time for them to go, so he kissed Momma underneath the mistletoe. Right after that, they went home.

James and I sat up talking about this past year, the birth of our son and daughter, how our love had grown, and what was in store for the new year.

We danced around to the Christmas music, held each other, and watched the tree, which was shining for its very first time in our very own home. It had been a good year, and my guess was there would be more good times and memories to follow.

Chapter 18

I could not have loved James any more than I did. James and the children were the most important part of my life, and my family was really all that mattered to me. I had the family that I had envisioned so often under that old willow tree.

On Christmas Eve, it snowed and snowed, and we had decided to have Christmas at our house this year. It would be James's first Christmas with a family he called his own. Later in our lives, we might have holidays at Momma and Daddy's house, but not this year. We wanted the children's first Christmas to be at home.

Before Momma and Daddy arrived, James and I took the children to the willow tree to put flowers down for the Andrewes's. We had resorted to artificial flowers because they would last her throughout the winter months. That was the first time that we had taken the children, and with the cold air, we only stayed long enough to clear off the dead flowers and replace them with the beautiful red and white artificial ones. James spoke only a few words to her, letting her know that it was Christmas and we had brought the children by for a short visit. He ended his conversation by telling her he had to take the children home before they got sick from the cold air.

When we returned home, Momma and Daddy were already there. The Christmas music greeted us as we come through the door.

Christmas Day was too beautiful for words. It had snowed all night, and we had a white Christmas. The floor was covered with gifts and wrapping paper and it was indeed Christmas at the Andrewses' house. Momma and I cooked like we always had, and Daddy and James played with Brandon and Hannah; they were enjoying the toys more than the children did. Brandon wanted to show off for his daddy and grandpa, so he took his first step. Hannah, being the curious one, pulled him down as she tried to follow his lead. Daddy and James laughed at the attempts they were making. We had our dinner, and later we all joined the children on the floor, playing with their toys and laughing along the way. Looking at where my life was a couple of years earlier to where it was now made me understand the true meaning of love. Christmas came and went way too fast, but there was a new year coming and we had to get prepared.

We were excited to stay up and watch the ball drop. Neither James nor I wanted to go to a party, so we took a nap in midday with the children, and the four of us watched the ball drop while the tree shone for the last time this year. We played with the children a little while after that, and then we put the two of them down for the night. I got on my knees at that point and thanked God for what he had given me this past year, and I told him what I wanted for the year to come. I also told him of my shortcomings with him, how I had put James first, but I promised to do better in the year to come. I hoped that God accepted my prayer that night and understood my love for my family. Surely, he did, I thought.

After I made love to James, he told me of his new year's resolutions. He told me that having a family of his own was all that he had hoped for in life. He then thanked me for making his life complete. I could hear the sincerity in his voice as he spoke. He told me that I was number one in his life, and he wanted to make every year a little bit better. He vowed that he would always take care of us, and if something was to happen that he couldn't, it would kill him. He thanked me once again for giving him the children and making his life complete. For a moment, our eyes met and locked in place; it felt as though we were reading each other's mind. James broke our silence by softly kissing my lips and reaching over to hold me. Within minutes, snoring interrupted the silence that filled the room.

The New Year 1989 started out life as usual—except James was working overtime now and we were saving money for that rainy day. We always paid our bills on time, we didn't have worries, and life was good. I was with the children more than I was with James nowadays, but that was fine with me because James was a part of the children and having a part of James was better than not having any at all. Daddy was talking about retiring in a couple of years. He felt his time for working was up; Momma and I felt the same. Daddy was getting up in years and he needed to enjoy life and his retirement. He thought he had saved enough through the years to carry him through.

For Valentine's Day, Momma and I cooked Daddy and James a dinner to remember. James liked steak and Daddy liked ribs, so we had a barbeque waiting for them when they arrived home from work. James had flowers and candy for me. Daddy had the same for Momma. James even had a card from the children telling me that I was their valentine. He wrote in my cards some of the most beautiful, sincere words that I had ever heard.

After dinner, we played with the children and then went to the willow tree to change out Mrs. Andrews's flowers. This time we gave her real ones. I often wondered if James would ever consider moving his grandparents' urns from our willow tree in the park to our willow tree at our home. Even though we had the other two urns placed on the mantle in our living room, I wondered if he ever thought of moving them closer to us. He never mentioned it and neither did I.

James made love to me that night in a way that I knew he was happy to call me his valentine. We also talked about our younger years, Mrs. Andrews, and our meetings at the tree. I spoke about his proposal to me and the promises we both made. We vowed again to keep those promises to each other. I thought it would be easy because of the way our love was there was nothing that could take those promises away. We were in love, we had love, and our family was God-given, so what else was there?

The twins were walking and talking now, saying Momma and Daddy. James was like a kid again. He loved it when he heard the word "dada." He would come get me no matter where I was or what I was doing and make the children repeat the word over and over again, "dada." I couldn't help but wonder when James was a toddler, if his father was as happy as James was to hear that word. It was a happy time. The twins were the showpiece of our creation, of our unity. Life was good, and I finally realized that James was my purpose, and he made our lives complete.

I didn't know what God's plans were for my life, but I did know at this moment, at this time, I was the happiest I had ever been watching James crawl around on the floor, sometimes just staring as if he was experiencing disbelief of the happiness he was experiencing. I was thankful that we were blessed with what we had, and even though this was all the children we were going to have, I knew that whatever God had in store for us was for the best.

Summertime was here again, and it was time to introduce the children to our tree at the park. We took a little picnic, just as I had envisioned so many times, to that old willow tree. We played with the children, each laughing and trampling on the grass. I remember making a promise to God that I would give him some of my time. I would start praying more, and I would spend some of my evenings reading the Bible to the children. I haven't yet, but I will, I thought. The last thing I wanted God to think was that he was not a part of this family. I surely didn't want to anger him.

James thrived on watching the children chasing the ball and falling, only to get back up and do it all over again. Hannah sat more than Brandon did; she found her pleasure in watching Brandon chase the ball and she giggled uncontrollably when he fell down. Watching the children interact with each other as if they had their own language going on brought joy to my heart. I knew one day they would be each other's strength. They would depend on each other. Even though Brandon was the boy, Hannah showed strengths of her own, and she proved to be the more dominant one. Watching them grow was an amazing experience that I would record in my journal as a special memory.

Time went way too fast this year, and quickly we were looking at autumn dead in the face. The twins were now communicating with each other, trying to form words and attitudes that we had never imagined.

It seemed like every night once I lay the children down, James and I made love. It was a different kind of love, a passionate yet caring love; it was a lovemaking that could go down in the books. I sometimes felt that James would make love to me better than the last time because he didn't want me to stray. I think he thought that I needed that in order to make me happy. Just knowing that he loved us, and I was able to make his dreams come true was enough for me. I enjoyed his lovemaking sessions, even though my body was crying for rest. He took his time, and it seemed like hours, orgasm after orgasm. We made love, and it was beautiful; it was well-waited for and well-deserved. I tried just as hard as he did; I wanted to please him just as much as he pleased me. Needless to say, I didn't want him to stray either.

There was no fear of that. I was a well-kept woman, and James was the man of my life, the man of my home. He was everything the children and I could ever hope for, and our lives relied upon James. My decision early on stood I would not return to work. James made enough money to take care of our family, and it was a difficult thought for me to leave my child with someone else for the entire day. Being a well-kept woman at the time didn't seem like such a bad idea.

The years had come and gone; the year was 1993, and the twins were fast approaching five years old. They were now eating table food and walking and talking from the time they got up to the time they went to bed. Sometimes you could understand them, and other times you couldn't, but that was a joy for James and me. We would spend hours at a time guessing what they were saying and laughing when they would get aggravated when we didn't understand fast enough. Our lives were good. The kids were growing up. I secretly wanted to have another child, but I didn't dare tell James; I didn't want to trouble him.

On May 24, we threw the twins a party for their fifth birthday. The previous birthdays weren't as exciting as this one. We just had cupcakes, but this was a birthday where they could tell that something amazing was happening. James and I had met a few parents at the park visiting with the kids, so we invited them. Since the park was where it all began, that was where we decided to have the party. The willow tree's blooms looked brighter. It seemed like it was more magical than it had been previously. Looking at the park in its entirety made me realize just how much it had changed. The swings had been replaced, as if to say new beginnings were on the way. The other trees looked like shadows compared to the willow tree. It was as if God himself was telling me that a new beginning was soon on its way. Funny how this birthday party made me realize the difference in the way I looked at the park versus the previous years.

Momma and Daddy came, of course, and James and me. It wasn't a huge party, but the children enjoyed it and we had enough pictures to fill a photo album. These are memories that will be well worth showing our grandkids one day, I thought.

Daddy retired in August. He said another layoff was coming at the plant and he wanted to spare someone's job. He had done his time, so he was giving someone else a chance to do theirs. He also wanted to enjoy the children and start living the rest of his life. He and Momma would travel some to visit their few brothers and sisters who were still alive. Work was still good for James; he worked a lot of overtime in spurts. It was nothing out of the norm. Daddy was so proud of him, and that pleased James.

Time wasn't standing still for anyone. That August the kids were starting kindergarten. I was hustling around in the mornings getting James off to work, and then waking the children, fixing their breakfast, and walking them to the bus stop. I remember crying the first day, and I didn't get anything done around the house. I kept wishing that time would hurry up so I could see my children again. It was hard at first, and I wanted another baby I think at times it bothered James too, but he never said anything and neither did I.

Work was slowing down at the plant. As Daddy had said, a layoff was about to come. The economy had gone sour, and people weren't buying things like they used to. This layoff just missed James; he would come home evenings and tell me about one of his friends barely making it. One friend lost his wife and family because he had lost his job. I think that was a big fear of James's, but he had nothing to worry about. I felt sorry for James's friend, but I knew that would never happen to us because it didn't matter to me as long as we had each other.

I remember the phone call that changed everything. It was a phone call that was never expected. I was making up the children's bed, and the phone rang brrrriiiiinnngggg, brrrriiiinnnnggg. When I finally reached the phone, the person on the other end had hung up. A few minutes later, just enough time for me to get back into Hannah's room, it rang again, bbrriiinggggg, bbrringgggg. I ran to it this time, and there was someone on the other end but he or she never said anything. Two hours later, while I was folding clothes, the call came again. This time the person on the other end asked if this was the residence of James Andrews.

"Yes, it is," I said to the shy voice on the other end.

"May I speak to him?" the little voice said. I could tell it was a woman, but why would a woman be calling James?

"He's not here at this time. May I ask who's calling?"

Silence remained on the line for a ten-second pause, and then the woman said, "I am his mother."

"Excuse me," I said, not thinking that I was hearing correctly.

"This is his mother, Sandra Robertson, and who am I speaking with?"

"I'm his wife, Victoria Andrews," I said, feeling ashamed for whatever reason. "James won't be home until five this evening. Would you like to give me your number so he can call you?"

"No," she said, "he won't call. You say you're his wife?"

"Yes, ma'am, I am. Is there anything I can tell him for you?"

"No," she said, "I am afraid he won't care. Can I try calling him back at five?"

"Of course, you can. You will get him at five o'clock or a little after."

"Okay, thank you. I will try then," she said, and she was gone.

How incredible is that? I thought, still holding the phone, my mind racing, wondering how James would react to the news that his mother had called. She found him; after all this time, she took the time to find him. Maybe now the twins would get the chance to meet the woman who gave life to their father. I was beside myself at this time. I couldn't wait to break the news to James. He would be pleased—or would he not care like she said on the phone?

James had barely made it in the door when the phone rang again. I hadn't gotten a chance to tell him the news. It was his mother again.

"James," I yelled, my voice carrying through the house and the telephone.

"Who is it?" he called back.

I didn't want to yell it through the house, so I ran to him holding the receiver. "She said she's your mother," I said, watching his facial expression.

"I'll take it upstairs," he said as he turned with a kind of uncertainty. James headed for the bedroom, and when I heard him speak, as badly as I wanted to listen, I hung the phone up. I should give him his privacy, I thought. He would tell me about the call later.

It was over an hour later when James came out of our room. He had already had his shower, and he had a look on his face that I would never forget. It was a look of concern. He seemed to have something on his mind. He sat down in his chair and watched the children, not talking, as if he was in deep thought. My first impulse was to wait until he spoke.

It was Hannah who made me realize that something was going on. I watched as she climbed up on his lap for her usual special attention, and it was as if he didn't even realize that she was there. He was looking at her, but he gave no reaction. That was out of his character; he usually welcomed her affection with kisses and hugs. She quickly got down, as if she sensed something was wrong, and she made her way back to Brandon. Every now and then, I would see her look up at her daddy as if to see if he noticed her so she could finish what she had started. Yet he just sat there. I didn't know whether to ask him about the call or let him tell me on his own. I couldn't tell if he was pleased that she had found him, or if he'd wish she would never call again. James then did something that I had never seen him do. He got up out of the chair, went over to the mantle, and touched the urn of Mrs. Andrews. That was the first time since we had moved into the house that I saw him touch her urn. The words from Mrs. Andrews came ringing back to me: One day I hope his mother and father try to find him and finally give him the love that he had missed all those years. Maybe that was what James was thinking; maybe that was what was beginning to happen.

It took several minutes for him to come back to the present. "Dinner smells good," he said as he walked over to the kitchen and sat down at the table.

I had set the table while he stood at the mantle, not mentioning at all the phone call that he had just received. At first, I felt a little shut out, but I shook that thought out of my head. I decided he would talk about her when he was ready. During dinner, he played with the children and talked to them about what they had learned in school. I cleared the table after dinner, and he put the kids in the bath, still without a word about his phone call, about his mother. I was getting ready to burst with questions after we laid the kids down for the night, but I still didn't say a word.

It wasn't until we bedded down and James made love to me that he brought the phone call up. He said, "Victoria, are you going to ask me about the phone call?"

"No," I said. "I figured if you wanted to talk to me about it, you would."

"It was my momma," he said. At that point, I wished that it wasn't dark so I could see the expression on his face, so I would know what to ask next. "She said that she talked to you earlier today. What did she say?"

"Nothing much. She just asked if this was your residence and could she speak to you. I told her that you were at work, and I was your wife, and then she said she would call back."

"Did you tell her about our children?" he asked.

"No, I didn't have a chance to. Did you?" I asked, not wanting to pry.

"No," he said, "and I don't want her to know just yet. I don't know for sure if she's well yet. I don't want that type of life around my children."

"What type of life?" I asked before thinking.

"She drinks too much to hide her pain. I went through it, and I don't want my children to go through it too."

"Well, what did she want?" I asked, not wanting him to clam up.

"She wants to come for a visit. She said she was better now, but I have heard that so many times before."

"Are you going to let her?" I said, not being able to stop the questions from pouring out of my mouth.

"I told her she could, but I am still unsure about it all."

"Well, we will be here with the children. I don't see any harm."

"We will see. She will call back in a few days. I told her I would talk it over with you. It's not like she has been a great part of my life."

Not being able to stop myself, I said, "I think it will be good for all of us. We have to move forward with the troubles she caused, and maybe this is her way of doing just that. Besides, I want the children to know your family."

"She didn't even ask about Grandma. I know they had words when she left, but you would think she would ask some type of questions about the woman that raised me."

"Did you tell her she passed on?"

"No, if she wanted to know or even cared, then she should have asked herself."

"You're still angry with your mother, James. We need to get past that. If she is well, she needs to be in the children's life. Your life, our life."

"We will see," he said, and with that, silence filled the room and we fell asleep.

Morning came way too early. I would be without James and the children again. I was hoping for the weekend to hurry and make its way in the week somehow.

The weekend must have heard my pleas because it came just as quickly as I had hoped. We had plans on going to the park for a picnic with the children. They were growing up so fast, and we were playing Frisbee and dodgeball with them now. Instead of watching them, we were all playing together. The phone call came just before we left the house; it was his mother again. This time James didn't go off by himself; he stood there in front of me carefully choosing his words.

"Yes, Momma," I heard him say, all the while searching me for guidance. "Yes, Momma, I have children, two; they are five years old now. I think we should have a relationship first before you come for a visit. Let us get to know each other first. There is a lot to talk about," he said, "but we will have those talks once a visit is established. I got to go," he said. "My family is waiting on me."

I knew James was angry with his mother, but who would have thought it would be seven and a half years and uncountable phone calls before he agreed to let her come for a visit.

I didn't ask or say anything else. I felt at that point enough had been said. We went on to the park as planned, but it was a more nervous time versus the fun times. After the conversation, James became silent. He was in his own little world, probably reminiscing about his hard life growing up. Even though I heard the brunt of the conversation, I still felt shut out, like he wasn't including me. It was like this was between him, his mother, and Mrs. Andrews. I felt a little uncomfortable. This was the first time that James didn't include me in something. I couldn't tell if I was jealous that another woman, even if it was his Momma, had gotten his attention, or it was the fact that he didn't feel the need to discuss anything about the phone call with me. I spent most of my time under the willow tree, while James spent his time playing with the kids; and at that point, he didn't seem to care that I was not involving myself in their activity. It was as if I wasn't even there. I felt offended at first, but when Brandon fell and he had a delayed reaction to his fall, I realized that he didn't know I was there because he wasn't really there himself. It was as if he was just going through the motions. James was thinking about something, and I was praying, praying that this time with his momma would be a time that we could put down as a good memory. Not like the bad ones I suspected he had in the past.

I didn't know that in the blink of an eye, it could be taken away. That in a blink of an eye the life you chose, the life you love, the life you need could disappear without a warning, without a sign. It could be gone. You might fight with every fiber of your being to get it back, but when it's gone, it's gone.

I wish I could turn back the hands of time and keep our God as the head of the family, love our God first and foremost, love James second, and then our children. It was James that I had put first, then our children, then God. I remember my momma telling me that if I put anything before God, he is a jealous god, and whatever I put before him, he would take away from me. I guess now I see in more ways than one that her words were true.

For ten years of our marriage, our family was on cue and, needless to say, it was perfect. Not God-like perfect, but perfect to us. Everyone knows that the only perfection is of God. Even though a life is thought to be perfect, something always happens to let you know that it is less than perfect. I came to that realization when tragedy struck our family.

It was late spring 1997. Summer was in the air, school was about to close for the summer, and the birds were nestling in the trees. Daddy was helping James in the garden while I was helping the children with their homework. It was then that I heard James's cry for help. He called out my name in a way that my heart fell. "Victtttttoriaaa!" I had never heard that tone from him, and that let me know that something was terribly wrong. With my heart preparing to make a leap out of my body, I ran as fast as I could to the outside, and I saw my daddy lying on the ground. "Call 911!" he shouted. "Now!"

His tone almost paralyzed me. It was so strong that my mind said run, but my eyes and body were fixed at their current position. I managed to get the phone and call 911. Then I called Momma. Within minutes I joined him outside. My daddy was lying on the ground, clutching his heart. He looked up as if he felt this was his last time seeing me. I saw a trickle of tears stream down his face as he gasped for all the breath that he could steal from the earth. James kept telling Daddy to stay with him, fear in his face and pain screaming from his voice.

Since it was my father, I was no good for anyone. My childhood flashed before me, as well as Mrs. Andrews. I followed James's lead and begged for my father to hang on; I had called the ambulance and I knew help was on the way. I was rubbing my daddy's now paling face while speaking. "Daddy, please hang on, help is on the way." I could tell that he was fighting with everything in his body because sweat was pouring from his face so hard that I couldn't tell which was sweat and which were tears. The same stood for James. My daddy had a stronger build than James, and he was holding on what seemed to me like for dear life.

I can't express the pain I felt watching my daddy slip away while my husband held him close. Mixed emotions ran through my mind. I was seeing my father hold on to dear life, while my husband held onto him, I felt, as well as having a flashback of Mrs. Andrews, and that hurt me as well. James had become close to Daddy, and now not only was I losing my father; he was losing his mentor, a man whom he had come to love as his own. Daddy was coherent from time to time. He would give a faint smile as if to reassure us, but it would fade quickly back into the pain that he was facing, and he kept fading in and out.

The ambulance arrived, and James insisted on being the one to ride to the hospital with Daddy. I felt that was good because, if I had lost my dad while on the ride to the hospital, I don't think I could have stood the pain that it would have caused me, and I had the children to think about. Knowing that James was going with Daddy was assurance enough. I also had to look out for Momma. I took the children with me, and thoughts of my daddy, my mother, and James came pouring through like an open sore. The children had questions about Grandpa, but I was in my own little world trying to give answers while trying to focus on what could or should be.

When we got to the hospital, Momma was already there. James met me in the waiting room. He was speaking words that I wasn't prepared to hear.

"It doesn't look good, Victoria. He's not breathing on his own. The doctors seem to think that he's had a massive heart attack, and only 10 percent of his heart is functioning."

I was now looking at my husband, probably with a look he had never seen, because I was in a mass of confusion. Two hours earlier, my daddy was fine. He'd never complained of a problem he was having, never had a concern to be spoken of—and now he was fighting for his life, and my husband was standing before me with that searching look he always had, waiting for me to react. I stood before him feeling a numb sensation take over my body, not wanting to respond to the look, not wanting to accept the fact that I was losing the only man who had ever been in my life besides him.

I just walked away. I had to see my daddy. I left the children in the waiting room with James because I wasn't prepared for what I was about to see. Daddy had a big tube shoved down his throat; he was hooked up to all kinds of wires, wires that I had no knowledge of. Machines surrounded his bed, and he was pale in color. Momma was covered with fear, and she looked like she had aged ten years. My heart wept for her. I couldn't imagine losing a man I had depended on all my adult life, not to mention her first and only love. The effect it would have on her, the effect it would have on our family, was indescribable.

I don't even think she saw me when I came in the room. Her eyes filled with tears, and her hand was holding his as she sat deep in prayer. My heart was full of hurt, pain, and confusion as I watched my daddy's life slip away, me not being able to do anything to save him.

Momma was about to lose the only man that she had known. That was more than I could bear. Flashbacks of James and Mrs. Andrews fell on my mind. I couldn't bear the thought of losing my daddy.

It was the decision-making day. We had to decide whether or not to leave Daddy on the machine. Even though this was a hard decision, I didn't want to see my father suffer. There he lay with tubes running out of his chest and mouth, not conscious as to where he was or why. When the doctor came in the room with the options of taking my father's life or leaving him to lie in that state, I saw my mother in a whole new, different light. She aged, and the blood looked as if it had drained out of her body. Her eyes filled with tears, and I could see her body trembling with fear, which had taken over her body as well as her mind. She was a God-fearing woman, and she knew that God's will would be whatever it would be, no matter what hurt, and pain was caused; but at that moment in that instance, I saw the light that used to shine within her turn into a shade of darkness. She didn't want to have to make that decision to take the only man she had ever loved, ever known, from this world.

She wasn't prepared for this, and to be honest, neither was I; but the decision had to be made, and I knew that if she couldn't make it based on her own beliefs, then I would have to make it for her. My world, the perfect life that I had known, had crumbled before me, and I wasn't prepared. I had to make a decision that would take away the man who gave me my life. Take away the man whom my momma loved and was used to. When I asked her what she wanted to do, the look on her face spoke to me in a tone that shouted to my heart. Her eyes were filled with tears, and her bottom lip was trembling. She wanted to be strong, and I know that was her every intention, but sometimes hurt is the ruler no matter what your beliefs are.

"Momma," I said in an almost silent voice, "when shall we do this? Shall we hope and pray that maybe God will shine his grace on Daddy one last time to give him breath so he can be with us? Is that truly what Daddy would want, for you and me to take care of him for the rest of his life? Should we wait until morning so that he can see the sun one more time?"

I said, losing control of my own emotions now, tears staining my own face. "What do you want to do, Momma?" I said.

"Victoria," she said, her blouse wet from her tears, "I know God has a will for us all, but I …" and her voice trailed off, "I can't let him go right now. We still have a lot to do. We have traveling to do. I know my God knows best, but can't we just have a little more time with him?"

"Momma," I said, grabbing her in for a hug, "what good will it do? He will just suffer more. Whether we take him off today or next week, he will only suffer. It won't get any better. It is what it is, and God's will is God's will. You taught me that. He will carry us through this, right, Momma? Isn't that what you always told me? Has your God changed because you are faced with this?" With those words, our tears became the stronger vessel within both of us. It had to be done, but how?

I wanted my daddy, but the doctors said that he would not have a value to life if he lived. It was a decision I never wanted to make, but it had to be made. Whatever the decision, I never wanted to be put in that situation again for as long as I lived, because it was the hardest decision I ever had to help make.

His brain was damaged, and the machines that he was hooked up to would be the only thing helping him to function. He wouldn't be able to talk again. He could still understand and hear, but it would only last for a few moments. We were warned by the doctors that, once we turned off the machines, he would still be alive for as long as his organs were functioning, but they would eventually shut down and then he would be gone. Those words meant that Momma would no longer have a husband, I would no longer have a father, and neither would James.

As hard as the decision was, it had to be made. Momma didn't leave him after the machines were removed; she stayed and prayed. I'll never forget Daddy's final moments. We were told that he was holding on with all his might and that he wasn't ready to go, but it wouldn't be long. I had decided to take Momma and the children to the cafeteria for something to eat to keep up their strength; James stayed behind with Daddy.

Once we finished our lunch, I settled the children in the waiting area and then returned back to the room. I will never forget James as he sat by Daddy's bed, talking to him like he had once talked to Mrs. Andrews. He didn't even realize that we were in the room.

"Mr. Adams, now you hear me," James said, tears welling up in his eyes. I knew he loved my daddy, and Daddy had come to love him. "If you must go, then go," he said. "There are still plenty of things that need to be done, but I will take care of it for you. I will continue to love your daughter and grandkids with everything I have in me. Victoria and I will take care of Ms. Adams. We will miss you, but I will make sure that they don't do without anything; their lives will continue to be as happy as you have made them. Don't worry; they will be fine. They love you, Daddy," he said, "and so do I. We will keep your values strong."

Daddy opened his eyes as if that was all he needed to hear before he left us. He then took two breaths, and he was gone.

Momma and I just stood there, crying and holding one another. It was hard to believe that life could be so unfair. We were still standing there crying when James came over to us and joined the hug. Momma then ran over to where Daddy was and lay on him, begging him to come back, but it was too late. He had finally gotten the okay to go; I felt hearing those words from James gave him the assurance that he needed to go home. I don't think Daddy could have left knowing Momma was in the room. He didn't want to see her hurting. I think when James made those promises, it gave my daddy peace.

The funeral was sad, but a homecoming for Daddy. He didn't want people crying over him; we knew that he wanted to go without any fuss. After the funeral service, Momma asked if James could take her home. "Victoria," Momma said, "I just want to go home and rest. I don't feel up to the ending. You guys go on and thank everybody for coming. There is plenty of food at the church. I just need my time now. I don't want to go to the place where he's going to be resting knowing that I can't touch him or bring him home with me."

"Okay, Momma," I said. "Do you need anything?"

"What I need," she said with a tear God saw fit to take so, "I just want to go on home and rest."

James took Momma home, and with worry in my heart, I did as she asked. The children and I went on to the burial ground, and James joined us. Then we went to the church, gave our appreciation, and then returned home. I felt sad for Momma, but I knew she had to manage Daddy's death in her own way.

Right after Daddy's death, James began to change. He wasn't the same. I guess in his mind, he lost yet another person who he thought loved him. I felt sadness daily for the loss of my daddy, but I had to be strong, no matter what my heart was going through. It was as though even though I had hurt and pain of my own, I was the stronger vessel of the two. James began to withdraw some. I guess with his promises, he felt the weight of the world was now on him.

Momma went into depression. She didn't laugh and joke like she used to. I knew it was hard for her, but I needed her closeness now more than ever. Now that Daddy was gone, I needed her close to me. I asked her to move in with me, but she chose not to. I knew it was hard for her to live in the house that she and Daddy had shared. I knew that Momma was too overwhelmed with losing the only man she ever knew, let alone the only man she ever loved.

We made a way to go on with our lives without the comfort of Daddy—or Momma, for that matter. We missed the way things used to be, and we often talked about it. We had our children to think about, and they were what kept us strong.

We tried visiting Momma on a regular basis, but sometimes she just didn't feel like company. We would go to her house, and she would be sitting in the living room without the TV or the radio on, yet she always had her bible in her hands. I felt that she was reaching out to God for his peace and comfort. The children would speak to her, and she would answer, but only in one or two words and she didn't seem to get really excited about anything. I told her about the children riding without training wheels, and her response was, "That's nice, Victoria." Momma was losing her will to live, and I didn't know how to help her get that back. I guess that was the way James felt when he lost Mrs. Andrews. Losing Daddy made me realize and understand more about the way James felt when he lost Mrs. Andrews.

We did continue to visit the willow tree and change out the Andrewses' flowers, but it wasn't the same because before or after we would visit them, we were now visiting my daddy too. Momma never wanted to go to the place where Daddy lay. I think that she had her own way of having closure. She read her Bible a lot, and after time went on, I saw that God was giving her the strength and grace she needed. Although Momma hurt, she never stopped going to church. She never stopped believing in God's will.

Chapter 19

Time had leaped forward. Almost three years had passed since I lost Daddy. James and I faithfully took fresh flowers to him and Mrs. Andrews every chance we got. We talked to both of them, letting them know the progress that we had made. Momma was doing a lot better, but she still had her days. James had kept his promise that he made about taking care of us, and I felt Daddy was pleased with that.

The twins were in their last year of elementary school. Spring was in the air, and so was their birthday. They were blossoming like two beautiful flowers. They were now preteens. Twelve years old to be exact. They were indeed twins; you wouldn't see one without the other, and Brandon guarded Hannah like a caged lion.

Momma came to our little birthday party for the twins. She brought a mountain of gifts for them. It was only the neighborhood kids and a few friends that the children chose who came. I could tell that God had given Momma grace and peace with losing Daddy. She laughed a little more, and she seemed to care about her surroundings a little more. Even though I knew she was hurt by losing Daddy, maybe even a little angry, she was more like herself nowadays. We had given her the time and space that she needed, and I always knew that she would come around when she was ready. The children had a blast, and it was the best birthday ever.

The only thing Momma really talked about at their party—to me anyway—was that the children needed to attend church. "Victoria," she said, "I know that you had to heal from your father's death, and so did I. The only way I healed was the help of God and the church. That was what was needed to help me get through. You haven't been to church since your father's funeral. Not wanting to put pressure on you, but when are you coming back to church?"

I tried to ignore the question because I really didn't have time to go to church; the kids were growing, and the biggest part of my time went to them. I even felt sometimes that I neglected James. He never said anything, but we didn't make love like we used to. I was way too tired once nighttime fell. I knew that God loved me and surely, he would understand. He was doing a good job keeping me and my family, so I gave my thank you from time to time, but I just didn't have time to sit in a church and hear some preacher tell me what I already knew. To me that was wasting time that should have been with my kids. I didn't read the Bible like I used to, and I didn't pray like I used to, but God know that I was thankful whether I went to church or not. Yet telling my mother that I didn't have time for God was like telling the sun not to come out and yet it was ninety degrees outside.

"We will," I said, "soon."

I wanted to leave it at that, but then she said, "Never put anyone before God. I keep telling you that God is a jealous God. You need to continue to read your Bible and pray—the New Testament, not the old. You need to focus on moving forward in God's word. The Old Testament is just a reference for what shall be. Read the whole Bible if you like but focus on what is to come."

"I understand," I said, kissing her on her cheek and walking away, excusing myself from the conversation.

Momma, knowing that I wasn't making time for God, started taking the twins to church, and I was fine with that. I knew we all needed to go, but James and I stayed behind. It was a good time for us to spend quality time together, and if it meant me staying home with James, then that was what I was going to do. The Bible said he was the head, so instead of pressing him to go, I would just stay home with him. It was good for the children to go because they needed to know God. I learned about him when I was growing up; why shouldn't they? It really didn't matter who took them as long as they went. That would help them later in life. I guess Momma thought that I would eventually join them, but I was much too busy enjoying James, and I felt that sending the children would satisfy God for now.

Twelve years of bliss and happiness as a family, and the only tragedy in our lives thus far was Daddy's passing. Our marriage was strong, Momma was becoming her old self again, and the kids were growing like wildfire. I couldn't hope for more happiness in our lives. But then James's work started struggling again, and a layoff was due to come. This layoff made the newspapers, and people all around town were talking about it. James and I had saved some money, so I thought we would be all right. James was a little worried, but I had confidence that he would keep his job. He has been with the company for over sixteen years, so surely, I thought, he will keep his job.

I remember exactly when the second trial of my life began. James came home from work the evening of the day the layoff took place, and he told me that in order for him to keep his job, he had to work temporarily at another plant, a job that required him to travel some through the week. The job would consist of troubleshooting in other plants, whatever that meant. Remembering how Mother and I had to pack up and follow Daddy, I knew that was something that I didn't want to put my children through. They had made a few friends here. I remembered how that moving had hurt me so. After James and I had a discussion, we decided that he could go alone, since this was only a temporary thing. He assured me that this was a trial run for the company, and if he did well, then the company would receive more contracts and that would create new jobs. This would allow the people who were laid off to be called back to work. If it fell through, then the plant would be forced to go through yet another layoff—or even worse, shut down for good.

I didn't think putting all that stress on James was a good idea, but there were three other men going also, so that made things a little better. I had given my children the bulk of my time anyway, so this would release some of the pressure off me. I would miss having James around every day, but at least I would not feel as guilty having to give him two nights versus seven. I worried about being alone, but I still had Momma. If I wanted adult company, I would just invite her over or go for a visit.

James was doing it for our family, and with the layoff, I just figured he didn't have a choice. I didn't have a choice. It was to start the next week, and he would have to be gone for a few days and then he would return home, only waiting for the next time that he would have to leave.

The night before he left, I had an uneasy feeling. Something I didn't understand had come over me. I knew he was leaving. We had discussed it and we were in agreement. Still, something didn't feel right. I knew he loved me, a so I knew trust wasn't an issue, but there was something that caused me not to sleep, something that made me feel that maybe this was not the greatest decision ever made. I felt like he was leaving, never to return. It was a feeling that I couldn't shake, a feeling that I didn't want to feel.

Getting him packed to leave was the hardest chore of our marriage. The children were sad too, but they knew he was coming back. That made things a little better. I just had a different feeling, and it was too sad to express. James gave me a kiss, a soft kiss, and he wiped the tears from my face. "Victoria, please don't cry," he said. "I love you, and I will return in three days. I will call every day, and you can call me when you feel lonely. This is just something I have to do for the children, for us." That uneasy feeling returned as he drove out the driveway, and that was the first time I asked God for peace. Something was either happening or was about to happen, and I needed to be prepared.

This went on for months and months on end. Fall came, and then the winter months. James was home for our usual traditions, but then he was back on the road again. The children were now young teenagers, thirteen years old to be exact. We were accustomed to James only being home a few days a week; he seemed excited to see us when he came home. Then, after almost a year of happy homecomings, something changed. The year was 2001.

I tried to talk to James about the happenings on his job, but he never said much. Nowadays his stress level was up. He even started drinking openly, something that he tried to hold secret before. I thought the only time he drank was in the shed with Daddy, and since Daddy had passed, I thought that had stopped. After James started talking with his mother again, I felt that he was totally against drinking, but that was just a feeling; now it seemed to be a welcome part of our lives. He would never let the children see him drinking, and as far as I could tell, they never knew; yet he didn't hide the fact from me.

I remembered that he would take a nip or two with my father and he never changed, so his drinking a few beers here and there didn't bother me at first. But then there were times that he would get short with me or the children, only to apologize later. It was a side of him we had never seen before and a side we didn't quite understand. As long as he was still paying bills, I had nothing to worry about, or so I thought. It had been a year and a half since the layoff and James was still going to work, not doing as much traveling as he had done in the past. He would still go for a day or two here and there. I felt we were out of the woods and his stress level should return to normal soon.

I had gotten the kids off to school one day and James off to work when a call came through; it was the bank. The lady on the other end asked if there was any way we could make a payment on our mortgage. This call would put us on a downhill ride; it was a call that I wished I had never taken.

"There must be some kind of mistake," I said. "We don't have a mortgage; our home is paid for."

She read out our address and asked me if this was the residence she was calling. It was. She then asked, "Does James Andrews still reside at this address?" I told her he did. She asked to speak to him, and I told her that he was at work and that I would give him the message. With that, I hung up the phone.

My mind went into overdrive. Mortgage payment? I thought. Something is terribly wrong. There is no way that we owe on our house. James didn't get laid off, he is still working, bills are getting paid. I'm sure James can clear it all up. I will keep my trust with him. I know our house is paid for; James paid for it with the money he got from the sale of Mrs. Andrews's home. It is clearly a mistake, and it can be cleared up. I will find the receipt for the payoff, and I will contact the bank tomorrow. Why would I receive a call like this? How could they make such a mistake? It happens, I am sure, but I thought it could be cleared up as soon as I told James what was needed.

James came home later than usual that evening; they must be working more overtime, I thought. I finished dinner and helped the children with their homework. It was after dinner and after the dishes had been cleared that James came home. He looked more tired than ever. I knew that they must be working him very hard, so I wouldn't bother him with the bank that evening. I would wait until morning. I felt that it could wait; it was just a misunderstanding that I was sure a phone call would clear up. After the kids went to their rooms, James and I sat on the porch. He had a few beers, and before I got a chance to tell him about the phone call that I received earlier, the phone rang.

It was James's momma. By now, they had a relationship. They had talked on the phone at least once a week since the first time that she called him. James had agreed that she could come for a few days. I knew that he meant only a few; even though they had a relationship, it was only over the phone. This would be the first time he had seen his momma in years. I knew he missed his momma, but he didn't trust her around the children because of her drinking. I guessed since he had picked up her old habit, that didn't seem that important anymore. Even with that thought, I was glad that he had agreed to let her come, because she had never seen the children and they often had questions that I couldn't answer. He said he only let her come because the kids knew right from wrong, and if she did or said anything out of line, they would be able to tell him.

His mother had a bad drinking problem, which is what he experienced when he was a child. I only got bits and pieces. I did know that she spent some time in rehab, but from what I got from my conversation with James, she was better now and had been for some time. I could tell this was something that he didn't want to discuss, nor did he want to remember. I would speak about his mother, and James would change the subject. He would say something like, "Victoria, let's not live in the past. We are heading into the future; let the past be just that, the past." That was the first time James, and I didn't agree on something.

I figured I could wait until after the visit before I told him about the phone call. It didn't seem that important, not as important as a visit from the woman who created James. Even though I thought James and I were rock-solid after fourteen years of marriage, I still felt a little nervous about meeting his momma. Now I know how James must have felt years ago when he was introduced to my momma and Daddy.

I was a bundle of nerves getting James off to work the next morning; standing at the bus stop was a chore too. James's mother would be there that afternoon, and I had a lot to do. I wanted to make the best impression that I could possibly make. I was wrapped up in my own emotions, so I didn't remember James saying much before he left for work. I guess he was a little nervous too. I was nervous yet excited. Even though James was stressing lately for whatever reason, the visit from his momma would be good for him, especially when she proved that she was finally sober.

I was sitting on the porch when she pulled up into the driveway. My first thought was that she and my mother were as different as night and day. She was an older woman in her late fifties or early sixties, I guessed. She wore a tank top and a pair of shorts, which my mom wouldn't dream of wearing in her younger years, let alone in her late fifties. Her face was painted up with way too much makeup for her age, and her nails were done. Even though she looked a little worn, you could tell she hadn't let grass grow under her feet. She had been on the move. Time had not stayed still in her life. By the way she dressed, she definitely kept up with the times. I had to laugh to myself. I was the total opposite of her too, and maybe that was why James chose me.

I went to meet her in the driveway to help with her bag. She was only staying two days, but by the luggage and the packages she had with her, you would have thought she was moving in. She had four suitcases and three bags stuffed with items that looked to be brand-new. "Ms. Robertson, hi, I'm Victoria, James's wife. I am so glad you could come," I said, trying to convince her that she was welcome.

"Hello, Victoria, I have waited so long to meet you," she said, looking me up and down. "You're an attractive girl, aren't you? Well, James never ceases to amaze me. I always thought he would be a whoremonger like his daddy, but from the looks of you, I can tell that you are the one who made him into a man, a man who has pride, the kind that his daddy always thought he had."

Walking up the steps to our porch, she stopped and gave me a second look. "Well, I must say James has done pretty well for himself. It's no wonder he didn't keep in touch with me. I guess he thought a loser momma like me would ruin it for him."

Once in the house, Ms. Robertson asked for something to drink. That made me nervous because I knew James kept a six-pack of beer hidden in the drawer of the refrigerator. I didn't want James to come home finding his mother a drunken mess, so I said, "Soda, tea, or water perhaps?" I walked swiftly, a little too swiftly, and passed her, as if to say don't look into my fridge. I saw the non-approving look on her face, which made me ease away from the fridge as if I was correcting an error.

"Tea, Victoria," she said as if she was a little irritated with my actions. I was thinking alcohol; she was thinking tea. I must find her out for myself; I knew she had a little trouble early on, and that was at the top of my head. I think she saw the expression on my face, because she immediately told me that she hadn't drunk alcohol in over fifteen years. Feeling a little embarrassed about my question, I told her that was something that she could be proud of, a big accomplishment. James, too, would be pleased.

We sat on the porch and chatted for a few hours before the kids were due to be getting off the bus. They were old enough to walk home now after school. We were on our second pitcher of tea when they came walking up the driveway.

"Oh, my heavenly father," Ms. Robertson said, "are those my grandchildren?" with hurt in her voice. I would say she was probably a little hurt; James wouldn't let her come before now, and she had missed thirteen years of their lives. She had a lot of catching up to do. "Victoria, they are truly a gift from God. Look at how they turned out; you and James must be very proud. Oh, what beautiful children; they are so well-kept. You and James are good parents. You have really taken care of these children."

I guess the children made her think back to the way she raised James. The look on her face showed that she realized it would have been much more rewarding if she had raised James herself, instead of leaving it to Mrs. Andrews.

The children walked up and gave her a welcoming hug. She started crying when Hannah called her Grandma. "Oh," she said, "that is the most beautiful name in the world. I never knew it sounded so good. Let's see if I brought my grandchildren something," she said, getting up and practically running to her luggage. I felt sad for her when I found out that she had brought them gifts from the time they were three years old up until now. She brought Hannah a few baby dolls, as well as Barbie dolls. Brandon had some big-wheel cars, as well as model cars with action figures.

"Even though you are young teenagers now," she said, "I bought them for you, and they are yours." She said she hadn't known if she would ever see her son again, or if he would have children, or if they would be boys or girls, so she bought gifts for both a boy and a girl. She had told me after rehab, she tried desperately to find James. If he had children, she wanted to be prepared, so she started buying gifts for both a girl and a boy, just in case. When she found out that he had twins, she was glad that she did. Just in case she ever got to meet them, she wanted them to know that she thought about them throughout the years. It was a good thing, I thought, because she was prepared for twins.

I left the children alone with her while I prepared dinner for my family. James would be home soon, and I didn't want him to think I was slacking because his mother was there. It was a good evening; once James saw that his mother was sober, it would be even better. Maybe, I thought, that would relieve some of his troubles.

When James came home, he was tired and probably a little nervous. We all ate dinner; he began to loosen up after conversation buzzed around the table.

"So, kids," their grandmother said, "what do you do for fun? Are you into sports?" she said, looking at Brandon. "Cheerleading?" she said, looking at Hannah. With the children just meeting their grandmother and not knowing her, the conversation was left to be simple yes and no answers, but that didn't stop her; she wanted to get to know them, and that was no secret. Their answers didn't seem to bother her a bit; she just kept the conversation going. After dinner, the kids asked to be excused from the table. With permission, they left, and Ms. Robertson followed them with her eyes as they left the room.

When the kids went to do their homework, I cleared the dishes and let James visit with his mother. I heard him ask why she drank so much in the years past. It took seconds of silence before I heard her say that she had been waiting years for that question, and if he had asked earlier, then they could have reunited sooner.

She explained to him that after their father left, she felt she had nothing to help her deal with life and that she turned to alcohol to release some of the pain. "When I found my life in such a mess, I drank to ease the pain, and it did. I know I neglected you but drinking to cover up the pain was all I knew to do. I knew you had your grandma to look after you, and since your father was in his own little world, I knew that the two of you needed each other. She loved you as if you were her own. There were times that I even thought she wanted to pretend that you were your father, just so she could start all over again, hoping to have someone in her life forever, and that she did. Even though you were my son, I didn't know any better. I felt that I had to look after me because at that point in my life, I had no one to look after me. I erased all the memories I had of your father with bottles and bottles of alcohol—that was my escape.

"I will tell you that I am sorry, James. I'm sorry for not being there for you; maybe it was for the best. I could never have done as great a job as your grandma did to raise you. I was so wrapped up in myself that I had forgotten that I even had a son. Once I remembered, it was too late, so I continued drinking until I made myself sick. It was then and only then that I made the decision to seek help, and by then you were grown. I put myself in rehab, and with the grace of God, I stayed there and received the help I needed. But by then you were a grown man, and I never got the chance to see you, nor did I know that Mrs. Andrews had passed away.

"I can't tell you how many sleepless nights after I got better that I wished that I had at least thanked her for doing what I was supposed to do, which was to raise you because you were mine. She did a fine job, and I wish that I had taken the opportunity to do the same. Now that you are a grown man, I see that her teachings fell on you. I see that you too have done a fine job; you have a beautiful family. I want to be a part of your family, James. I want to be a part of you."

James looked down while mumbling something to his mother. I couldn't make out what he said, but I know it brought more tears to her. Whatever he was saying brought pain to her soul. I got a few pieces of his conversation with her, something to the effect that he understood more than she would ever realize. I was trying to listen in. I wanted to hear what was on James's mind, what had been on his heart so heavy, so I decided to join them on the porch. When I got to the door, they were embracing, and both were crying. I felt that I should leave them alone; there was a lot of catching up to do. I felt if he wanted me to join, he would call for me to come outside and be with them. I just backed away without them knowing I was there. I wanted them to have this time together because as a mother I couldn't imagine not being a part of my child's life until he had a family of his own. I sat at the kitchen table, where I could at least hear a part of the conversation but far enough away that I would not disturb them.

I heard James ask about his father. She told him the last she'd heard, he was living in this area, doing well, probably drunk and still whoring around. "It doesn't matter how good he's doing now," she said. "He is still a loser in my book. I don't want any part of him. He ruined my life, and for that I want no part of him." I could tell she held anger in her heart for James's father. Maybe that was why James held his anger in. He probably picked up that trait from her.

The next morning, James showed his mother the Andrews urns, and then he took her to the willow tree to set out fresh flowers. I let them go alone while I prepared for a cookout.

It seemed like she hadn't been with us any time before she was backing out our driveway, traveling the roads to take her home. The kids stood waving, while James held my hand. I was glad for the visit, and I was sad to see her leave. Her last words to us were, "I hope you have me back," and I answered for both of us, "Anytime." Then the dust flew, and she was gone.

It was a memory that we would be glad to share at a later time.

Chapter 20

School was out for the summer, and the children were going to Christian camp for two weeks. It would be their first trip away from home. Needless to say, my nerves were a little scattered. Yet I was excited for them to be able to finally get the opportunity to interact with children outside the eye of their father. Getting the kids ready for their trip was a little hard to do. James was a little overprotective with the children. I would say his childhood played a role in that. He would let kids come over, but he was very reluctant for the children to go visit their friends. He just didn't trust people, and I sometimes felt for the children, but he was their father. Although I had friends growing up, the only true friend I had ever known him to speak of was the one that he married or Mrs. Andrews.

James and I drove the children to school for the ride to camp. They were waving and hollering out the window when the bus pulled out. I was crying, and James was comforting me. I didn't want them to go either, but only because I would miss them, not for the same reasons that James had. But I knew if it was Christian camp, God would watch over them. Deep down, I felt that was the only reason James agreed to let them go. It was hard enough on the children because I didn't want them to do sports for fear they would get hurt, so they didn't ask to do sports and I didn't encourage them. I guess they sensed my feelings. James, on the other hand, didn't want them to hang out with kids for fear something would happen. It was unfair to the children, I felt, but we were learning as we went, and we wanted to be careful. Although sometimes we were too careful, we didn't want to make any mistakes because we didn't have the opportunity, like most parents, to correct our mistakes with the next child. They were all we had or ever would have.

James and I sat on the porch that night, he with his beer and I with my thoughts. I felt a little distant, and he seemed a little distant also. He had something on his mind, and I thought it could have been a number of things—the children, his mother, his job—so I felt it best just to snuggle up and watch the night defeat the day.

I got up early the next morning, earlier than usual. I didn't sleep well because I was missing the children. Before I realized that James was running late for work, I had drunk my morning tea. In the past, I didn't have to wake him up; getting up on his own was a given—he never missed work.

"James," I said, "honey, you are going to be late for work."

"I'm calling in," he yelled back at me. "I just want to spend the day with you."

I could go along with that. It would be nice to have him home with me. We could work in the yard together, or just spend the day in bed. When I first thought we could spend the day in bed, off I went, back to bed with James. He made love to me like we were newlyweds again. It started out as the perfect day. I couldn't help but wonder what the rest of my day would hold for me.

After a few rounds of passionate love, we went back to sleep, only to be awakened by the phone. James got up to get the phone; not wanting to, I soon followed him. He was rather quiet with his phone conversation; he agreed a lot and told the person on the other end that they would hear from him soon. With that, he hung up the phone. I didn't ask who was on the other end; I just assumed it was work or something of that nature.

We went about our day like the phone call never took place. He was a little distant, and I noticed it from a distance, because James acted like he didn't want to be around me. Something about that phone call changed our beautiful day, and my curiosity finally got the best of me.

"James," I said as I went to his side, "what's wrong? You are acting different all of a sudden. Do you want to talk about anything?" That question caused James to start his searching; he was searching my face again as though he had something to say. I could tell there was something on his mind, and yet he said nothing.

Days went by, and James still didn't tell me what was on his mind.

When it was time to get the kids from camp, they were excited to be home. We all went to the park that evening and I could tell that James still had something bothering him. Ever since his mother's visit, he had seemed distant. Had their talk on the porch been so devastating that it took him back to the days with Mrs. Andrews? Was he hurting all over again? Something was wrong, and he had put up a block so I wouldn't know.

It wasn't until August when school started again and I went to wake James and the kids to start their day that James told me that he wouldn't be going into work that day, that when the kids left for school, we had to talk. His tone was one I had never heard from him before, a tone that let me know that troubles were on the way. I hurried the kids off to school, wanting but at the same time not wanting to have this talk with James. I just had a feeling that the happy days had ended, and the trouble days were gearing up to start their season.

James stayed in bed until the kids had left for school. He found his way into the kitchen, grabbed a cup of coffee, and sat down at the table. I eagerly wanted to know what had been bothering him. I sat down across from him; I wanted to see his face, and I wanted him to see mine. I lifted my tea to my mouth, glancing at him, waiting for whatever to fall from his lips. I sat there letting him know that he had my full attention. Whatever it was that had been such a secret, had been serious enough to bring this distance, I wanted him to see my reaction. I had to prepare myself for what was coming next, even though I didn't think I would ever have had enough time to prepare for the words that were going to bring unsought troubles to our lives. I had to bring strength from within to help support my family. I had to bring forth the fight in me to help keep us together.

"Victoria," he said, "I haven't been as truthful to you as you deserve. There is something that I need to tell you, and I needed to tell you a year ago, but I felt like such a failure. I didn't know how to bring myself to tell you of the things I did and didn't do." His voice made goose bumps jump upon me as big as chicken pox. I couldn't imagine James doing anything to hurt the family, to hurt me. I feared what he was going to say next, but I needed to know. He paused long enough for a tear to run down his face. He then got up and turned his back to me. I knew he didn't want me to see him crying, and that was what brought my own tears. If James was crying, then whatever he had to tell me was bad news. He raised his hand to his face as if he was wiping tears, then he turned to me and said, "Remember the layoff?"

I nodded my head yes, my eyes planted on him.

He dropped his head, not being able to make the words come out. "I was in that number," he said. "I got laid off like the rest of them. The job that I told you was for the plant was really with a few, guys, but it had nothing to do with the plant. It was to work construction," he said, now lowering his voice. "I was hoping that the construction job would last longer than it did, but it ended, and I was unemployed. Remember my friend that I told you about who lost everything including his family because he was laid off? Well, my fear was that if you knew, then I would lose you and the children too. I would get up in the mornings and look for work because I didn't want you to worry," he said with sincerity. "I didn't want to worry the kids. I didn't want to keep this from you. I was receiving unemployment; that was the way I was paying the bills while I was looking for work, but it since has run out. This has eaten me alive for months. I didn't know what else to do."

"How did we make it this far, James?" I asked, now concerned from what I was hearing.

"I had unemployment for six months, and then I refinanced the house after my unemployment ran out to keep us going. I was thinking that they would finally call me back to work. Now," he said, searching my face as if he was counting my tears, "we are behind on the house, and the bank is threatening foreclosure. There is no …"

"They want to take our home, James?" I said, cutting his words short, tears now streaming down my face. I tried not to cry, but the tears came with a blast. I could feel the hurtful groans I had tried to keep hidden in my heart take control and seep out. My mouth wanted to yell, but I held back, holding in the hurt that I felt at the present time. James couldn't bear to see me crying; he ended the conversation by getting in his car and leaving. My guess was that he was going to get beer. I wondered if that was what he was telling his mother on the porch. Had he confided in a stranger before confiding in me? I felt my life unraveling at that point. What used to be a happy family was slowly becoming a thing of the past.

An idle mind is indeed the devil's workshop. Things started to get worse once the news about the disclosure rang true. Weeks went by, and the more time went by, the more James seemed to drink and sink further into depression. I think James didn't feel like he was the man anymore. He would always compare himself to my dad and talk about the promise he made to me the day at Mrs. Andrews's graveside. The plant finally shut down, and James considered himself a failure. He criticized more than he loved, and he distanced himself from our family. After I let a few months, pass hoping James would snap out of his depression, things got even worse. Nothing seemed to make him happy, and nothing seemed to make him care. Instead of a few beers, now his drinking doubled.

With no income coming in, I had to resort to welfare, which took a toll on James and his pride. He said the day I received my food stamps that he didn't want the government raising his kids. I understood how James felt, but with no jobs and bills coming every month, what was I to do? Let the bank take the house and lose everything that signified our family? I made arrangements with the bank and applied for welfare the very next day.

James would go look for work, or so he would say, but I was starting to doubt him, because when he came home, I could smell the beer on his breath. He was never dressed for work, and he never left the house until around noontime. How do you approach a situation like this? I was with a man who lived by my daddy's words, who lived by the Bible words, the words that said the man was to be the head and the woman was the helpmate. A man who demanded nothing less than respect, he had deserved it for all those years that had gone by. He had it, and I wouldn't take it from him now. I would not doubt him. I would do everything I could do to make these pages in our once-happy life as painless as possible. The welfare check wasn't much, but it kept us in our home, and the food stamps kept food on the table, with little more to hope for.

I decided that I needed to talk to my momma, gather from her words of wisdom, and keep our love together. Make it strong again. I waited for James and the children to leave for the day, and I called my momma. Momma believed in Daddy's guide to life. It was the guide that James once followed and once believed in. Even though her voice was calm and subtle, she was a strong woman. Since Daddy passed, if anybody knew the answers, it would be her. She could tell me how to deal with this situation, how to move forward.

It always felt good to hear her voice; she spoke in a tone that told me she was sure of herself, choosing her words carefully before she spoke. When I was a teenager, she would say that I was her biggest challenge.

We used to argue sometimes because she said that I always had to have the last word. I did, but there were many times now I wished I had just shut up and listened. I had to learn a lot the hard way because I didn't listen. I was listening now because I didn't have the time or the strength to learn the hard way. My marriage was failing, and I couldn't afford to figure this out on my own. I had to go to a deeper knowledge, someone who had wisdom, and that was my momma.

This gave me the opportunity to look at things for what they really were. My life was now falling apart, and the one person that I should be able to turn to was causing this. As I listened to Momma's words, she told me that I had been on her mind, and she was just praying and waiting for my call. It was as though she knew that I had something on my mind, and she was always willing to help. Momma loved for me to come to her for advice. I think that was one way that she felt needed.

Before I could get out what I was going to say, she said, "Victoria, pray, just ask the Lord to guide you. Ask the Lord to show you what you need to do to get through this. No marriage is perfect, but it's up to you to get the answers from God. You just need to ask for God's grace and peace while he is doing his will. His will is going to be done, and there is no way you can stop it. Everything happens for a reason. Read Corinthians one and two; it will give you guidance. Everything will happen according to his will. Wisdom is what you should look for from God, and strength to endure whatever his plans are. I can't fix this, but God has a purpose for everything. I'm here if you need me, but your extra time right now needs to be with God. Put him first, and the next thing you know, it will all work out. He will give you the courage and the peace you need."

Her words were like music to my soul. At that instant, I felt the peace that she was speaking to me about. I knew my momma had a relationship with God, which the devil knew not to touch. Instantly I felt God's arms wrap around me, and I felt a peace so strong that it brought a sense of joy back into my spirit.

The song that the church choir used to sing came rushing through my mind with such force it brought chills through my body. I couldn't get the words out of my head; it was so powerful. "He may not come when you want him, but he will be there right when you need him. He's never late, always on time." Thinking of that song kept me in good spirits. I knew that God had a will for everybody, and our lives would be according to his will, whether good or bad it would be.

Later that evening, the house was rather quiet. James was watching television and the kids were in their rooms doing what kids do, so I decided to take a little time and spend with God. No time like the present, and I needed him to show favor over my family and be quick about it. I went by my bedside and fell to my knees, and words of prayers just came rushing out of my mouth. "What to do, Lord Jesus, what to do?" I prayed. "Help me find the strength to keep this family going, to keep my family together. I feel weak and I feel that I have no one to turn to. I don't want to involve the children because this could be a passing thing, but I need to understand how something so good could turn and keep turning for the worse. We have gone from a happy family to a family wondering what the next day will bring. Please step in and show me something, so I will know what step to take next." I felt somewhat exhausted after my prayer, and I counted that as praying from my heart. God knew that it was my heart talking. It was up to him to hear it and move on my words.

Chapter 21

The next morning, I had my tea on the porch, and the birds seemed to be singing louder than ever. I knew God had a hand in our future. I just needed him to give me signs that I could understand. I felt that I didn't quite understand a sign from God, and I would mess up his plan for me by doing the wrong thing. I needed at this point for God to treat me like a five-year-old because I didn't have time to mess up.

Since James's news, I went faithfully to the welfare office every six months to renew. James wouldn't take me; I had to drive on my own, and sometimes it took up the whole day. It was usually depressing for me, but once I got there and saw all the other people who were struggling just like we were or worse, I didn't feel so bad. Even though sometimes it took my whole day, it was worth it. We had food, and the state provided us with insurance because James wasn't working and a little check every month to help with our bills. Renewal was coming up again in a few days.

Even though James's drinking was heavy now, it always became heavier on the day I went to the welfare office. He stayed in our room and drank all day long. When I got home, I usually had to raise the window because the smell of alcohol was so strong. It didn't seem to bother James that all he did was just drink and drink and drink. I found myself praying, praying, praying; the more he drank, the more I prayed. I knew that my pride had hit rock-bottom, but in the reality of it all, my pride lay within my family; I really didn't care what other people thought. My family was now in a sense depending on me, and really at the end of the day, weren't they what really mattered?

Since the room was filled with needy people, the welfare office was a bit depressing at this time. Some were needy; some were just there for the ride.

Mr. Wallace was my caseworker. I never looked forward to seeing him. If my mood was good, I could always count on my mood changing after I saw him. He had a stern-looking face. He didn't wear a wedding ring, so I assumed he wasn't married. I remember thinking that I was before a man who really didn't have a family, so he didn't know what my heart was feeling. Every time I went into his office, I felt as though I was borrowing money from him personally. He looked to be in his late thirties, nothing wet behind his ears, not a caring bone in his body. He always made me feel dirty, as if I was just another case. When he spoke to me, I could hear the dominance in his voice. He treated me like I had other options and I was just using the state's money because I was too lazy to find a job on my own. I guess he came from a rich family and never had to understand a struggle, unless it was with a poor kid, whipping his hind parts for being haughty or downright disrespectful. No matter the season, summer or winter, he always had on a suit, and you could tell that it didn't come from a cheap store; it was probably tailor-made.

He had ton of questions, and they were always the same ones. You would think that after two years, he would realize my answers weren't going to change.

"So, Mrs. Andrews," he said in his stern voice, "your family has been leaning on the government for two years now, correct?"

"Yes, sir, that is correct," I replied, trying not to roll my eyes. If it wasn't for feeding my kids, I wouldn't be here; now lean on that, I thought. I was glad he couldn't read my mind.

"Well, after two years, the government requires you or Mr. Andrews to go under a work-study program. That is a program that requires you to either attend school, college, or what have you, or get a job in order to continue receiving benefits. Is Mr. Andrews just not able to work?" he asked, looking at me as he leaned forward against his table, as if he was getting ready to catch me in a lie.

"No," I said almost in a whisper, "not at this time. Although he has looked for work, he hasn't had any luck thus far."

His voice trailed off, and I went into deep thought. There was no way that James was going to want me to work. If I didn't work, I couldn't receive a check. If I didn't receive a check, we would have no food and the bills wouldn't get paid. I didn't realize my thoughts had brought tears until Mr. Wallace nudged me with a tissue.

"Do you understand, Mrs. Andrews? You have approximately two weeks to report back that you have a job and four weeks to produce a pay stub. Now, you will have to report your earnings each month, and your check will be adjusted according to the amount of your earnings. You will receive next month's check, but then after that, you will have to report your earnings on a monthly basis. Do you have any questions?"

"No, sir, I don't," I heard my mouth say. I wanted to give him a piece of my mind and tell him exactly what I thought about him, but that wasn't proper. I decided I would carry my thoughts of him with me, and with that decision, I got up and left the room.

The drive home was quick. I was so deep in my thoughts that I got home quickly. One would have thought that my house was next door to his office. I sat in the car long enough to wipe my face and eliminate the trace of my tears before I entered into the house.

James was home, and the last thing I needed was for him to see me crying. He knew where I had been, and to come home crying would be unheard of. I didn't know what he would do, and I really didn't want to find out. I knew that he would have been drinking, and I didn't want to face that right now. I didn't need that reality hanging over my head along with what Mr. Wallace had told me.

The instant I went into the room, which smelled of alcohol, and saw him sleeping, I became angry at him. I had to immediately wipe those thoughts from my mind; because it wasn't his fault fate had dealt him a bad hand. I had to understand that with such a blow to his life, he was doing the best he could. I would tell him what Mr. Wallace told me; maybe that would hit home to him and make him snap out of whatever he was going through.

I couldn't continue to let this go on. He had to put the beer down and pick the paper up. He had to start being a positive part of this family and making excuses for him was a bit overrated right now. I went to where he was lying on the bed. "James," I said, "we need to talk about some things."

He immediately turned to me, sat up on the bed, and rubbed his head as if to say, "Here it goes."

"I know things have changed in this family," I said, "but there are decisions that need to be made. Mr. Wallace gave us two weeks to find a job, or he is cutting off our welfare. One of us needs to work, and we need to find it right away. I am going to start looking for work tomorrow." Waiting for a reaction, I sat down beside him.

He said nothing. He just looked at me with a sort of blank look, and I could tell that he had been drinking. His reaction was not very surprising, so without saying another word, I just got up and left the room. I could tell my blood pressure was rising, and I was thankful that Hannah and Brandon had gone to the park because I needed their rooms. James and his used beer had crowded mine. I decided to go to Hannah's room and get on my knees and spend a few minutes with God.

Hannah and Brandon, now fifteen, gave their father his space. They would only spend time around him when he approached them; they didn't want to bother him. I knew it was completely obvious to them that something was wrong. I knew the children were sometimes angry at our situation, but most of the time, I think it was sadness for their father. When I thought they were getting angry, I would tell them not to think bad thoughts of their father. "This too shall pass. We will be back to normal; just love him, but at the same time give him space. We will make it. One day you will look back on this and see it wasn't so bad." Was I telling the children that because I believed it was so, or was I merely hoping that my words were true?

Even though the kids were in the prime of their teenage lives, their father's struggles took a toll on them. The love that they had once shared with their father was a love that most children never see now. It seemed to be a love of concern, and I could expect nothing more at this passage in our lives because he never gave them any of his time. I think if he would have given them just a little bit of his time, even if they did know that he drank, they would love him just the same. It was I who was under the microscope all the time. The pressure was on me to keep the family going, and pressure it was.

Disconnect notices would come often, and James finally started leaving them lying around, I guess so I could see. I couldn't understand why he made it a point to show me the bills. Did he want me to realize that he was failing our family and wanted me to make the choice to leave him? Did he want me to get so mad at him for the way that things turned out that I would fall out of love with him, and it would be easier for him to leave me? I didn't know what he was thinking or what he was expecting. Since he wanted nothing to do with the welfare money, I took over the bills. I would have to switch the bills around to keep something from getting turned off. To have the lights or the water turned off, there would be hell to pay, because that wasn't proper. James's pride was getting to be a bit much. It had been instilled in him for years, probably from birth. He wanted his family to be the opposite of what he had as a child, but all the while he was not doing anything to contribute. I could see now that he was following in his mother's footsteps.

Somewhere along the line, James forgot that the bills were due on a monthly basis, yet he expected them to be paid. I didn't dare complain of his drinking; that was what he felt he needed to cope. When he didn't drink, he was unbearable. He would complain about everything. He would be short with his speaking. He was turning into a man I never expected to be in my life. He didn't approve of the welfare, so I thought many times to ask him how he thought he was getting his beer, yet I had more important battles to fight.

My focus couldn't be on James and his problems. I needed a job, and I couldn't wait for him to snap out of his misery before I found one. I would fight that battle once I conquered the most important battle at hand, which was finding a job that could substitute for the welfare that I had been receiving. Thoughts of how he would react and the things that needed to be done flashed up against my brain to the point I became angry at him.

A battle was what I was in; there was so much at stake, and I felt like I was under attack. My children didn't deserve that their father had turned into a drunkard; he had turned his back on his family, and I was tired of him and his beer smell. I wished he would just leave if he couldn't do any better than that. Beer was all he thought about that; it was his out, his refuge. Where was my out, my refuge? I couldn't take much more of this. I just wished he would just go away.

I immediately wiped those thoughts from my mind. I loved him, and he had tried to find work. He didn't drink the expensive beer. He bought the cheapest beer on the market, and when I went to the store, I found myself buying beer for him too. I could be adding to his troubles. I just wanted him to have some type of happiness, even if it was at the expense of mine. I didn't want him drinking; I just thought that was something he needed to help him function. Without it, he slept all the time. He was cranky and very unhappy, which made all of us unhappy. I would buy him beer for a little piece of happiness.

I knew he was under pressure, pressure that even I couldn't understand, but we had to get past that and move on. It was up to me to help pull him through, even though I was the helpmate. I was his better half, and we had to stick together because I loved him so, not the man that he was now but the man that he was before the loss of his job and his drinking. I knew that he needed a job soon, not only for us but for himself. I couldn't force him. There had to be a better way; force or pressure wasn't what he needed right now.

We had a mortgage and a car payment. That didn't seem a concern of James's now; he had his drinking to do. He had to make sure he had his drinking supply, or he just wouldn't function.

If he was in a better mood that evening, with Mr. Wallace's words on my mind, I thought it would be time for me to talk to James about my getting a job. It wouldn't be easy, but this was something that we needed to help with the stress, to help with the bills. I was running out of time. Mr.

Wallace gave me a deadline, and if I didn't make it, I knew our troubles would magnify.

I got on my knees and prayed so hard that the tears swallowed the side of my bed. It was as if God himself again picked me up and walked me to the table, where a newspaper was lying open to want ads. I scanned the paper to see what God was showing me, and there it was in black and white: a job at the pharmacy store.

Sometimes it is easier for a woman to get a job than a man. I had to find a job to take care of these bills. I remembered Ms. Fable at the pharmacy store said if I ever wanted to come back to work, she would hire me. I wondered if the offer still stood. I knew that she now ran the store herself and she had a pharmacist, so maybe she would consider me an asset.

Ms. Fable didn't always come off as a pleasant woman. I would sometimes see her in passing and she would always ask about my family, yet she was all about business. Rumor had it that she had tragedy strike in her life; she had lost her sister and nephew when she was a young woman. There was a fatal car accident that took their lives, so surely, she could understand that different people go through different things. She was the kind of woman who always carried herself with dignity and pride. She was always nice to me. I only knew her for a short while when I worked there because I never went back to work after the children were born. I wished now that I had kept working there and hoped that she didn't bear any hard feelings against me for leaving the pharmacy. I decided before I spoke to James again that I would visit her store.

It was like she had read my mind when I came into the store. I didn't frequent the store, but that was only because I didn't have the money to.

"Victoria," she said, "are you here to get put to work?" That was easy enough, but I had to make sure that she wasn't just teasing me.

"As a matter of fact," I stated as sure of myself as I could be, "I was just about to ask you about the ad that you ran in the paper about needing help in your store."

With a smile that I wasn't expecting, she said, "I was just about to put the sign on the door, but the job is yours if you want it. Now I can't pay much, but it can help you get by. When can you start?"

Everybody in town knew that James was laid off; I knew this because I saw the majority of them at the welfare office. Bad news traveled fast in our little town. Good news was never discussed. I had to take what I could get; maybe that was what she was talking about when she said to "help you get by." I knew that her business had slowed down there weren't any jobs and people weren't buying things like they had the past years they couldn't afford it. She had since sold the pharmacy and she was the only one running her store. "Well, I have to talk it over with James. Can I let you know tomorrow?" I said, trying to keep my pride intact, because that was what James would have expected me to do. "Will that be, okay?"

"That will be fine," she said. "I will hold it for you. Just let me know within the next day or so."

I left the store feeling positive, but at the same time, wondering if she knew about my welfare visits. Bad news seems to travel fast.

Cooking dinner that evening was a chore. I had a lot running through my mind. At the same time. I knew I had to speak with James about my job. I didn't know how to approach him, but I knew behind all the troubles with the drinking, he was a kind man and he loved us. The only thing I was worried about was his pride. Yet I was feeling, and from what I had seen in the last couple of years, his pride lay in his drinking. In the beginning of our relationship, James wanted me to be a well-kept woman. I didn't think he would be equally as satisfied being a well-kept man. I didn't know what he would think was worse: being on welfare or me finding work. I would have to speak to him. I thought I would speak to him when the smell of alcohol wasn't present.

After dinner, I felt James was distant. He looked like he had a lot on his mind, but I had a lot on my mind too. There was no sense of neither of us sleeping that night. He had his beer as his sedative. If I didn't talk to him, it would be I who had the sleepless night. Before I decided to speak to him, I thought he had had one or two beers, but he was trying to hide that fact.

As the evening wore on, I decided that I had better get this off my chest. I knew it wouldn't be long before James would go out for the evening, so I thought better two beers than six. At that point, I thought it was a good opportunity to ask him about the pharmacy store. I didn't know how to approach him, but I knew this was as good a time as any, and I knew that I couldn't keep Ms. Fable waiting because that wouldn't be fair to her.

"Honey," I started, trying to sound positive and excited, "Ms. Fable offered me a job today. I have been thinking on it. What do you think?"

Silence filled the room for what seemed to me as forever, so I continued on. "We don't have any money saved, and jobs are few with the economy and all. I think before we lose the house and everything that you have worked for, I should try to get a job. Women do it every day. It would be good to have money coming in—no more welfare—and it will just be temporary. Is that something you think I might be able to do?"

"Vicky, it isn't proper for a woman to work and keep a man. I know right now times are hard. I know finding a job isn't easy, but I don't think I could stand you working and me staying home. How would it look for you to be taking care of my family? That is what a man is supposed to do."

My first impulse was to say, "That is right, James, and you are not doing that right now," but James spoke so low, I could barely hear him. He was hurt, and I could feel it. I didn't know at that point what to do or say. I just prayed for the Lord to guide my words. "That is what you have done, James, but the good Lord also knows that work isn't easy for you right now, and I have the opportunity to help my family. I feel that is the proper thing to do."

Silence filled the room again. It was as though James was struggling, trying to get his words out. He was struggling to speak. He was hurting and I knew it, but we needed an income, and I was able to help and that to me seemed like the best thing for us at the time.

Finally, James said, "I can't allow my family to suffer because I can't find work, I just wish there was another way. I just wish that I could provide for my family and be the man that I used to be."

"Not having a job," I broke in, "doesn't make you less of a man, especially if you are willing to work and can't find a job. It makes you less of a man when you don't care. I know what kind of man you are, James. I know that if you could, you would. You have always provided for this family, and you will again. Just let me do this for us. In time, when the economy picks up, you will find a job. You will be able to provide for us again and I will quit working. In the meantime, I will work at the pharmacy store just to keep things going."

James stood up as if he was going to leave the room, but as a second thought, he turned around, and it looked as if the color had drained from his face. "I have failed this family," he said, "and I don't know what road I need to take to get it back. It seems," he said, eyes now filling with tears, "that every road I seem to take is a dead-end."

I got up off the bed and went to him. I had never seen him in this light since we were sixteen, the day we broke up years ago. Chills ran down my spine. It was as if God was telling me something. I knew James needed help that I couldn't give him. Trying to reassure him, I said, "You didn't fail anyone, James. You are just going through a tough time. It will pass. You have to want it to pass; you have to beat this thing."

I grabbed him by his arms, and this time it was me who was searching, trying to figure out exactly what was on his mind. "We are a family. My circle consists of you and the children, and when you can't support us, then I can. That is the way life is. That is why God gives us another person to be the helpmate. I will help us get through this, and we will one day look back on this and realize it's not so bad, but we both have to be strong; I can't be strong by myself. I need you to be the man you were before you lost your job. I need that man back, and you can do it, but you've got to really want to."

While I was talking to him, he seemed like he didn't want to make eye contact with me. He was looking up, as if he was talking to God or looking to him for answers, so I continued on. I thought that the breakthrough was finally coming. I could tell that James was hurting and that hurt me too, but even though tears were trying to break through my eyelids, I refused them. I didn't want James to see me cry at that point. He needed to see that where he was weak, I was strong and I could do this for him, for us, for our family.

With that conversation, James and I returned to the bed. He didn't go out like I had originally thought, or he had originally planned. It was time to bed down, and right now he needed to be held. I positioned myself to hold him, and with prayers in my heart, we fell asleep. We both moved about, not being able to get comfortable. Not much sleep occurred. We will get through this with prayers, I kept thinking.

As soon as my foot hit the floor in the morning, I called Ms. Fable. She seemed pleased that I had taken the job. That made me a little more comfortable. I told her I would be able to start right away, and that was fine with her. I had two years with James not working and drinking. Not only was I now able to have money coming in without the extreme help of welfare, but I would have an out for myself. I would have a breather from James and all the sadness that this sickness had brought me, so now I had to step it up and focus on keeping our lives on the level.

James left early that morning. He didn't say much, but I guessed he was looking for work. Soon after I told him I'd accepted the job from Ms. Fable, he put on his work clothes and headed out the door.

It was almost dark when James came home. I was waiting on the porch for him. I had kept his supper hot, and when the kids questioned where he was, I told them that he had evening shift interviews for work. I never would have told them that I thought he was out drinking, because they didn't need to know that.

I didn't want them to know the troubles their dad and I were facing. I was so glad that they had already gone to their rooms when James returned home drunk. I quickly put him to bed and sprayed the house so they couldn't smell the lingering smell of alcohol. He was asleep as soon as his head hit the pillow. It was so sad to see my James like this. I could only keep praying that he found a job, that God had mercy on my family.

Sleep was a little more than impossible for me, with the alcohol, the pain that filled the air, and the hurt I was feeling for myself, for my family, and for James.

I was excited to tell the children about the job even though I didn't know what their reaction would be. I knew that they would much rather have me home instead of their father, but they were at the age now that they spent most of their free time at the park with the other children. James didn't seem to care, and I knew that without me being home, they would spend even more time with their friends. James was not the best company now, and I knew they needed an out to all this change of life. They had gone with the flow, and they had not asked any questions thus far. That was the way they were taught, and I was glad about that.

They knew grown-folk business was just that: grown-folk business and they shouldn't interfere. They knew something was going on with their dad, but they didn't ask, and I didn't tell them. I wasn't going to lie to my children, but I wasn't going to burden them with our troubles either. I would just have to pick up the slack and try to make their lives as normal as possible. At their tender age of fifteen, they had adolescent things to worry about; the last thing they needed was our problems added. James was always in bed when they got up, and they were in bed when he got home. So I just prayed that they didn't know.

Brandon was the one I was most concerned about. I could tell he missed his father, and so did I. Walking into Hannah's room and finding both of them together seemed like the perfect opportunity to give my news. I just started the conversation up and hoped they would be as excited as I was.

I had to let them see my presence. Even though they were in the same room, they were in their own little world. Brandon had on his earphones listening to music, and Hannah was engulfed in her computer. I guess twins like the feeling of closeness, but at the same time, need their space.

"Hey," I said, grabbing Brandon on his leg to get his attention. My voice prompted Hannah to swing around and notice my presence. "I got some wonderful news today." No one spoke a word; they just looked at me, wanting me to go on. "I got a job," I said, hoping for hugs and smothering kisses.

Brandon's reaction surprised me. He looked at Hannah before he spoke, and the irritation filled the room. "That's great, Mom," he said. "That is good news. Funny, though. I was thinking about doing the same thing, you know, to help out around here. When is Dad going to think about doing the same?"

His words cut me like a broken glass bottle.

"Brandon," Hannah said, "just be glad that Momma has this job. Be glad that she is doing what she wants to do."

Looking as if he wanted to tell her to leave the room, he turned back to me and said, "Is that what you want to do, Mom, or is that what you have to do? There is a difference, Hannah," he said. "I mean," he continued on, "I see Dad is doing what he wants to do, which is nothing." I couldn't say a word. I could only see that this little boy was finally growing up. He never voiced his opinion on his father before. This was a real moment. This showed me that even though I was the one pretending that we were a happy family, all along my children knew that there was more going on than what I was showing them or at least trying to hide from them. Brandon too was hurting, and this was the first time he ever really showed it. I guess you get what you ask for. Should I break it down for them, that it was a sickness, a disease, or should I just keep praying that he would soon change, and it would all be a bad memory, one that I would hope they would forget? I had never lied to them, and I couldn't start now.

"Brandon, this is something that I want to do. I know your father is not what he used to be, but we are still a family and one day, once he's better, it won't seem so bad. You guys are growing fast, and now that you are in high school, there are things you are going to want to do. We have to plan for those things. Please, don't feel 'against' your father. He is battling all on his own, and the last thing he needs, in spite of how you really feel, is to know that you are angry with him. Just please look past his battle and see his needs. What his needs are is for his family to love him in spite of what they see. You have been to church with your grandma, and you know what prayer can do. Just pray for him."

"She is right, Brandon," Hannah said. "I pray all the time. I know that God will fix this."

Another wake-up call; listening to Hannah showed me that she too had matured, and I was a little downhearted to know that somewhere during my own self-pity and sadness from James, I missed this transition. "Momma, you may not know this, but I have been learning a lot by going to church. There is a lot that I have wanted to share with you, Momma, about what I have learned from Grandma, but I remember how when Grandma would ask you to go with her, it bothered you because you weren't ready. I made this decision on staying in church on my own, and whenever you are ready, you are welcome to join us."

She gave me a wink and continued on. "Pastor Clark said that things happen for a reason, that our time is not God's time. He says that everybody goes through trials and tribulations for God to use them. He says count it a blessing to go through a life's storm, because God is shaping and molding you, he says, and I know that Daddy is not what we are used to, but I count it a blessing and I trust in God that he will bring us through this. I read the book of Job, and I see what could happen and what God allows. I am not going to doubt the Bible, because that is the oldest book around and it never changes."

I could not believe my ears. My daughter was teaching me what I should have been teaching her. She had taken her sadness and turned it into strength. She was doing what I was supposed to be doing, and how bittersweet that was.

"Brandon will be all right," I heard her say as I tuned back into her voice. "He is angry, but he will be all right. He needs to pray and ask God for peace. You go to work, and you do whatever you have to do, Momma, and keep God first and see what happens. Next year when you and Daddy get me ready for my school activities because you worked to make it happen, remember this conversation when everything is better for our family because all things work together for the good," she said. "Smiling brother can sit home and remember this conversation too," she ended with a giggle. He threw her pillow at her, and we ended that meeting in a group hug.

Working at the pharmacy store was a good experience for me. It had been years since I'd worked. It was a challenge, and it took my mind off my troubles. I wanted to do a good job for Ms. Fable, because it was, she that gave me the opportunity to help my family. She would come by throughout the day to see if everything was okay. She would stop if we weren't busy, and we would chat for a minute. I enjoyed my job, and it seemed like things were finally looking up. James wasn't happy, but I just figured that in time, he too would adjust to me working.

Chapter 22

Winter had set in. Snow was on the ground, and it was cold on the outside of the house as well as the inside. The light bill had tripled. It was taking every penny I made just to keep up. I was not getting a check from welfare since they had made the adjustments. James, of course, was warm. He had his alcohol to keep him warm. He stayed to himself more than ever before, and we were all now functioning the best we knew how.

Waking up the next morning was a chore. I immediately took a shower upon waking up. I felt as though the alcohol that sifted through James's teeth and body had stained my clothes. I didn't want the kids to smell it. I didn't want to smell it any longer than I had to.

When James woke up one morning, he grabbed the paper, looked it over, and headed out the door. My prayers followed him: "Please, please, Lord, let that man find work today. If he keeps this up, it will kill him. It will kill me."

I worked around the house and prayed all day. Something had to give, and something had to come through for my family.

A week before Thanksgiving, I decided to cook James's favorite meal, hoping I could strike up a new beginning before Thanksgiving so we could all be thankful for something. I was hoping he would snap out of the depression that he had allowed to come over him. I cooked fried potatoes, pork chops smothered in onions, corn on the cob, and fresh rolls. They weren't my mother's rolls, but I had watched her make them enough that they would serve their purpose. I felt that would make him happy, that it would make him feel better.

I found myself on the porch again; I took a blanket and some warm tea with me to the porch, to keep me warm so I could wait for James to return home. The kids going to bed while I waited on James to come home had become an everyday routine. I wondered what was going through their minds. I knew at some point I had to talk to the children about what was going on. I couldn't keep them in the dark forever.

James came rolling in about one thirty in the morning, I had already bedded down; I realized his time to come home was later and later and he came home drunker and drunker. It seemed like he was falling into a deeper depression, a depression I never knew, a depression I hoped I would never come to know.

I awoke the next day to tea in bed, served by a very handsome man all dressed up to find a job, with a smile on his face. At first, I thought I was dreaming, because I hadn't slept well the night before, tossing and turning. I couldn't get used to going to bed alone and tossing and turning; it was hard when you have spent years going to bed together. Being alone in the bed takes a lot of getting used to. I was having flashbacks of when James was supposed to be working out of town, only to find he'd been lying about the work he was doing. I couldn't help but wonder what he was doing these days while he laid out drunk. Days went by with James leaving to find work only to come home drunk.

At two thirty last night, I heard him stumble into the bedroom, breathing like he had run a race, and covered by the smell, oh God, the smell of used beer, used liquor. I wasn't familiar with that smell, and it was dreadful. He slid in beside me like he had before, and he shaped his body with mine, but the smell, oh, the smell was stomach turning. I lay there as long as I could, hoping that he would fall asleep. Then he started to talk, a talk I never knew, a sound from him I'd never heard, and it only made the alcohol smell singe my hair and magnify.

"I love you, Victoria, I love you so much," he said, struggling to make sense with his words. "I am not the man I used to be. I feel myself slipping further and further away. I'm not even half the man I used to be. I feel I am no longer the man you need."

"Stop that nonsense talking, James," I said before he could finish. "Go to sleep, and we will talk in the morning. That is just alcohol talking."

"No, no, no, no," he said. "We need to talk now, while I have my nerve up."

"James, please," I said, managing to talk through the smell of his breath sliding down my back and flashing around to my face, "go to sleep. We will talk as soon as I get home tomorrow evening."

Silence filled the room for about two minutes, and then he said, "Shoo don't vaunt to talk to me."

At that point, I got out of bed, not knowing if it was disgust from the smell or pain for him; but I got out of bed, turned on the light, went to the edge of the bed, and rubbed him. I felt like his mother at that point, and I didn't want to wake the kids. I felt as though I was outside of my body. I was a mother to him, not his wife.

"Go to sleep; it will be okay in the morning. Tomorrow is a new day. Things are going to work out. Things are going to be just fine. You can go get a job. I feel that you will find jobs soon; just keep trying. You're just aggravated right now; stress is a bit overwhelming, shhh. It's okay. We are going to be fine; everything is going to be okay."

That point was the start of the worst night of our unity together. I felt that all he needed was to sleep off his drunkenness. I felt as though something more was happening. Tears were rolling down James's face as if he knew it was ending, as if he thought that our love was failing us. James was absolutely pitiful at first; then something got in him, and he was angry, he was mad that fate had dealt us this hand. The main problem with that was his anger wasn't shown toward fate; it was shown toward me.

"What's the matter?" he shouted. "You think I'm not the man no more. You are going to leave me, aren't you? You made a promise to God, a promise, Victoria," he said as if he was trying to make me remember. "What about the promise, Victoria? What about what you said?"

He was talking so fast he wouldn't give me the chance to respond to his questions. I don't think he wanted me to respond. He had things he wanted to say, things he needed to say, and I was going to let him have his say. This told me what he had bottled up on the inside. I felt it was good for him to get it out. I couldn't talk to him at that point; I could only listen.

"Did you forget, Victoria, did you? You think I'm weak, don't you? You think I'm weak because I drink. Well, I am a man; I will always be a man. We are a family; we will always be a family."

He kept on and on until it got downright scary. I had never seen this side of him, and the anger that he had bottled up inside of him was finally coming out. It might have been a good thing, but he was scaring me. I didn't know where this was heading. I didn't want to find out.

"James, you're scaring me. Please stop—the children," I shouted, but he kept on and on. At that point, the way I felt, the way I thought, didn't matter to him. How long had he held this anger in, and why was it toward me? His anger was so wild that it could have turned violent. Being a family, even our children, didn't seem to have any leverage at that point. I was looking into a stranger's eyes. The pain was so much that I decided at that point I needed to leave his presence; I would let him calm down, and later return when he was asleep.

That was a big mistake, because when I got up to leave, he grabbed my arm, led me to the light, and then led me back into the bed. He then reshaped his body with mine and held me until I could barely breathe. His hold was so tight that I completely forgot about the smell, and within minutes he was asleep. It was then that I felt that our love was ending, as if the love that I once knew was dying. It wasn't until he released his hold that I realized that the smell wasn't gone; it had just faded because of my fear. Once he was asleep, the fear eased up, and the smell came back.

Now I was waking up the morning after, in bed alone, but at least James was in a much better mood. He was fully dressed, and he seemed happy. I didn't understand why, but did it really matter, as long as we were getting back to normal? I didn't bring up the night before, and he didn't either. I probably won't bring it up; I hope he doesn't either. Maybe that was all he needed—to get it off his chest.

I rustled around as best I could to get him off to look for a job. He left the house like he normally would. We gave each other a big hug, and he kissed my lips repeatedly, softly like he always had.

Was I so overwhelmed with his drinking that I dreamed of him forcefully putting me in bed, holding me with fear, crying like a newborn baby—was it all a dream? Confusion filled my mind. I didn't know whether to laugh or cry, but when I looked down at my arm, I could see the faint bruise that was left from James's hold. In that instant, I knew it wasn't a dream. It was real, it had happened, and I didn't know why. Why was he acting like his old self this morning, and would this sad, depressed, angry person return? The thought of it took my breath away.

James left early that morning, and I took a short shift at the pharmacy store for extra money. When I got home, the children said that their father had been there but left again. It seemed like James was gone for days, but he was only gone for hours. The sun had finally bid farewell and the lightning bugs were starting to gather in the yard. I counted every minute, every second, every hour, praying, praying that James would come home with the news that he had found a job. When he finally returned, I would have sworn that it wasn't beer on his breath but liquor.

When he got into bed, the smell made me nauseated, but James started his talking again. It seemed that the only time we talked anymore was in the bed once he got liquored up. If he didn't have alcohol in him, he had nothing to say. They say that when you are drunk, you speak your sober thoughts. Was he going to give me a repeat of the previous night? This time, would his force be stronger?

At first, I pretended that I was asleep, hoping that he would go to sleep too, but that didn't work. He nudged me in my back until I responded.

"Victoria are you awake?" he kept repeating until I answered. His speech was slurred, and his breath reeked. "Hey, hey, Victoria, I need to talk to you."

"Yes, James," I said, praying he would be silent.

"I'm sick," he said. At first, I thought he meant that he was going to get sick in our bed. I intermediately jumped up and put the trash can beside the bed. The last thing I needed was to have to clean up after his drunken night.

I turned the light on, and I saw tears streaming down his face. "No, not now," he said. "All the time I'm sick, and I can't get better. I don't want to drink, but I need to drink. It's killing me, and it's killing my family. Please, Victoria, help me. Help me be the man I used to be, or I will die. I have these thoughts all the time of death. Maybe I would be better off; maybe my family would be better off. I'm scared, Victoria. Please, help me. There is a family curse that is now upon me, and I don't know how to fight it. I don't know how to get past it."

I couldn't help but cry too. He wasn't fighting anymore. It was as though he was claiming his family curse; it was as though he felt defeated. The pain I saw in his face was surreal. I felt so helpless at that moment. The smell of alcohol was very strong. The smell of alcohol was as strong as ever, but it went away long enough for me to hold him. I took him in my arms, and he cried like a newborn baby. It was then that I honestly felt that he was reaching out to me.

"I will find you help, James," I whispered through my own tears. "I will make an appointment for you, and I will get you help."

"Thank you, Victoria." His voice was so humble. "Thank you for not giving up on me. If you give up on me, what will I have? Please don't hate me; I hate myself enough for the both of us." With those words, he lay back down and went to sleep.

I waited until he was asleep, and I went for the phone book. I had no time to waste; I didn't want to give him time to change his mind. After looking through the phone book and finding a doctor that accepted Medicaid, I felt content with Dr. Graves. I marked her name and address down and put it on our dresser. I would call her first thing in the morning. There wasn't any time to waste.

The smell of alcohol filled the room, but surprisingly enough, I slept through the night. I didn't know if it was the feeling of relief that finally James was going to get help or if I was drunk from the smell of his alcohol. I didn't care what the reason was; I had sleep that was long overdue, and it felt really good.

James was depressed in the morning, but I was going to fix that. It was just a matter of time before he would be his old self again. I hurried the kids off to school and made the call to Dr. T Graves's office. I made the call-in front of James, so he would know that even if it had been the alcohol talking, I was going to follow through and get him some help.

Once I got off the phone with Dr. Graves's receptionist, I looked at James, and tears were streaming down his face. I knew he was hurting, but this was the only way. I knew he hated doctors—he didn't believe in them—but he needed help that I couldn't provide. I don't doubt God's work, but sometimes you have to use common sense. The doctor just might be God's will.

"Doctor Graves can see you this afternoon, James," I said, hanging up the phone, "and I will go with you. I'm sure once you see her, she will give you some medication, and it will all be better."

James's tears stopped, and he seemed angry. "I will go, but I don't want any medication. I just want to talk to someone about my troubles. I don't want to put the burden on you any longer, but I will not take medication."

"I know you don't like medication, but sometimes it's needed to help us feel better about situations, about ourselves. Just try it, and if it doesn't work, then don't take it." With that, I left the room before an argument started. My mind was too tired to argue; that was something we never did until these days. It was too exhausting, and I had to keep my strength up for the doctor's visit.

I called work and took the day off to take James to his doctor's visit. I really couldn't afford to do that, but one day of work compared to James getting help didn't seem that important. James was silent on the way to the doctor's, and I didn't speak either. I knew he had a lot on his mind, and I did too, but my thoughts were happy ones. Things would get back to normal, and we could put this all behind us.

We sat in the doctor's office for what seemed like hours. I filled out the paperwork for James. He could read and write, but I wanted to make this as painless for him as I could. I didn't want this visit to seem like a chore to him. The less he had to do, the better. I thought a time or two that James was going to get up and leave. Just when he stood up and my thoughts were that he was really leaving, the nurse came to the door and called his name. "Thank you, Jesus" was all I could say at that point.

"Mrs. Andrews, you may come in for the initial visit, but the doctor would like to spend time alone with Mr. Andrews." Her words cut me like a knife. I wanted to be in there for the whole visit because I wanted to know, wanted to hear, what James had been feeling. I also wanted to make sure he told her about his drinking. I had to respect the doctor's wishes, though, because after all, she was going to help him. Whatever she needed to pull him out of this, I was willing to give her.

After James was weighed in, the nurse just asked him general questions. I was careful not to answer for him, because I thought she would make me go sit in the waiting room. She just asked his age, date of birth, and reason for the visit. That was when James looked at me, and I spoke for him: "depression." That was all I said; he could get into the whys and how's with the doctor. After a few more general questions, the nurse left and told us the doctor would be in soon.

James looked nervous, but as long as he had gone this far, I felt he was going to be okay. It wasn't long before the doctor entered the room. She was a pretty woman. She had long strawberry blond hair, and I would say she was in her late thirties or early forties. She had a warming smile and a soft voice. I was pleased when I saw her. I didn't want a male doctor for James because I didn't think he would want to tell a successful man his troubles. A woman was different; he wouldn't feel as intimidated.

"Hello, Mr. Andrews, I am glad you came in. I will do everything medically possible to help you with your situation. Mrs. Andrews, I will need you to leave me with Mr. Andrews, so I can get a real feel of what's going on with him. If he chooses, we can recap with you once our session is over."

Her words were from a woman who knew what she was doing. She was professional and she seemed sure of herself; if anybody could pull James out of this, it would be her. I didn't know what to say in response; I just kissed James on his cheek and left the room.

The wait seemed like hours. Finally, James came through the door carrying two pieces of paper. The doctor told him to check back with her next month once the medication had time to go through his system. I didn't know what the prescriptions were or what the diagnosis was. I guess the doctor felt that James would tell me if he wanted me to know. She was private when it came to James. I guess I had to respect that he was her patient; even though he was my husband, that didn't seem to matter. Confidentiality is just that. She told the receptionist to set him up with an appointment for the next month, and with those words, she was gone.

I felt cheated she didn't recap with me. I didn't even know what he told her. I became a little angry, and I think James knew it too. He didn't say one word on the way home, and that just sparked the fire burning inside of me.

Once we got home, I asked James if he wanted to talk about his visit with the doctor. He said there wasn't anything to talk about. He said I knew he was sick, so what else was there to say? I didn't feel comfortable with his distance, but I could only hope that God was in the middle of this. James headed back out. He said he was going to get the prescriptions filled. I decided to give him the benefit of the doubt, even though my heart was telling me different. My heart was right. Even though when he came home, he had the tiny bottle that held his prescription, he had also been drinking.

Thanksgiving came way too quickly this year. It went just as fast as it came. Momma came for dinner, but she didn't stay long. She knew we were going through something, and I could tell that she too was saddened by James's demeanor. She didn't let on like she knew the situation because she wasn't one to stick her nose where it didn't belong. She spoke to James as she always had; and when he didn't respond, she just sort of shrugged it off and continued talking as if she hadn't noticed a thing.

Ms. Fable gave me Thanksgiving dinner on credit. That way we could celebrate with a feast. She said she would take ten dollars out of my pay each week until I paid it back. I was glad that she allowed me to pay it back through my paycheck, because of the waybills were pouring in. It would have been hard for me to pay it back any other way, and I didn't want to let her down.

Hannah, as always, helped me prepare the feast, and we got to spend quality time together. James spent most of the day in bed, but he managed to get up to watch the football game with Brandon. That was a tradition that never failed. Brandon always chose the opposite team from Dallas, which was James's favorite team, and they would compete with each other throughout the game. Then we would sit at the table, and James would lead us in prayer and cut the turkey. For the duration of our meal, Hannah and I would have to hear them discuss the game. They discussed who cheated at what play and why the other team lost or won. That was the same tradition that James and my dad had, and I was sure Brandon would carry it on to his son as well.

After a while we learned to deal with it and kind of looked forward to it. This year, they watched the game, but James wasn't very challenging; he didn't feel up to leading us in prayer or cutting the turkey. He ate only enough to fill up a baby. Even though Brandon tried to keep the dinner-table tradition going, it seemed like it was a struggle for James to even be there. He seemed distant, and his answers were short, either yes or no. There was no conversation coming from him at all. One minute when one of the children would say something, he would look at him or her as if he was going to respond; and then it was as if he thought against his thoughts, and he just continued eating. If Brandon made a joke about the game, James would just agree quietly.

Seeing that the children were feeling down after about thirty minutes of noncommunication from their father, Momma looked at me and then said, "I have a family tradition that we used to do when your mother was a young girl. We would each go around the table and tell what we were thankful for. I will start," she said. "I, Rebecca Adams, am thankful for another day that the Lord has made. Let us rejoice and be thankful for this day. I am thankful that God has given me grace and peace, that I have a wonderful daughter and son-in-law, two amazing grandchildren, and a God that counts me worthy enough to serve him. Victoria, your turn."

She looked at me and I said, "I, Victoria Andrews, am thankful that I have two wonderful children. I have a great husband, and I am so very thankful for my family." Looking at Hannah, I prompted her to go next.

"I, Hannah Andrews, am thankful for my family and for the love that we share." She stopped long enough to look at her father, and then she continued, "I am thankful to just have a family. Most kids don't have a mother and a father. Brandon," she said, looking at him.

He looked at his father, I could see anger whaling up in his face like a shark going after his prey, and he said, "I am thankful for Momma, who keeps us going as a family. I am thankful for Hannah for being my better half," he said, barely smiling, almost in tears. "I am thankful for my grandma," he said, again looking at his father in advance, "and one day I will be thankful for having my father back the way he used to be." With that he got up and left the table.

James just sat there. Hannah did not want her father to go without saying something; it was like she needed him to be thankful for his family. "Daddy," she said, "what are you thankful for?"

In that moment, James glanced at her and then at me, and then he said, "I, James Andrews, am thankful that my family haven't given up on me. I, James Andrews, love my family, and I want what we had. I am angry for what has happened, and I hope that, whatever the future holds for me, my family will forgive me." After those words, James got up from the table and went back into our room.

Needless to say, at that time, dinner was over. Momma and Hannah helped me clear the table. Washing the dishes, in a soft voice that I could barely hear, Hannah asked, "Momma, what's wrong with Daddy?" My first impulse was to ignore the question, hoping she wouldn't ask again, because I really didn't want to answer; but I couldn't bear making her repeat it. I had to face it, and she had a right to know. Momma excused herself and went to check on Brandon while I spoke about our problem to Hannah.

"What you are seeing from your father, Hannah, is a case of depression. It comes along when the stress is too much to bear. It doesn't mean that he loves us any less; it just means that he doesn't know how to cope with what he's going through, so he says nothing or as little as possible. I know it's hard for you and Brandon, and I understand. I just hope you and Brandon understand it's nothing we did. It's just something that he's going through, and we just have to, as hard as it may become, we just have to accept it for what it is."

I could see tears forming in her eyes, so I told her that I would finish up if she wanted to be excused. Without another word, she just turned and went to her room. It was far from our traditional Thanksgiving, and I was glad it was over. All kinds of thoughts were in the air, and I was inhaling them with every breath I took.

I was angry at James, although I shouldn't have been. I knew this was hard on him, but I thought he was a stronger man than what he was showing me now. I didn't feel like going into the room and facing this tired-looking, sad man, so I went out on the porch. Moments later, before she left, Momma joined me.

She said, "Victoria, just pray. God has got control of this. I know that it has to be hard for you and the children, and even James for that matter, but for years you have put your trust in James. Now it's time, past time, to put your trust in God. The children are hurting, Victoria, and this is not healthy for them. Brandon is angry and he misses his father. Something has to break through for this family, and it can only be done by the grace of God. I will leave you with that thought. Call me if you need me."

As she pulled out of the driveway, I thought about what she said. She was right. I had put my trust in James, and now I sat wishing I knew what was going on in his mind. Whatever his thoughts, the way James was acting wasn't healthy for him or us.

One week after the children had returned to school after Thanksgiving break, James had left for the day and I had the day off, so I decided to clean our room and do some laundry. While changing the bedsheets, I noticed some wilted, yet not dead, rose petals that were lying within his pillowcase. That told me that he had been to the willow tree. Mrs. Andrews's words came into my mind: "Persevere." Maybe she told those words to James too; maybe that was what he was trying to do. My curiosity at its peak, I decided to look about the room for more clues as to what James was thinking or doing, since the room was where he spent most of his time.

I looked underneath the bed, and there was a half-bottle of liquor and several empty ones. The sight of those bottles hidden behind his shoes angered me. Feeling my blood pressure rising, I looked for his prescription to see exactly what it was that he was taking while he was drinking. I found his medication in the bottom drawer. It was Prozac, prescribed for depression. I remembered that drug when I used to work in the pharmacy part of the store, and that was the drug of choice for depression. I counted the pills. It had been two weeks since his doctor's visit, so at least fourteen pills should have been missing. Only one had been taken.

Was he even going to try? I thought as I closed the bottle of pills and carefully placed them back in the drawer. He needed to take the medication that Dr. Graves prescribed for him. The medication was the only thing that would help him through this. I decided to have another conversation with James. He had to want to get better, and that meant taking his medicine. If he did not want to get better, then what was the point of putting the family through this? I entertained those thoughts for the rest of the morning. I managed to get the rest of the house cleaning done, the laundry and make dinner before the children arrived home from school. My thoughts consumed with my findings of the day I wasn't much company for the children although I tried to conversate and act normal not knowing anymore what normal was. After a semi quiet dinner, they went to their rooms within minutes I heard Brandon's music playing so before I entered into my self-pity I checked in. Hannah was on the computer in her room and Brandon was reading a magazine listening to his music. I cleared away the dishes made a pot of tea then went to my usual spot on the porch and before I knew it, the stars had come to sit with me as well as the darkness, so I retired to my room.

It took the reality of it all to smack me in my face. Days had passed, and I still hadn't had that conversation about the medicine with James. When I talked to him, it drained me to the point that I would lose sight of our children and focus on his issues. I had to come to a happy median, because the kids were growing up and I didn't want to miss that in the midst of helping James with his problems.

Late one evening, I felt James was distant; he acted like he had a lot on his mind. At first, we were all sitting in the living room. Conversation was vague with him. He would become engaged, as if he was trying to be a part of the conversation, and then would simply stare at something. One time Brandon acted like he was going to the kitchen, but instead he picked up a pillow and smacked Hannah on the back. That prompted her to jump, and we all laughed. James had a delayed reaction, but he finally laughed too. I think he had had one or two beers, but he was trying to hide the fact that he'd been drinking, so I pretended that I didn't know.

Brandon put his coat on to go outside, and James followed him. I looked through the window to see what they were doing, and I saw them standing beside the willow tree talking. I felt as though Brandon would pull James out of his troubles or at least take his mind off of them.

I left the two alone and put all my focus on Hannah. We talked, I did her hair, and we felt like, just for a moment, that we were a functioning family again, that our lives were getting back to normal.

I know the kids missed their parents. Even though we were in the same house, we were in different worlds. Staying focused on the children had always been important to us, and that was one thing among several others that we were lacking. James was so caught up in his self-pity and I was so caught up in James that we were just going through the motions.

Later that night, we were lying in bed, and James told me that he was proud of our children. He told me that he remembered when he took part in raising them, but he knew that I was raising them now. He told me that he missed the kids' transitions as they were growing up, but he felt that he was only a burden now.

I assured him that he played a big part in raising them and as long as he did what Dr. Graves told him to do that, he would be able to see more than he had missed. In time we would be doing all the things that we originally planned for the children, and this period of trial would become a thing of the past. He kept on talking as if he didn't hear a word I said. He was telling me how he hoped the children didn't think less of him since he didn't have a job. All he wanted in life was to be a provider for his children, and a good man to me. He spoke about the earlier conversation that he and Brandon had. He knew Brandon needed a father figure and he wished he had the energy to be there for him. He felt that the sickness dominated his life, and he didn't know how to control it. He said he wanted us to go on trips and see things together, go camping, go fishing. He talked about how the children were getting old enough to stay home alone, so maybe we could go away for a day or a night. He had a lot of positive hope, and I felt that my prayers were beginning to be answered. He was going to be a good man to me and a great father to the children; we loved him then and we love him now. I tried to make him understand that. I didn't think he was grasping the fact that he was still the head of our home and we still needed him in our lives.

"James," I asked, "are you taking the medication that Dr. Graves prescribed you?"

He paused before he spoke. "I tried to take it, but I have these thoughts. I stopped taking it."

"Thoughts?" I asked. "Still thoughts of death? Maybe drinking with the medication is hurting you more than helping you," I said, trying to choose my words carefully so I wouldn't anger him.

"I don't like the thoughts, Victoria," he said. "I don't like the medication, I still drink, but not as much, and I try not to, but I need to; my body craves it. Some days I am up, and others I feel down, and I am tired of this roller coaster that I am on. I just want it to all go away."

I had nothing else to say because I too wished it would all go away, so we could have our lives back.

I did know that the children loved their father, in spite of his distance toward them and his drinking. He was a proud man, and what he was taught in his earlier years was something no one could ever take away, not even fate.

After Thanksgiving, Christmas went by in a blur. I didn't feel the need to put my children through the same activities that we had for Thanksgiving, so I told them we would just open presents the day before Christmas. I could only hope that the gifts that I was able to get them would take away the pain of not actually celebrating Christmas like we had in the past. I did manage to sit with them while they opened up their gifts, faking a smile just to show a little joy, while my heart was torn apart, knowing that their father had a sickness that neither he nor I could take control of. My family was drifting apart, and I was feeling like a helpless soul. I felt that I had stepped away from my body and my mind; I was just a bystander looking on as we all fell apart.

Chapter 23

The New Year had come and gone; we had lost another year waiting and wanting to get back what seemed to be gone. It was now the year 2004. The children were getting older, maturing at a fast pace. They would be turning sixteen this year, and James and I were missing the best years of their lives because of our own self-pity. This had to stop. It was time to stop waiting for an unpredictable miracle to happen and make something happen, even if it wasn't God's will. I was beyond tired of the way life was going, and something had to be done.

As the days went by, I found myself in a robotic routine: working in the mornings, sitting on the porch waiting for James to come home in the evenings, crying, wishing the heavens would open and gobble me up. In spite of how I was looking or feeling, never once did my mind stop working on what could be done to get us through this. I had tried everything. The more I tried, the less he tried. I couldn't nor would I finish up my children's high school years worried about what James was going to do if he was going to get well. A change had to come.

As the months passed, my knees were becoming more familiar with the floor. I got down on my knees, and I asked the Lord to change James to be the man that I longed for, the man that I needed, or give me the strength to get over him, give me the strength to move on.

"Please forgive the promises I made to him, for I can't take this anymore. I love him so. It is somewhat of a passionate love that allows fear to grip my soul, and just thinking about it terrifies me. I can't stop loving him, no matter how hard I try or how much I need to. With every stroke of his hand, my love for this man grows stronger. It didn't used to be this way, the fear I mean. With every waking moment, we were in each other's arms. We were considered to be one; we were soul mates. Where is my out? When are you going to show mercy on my family? When are you going to show mercy on me? How much more do you expect me to bear? When is the change going to come? This didn't catch you by surprise, so why hasn't your glorious plan shown its face? I have given all my burdens to you. I have let go so you could fight this battle. Why don't you make haste and prioritize my family? Put us above others who need prayer. This has gone on for too long; I need an out. I need to know that you are working things together for my good. I need the sign letting me know that if I endure, joy will come. Please, Lord, show me what it is you want me to do if that is what is hindering our family's blessing. Just show me, and I will do it. Please make haste in Jesus's name. Amen."

A few days after I said my heartfelt prayer to God, I tried talking to James about his drinking and how it was affecting Brandon. This wasn't hard to do because he needed to stop drinking so much. If he knew it was bothering the children, it might jolt him back to reality. When I brought this to his attention, he just said that he loved us and that he would do better. He said he didn't ever want to hurt the children, that we were his life.

That was his only response to me each time I would try this conversation, and I had done it weekly for at least two months. The response would always be the same, so I decided to quit asking because every time I asked him, the same thing would happen. He would go off into deep thought for hours; he wouldn't talk or come out of the room after that conversation. This would last sometimes for days, him lying in the bed in a fetal position. I didn't know if it was embarrassment or just plain pity. I never bothered him with it again.

Sometimes he would stop long enough to give the children his attention, but as soon as he felt they were content again, he would start back drinking, each time heavier than before.

No matter what the change was, it had to come. I just needed to keep my focus on the children and let whatever was going to happen, happen. Summer had come and the children were out of school. I was glad that they at least had a few friends that they hung out with at the park. James never really wanted them to be away from us but nowadays that didn't seem to matter either. They would wake up in the mornings spend a little time rustling around then they would head out with some friends. The sad part is that they never invited them to come in. If I was at my car or on the porch they would introduce me, the children that they were hanging out with seemed nice enough that I didn't worry. A part of me was just glad that they had an out to all this madness that was forced upon them. Hannah and Brandon was always together so that made things a little better I knew that they would protect each other, and I knew most of all that Hannah was a church going girl so if something was going on that she thought was against God, she would make it known. Brandon on the other hand didn't go to church like Hannah did momma picked her up faithfully every Sunday and Wednesday I felt Brandon would only go when Hannah or momma asked him to. He was in his own thoughts and being a young man without a father I had no choice but to try and understand.

I spent the summer working as hard as I could picking up extra hours when Ms. Fable offered them. I tried to put a few dollars back because I didn't know what our future held. James on the other hand didn't change his routine. Why would he, he was now set in his ways. He would get up some mornings like he was looking for work then he would come home late at nights drunk. Somedays he would not even leave the room I felt that was only because he kept him a stash of whiskey underneath the bed. I was getting to say the least fed up with the way things were and the children deserved better if not a father at least a mother. I had to weigh my options more carefully and somehow find the strength to be the mother that they needed. They would be juniors when school started back up this year and looking back on the past years, I had lost track of their lives because I was so wrapped up in mine. If James didn't feel up to giving the love that his family deserved, I had to put him on the back burner and focus on the two people who really needed me the most. I just hope they weren't too scarred from what James, and I had allowed.

After all my praying and thinking on the children and trying to figure out how I could focus on the children I found myself getting into a routine similar to James'. As the months passed by there would be days that I would focus on the children, and we would spend the evening together and try and do family things without their father. Then I would become so overwhelmed with things not changing that I would find myself alone on the porch. These children were on a rollercoaster ride first with their father and now I feel I was unconsciously doing the same thing. Something had to happen, something has to give.

We had gone through the whole year, changing only for the worse, so I vowed that I would not do this again next year. The children were of the age to get their license, but again we failed them. We didn't make the time or have the energy to take the time to help them learn how to drive, much less get their licenses. They didn't complain or even bring it to our attention. I knew that it was time, but I was just hoping that they would understand and give me just a little more time and I would do whatever I had to do to make that happen for them. A license was an important part of their teenage lives, and once again we had failed them as parents.

Holidays were not even holidays. We just went through the motions. It wasn't fair to our family to keep this up. The good memories had faded, and the bad memories had taken over, and the children deserved better; I deserved better. James deserved better. And since I couldn't control what his situation was, I had to make a change for the children's sake.

There were nights James would come home when I was sitting on the porch waiting for him and he didn't even get out of the car. I would just go in the house and bring out a blanket to the car and cover him up. He would then sober up enough to come into the house only long enough to wake me in the early hours of the morning. The pain I felt, along with the smell, wouldn't allow me to go back to sleep; something kept telling me a change was about to come. I didn't know it then, but I remembered Momma telling me as a child, "When you can't determine something, whether it's someone or something, then it must be God." God comes in many forms. He can come as someone you've never seen or something that you don't know. So, when the something kept coming in my mind, I prayed more for strength and peace, as well as understanding, because I knew I would need help no matter what the change would be. I knew that the change would be from God because my dreams always included someone or something. Yet I could never identify who the something or someone was.

Thanksgiving came and went; it was just like a regular Sunday meal. We didn't even eat it at the table. We all just ate when we felt like it—no thanks for anything, no setting the table, no football.

Christmas would be the next holiday to come, and I had to make a way to get presents for the children and for James. He would always decorate for the Christmas holiday; that was something we all enjoyed doing together. Hannah and I would separate the lights for James and Brandon, and they would put them up. Later we would go out, find a tree, decorate it, and drink hot chocolate while sitting and watching our masterpiece. James would do the honors of plugging in the tree. We tried to outdo ourselves year after year. That tradition slowly dwindled down. The past years he didn't take the time to get the lights up I would bring them out and unravel them hoping that he would take a little time to put them out, but he did not. I guess his thoughts were as long as he prepared the tree for decorating that was enough. Even on the nights that he wasn't drunk he didn't want to help us decorate. He didn't offer and I didn't ask. Of course, that would be asking too much but he would prepare the tree for decorating.

This year was different; James didn't mention getting a tree. I got the boxes of lights out hoping that James would put them out. I guess I should not have bothered. No matter what was done, he didn't seem to care. He never mentioned decorating, and I didn't either. The kids were big enough that the outside lights didn't excite them as much as they had in the past, so I figured a tree would suffice. I kept telling myself, "Just get through this year; a change is going to come."

We did manage to get a tree; the children and I picked it out from the corner store. I left it on the porch so James would know he had to trim it and put it in the stand. He was not concerned with that either. I finally asked James if he was going to put up the tree this year, and he told me he didn't feel up to it. After work, while I was on the porch waiting for James to come home from a night of drinking, I prepared the tree for decorating. I kept telling myself that my Christmas this year would be much better than my regular Sunday meals; we would enjoy this holiday if it took all the strength I had left, and I was going to see to it.

The kids and I finally decorated the tree the week before Christmas, without James. He was gone now more than he was home, and holidays that once in our lives meant everything to James, now meant nothing. Decorating the tree wasn't the same, and Brandon was the one to plug in the tree. We sipped on hot chocolate and sat quietly. James later graced us with his presence, but he was drunk. I was hoping that the kids didn't notice, but I saw them look at one another, so I put James to bed without a sound.

When I returned to the room, I wanted to continue on like nothing had ever happened, and I didn't want to go back into my room until James was asleep. The kids had retired to their rooms, and it was a sad time for me, an angry time. I made the eggnog, according to the tradition we always had, and I turned on the Christmas music, sat down on the couch, and cried as I watched the once-beautiful lights turn into a blue Christmas. I guess you could say that was the straw that broke the camel's back.

I went into our room, and James had fallen asleep. I decided not to wake him; I wanted him sober, and I didn't feel up to dealing with his drunken self-pity. Yet he was drunk every day, so playing to his beat could take another year and I wasn't going to do that. I couldn't help but think as I watched him lie there like he didn't have a care in the world, the impact this had caused to our family and all the caring, or shall I say the lack of caring, he showed. I wanted to dive right in and tell him exactly why his family didn't consider him a part of them anymore. I wanted him to know that he had self-destructed, and we were the ones who were suffering through it.

Something came over me and said, "Wait. It is not yet time. Doing it that way will accomplish nothing. Even though you feel you have waited long enough, it is still not yet the time. Don't you be the cause; just let it happen."

That was the strangest feeling I had through all of this. I didn't understand it. I wanted to just dive in, but something was holding me back. Our way is not the Lord's way. I knew that, but enough was enough. Just when I thought God wanted me to act, something held me back. I found myself waiting and waiting, and I didn't know for what. I knew I was fed up. God knew I was fed up. What else was there?

I just said a little prayer for strength, and God spoke to me again, saying, "Lean not to your own understanding. This battle is no longer yours, and when I see it's time, then it will be time." Not acting didn't stop me from thinking, and even though I knew that God heard me, at that moment I really didn't care. I thought, if death is what he wants, then he needs to hurry up and do it so we can bury him and move on. Was that God's plan? I thought he didn't want me to be hard on James because death was the outcome, and he didn't want the children to blame me. Did he really carry on the family curse? Was he going to go on in his drunken state, or worse, kill himself, and if I pushed, would he do it while we were all home? So many unanswered questions, and I was so tired of this. We were due for a change. His feeling sorry for the way his life was, and his self-pity had gotten the best of me. He was hurting the children; he was hurting me for that matter. This had become an everyday thing. It was not getting better, only worse.

Lately James had gotten up before me, but I felt that James knew I was angry, so when he felt the anger, he would stay in bed, probably pretending to be asleep, until I left for work the next day. Work was a little hard that day. I felt that I should have stayed behind and had the talk with James.

Something had to shake him back into our family, and I prayed to God that he would give James some kind of wake-up call before he destroyed us.

The children were home with James, and that made me a little uncomfortable because I didn't know what kind of mood James would wake up in. I called the house on my break, and Hannah told me that Brandon and his father were on the porch talking. I wanted to tell her to go out on the porch and tell me what they were talking about, but I didn't want her to know that I was worried. I did ask her what she had been doing and if her dad had been in a good mood today. She said that she had thought that he was because he and Brandon had been laughing and talking all morning. She told me that their father was going to take them to the willow tree to put fresh flowers down for Mrs. Andrews and then maybe go to Daddy's grave. Her words gave me comfort, and I was able to finish out my day at work. Maybe, I thought, spending the day with the children would pull him out of this depression that he had come to enjoy so well. Peace was what I felt, a sense of peace. I didn't realize it was the calm before the storm.

When I got home, my whole family was on the porch. In spite of the December air, they were on the porch bundled up in their coats and hats. I couldn't see their faces, nor could I hear the conversation, but being on the porch was a step in the right direction. Breathing easy, I couldn't wait to be a part of their conversation. Maybe the medicine had finally kicked in and we were finally getting back to normal. My joy didn't last long; once I reached the porch, the horror of what I was seeing took control.

All of them were crying, and it wasn't from joy. James was on the swing, tears streaming down his face. Brandon brushed past me, flushed with anger and a tearstained face, swiftly heading for the yard. Hannah just kept burying her face in my shirt, crying uncontrollably. It made me sick to wonder about what had happened in those hours after I spoke to Hannah. I didn't know what to say or what to think; I could barely speak.

When I found the courage to talk, all I could get out of my mouth was, "What's wrong?" Before I could force anything else to come out of my mouth, I was making tears of my own.

It was Hannah who shared the horror with me. "Daddy's, dying, Momma."

Chapter 24

Mixed emotions came flooding through the blood in my veins like thunder during a rainstorm. I felt fear, anger, and pain all at the same time, and it was fear that would end up being the strongest force.

"What do you mean Daddy's dying?" I managed to say.

I turned to James for answers, and when his eyes met mine, he just got up and went into the house. I didn't know whether to go after him or stay with the children. I had never felt so torn in all my life. I ended up staying with the children. I needed some answers, and I knew I couldn't get them from James. When James went into the house, Brandon returned to the porch. I turned to my son, who was now the strongest man in our home. "Brandon," I said, "what happened?"

Brandon looked at me in a state of confusion. He was searching my face like his father once did for some type of answers, answers that I couldn't provide. "Everything was good," he started. "We laughed and talked this morning. He was talking about fishing in the spring and teaching us how to drive so we could get our learners' permits next summer. Then it all started falling apart at the willow tree. We never made it to visit with Grandpa.

"We cleared off the leaves that had fallen from the tree, like we always did, and then he spoke to Great-Grandma. He was talking about failing everyone and said that he no longer wanted to live. He said that he wanted to go be with her, where happiness still existed. He told her that he had something to tell us, and if she could help him with the strength to do it, things would be better for everyone. He started getting upset and said the only two things that she had ever told him wrong was that he could break some family curse and that you understood him and would always be there for him no matter what.

"Then he told us to wait for him in the car. On the ride home, he told us that he couldn't go to Grandpa's grave because he felt sorry for letting him down. He told us he didn't keep his word to Grandpa, but soon we wouldn't have to worry because he would no longer be with us. He would no longer be here to cause us pain and hurt. He said something about ending a curse.

"We rode home without another word," he said. "When we got back home, he called us both to the porch, and he told us he was sorry for not being a better father for us. He told us to take care of you, and when Hannah asked why he was talking that way, he told us that he was dying, and he wouldn't be around much longer. He told us that he loved us; he said he was sorry. He said promises are meant to be kept, but if we weren't careful, promises can turn into miserable lies, lies that cause hurt and pain. Then he made me promise to take care of you and Hannah."

Hannah just sat there, resting in my arms. Her tears had slowed down, but they hadn't stopped. I wanted to sit there and hold her while she let go of some of her pain. Brandon's tears were gone, but as he watched Hannah cry, I could see the anger well up inside of him all over again. I sat and listened patiently, although I was confused and felt somewhat afraid for the children, for me, and even for James. It wasn't long before fear left, and anger took over. Why would he say such a thing to the children? Why couldn't he have brought that pain to me instead of the children? Those nights that he was breathing the alcohol down my back, why couldn't he have shared his thoughts with me? Before I thought, I asked the children, "Had your father been drinking?"

Brandon just looked at me, as if to say, "What do you think?"

It was Hannah who said the painful words. "Yes, Momma," she said, "he was drinking a bottle of liquor." As quick as those words came out of her mouth, it was even quicker that I felt the life drain out of my body. I had to sit down before I passed out in front of my children.

"What's wrong with Daddy, Momma?" Hannah asked again.

"He's sick from depression. That is all I can tell you right now. That is why he drinks: because he's depressed. He's not dying; he may feel like it, but he's not. He's going through a stage of depression, and that is how he feels sometimes, but he's not dying. What your father is going through, only the doctor can help him. We can only support him, but it's up to him to get better." I knew I shouldn't be having this conversation with the children, but I couldn't leave them in the dark forever. It wouldn't be fair to them.

We sat on the porch barely talking, and Brandon's anger slowly drained back down to pain. I didn't know if it was anger or pity for me, James, or the children, but I felt the need to be close to the children tonight.

Weighing my options, I decided to sleep with Hannah instead of James. He exhausts me, and I could better deal with this situation in the morning.

When the children and I awakened in the morning, James had already left for the day, and for a brief moment I didn't care. I didn't sleep much through the night, but I can say it felt good to close my eyes and not have to smell the stench of alcohol. His self-pity was beginning to weigh on my nerves. It was starting to take everything in me to get through my day without the drama. God knows I prayed. Whatever God had in store for me, he needed to bring it quickly, because I couldn't take any more of this. If God doesn't put any more on you than what you can bear, either my prayers stopped in the clouds, or God was trying to teach me a lesson. Well, I thought, for what it's worth, I got it, Lord, I got it. I don't want to learn anymore.

James came home after dinner was over, and I think the children were just glad to see that he was alive. Anger welled up in me to see the concern they had for their father. This was a man who, instead of putting down the bottle and taking his medication like he was supposed to, decided he would rather put fear in his children and gather all the self-pity from them that he could; he wanted them to excuse his drinking with the fact that he needed it because he was dying. Instead of protecting them from his madness, he chose to roll them into his self-pity. This was the first evening since this downfall started that I didn't wait for him on the porch. Looking outside my window as if noticing it for the first time, I could see the porch was losing its shade. It had kept it through the years, but the magic that it once shared with James and I playing with the children had now turned into a dreadful place full of sadness. I had sat out there many nights waiting for James, and now it was as though its purpose had been lost. Part of me wished that he wouldn't return, but that was only a small part of me. The rest of me wanted God to step in and have him return—to the James I had years earlier.

I knew I had to address the fact that he frightened the children, but I also knew that by the time I had finished the conversation, I would feel sorry for him, and I didn't want to feel that way right now. I wanted a change. We needed a change, and when the new year came in, he had better have a list of resolutions to fix these past years, or I would make arrangements to leave. I would just move on without him.

I went into our room, and once again, he was sleep. He had been to visit my father, I knew, because he had two flowers a red and white carnation. Those were Daddy's flowers when we buried him, and now they were lying on the floor beside his side of the bed. I decided again not to wake him, but we had to talk about this sooner rather than later.

I guess I must have been thinking out loud or talking in my sleep, because when I woke the next morning, James had already taken the morning paper and was gone. Let my prayers follow him, I thought; please let him find a job today. I had the day off, so I worked around the house getting ready for the holiday and prayed all day. Something had to happen; something had to come through for this family. Maybe God was trying to tell me something; maybe I needed to take a different approach.

While cleaning the room, I saw that James had taken the flowers, There were a few petals on the floor, but the flowers were gone; only a few had fallen off. I instantly thought of Daddy. What would that wise man do in a situation like this? What would Mrs. Andrews do if she had dealt with James in a manner that he only had respect and love for her? How could I get that? God must have spoken to me because all I could think of was when James wanted the kids to mind, he would say we had to show tough love. He got that from my daddy. Daddy used to tell us you have to teach the children young and not give into them; if we wanted our kids to do good in life, we couldn't let them run over the top of us. Thinking of how the children had turned out, he was right. Tough love, I thought, your turn, James, because I can't allow you to keep hurting the family that loves you. I looked underneath the bed, and the same bottles were still under there, with a fresh one added. I went into the kitchen, got a trash bag, and loaded all the bottles up except the new one. I left that. My thought process was only to let James know that I knew his hiding place. It was up to him to feel ashamed; maybe he could be shamed enough to pour the other one out. I found myself waiting on the porch again. I took a blanket and some tea with me to keep me warm while I waited for James. While waiting on him, I thought of the children. I wondered what was going on in their minds, and whether their tears had caught up with mine. Thoughts of them and a pot of tea kept me warm while I watched out for James.

James came rolling in around twelve thirty, right after midnight. Even though he was earlier than usual, he was still drunk. He came home drunker and drunker. I didn't know if he was still seeing Dr. Graves.

Considering that he wasn't taken any of his medicine and no new prescriptions had showed up, I doubted it. He never talked about it, and she wouldn't talk to me. Regardless of what he was going through in his life, he had shut me out, and we would discuss it tonight, because the time had finally come.

I got into the house before he came on the porch. I sat down in the darkened living room, and I watched him stumble across the floor and into the bathroom. I then got up and went to our bedroom door, leaving the door cracked just enough so I could see in and hear. I heard him urinating, probably all over the floor, probably on the walls. The longer it took for him to get into bed, the madder I got. Once I saw him sit on the bed getting ready to bed down, it was like he didn't even notice that I wasn't there, nor did he seem to care. I walked into our bedroom at first, I just looked at him like he had me so many times, searching, hoping he would say something to start the conversation. Whether it was "I'm sorry" or "I love you" didn't matter, but he just sat there looking at the floor. I knelt down in front of him, wanting him to look at me. When he didn't, I broke my silence.

"James Andrews, what were you thinking, or were you thinking at all?" He then looked at me with a blank stare, a stare that brought fear but not enough for me to shut up. "Who have you become?" I continued. "What would Mrs. Andrews think, right now, if she saw you? What about those promises you made years ago? Have you let alcohol take over those too?" I said. "Please," I said, "please, James, tell me, and help me to understand. Why on God's green earth would you tell the children that you were dying?

What possessed you to want to hurt them just as much as you have hurt me? How could you put our troubles on the children? Family curse—is that your poor excuse? You are carrying a family curse? Really, James, is this what I had to look forward to when I said I do? Liar!"

As I was speaking, at times probably yelling, he had a blank look on his face, but with tears added. Something told me to stop, that I had said enough, but I couldn't. I had to use this time that I knew he was listening to let him know everything that was going on in my mind.

"Look at yourself," I said, pointing to the mirror. "You are a walking mess, James, and this is what you want your family to love and respect? This is who you were talking about when you told me in front of God, your grandma, my father, and everybody that you wanted me to keep my promise to? This is the man who is going to take care of his family, love and cherish us? Is this the man you were referring to, because if it is, you have really confused me? I never thought when I made my promises that this is what I was looking forward to, that this is what would be the head of our home, that this is who my children would call father. Helpmate is what you expected me to be. Well, Mr. Andrews, I am all the help this family has. The head is what you are expected to be. Yet you are not even the tail!"

He stood up as if he was going to hit me, but he decided against it and walked past me as if to start out the door.

"Stop, James," I heard myself shout. "Don't you dare go out that door! Don't you dare ignore me. I have had to put up with your pity and self-destruction for almost three years. You are going to give me ten minutes of your precious time, and you are going to listen to me. You don't try! You don't want to try. You enjoy watching your family suffer. Why? Tell me why. Help me understand, James, how once this family was your everything, and now we have turned into your nothing. How could our dreams be one, and now our outlook on life is so different? What do you want from me? What do you want from the kids? Yes, promises do turn into miserable lies, but how do we, your family, fall into that category? We clearly see how you do."

He walked back across the room and sat back down on the bed; eyes focused on me. He had never seen me act this way, and I wanted him to know that this was the last attempt at saving our family. Knowing that I had his attention, I continued.

"If you think that I will keep my promises to this man, well, think again. My promises will be the ones that turn into the miserable lies that you speak about. If you ask me, it's all lies. I want the one man that made me those promises back. I want the man I had, not this man that I am looking at now. I want a strong man, the man I had, not this week, pathetic man that you have chosen to be. That man is who my promises were for, not this man," I said, again pointing to the mirror.

James didn't budge, so I went to the bathroom and got my vanity mirror. I put it up to his face and said, "Look at this man, James; this is who you have become. This is who you expect your family to love. Look at him." I didn't know this man that I was now yelling at or what he was capable of, and it really didn't matter at this point. I had something to say, and it was time for me to say it. He could have choked the life out of me, and it wouldn't have mattered. God gave me the strength to tell him what was on my mind, and that was what I was going to do. I wanted some type of reaction, but I got nothing but tears.

My heart was telling me to shut up, but my mouth wouldn't allow it. It had something to say, and it wouldn't stop until it was done. James took his hands and rubbed them hard across his hair and then over his ears, as if to tell me he didn't want to hear anymore, to shut up, but I couldn't stop. He finally said the words that I dreaded to hear. He looked at me with anger in his face, and he said, "Do you think I want to be like this, Victoria?" He screamed with all his might. "Do you think I chose this life? Now you look at me," he said, standing up. "Is this the man who gave you those promises? Is this the man that you thought I would be? Well, Victoria, I didn't think I would be this man either, but I am, and I will be until the day I die, I may not be dead to the point that you can place me in my grave but the man you married is dead this is who I am now, and I will be this man until the day you place me in the ground. Stop trying to bring him back because that man is no more. So now what, Victoria, what? Now I wish I could be with the only woman who could ever help me! You are not her; you are not my grandmother, Victoria, and I am not your father. I am James Andrews, and I am a man."

His words stopped the blood that pumped to my heart. I stood there, and all I could think was, After all these years, James, that we have put up with this, you are willing to accept this life until you die. Oh my God in heaven.

But what I said was, "Take your pills; drink your liquor. I remember, James, when you told me that Mrs. Andrews thought you should choose me. It was cute to me then, but tell me, James, is that why we are together? Did she choose me for you? Tell me, are we only together because she told you to be with me, because I would understand you, because I would stand by you. Did you marry me because she told you to, James? I'm not Mrs. Andrews, and there are things I won't accept, and I will never understand. Oh, and the family curse that you were so supposed to change, well …" I paused long enough to reach underneath the bed and pulled out the bottle of liquor that he thought he had hidden. I took the top off and took a big drink myself. "Let's share, James. Let's both ruin the children's lives. Let's do it together. Let's not make a change; let's keep the curse going. The kids are just kids. I am sure my momma will raise them."

Not only was I surprised at what I had just done; he was too, and he jumped up and knocked the bottle out of my hand. I thought he was going to hit me, so I flexed back, and fear left me. "Hit me, James. Is that what you want to do? Hit me. If that is what it will take for you to come back to us, then do it, James, just do it. Put all your blame on me. Is that what is coming next? I can take the pain, James. I have been taking it for years; I'm not afraid anymore." Tears were now streaming down both of our faces, and his tears this time didn't bring pity; his tears made me angry that we had to result to this instead of him using the help that was provided by his doctor.

I became angry all over again, which prompted more words. "If you want to be the alcoholic that you were used to while you were growing up, you will have to do it in the streets. If it's death you're seeking, if you are wanting to be with Mrs. Andrews that bad, then you have to do it somewhere else. Don't expect me and the children to continue to watch you self-destruct. If you choose to give up and die, my promise to you right here and now, is that you will not kill your family too. I won't allow it, and that is a promise that takes precedence over any promise that I ever made to you before. You will not die in front of us, James. I won't allow you to. Do it somewhere else if that is what you're choosing.

"Just in case you don't know," I continued, just about out of breath, "Christmas is in a few days, and you will be a part of this family, a family that deserves a holiday with the old you, not the one who is here now, a family that you are killing, a family that has watched you sit back and allow the devil to put this illness on you, a family that has watched you wither away to almost nothing. You, James, let yourself become too weak to fight. Our family would rather take death themselves rather than see you go through this. We have been your strength, we have fought on your behalf, and you will become a part of this family this new year, or you will continue dying somewhere else by yourself. I will not sleep in this bed with you while alcohol is running down my back, lying awake while you fight for breath, any longer. I will not smell the stench of used beer or used-up alcohol. I will sleep on the couch until you decide what you want to do.

"You have wanted understanding and love all these years; you have expected respect. When are you going to understand that we need you that we need your love? That after all this time I deserve a husband, the children deserve a father. We deserve someone who can give us the love and understanding that we have shone. Jobs are hiring, James, every day, even if they are only temporary. You say you can't get a job because they aren't hiring. The truth is you can't get a job because you are always drunk. Nobody in their right mind will hire a drunk. We've got pride too, James, and you are embarrassing your family. So here are your options: you are going to be a part of this family or find somebody else to share your pity. When the new year comes in—and it's coming soon, James—you have to decide what is the most important, and we will go from there."

I had said more than enough, I thought. I stepped back, with tears still streaming down both of our faces. I walked to the door and looked back to see if he had moved, and he had not. I then walked out of the room, shut my eyes, and let the tears roll as hard as they would come.

When I opened my eyes, the children were sitting on the couch holding each other, with tears of their own. Our arguing and yelling had awakened them. After staring and apologizing with everything in me, I went to them. Did they hate me for what I had just done? Could they realize that I wanted their father as much as I knew they did? Could they see that I had done all that I could do, and this was all that I felt was left? James had never seen that side of me, and neither had they. Had I gotten to James, but had it caused them more pain and fear?

Holding the children while sharing their pain, I couldn't help but to ask the Lord why he had allowed James and me to give birth to these two beautiful children, only to destroy them in their teenage years, to scar them with a scar that could have been prevented had we had our old lives back.

It wasn't until the next morning that I fully realized that what had happened the night before was not a dream, but real. I remember crying myself to sleep. I awoke on the couch praying that what I had said last night was merely a confused dream, only thoughts that I would say out of the children's presence. When Hannah woke and I saw her face swollen from crying, I knew it wasn't a dream, but reality. Fear and sadness were all over her and immediately transformed into my body. When she looked up at me, I whispered, "I love you, Hannah, and I am so sorry."

She looked at me as if she didn't know what I was saying, and then she spoke words that would comfort my soul. "No, Momma, I am sorry. Brother and I know that you are doing your best. We love both of you. We just wish Daddy could get better. He's sick, and we realize that we just want things back the way they were. He can't help it." She said, "Momma, it's the sickness."

I felt as though she was my momma, and I was the daughter. I felt so foolish because she was right. I was focusing more on James, and not enough on the illness that took him over.

"We don't blame you, Momma. We don't blame Daddy either. We just wish he could get better so we can go back to the way we were."

All I could say was, "Me too, baby, me too. I don't blame your daddy; I just wish it was different for all of us, that's all." With that we started into the kitchen to fix breakfast.

I looked out the window to see if James had left or if he was still in bed, and he was still here. His car was parked in the same old spot as the night before. I wondered with his state of mind, was he thinking that last night had been a dream, or had reality finally sunk in? Would he understand what I was trying to say, or was he just angry for the way I stood up to him? I just wished I could take it back and give the Lord time to do his work, but it had been four years. The twins were high school juniors now, and I didn't want the best days of their teenage lives to be memories of the way things were now. Maybe the Lord had tried to help James, and he shut him out. I thought maybe that was why the changes in him had been for the worse. I couldn't understand why the Lord allowed James to take it this far.

The snow on the ground reminded me that Christmas was only a few days away. Would James be his old self, giving us a Christmas to talk about for years to come? Would he help me wrap the children's presents like we had in the past? Would we stay up late, waiting for that beautiful day when the children would burst open their gifts, talking about it was what they always wanted?

I could only imagine what this Christmas would hold, and I could only pray that it would be a Christmas that we would remember and cherish for years to come. Or would he sleep through it waiting for the new year to come to make a big change?

Brandon came into the kitchen and interrupted my thoughts. "Is Daddy here, Momma?" I nodded my head while studying the concern on his face. "I suppose he's sleeping?" Brandon asked.

"Yes," I said.

"Are you all right this morning?" he asked me, wanting to know that I was.

I could look at his face and tell that sleep didn't come easy for him last night, and I wished I could take the pain away from him, but it was what it was. I knew that until James made a change, this was how it would be.

"Brandon," I began, "I know you heard me and your father arguing last night. I know you were hurt by our words, but don't blame yourself or think that you had anything to do with this. Your father is sick, and he has let this sickness take control of him. I love your dad and I love our family, and I just wanted to let him know that this sickness is getting the best of all of us. I know you heard some pretty hurtful things, but I said them with good intentions. I was hoping that they would make him see that he had to fight this illness that he faces. Please, son," I continued, "don't think bad of your father because of this sickness, and please don't think bad of me."

Cutting my words off, Brandon said, "I don't think bad of you, Mother, but Daddy has to want to get better. He has to try for himself, for all of us. We can't keep feeling sorry for him. I think that is what he wants, and I think that is why he hasn't tried thus far, because we accept all that he does, and he thinks it's okay. Somebody has to get through to him, and he has got to want to get better. I don't like the way he is. It's like he doesn't want to be a part of our lives anymore, so no, Momma, I am not mad at you. If he doesn't want to be a part of us, then he should just leave and stop hurting us." He reached over, gave me a hug, and went to finish getting ready for school.

I sat there for a few more moments pondering Brandon's words. We had accepted the way James was, and that could be why he was only getting worse. We didn't make him try; we were just hoping he would. My children had really been through a lot these past years, and all the while, I thought that I was hiding it from them. They knew all along what was happening. Sitting there until I saw the children off to school, flashes of the day before Mrs. Andrews died and I was standing by the doorway listening to her and James talk came rushing back. She told him that he should choose me and that I would help him and understand him. Had she been the reason that James chose me? Had he wanted me to continue what she had started in his life—the caring and the understanding—and was she as well as he expecting that I would stand for whatever just because? I had to get ready for work, but I waited until the children left for school because I didn't know what I might find this morning. I was glad when I saw the bus pick them up. It was then that I opened the door to our room.

When I walked across the room, I saw James staring up at the ceiling. I tried not to stare, but I noticed that he didn't blink. I got my clothes together, feeling a little nervous. I continued on with my shower, and when I came back into the room, James was in the same position, still staring at the ceiling. For a minute, panic rose in me: I thought he was dead. I moved close enough to him so that I could see that he was breathing, and he was still in the same position when I left for work.

Even though I loved James, I couldn't deal with his self-pity this morning. I could only hope that he was thinking about what he had done to the family, and I hoped he realized just how much we loved him and how he was hurting us. Maybe this would make him snap out of his self-pity and return to us. That was what we needed, and that was what we were hoping for. I found peace and went on to work.

Ms. Fable was in a great mood that day. Even though the pay was much more than I deserved, she added a Christmas bonus. It was a bonus that was well appreciated, and well needed—and one that I wasn't expecting. With the bonus, she gave me half the day off to Christmas shop for the children.

The thought of going shopping and then being home with the kids just in case James was still there overwhelming to my mind. Nowadays I didn't feel safe leaving James home with the kids, because I just didn't know what to expect.

With the car full of gifts and wrapping paper, I headed for home. The closer I got, the more depressed I became. It was hard to tell what James would be doing, and I didn't want any more unwelcome surprises. I hoped he was still alive; I prayed he was moving about the house. Even though I didn't have the James that I desired, I couldn't dare lose him to the point that there was no returning.

Erasing those thoughts from my head, I pulled up into the driveway. I noticed that James's car wasn't there. With a sigh of relief, I took the presents into the house. The children would be home soon, and when they went to sleep, I would wrap the presents and wait for James to return. My only prayer that evening would be "Lord, when he returned, let him be sober."

The children came home, and we had dinner together. After dinner, we made holiday candies, even though we took turns looking out the window for James to come home. He never returned, but in spite of that fact, the children and I had a wonderful time. We finally managed to bring the Christmas spirit in, but it would be James who would take it away.

Once the children retired to their rooms, I started wrapping the presents. It was getting late, and I didn't have the energy to wait for James. Even though I could do without the smell of alcohol and his depression, I still loved him, and that wasn't something easily ignored.

When James finally came home, I decided to sleep in our bed. This particular night when James came home was different. I should have seen the signs; I should have known that something was about to change. Blinded by his love and depression, I never would have expected what was to come next, especially after the previous night.

When he came home, he wasn't drunk, but I could tell he had been drinking. He came in the house, took a shower, and climbed into bed. He then whispered that he loved me and made love to me like it was our first time. He was gentle, caressing each part of my body like it was a fine piece of jewelry. Even though I was still a little angry, I submitted myself to him, melting my body into his. For that very hour or so, we were one, just like we once were. James had to be feeling better, I thought, to be able to perform like he did. He was snapping back to reality. Being so caught up in our troubles, we forgot to make love. It wasn't even considered. But even though we forgot to make love, James didn't forget how to make me feel.

After making love, James whispered, "I am so sorry for hurting you, Vicky. I never thought I would turn out this way. If I had known it, I never would have included you in my life." He hadn't called me Vicky in years. I didn't say anything because I didn't know what to say. I thought, yes, things were changing. I slept like a baby, sleeping in James's arms.

When I woke up the next morning, I woke up to James looking down at me, rubbing my face like he was trying to make a memory. I longed for those strokes with his hand and his touch that had been almost forgotten. I pretended to be asleep so he would continue on. After he rubbed my face, he took his hands and explored the rest of my body, and that told me that he wanted to make love again. In spite of the fact that my body was exhausted from last night, I submitted myself to him again, feeling every inch of his body slowly mixing with mine. I didn't want it to end; I didn't want him to stop. I wanted him to know that I needed him because I knew he needed me.

When we finally got up, I was running late for work. I wanted to call in, but that wasn't an option after the bonus and the half day that Ms. Fable had given me the day before. James kept looking at me, asking me for forgiveness. He kept saying how much he loved me and the children, and he kept asking me if I still believed in him. I just wanted him to know that the love was there for him. I was hoping, while his eyes was searching my face, that he would reach into my mind and know that I couldn't live without him, that he was everything to me and the kids, that whatever was in our future, we would do it together. Whatever God's will was, we would endure and have the joy together.

I knew he was going through things, but he had to get better. That was on my mind, but we would talk more about that after I got home from work. Now was not the time to say those things because I didn't want to put him back into his depression.

Before I left, he stood in front of me and said, "I know I have let you and the children down, Vicky. I know that I'm not the man to whom you made those promises years ago, but you are the woman that I made those promises to and much more. You and the children deserve much more than what I have to offer, and I pray that happens. You don't need my troubles, and I know more than ever that I have been only that. You deserve better, much better than I can give you right now. I know that I have to deserve to be a part of your lives, and I am going to fix that because right now, I don't deserve a family like the one that God has given me. Until I am, I promise you all over again, I won't put my troubles on you or the children. I love you and the children with every breath that God has planned for me. I promise that one day I will make it all up to all of you. Right now, I know that I am sick, and I will do all I can to get better, so I can be that father, that husband, that you all deserve."

His touch and his look were different. I was glad that he was finally coming through, and reality was finally sinking in.

He continued, "I want this Christmas to be for you and the children a peaceful one, one full of love, and the new year full of welcome changes." His words put a smile on my face. Those were the exact changes that we had been searching for. It was exactly what was needed in this family.

"James," I said, once he was finished, "we want you to get better, and we love you. We will stand by whatever you have to do to get better because we love you. We want you in our lives."

"You mean it, Vicky, that you will stand behind whatever I feel I need to do to get better?" he said, searching my face, his eyes tearing up.

"Yes," I said. "We will stand by whatever you feel you need to do, James—whatever it takes."

With that he kissed me with the passion that his lovemaking gave, and I left for work.

Chapter 25

I had a great day at work. It was Christmas Eve, and James had given me the best present that I could ask for. God must have heard my prayers, I thought, and now I could see the light at the end of the dark tunnel. The darkness was now slowly disappearing, and the light was shining brighter. It seemed like I was at the pharmacy store for days instead of the usual eight hours. I couldn't wait to get home to James again. Tonight, we would be back to making memories, good ones this time.

I don't remember the drive home; I must have broken every speed limit I went through. I was feeling like a teenager myself. My mood was so lifted when I got home, it didn't matter that James wasn't there. The children and I started dinner and sang Christmas carols. My thoughts were that James would be home soon with presents for the children, ready to start rebuilding what his depression had torn down.

For the first time in a long time, I felt a sense of satisfaction, a sense of deep love for James. The kids stayed up as late as they could, waiting for their father, but I assured them that he would be in a better mood and things were getting ready to change.

James still wasn't home at two o'clock in the morning. By then, I was starting to worry. "Please," I said out loud so that God could hear me, "please don't let our talking and lovemaking be in vain. Please let him come home the same way he left this morning." I felt content that God heard my prayers, and again I had the feeling that things were headed in the right direction. I knew that he would be home soon, so I just ignored the time and jumped into the shower.

With memories of the previous night, our conversation this morning, and our past happiness, after my shower, I put the gifts underneath the tree and went to bed. I decided to sleep naked so I could give James his Christmas present as he had given me mine. My mind took me back to when we were actually a family. We would take the kids to the park, and later James and I would talk about the progress they were making. We would sometimes sit in our yard picnicking under our own willow tree. Brandon and James would plant our garden, and Hannah and I would cover the plants up with dirt. Then we would spend time looking at our creations. After the children would bed down, he would make love to me like he did last night. With so much happiness and peace in my heart, I fell asleep.

When I woke in the morning, I jumped out of bed and threw on my robe, thinking that James was in the living room on the couch. He must have fallen asleep wrapping gifts. When I went to the living room, James wasn't there. I looked out into the driveway; James's car wasn't there. All kinds of thoughts entered my mind. "It's Christmas day, James," I said to myself. "Please don't ruin this day for me and the children." Maybe he had been in the bed, and he had gotten up early for whatever reason and gone out. I didn't think to look if his pillow was ruffled any.

As I went back into our room, I saw that his side of the bed hadn't been touched. At this point, anger welled up in my body like an ocean floor getting ready to erupt. Hadn't our past Christmases been bad enough? Couldn't he at least have given us one day? What could he be thinking, or was he thinking at all? What would I tell the children? They would be up soon, and I wanted time to stop and wait for James to come home. I wanted God to open up the heavens and pull me through, because I just couldn't take anymore.

When I heard the children waking up, I went back into my room. I didn't want to face them with the news that their father didn't come home. This was Christmas day. I stayed in my room long enough to get on my knees and pray. I asked the Lord to give me some kind of strength to help me with my struggle. "Jesus," I said, tears presenting themselves, welling up, unstoppable, "give me just a moment of your time. Count me worthy just long enough for me to speak with you. You know that we have been through a lot, and I knew that a change would soon come. I didn't know what to expect, but I knew that a change was coming. Now that it's come and I don't know what else to expect, please, please give me strength and watch over him. Whatever he is thinking, please intervene in his thoughts and give him peace. Allow us to get through this day and bring him back to us safely. Strengthen me, if only just long enough to get through this Christmas day." I also prayed that when James came home, to let him be as humble as he could be, and not bring home any drunken drama. "I know he will come back. There is no way he could just leave us, so when he does return, let him be the man that I desire, that I need, that the children need. In Jesus's name, I pray. Amen."

Before I returned back into the living room, I decided to call Momma. At that point I needed some type of guidance, something to help me understand. I needed help in figuring out what I would tell the children.

"Merry Christmas," she said when she picked up the phone.

"Momma," I said, fighting back tears but trying to sound as strong as I possibly could at that point. "James didn't come home last night."

"Oh, Victoria, no!" she said. "Do the children know?"

"Not yet," I said.

"Well, I am on my way. Just try to hold on until I get there."

After we hung up, I went to the bathroom to wash my face so the children wouldn't know that I had been crying. When I went into the living room, I was greeted with the kids opening up their gifts, tearing into the presents, not knowing that I would be the only parent attending the excitement. Brandon looked at me long enough to thank me for the pants, shirt, and shoes that matched before he tore into another present. Hannah got the pedicure kit that she had asked for so many times before. She started doing her nails, so the rest of the presents didn't matter. I managed to smile. I was not going to take this time from them, knowing that troubles were coming in full swing.

The excitement of new things filled the air, and it was so good that they didn't notice that their father wasn't there. Finally, Brandon asked the Christmas-stopping question: "Momma, where's Daddy?" I think the reason he asked was because he had picked up a gift that I had signed from his father. "Is he still asleep?"

The look on my face must have given the answer. I told him the truth. I didn't know if it was a good idea, but I didn't want to lie to him. I tried to sound as normal as possible. I tried to hold it together, but the words "he didn't come home last night" started to fail me.

Brandon and Hannah were now at my side, holding me; we were all letting our tears fall. We were sitting on the couch, feeling confused and numb, when we heard someone on the porch knocking snow off their boots. Our eyes turned to the door, silently hoping that it was James. The door was flung open, and it was then we realized it was Momma.

"I just don't know what to say," she said, seeing sadness on our faces. "The roads are bad. Have you called the hospital?"

"Not yet," I said. "I was just hoping that he would come home before I took that approach."

"Time's wasting," she said, taking control. "Something has to be wrong. We need to go look for him. I just can't believe that he would just not come home on Christmas day. Brandon, you ride with your momma. Hannah, you ride with me. We will look around town and meet back here at …" Looking at her watch, she said, "It's eight thirty now; we will meet back here at eleven o'clock."

That was how we spent our Christmas morning, looking for their father. We didn't really know where to look, so we just rode the streets and looked in a few parks. I even went into the Country Kitchen bar, but still, no James.

When we entered our street at five minutes till eleven, I was praying that his car would be in the driveway. As we reached our driveway, there was still no car, no James. Momma and Hannah were there when Brandon and I arrived. Hannah had grabbed the phone book and was thumbing through the pages for the local hospital. When she found the number, I dialed it.

Was he trying to get home? Was he somewhere run off the road? Was he at the hospital? When the phone started ringing, the lady on the other end of the phone said, "Pear Heart's Memorial Hospital, can I help you?"

"Yes, um," feeling a little embarrassed, I said, "do you have a James Andrews at the hospital?"

"Let me check; one moment please. No, ma'am, we don't have anyone by that name listed as a patient. Is he visiting someone?"

"No," I said, "thank you." With that I hung up the phone.

I looked at the children as if to say he's not there, and they read my mind because they each got up and went to their rooms. I made a pot of tea for me and Momma. By now she had joined me in the kitchen. In a low voice, as if she didn't want the children to hear, she said, "Victoria, what happened? Did y'all have a falling-out?"

"No, Momma. As a matter of fact, I thought things were getting better. We even talked yesterday morning before I went to work." Then the conversation that morning came rushing back, paralyzing my heart. "Will you stand behind whatever I have to do to get better?" The tears returned, and I had for a moment forgotten that Momma was there.

"What, Victoria, what?" she asked.

"Oh my God, Momma, James was trying to tell me something yesterday morning, and I didn't understand until now what he was trying to say. Even worse, I agreed to it."

"What did he say?" she asked.

"He said, 'Will you stand behind whatever I have to do to get better?' He also said that he didn't want to hurt us anymore. He told me that what we wanted might not be what we needed." Then I told her about the argument that we had two days before that, and the blame instantly fell on me. "It's my fault, Momma, that James is gone. I told him that if he didn't make a change by the New Year that I was leaving him. Instead, he left me. Oh, Momma, what have I done?"

Her shoulder was the perfect place for my head at that point, and I just cried and cried.

"Victoria," Momma said, "he will come back. Maybe he left to try to figure out things on his own. He knew he was hurting you and the children. He probably wanted to get better on his own, and if he couldn't, he just didn't want to put you and the kids through any more pain. Victoria, he is a grown man; he knows what he's doing. Don't blame yourself. The only thing that gets my goat is he could have waited until after Christmas. Just pray God has got this thing under control. It will all work out for the good in due time."

The children spent the rest of the day in their rooms. I went in from time to time to check on them and found their faces stained with tears. At times they would be in each other's rooms when I walked in. They would stop talking, and my thoughts were they either blamed me or they didn't want to worry me with their own thoughts. I left them to themselves and rejoined Momma.

"Do you want me to stay?" Momma asked as I came back into the living room for the umpteenth time.

"No, Momma, go on home," I said. "If he returns or if we need you, I will call you."

After that she left and I retired to my room for the rest of the day, at times finding myself looking out the window watching the snow fall, wondering where he was or what was on his mind. While standing there, Mrs. Andrews came to my mind. The urns! I thought. Are the urns still on the mantle where they've been all these years? I rushed to the living room, and they too were gone. I hadn't noticed them before. Had they been gone before now, or did he take them when he left? Sadness took hold of my body yet again.

James's mom called like she always had since the visit. When she asked to speak to James, I told her he was out. So that told me he wasn't there, and I didn't say anything else at that point. James didn't like for me to tell his business, and when he did come home, I didn't want him to know that I had told other people about his troubles.

Later that evening, Momma called. "Have you heard anything, Victoria? I have been praying."

"No, nothing," I said. "The children are still in their rooms, and I am in mine."

"Well, if you need me, call me," she said again. With nothing else to say, the phone call ended. I never mentioned the urns being gone; I thought I had worried her enough with my problems.

The kids stayed in their rooms, and I stayed in mine. There was nothing to say, nothing to do. We didn't eat dinner. I just kept looking out the window, hoping that one of those cars that passed by our street would be their father. To my disappointment and sadness, it didn't happen. I slept on the couch with the television on the news channel just in case there was something on there about James. Still nothing, and every hour I was up looking out the window, but still no James.

The next morning the pharmacy store was still closed for Christmas. I managed to put on a smile and wake the children. The gifts were still the way they were left the day before. I knew the children were still hurting and probably had as little sleep as I did, but they still had presents to unwrap and we still had to make ourselves go on. I decided to put on the Christmas music like I had planned on doing the day before, and I put on a pot of tea.

Within moments they came into the living room looking at me as if I had lost my mind.

"Guys, look," I said, "there's nothing on the news. We have to hope for the best. Your father knows what he is doing; he is a grown man. I don't think he wants to hurt us. I honestly think he is trying to get himself better," I continued, using Momma's words and trying to sound as convincing as she had convinced me. "Instead of letting all these presents go to waste and instead of being sad, until we hear otherwise, let's just think positive that your father is trying to get help because he doesn't want to hurt us anymore."

Without another word, I sat down under the tree and started handing them their gifts. Whether I was convincing, or they just wanted to please me, they sat down and started tearing into the gifts like nothing had ever happened. I tried to be excited for them and discuss something about each of the gifts they were opening, and they joined in. It wasn't as happy as it could have been if James was there in his right mind, but in time, I thought, in time.

After the gifts were opened, I made breakfast for me and the children. We sat down and ate. While eating, Brandon asked a question that tied my stomach in knots, almost to the point that I was going to be sick. His words were faint but sincere. "Is it my fault, Momma, that Daddy didn't come home?" Brandon said, with tears filling his eyes.

"No, Brandon, neither you nor Hannah have anything to do with it. Your dad is just going through a tough time, and by him not having a job, he felt that he isn't the strong man that he used to be. He's just going through something, that is all, and he doesn't want us to see him hurting anymore. I'm sure he will be home soon; in the meantime, we have to remain strong." With the children, I had to stay positive, but thinking back to the last day that James was here, I knew in my heart after his conversation with me that he would not be back, that he felt that he was hurting us more than loving us.

Hannah never said a word. She just sat and listened as if she was soaking it all in. After breakfast, the children spent some time with their gifts, and then they went to their rooms. Momma called again asking about James, and I told her about Brandon's conversation and then I went to my room. Around five o'clock, I forced myself to get up out of my bed and heat up our Christmas dinner. While heating up dinner, I decided to check on the children. They were both in Hannah's room playing on the computer, so I told them that dinner was about ready and that they should wash up so we could eat.

We sat down to a quiet dinner. Hannah helped me clean the kitchen afterward, Brandon took out the trash, and we each went to our own rooms.

Morning came a bit faster than I would have liked. It had been three days since James left us, and I couldn't go to the pharmacy store today. I called Ms. Fable and told her that I had a family emergency. The kindness in her voice made me regret lying to her, but it was a family emergency: my husband was missing.

The joy that I had forced the day before had left, and sadness and confusion set in. Why couldn't I have seen this coming? Why didn't I know that with his last words to me, he was talking about leaving us? I could have convinced him to stay. Why did he wait for Christmas to come before he did this? Were my words so misunderstood that James thought I wanted him to leave, versus just trying to get better and be a part of our lives?

Mixed emotions were filling my heart. I found it best to spend time in my room alone away from the children. One minute I was angry, beating my fist against the pillow that I held while sitting Indian-style on my bed. The next minute, fear would grab hold of me, letting me know that any minute somebody was going to knock on that door with news of his death. Then tears would fall, as I wondered not only what else was in store but where did we go wrong? Is losing a job so serious that it broke our family up, or was losing the job just an excuse, an escape from being a part of our lives?

Confused, that was how I could be described, in a state of confusion. Could he have been so hurt and confused that he thought this was all he could do? Was there another woman, a drunken woman, who could deal with the depression, because she was depressed too, who talked him into leaving his family to be with her? Was there a woman out there who was going through something similar, so that James felt that they were two of the same kind?

We started our search for the day. We looked in ditches and behind buildings. We didn't dare ask anyone because we knew James did have a little pride left. How embarrassed he would be if he did return, and people were all talking about his family looking for him like a pack of wolves looking for their prey.

We didn't report James missing until New Year's Day. Momma was so supportive. I don't think I could have made it through my struggle without her. She went to the police station with me; we thought it was best that the children stayed home.

The police had a lot of questions for me that I didn't understand why they were asking. Questions like were we having marital problems? I felt the officer was trying to imply that he left me for another woman. The way he looked at me made me a little uneasy. His forehead was crinkled, as if to say, "You are lying." Did I know of James having an affair? Did he work, and if so, where? Was James a person who was wanted by the police? Did he have a violent temper? Did James go by any other name besides James Andrews? All the answers to the questions were no. The police saw I was aggravated, so they changed their line of questions. They wanted to know what he was wearing, the color of his eyes, hair, was he black or white? What places did he usually frequent? I felt in my heart that I was violating James's pride, but I had to do what I could to bring him home.

After two weeks, the kids were more and more concerned; they, like me, feared the worst. Yet they returned to school. The school break was over, and we had to get our lives back on track. James still hadn't returned. He was out there somewhere, wandering around homeless. I spent my mornings looking through the obituaries for an unidentified man. My days were spent on my knees, and my evenings were spent on the porch waiting and praying for his return.

I took a leave of absence from the store. Ms. Fable was more than understanding when I let her know what was going on. She even told me that she would pay me as if I was there and I could make it up to her later. I couldn't miss a phone call if it came through. We couldn't afford voice mail or caller ID, so I had to stay by the phone. There were all kinds of thoughts I couldn't get past. There were so many questions that I didn't have answers to—and it looked like I never would. How could he leave our family, making life a living hell for me? How would I carry on and raise this family by myself? How could I face the world without him by my side? Didn't he even think that leaving us would hurt more than him staying? I really didn't think James thought about this at all.

The police supposedly looked for James for two weeks before my persistence took a turn for the worse. I called at least twice a week. It wasn't until I asked them what exactly they had done that the unthinkable happened. It had been two weeks with no word on what they had been doing. With anger in my voice, I told them that if they didn't prove that something was being done, I was going to the chief with my concerns.

As if they were punishing me for my actions, the next day, in big bold letters on the front page, was MISSING ON CHRISTMAS DAY and a picture of James. The kids had to see it. I had to see it. This was the most humiliating time for us. What was everybody thinking? Now everybody knew that our family was torn apart. All James's adult life, he lived by his pride, and with numerous cases of beer it had been stripped away. I didn't think James was alive because, if he was, he would have seen the paper and he would have known that we were looking for him. If he was alive, then he didn't want to be found.

Reality had finally sunk in. James was not coming back. My prayer was still for his safe return, if only for a little while, to face me and the kids, to let us know why he left. It was not James's love I needed right then, because it was obvious that, for whatever reason, he didn't want to be here. It was closure; I needed to close this chapter in my life and force myself to move on. If he returned now, it would never be the same.

I heard the children the night that the newspaper came out. What is 2005 going to hold for us? I thought, listening to the sniffles and crying of my children. James, what have you done to this family? It was like they took turns crying themselves to sleep. I tried to comfort them as best I could by going into their rooms and kissing them on their foreheads, but I didn't have the strength or the energy to give them the comfort that they needed. Who was going to comfort me? Who would be my strength? I couldn't lean on the children—they had enough to deal with going to school and trying to stay focused. Momma was the only one I had to share my pain with, and pain it was. James had been my strength, my comforter, and now he was gone. Turning to the Lord would be my only hope. God said he wouldn't put any more on you than what you could bear, and he was really taking me to my limit. God also said he would not leave me or forsake me. All I could say was he had his work cut out for him. James, too, said he wouldn't leave me, but now he was gone.

The principal of the school called wanting to know if there was anything that he could do. The embarrassment, I thought, for the children. I wondered what the teachers were thinking, what the children were saying, as they passed my children in the hallway. Something that I had wanted to keep secret for the sake of the children, now everyone knew, and to top it off, the school knew. A particular teacher came to my mind. She has been known for her gossiping and judging of others. My mind took me back to one of our conversations she was telling me about one of my students and I remember thinking how miserable she must live for finding joy in other people's sorrow. I was just wondering what the teachers were saying about me and about the children. Were the teachers going to be caring, or were they gossiping with one another? Were they sharing our pain with the other parents, or were they secretly saying a prayer for our family?

Then my mind took over, and I remembered something my mother had said. "You reap what you sow if you ever take joy in someone else's pain. Be careful because 'vengeance is mine' saith the Lord." Those words gave me comfort because if there was talk—and I am sure there was—then I would just let God handle that part of the battle. He could do more than I could ever imagine.

Chapter 26

A month to the day after James had left us, there was still no word on him returning. Ms. Fable had been great, but I had to return to work somehow. Bills were piling up, and I didn't see a light at the end of this tunnel; all I could see was pain and hurt. I thought I was all cried out; I didn't feel I could cry anymore. I wanted to, but the tears wouldn't come. I thought I was getting angry now. I was getting to the point that if he did return, I might just ask him to leave. I just couldn't get past how easy it was for him just to walk out and discard us like we never existed. Why would he hurt us like this? How long had he been planning this?

I had been so crossed up in my emotions that I didn't even think to call his momma. It had been a month now, and she was the furthest thing from my mind. I guess I didn't call because she hadn't been in our lives like my mother, and I didn't want to worry her. I knew in her past she had struggled with drugs and alcohol; I didn't want her to know James was going through the same things. Even though he now had a semi-relationship with his momma, he kept our business from her. Surely, I thought if he was there, she would have at least called. Maybe he was there, not thinking I would check.

Not giving it another thought, I phoned his mom. "Hi, Ms. Robertson, how are you?" I heard myself say.

"Oh, Victoria," she replied, "I'm fine. How are you, dear?"

"Oh, pretty good, considering." She sounded as though she was healthy now. I knew she'd always wanted to be in our lives, but James kept her at a distance, thinking she might return to her drunken ways. He didn't want the kids to experience what he had growing up.

"How are the children, Victoria? You know I would love to see them."

"Yes, ma'am, they are fine," I replied. "Ms. Robertson, have you heard from James?" I said, getting straight to the point before I lost my nerve. I didn't have time to chitchat.

"Why yes, dear," she said. "He called just the other day. He's got troubles, don't he, Victoria?" she asked.

"Yes, ma'am, he does."

"He told me all about his sickness, and sickness it is," she said. "You know, I know better than anybody."

I wanted to know their conversation. I wanted to know if she knew where he was. I knew he had troubles, but maybe she could help me find him, I thought.

Interrupting her, I said, "Ms. Robertson, what did he say when he called?"

"He asked if I had heard from his father. I thought that was odd, so when I asked him why, he told me about his troubles. He told me that he was taking medication from a doctor. I told him to stop the medication while he was drinking, because that was what started my troubles way back when. He told me that he was about out of them, and he wouldn't get anymore."

"Do you know where his father is, by any chance?"

"I told James that I had talked to his father a few times. He was the one trying to find James. I didn't give his father too much information because he still has his troubles. He only calls me from pay phones. I guess he doesn't want me to know his home number, for fear I may want some of his blood money, so those numbers wouldn't do James any good. He then told me that if I was to speak to his father, to tell him that he was with an old friend of his and he wanted to talk to him. That was all he told me, dear. I can't for the life of me think of his friend's name; he told me, but I can't think of it now. When his father called back, I just gave him the message …" Her words trailed off as if she was thinking. "Willy, that's the friend's name; he told me to tell his father that he was with his old friend Willy. Now where his friend is, I couldn't tell you that. I don't remember his father mentioning to me a friend by that name."

He is alive, and if he is alive, he is probably going to come back home soon. Tears trailed down my face. This time it was tears of joy, tears letting me know that there was still that little inkling of hope. I cleared my throat and wiped my tears because I didn't want her to know that I was crying.

The reason I called her was the reason my tears started. I didn't want to cry, but I couldn't hold it together anymore. Tears returned, and before I knew it, they were uncontrollable.

She too was crying at this point, and she told me she would call around to people she knew to see if they had heard from James or knew who Willy was. She would call me back. She also said that she would send money to help us until I could get back on my feet.

Her concern shifted toward the kids, and I told her the truth: they were devastated. She also told me that she knew James loved us and one day he would return. Something similar had happened to her years ago, and she knew that he would find his way back home because she did.

I wanted to know all the details and maybe that would help me to understand this better, but I didn't ask. I felt if she wanted to tell me she would, and she didn't go into details, so I left it alone.

The money she promised came in a matter of days. I immediately called the phone company and got voice mail. I was working again, and I couldn't stay by the phone. Ms. Fable was the only person I dared talk to about this. I had to talk to her because she was my boss, and it was already well-known. Ms. Robertson never found out who Willy was, and James never called her again.

Two months passed, and I had a desire to talk to Dr. Graves. James had plenty of time to return if he wanted to, and yet he didn't. I needed answers, some assurance so that I could at least move on. Snow was still on the ground, but a hint of spring was in the air. I knew that Dr. Graves wasn't going to break her confidentiality with James, but surely, she could give me some kind of understanding. I would talk to Ms. Fable the next day at work, and then I would take it from there.

The children were adjusting to their father's leaving. Hannah was all excited when she came home from school that evening; she wanted to go to summer camp. It was going to cost two hundred dollars that I didn't have, but I was going to make a way to get the money so she could go. I had several months to prepare, but I also had their prom coming up. Not to mention their birthdays. I had to put my ducks in a row and make these things happen for my children. Going to summer camp would be a great idea. It would give Hannah a taste of being away from me before she started college next year, and besides, it was a good opportunity to take her mind off things. It would be good for her to get away and be with friends.

James had left me right before my junior year of school, so I had to make this the best prom ever for my children and for me. Their father had now been gone for a little over three months. I promised myself that I would teach them to drive this year and try as hard as I could to make their lives as normal as I possibly could—if for no other reason than to make up for the years that I missed with them dealing with James and his troubles. It was their time now, so why not live and try to enjoy things? It was past due and well-deserved. The children were maturing at a fast pace, and I wasn't getting any younger. Before I knew it, I would probably be a grandmother myself. James, we knew, on the other hand, if he was in his right mind, probably would not want her to go; he would want her to stay around the house and learn things from me. She didn't have to be a well-kept woman. She would be able to make her own choices about her life and not have the pressures of trying to please us.

Brandon was in a better mood this evening too. He came home with good news, and it was a welcome change. "Mom," he said after busting through the door, "Devin, a senior at high school, has a paper route, and he was wondering if I could take it over because he was going to college." Of course, I told him yes." The excitement on Brandon's face and in his voice was confirmation enough, letting me know that this was a good thing for him. He found something that he could get excited about, and I thought it would be a good experience for him. I suddenly got angry at James again because, look what he's missing. I thought, his children are growing up, and he's too stuck on his troubles to be a part of it.

I spent that evening back at my familiar place, the porch. I took a pot of tea with me and sat in my usual chair. I was thinking of how miserable my life had been in the past. I thought how the number sixteen was like a bad omen in James's life. His troubles started at sixteen, he left me when I was sixteen, and now that the children were sixteen, he was gone out of their lives too. Maybe it was a family curse; maybe that number had a bad significance in his family's life. I would break that chain. It would be I who would break the Andrews family's curse.

What I was hoping would be a nice, relaxing evening turned out to be a tear-jerking evening. I sat there listening to the frogs croaking, and the thought of how fast the kids were growing just hit me like a diesel truck. I was glad they had retired to their rooms, and I knew once they entered their rooms, I would have to call them before they came out. How many years had I missed? If I had thought that it was all for nothing, I would have let him go a long time ago. If I had known that my love was in vain, I would have never waited for that unmistakable love. I heard myself laugh out loud to the point I thought I was losing my mind. What a fool! I was so blinded by the flow of love and desire that I couldn't see the red flags. I didn't want to see the red flags. All I knew was that I wanted him, and he wanted me—or so I thought.

After the children bedded down, I wrote James a letter telling him how he was missed and about the kids and how they were growing up now. I remember Momma used to do that when I was younger. Whenever she had something to say and she didn't want to anger Daddy, she would just write it down and put it in a box. So, I thought that I would do the same. I wrote a long letter, a few pages. Even though James had wronged us, I wanted to know where he was and what was on his mind the day, he left us. If nothing else, after seventeen years of marriage, I thought I needed some type of understanding for closure. I fussed and cried and wrote so much that I fell asleep.

Moods in the house the next morning were cheerful. Brandon could accept his job, and it would start right after school shut down. Hannah could get all the details about this camping trip. I was going to find out information on where James could be, and things were looking better.

On my way to work, I felt like a weight had lifted from my soul. I would speak to Ms. Fable about things that were going on, and I would ask her about how she would go about talking to Dr. Graves. I would go visit with Dr. Graves and try to piece things together.

It was midday before I got up my nerve to talk to Ms. Fable about finding out information on James's condition. I walked into her office, and she looked at me over the top of her glasses, motioning for me to come in.

"Ms. Fable, I was thinking about going to talk to James's doctor, and I don't know how to go about doing it," I said, feeling kind of nervous. "I figure if she could tell me about their conversations, I could get a better understanding of what's going on."

"Victoria," she said, "please sit down."

I did as she asked and continued. "I know that she won't tell me much, but anything that she will tell me will help," I said.

"A doctor is limited on what they can say to others about their patients, but I don't think it could hurt. I just don't want you to get your hopes up, because she may not talk to you at all. It all depends on what James told her and how far she will take the confidentiality business.

"Some doctors will tell things; others won't. It all depends on her and what she feels. She will be breaching patient confidentiality. It never hurts; just call her and set up an appointment. Never try to do it on the phone. It's more personable in person, and it will be harder for her to turn you away. Furthermore," she said, "once she sees how hurt you are, she will probably listen to you and feed off of your conversation.

"Now, when you call her, don't give your name; give mine. That way she won't be expecting you. Matter of fact let's do it now. I will call and make an appointment for you."

I was glad she decided to make the call; my nerves wouldn't allow me to do it.

We looked in the phone book and got the number, and then she made the call. She always was professional, so by her doing it, they might see me right away.

"Yes, I would like to make an appointment to see Dr. Graves," she said. "Yes, I will hold." She looked at me and winked.

"No, I haven't been there before.... Yes, I have insurance.... I would like to see her right away," she said.

"No, two weeks from now will be too late. Put me down for that day, and if you have any cancellations, would you please call me at 553-0005. What time does she close?" Ms. Fable asked before she hung up. "5:00 p.m. Thank you so much."

I could tell by the look on her face that she had a plan.

"Victoria, they couldn't see you for two weeks, so this is what you need to do. Go there at 4:45 p.m. and ask to speak to her before she leaves for the day. If she has time, she will see you. If she doesn't, we still have the appointment. Apparently, Dr. Graves is going on vacation this afternoon. If I, were you, I would be there at the time of closing. Surely if she is a good doctor, she will make time for you before she starts her vacation."

I thought that was a great idea, even though I wouldn't know what to say. I would still go, and maybe, just maybe, I could make the questions flow. I owed it to the children and myself to get the answers that would allow us to move on.

I didn't really hear the customers that day. I was just going through the motions; my mind was on Dr. Graves and James. Would she be upset that I had come? Would she turn me away with no answers? Could I face her, knowing that I might leave worse off than I came? Questions filled my head, and with that time flew. Before I knew it, Ms. Fable was telling me the time and that I must hurry if I was going to reach my appointment.

"I will take care of the rest of the customers," she said. "Hurry along."

With that, I grabbed my purse and was on my way.

When I approached Dr. Graves's parking lot, I felt fear grasp me. Should I go in, or should I stay and wait for her in the parking lot?

I decided to go in because I didn't want her to think I was a stalker, and she would probably be mad. Inside her office, I knew she wouldn't make a scene and embarrass me.

As I went through the double doors to her office, I felt as though weakness was my friend. It held onto me until I reached the receptionist.

"Can I help you?" she said, looking through the glass.

"Uh, yes, I would like to speak to Dr. Graves," I said, barely forming the words.

"Do you have an appointment?" she said.

"Uh, no, ma'am, I don't. I just need a few minutes of her time before she leaves for the day. Would you please check and see if she will see me?" I said, wanting the girl to get off her butt and check for me before she left.

"What's your name, please?" she said.

I wasn't expecting her to ask my name, so I had to think in a hurry. "Lauren Justise," I said, stalling. I don't think she believed me.

"Okay, Ms. Justise, please have a seat, and I will check for you."

"I blew it," I said to myself. As I was sitting down, I was sure the receptionist knew I was lying, and she was probably telling Dr. Graves I was a nutcase. Dr. Graves was probably going out the back door.

Dr. Graves walked by the door where I was sitting, and she saw me. I wondered if she remembered me. I wondered if she was calling the police. A few minutes later, the receptionist returned to tell me that Dr. Graves would see me in a few minutes. Relief was close by, but I had a way to go before I could relax.

The door opened, and there she stood. She had her long strawberry-blond hair in a ponytail, her glasses hung off her nose, and she wore a lab coat the length of her dress. This was the woman who was about to give me all the answers I needed to get through this. I felt like I was being interviewed by God himself, but I managed to look at her when she called me by name.

"Victoria, please," she said, "come in."

She knew my name. She remembered me. She probably had the receptionist call the police and allowed me to come in so she could detain me until they got there. I would be arrested, and the welfare would take the kids away. I thought once to turn and run out the door, but her words stopped me.

"I was expecting you," she said. "I thought you would have been here way before now."

I couldn't say a word. I knew she was going to give me the whole drill about the confidentiality policy and how James would have to okay it before she told me anything. My attention was back on her now. She was talking, and I had to push the thoughts aside because I didn't want to miss a thing.

"I know you must be hurting," she said, "and you know that I am limited in what I can say because of my patient confidentiality contract. I will tell you this: James loved his family very much. He wanted to get better so he could take care of you and the children. I can explain to you as best I can about the depression that James is going through without giving you, his information. Depression is a beast, Victoria. It can and will take control of your mind and body with such a force that you may not be able to think straight. It comes in a form that makes you dependent, whether on drugs or alcohol or even food. People react to it in different ways. You don't feel worthy and sleeping or your addictions is all that you feel up to doing. Some people take it out on the ones they love, and some people become self-absorbed in pity. Some people do one and then the other; some do both."

"James left us," I interrupted.

"I know," she said. "James kept a couple of his appointments after he left his family, and that is how I knew that he loved you. Please let me finish."

"Sometimes depression causes people to think that the only thing they can do is to run away from it all—family, friends, even themselves. They can find better peace pretending that the ones who love them don't exist. They can feel that they are a burden, and they leave only to find once they have left that they don't know how to come back. They're hurt and they hurt the ones they love, so to make it all go away, they leave. They sometimes return just as humble as they left. But it's up to them to make that decision. You can't force them back because that only pushes them away. They have to come on their own, and if they do return, then they know that they have to make changes to be accepted back into the loved ones' lives. If they don't come back, it's because they are not willing to make the change or they don't know how to make the change. It differs from individual to individual."

"What you need to do now is pray and ask God to watch over him. It has to start with him. Drinking and medication don't mix, and it could cause more health problems. Sometimes medication and alcohol make the situation seem better, but in the long run, it does more harm than good."

"We love him," I said, with tears flowing, "and we can't get past him leaving us. We want him to come home," I said, not able to control my mouth. "I want him home, Dr. Graves. We have children who miss their daddy, and life is not the same without him. I have looked for him, but I can't find him."

"He doesn't want to be found, Victoria. If he did, he would come home. Let him go, and one day maybe he will find his way back to his family. On a personal note, I think he will return. Leaving the family, he felt, was the right thing to do. He felt he was a burden, but it's up to him; he has to make the decision. If you force him back, things will get worse. Let him have this time, and he will one day return."

Dr. Graves was wonderful. She eased my mind with her words more than I thought I could have done on my own. I left her office with thoughts of missing James, but also with hope that one day he would return.

Leaving her parking lot, I felt a presence like I was being watched. Out of the corner of my eye, I saw a figure standing there as if it was waiting for me to do something. It was so real that it gave me chills that took over my body, but when I turned to look, no one was there. My imagination getting the best of me, I thought. I'll just count it as my guardian angel. Feeling grateful that the doctor took the time to speak to me, I felt a lot better about the situation.

Chapter 27

Before I could sink into self-pity, spring had sprung. The children were going about their lives as if they weren't missing their father. May had arrived. The prom was fast approaching, and the children wanted to go. Since neither of them could drive and it was their birthday month, I thought I would combine everything together. I would be better able to afford it, and this would be the best prom ever. Considering they didn't have their licenses and they would be a bit embarrassed by me dropping them off and picking them up, I thought I would surprise them with a limo ride. They never talked about dates, so I guessed they would go with each other, but I would make this a most memorable event. I would make Hannah look like a princess and Brandon a prince. This would be an event to go down in my journal, I thought. I would talk about their father once the prom was over. I wouldn't dare tell them now; it might spoil it for them.

I told Ms. Fable about the children going to the prom. She told me that she would make all the arrangements for the limo. I would pay for it, of course, but she would make all the arrangements. Momma was excited too. She wanted to go shopping with us to get the tux and the gown. This was a happy time, and it would be so good for the children.

As the weeks passed, we got closer to their birthday. The prom was the preceding Saturday, so it was going to be quite an exciting month. We hustled around looking for this and that as time raced forward. We had to finish our shopping the weekend before the big day.

When I got home from work Friday evening and checked the mail, there was an envelope that didn't have a return address on it. In fact, it didn't even have a stamp on it. My first thought was that it was a letter from James, but it was a little thick for a letter. My curiosity piqued, I hurried in the house and tore it open. Money fell on the floor; it was crisp new bills totaling five hundred dollars. Ms. Fable, I thought—she sent this money to me so we could shop for the prom. Excitement filled my head. What a wonderful prom the children would have! I tossed the money in the air, only to scoop it up and toss it again. She knew I wouldn't take it if she handed it to me. What a friend she was to do such a thing! I felt that I would be in debt to her for the rest of my life.

Momma came early Saturday morning. She wanted to beat the crowd and shop without all the rush. We all loaded up in the car to hit the stores. We would make a day of it. It was fun watching the children try on the clothes, and they each judged the other and we really enjoyed that day. Hannah decided on a gown fit for a princess. It was peach in color, cut low in the back, with a split in the front. It showed a little cleavage, but not enough that would allow her to disrespect her beauty, so I let her get it. She chose a white handbag and white shoes. Brandon had a black tux, and he wore a peach shirt, so he and Hannah could match. He looked so handsome; he was indeed a prince. I felt a little overwhelmed leaving the store. I thought how proud their father would be if he could see how beautiful the children were.

The day before the prom, with all the excitement, the children realized they didn't plan on how they would get to the prom. It was Brandon who approached me with the question that made my heart laugh. "Momma," he said, "you are not going to drive us to the prom, are you?"

"How else do you plan on getting there?" I asked, laughing to myself.

"Well, can we go early so the other kids don't see us getting dropped off?"

"Why, Brandon, you are not ashamed of me, are you? I thought I would chaperone; that way I could be there with the two of you." The look on Brandon's face was so pitiful that I had to laugh out loud.

"I'm not going to drive you to the prom. I have made arrangements for a cab to come by and pick the two of you up and drop you back off."

Even though Brandon was relieved that I was not taking him to the prom, I could tell he wasn't excited about the cab either. The limo surprise would be a memory worth keeping for my grandchildren.

"Happy Prom Day," I yelled across the house as I woke up on their special day. The kids were already moving about the house. "I wonder what this special day will hold for the two most important people in my life," I said as I met up with them in the kitchen. Smiles was all I got. They knew we were struggling financially, but their smiles led me to believe that they knew I was up to something. I had held us together this far, so they knew that they should expect something wonderful.

Hannah had been up at the crack of dawn Saturday morning doing her nails and prepping for the most exciting night of her life thus far. Momma and Ms. Fable came over that evening and helped them get ready. Ms. Fable brought corsages, and I was glad; with all the excitement, I had forgotten to get them. Momma brought the video camera, and I took pictures. Hannah and Brandon looked amazing. They would be the best-looking couple at the ball, I thought. What a shame that James was missing this.

The knock at the door was the highlight of the evening. It was their chauffeur. When Hannah opened the door, she shrieked with happiness.

"Brandon, come look!" she shouted through the house. He wasn't in any hurry because he thought it was a cab driver. He lit up when he realized it was a limo instead of a cab.

"Momma, you tricked me!" he said.

"That was only because I wasn't invited," I said, teasing. "This, my children, is your birthday present from me!" Watching the light in their eyes twinkle and the happiness that was shared at that moment, I continued, "Now get going before it turns into a pumpkin. By the way," I said as they were leaving, "it returns at 1:00 a.m., so don't be late or you will be walking."

I watched as Brandon handsomely grabbed his sister by the hand and gently guided her down to the limo. He and she looked like a prince and princess. The neighbors gathered outside of their homes to see exactly who got in or out of that limo. The neighbors were also awestruck as Brandon held his sister's hand and led her to the limo. The limo driver held the door open as they got inside. You could see the neighbors watching from their sidewalks and driveways. As the limo pulled out, they showed approval by waving at the children as if they were movie stars. I watched the limo drive off with the happiest children in town. It brought tears to my eyes knowing that I had pulled off the most exciting night of their lives. Even more so because I had to do it without their father

Momma had put on a pot of tea, and we sat on the porch until the sun 9 down. When Momma and Ms. Fable went home, I went to my room and wrote in my Journal. This was indeed a day to remember.

It was 12:58 p.m. when I heard the limo pull up in the driveway. I got up and went to the door, anxious to hear about the children's night. They had a wonderful time. They danced all night long, and they took pictures. To hear them tell it, they were the most popular couple at the prom. There were other kids who had limousines, but they thought that theirs was the nicest. They later went and had pizza and then returned home. They thanked me for that evening, and Hannah whispered in my ear before she went to her room that she wished her father had been there to see her. She gave me a kiss on the cheek and disappeared. That hurt my heart and made me a little angry, but I shook it off and went to bed.

On the following Saturday, their actual birthday I got up fixed breakfast HAPPY BITHDAY I yelled across the house hoping to wake the children. I was all money and presents out from their prom, but I felt I had to do something special for this day. As they entered into the kitchen, I had placed a couple of candles on their beautifully browned pancakes and was singing with everything I had in me. We ate our breakfast and I said,

"Today is your day what do you want to do I have an idea and it won't cost us a thing."

"We can do whatever you want to do momma because you have done enough for us" Brandon said. Hannah chimed in I don't have any plans so whatever you decide as long as we are doing it together, I think it will be a wonderful day."

Very well then go put on some old clothes and meet me in the back yard" The look on their faces were priceless. They didn't have a clue as to what I was planning.

About a half hour and plenty of whispering later they were standing beside me in the back yard like I had lost my mind.

Hannah and Brandon, I said looking at the anticipation on their faces lets go fishing. We always wanted to go but we never took the time. Up against the house were several fishing poles that I had gotten when my father passed away. We can dig for worms this morning and by afternoon we can have a lunch packed and go to the creek for some family fishing. "Now that is what I am talking about" Brandon said. Worms momma really can't we use corn or bacon or something like that my nails were just re-done last night."

"Baby" Brandon said teasing her "I will bait your hook all you have to do is hold the pole."

With those words she said, "I will let you guys dig for worms and I will prepare the feast for our lunch."

I hadn't thought that Hannah would be scared of worms I didn't like the little squirmy creatures either, but I wouldn't dare tell Brandon. We dug and dug and gathered and gathered once we were almost done our yard looked as if a mole had a field day. We had enough worms to fish all-day and with basket of food in hand Hannah met us at the car.

"This may be fun after all she said we always wanted to go fishing and a picnic by the creek sounds exciting along as none of the fish water splash on me."

We arrived at the creek around 11:00 o'clock there were already fishermen there fishing some were wading in the creek with their poles other were sitting on the bank. We found our spot and Brandon grabbed the worms and baited our poles.

Hannah was the first to get a bite on her line she shrieked and laughed and hollered Brandon help me. They pulled and pulled tugged and tugged and out came a tiny fish. We all laughed the way they were tugging and pulling we thought that we had a shark. That was the beginning of an exciting day. We sat there and we watched as other fishermen caught there fish and we caught our share of course. We stopped fishing long enough to eat our lunch and then we were back at it again. It was disappointing to find out that we had only one more worm left. At the end of the day, Hannah caught five. Brandon caught eight and I caught two. I barely got to enjoy my fishing because I was enjoying the excitement of the children.

As we were leaving this little boy and his father was walking past us and we heard the father tell his son you will catch some son. We will come back another day. Walking away empty-handed Brandon, Hannah and I looked at each other and as if we had the same thoughts, Brandon and Hannah quickly went to the little boy and Brandon said would you like to have ours we were just going to throw them back. "Really" the boy said, "you mean it." The father thanked the both of them and we got into our car fish smell and all and headed home each with a smile on our face and much conversation about our exciting day.

More surprises came once we pulled up in our driveway momma and Ms. Fable were sitting on the porch waiting for us. "Where have ya'll been" momma said as we got out the car "fishing" Hannah said "it was fun"

"Sounds like it" Ms. Fable said. "Where's the fish?." "We gave them away" I said fishing is one thing cleaning them is another and that brought laughter because at that point I think we all were in agreement.

"Well, aren't there some birthday's today momma said. Yeah, replied to Ms. Fable "we were all set for a party, and no one was here."

"We had our big birthday present last week remember" Hannah said.

"Well, someone should have told us" momma said "we were thinking the party was this week" momma said teasingly "Yeah Ms. Fable said well we had better take our gifts back to the store and get some of that money back right away"

"What" Brandon said "no way"

After the laughter subsided Ms. Fable said, "Then you better get inside and get them before we change our mind." "Yall shouldn't have I" said with my heart filling with much appreciation. They each just shrugged their shoulders as if to say what did you expect.

Without another word the children raced into the house to see what presents they had gotten for their birthday

Once inside the house it looked like Christmas. There was lots of presents and a cake dedicated to both of them, and Joy filled our home once more Hugs and thank you followed the tearing into the gifts after washing off the fishing smell, we all spent the rest of the evening on the once depressing porch with joy in our hearts laughing and talking about plans for their future and that was the way we spent their seventeenth birthday just enjoying the children.

That wasn't the end of it because on Monday they each got a card with two hundred dollars apiece from their other grandmother. So far this was the best birthday ever for our kids and it was worth putting down as a memory. Shame, Shame James Andrews your missing out on somethings that could give you a whole nother perspective on life.

It was the first of June before I decided to visit the willow tree in the park. I decided to go there so I could tell Mrs. Andrews about my visit with James's doctor, and I also told her about the children going to the prom. I put down fresh flowers and headed to Daddy's grave. I told him the same thing that I had told Mrs. Andrews except I added their birthday and the fishing trip. I wished that they were closer, so I didn't have to repeat myself, but it was what it was. I cleaned off his graveside, gave him fresh flowers, and went home.

When I got home, the children were already cutting the grass. Hannah would be leaving in a couple of weeks, going to camp. Brandon hit me head-on when I got home about getting his license. He was becoming a man, so I thought it was time. I finished helping the children with the grass, and we put hotdogs on the grill. I still felt like I was being watched, but God had given me such peace that it didn't matter. I knew he was watching over me, and I knew that he loved us.

I spent Saturday testing with Brandon on his exam for his learner's permit; we were going to take the test on Monday. In between testing and cleaning, I decided to talk to the children about what I had learned about their father's depression. We had taken a break from testing, and we decided to sit on the porch and soak up a little sun. We talked about the exam and just things that they wanted to talk about. After we'd chatted for half an hour on the porch, I thought it was a good time to discuss their father and his condition. "Guys," I began, "I went to see Dr. Graves a few weeks back." I looked at their facial expressions as they expected news about their father before I continued on.

Hannah was all ears. She was just as curious as I, and I tried to fill her in as much as Dr. Graves did me; Brandon, on the other hand, couldn't care less. He was angry at his father, and I understood. "He's a coward, Momma," he shouted as he walked into the house. He shouted back over his shoulder, "He could have stayed and allowed us to help him. But, instead, he chose to leave; and since he has been gone, we have been much happier. I am glad he is gone, and I hope he never comes back."

I hurt for him, but that was his feelings, and he had to sort through them on his own. I wished he had felt differently, but he was a young man now and he had been hurt by his father. Hannah and I watched as the door closed behind him. I started to run after him, but he was a young man now and I had to let him sort out his own feelings.

Hannah, on the other hand, wanted to soak it all up. "I miss him, Momma," she said. "Sometimes I am angry, and there are other times I hurt for myself, for you and brother, and for him."

I gave her an approving nod. "I understand," I told her. "I get like that most of the time." We both laughed. "He can still come back, Hannah," I said, not wanting to give her false hope. "But he has to on his own. We can't force him. He has some sorting out to do, and when he is ready, he will come back, and we would be back to normal."

The biggest smile filled her face, and that let me know it gave her joy, as well as a little hope. She was happy to get the news, and I was happy that I saw the sparkle back in her face.

That same night, I wrote in my journal to James. I had to tell him how Brandon was feeling and what I felt about visiting with his doctor. He had to know, and I felt that if I put my feelings on paper, God would tell him. I wrote until I went to sleep.

Sunday came with Hannah running around the house looking for her clear nail polish to fix the hole in her stocking. "Join me, Momma," she said, squinting up her face. My first thought was to go with her, to join her this morning at church, but the devil crept up to use Brandon as an excuse. "I think Brandon will need me to help him study, so he will do well on his test tomorrow." Every time I quizzed him, he would only miss a few questions, so I knew that he would do well. I guess one could say I was just a little angry with God about the way things were going in my life. I didn't feel like giving praise to someone that only showed me sadness. Changing the subject, I said, "I also think that Brandon has a little girlfriend. A call came in today for him from a Jasmine. He took the phone and went into his room." I had to smile when he took the phone, and that sent me back to the time that his daddy and I first met. After Hannah went to church, I helped Brandon study for his test. When she came home, she and I went to the park. We invited Brandon to come, but he was on the phone again. I asked Hannah about the mystery girl, and she told me what little she knew.

"She's pretty, Momma," she said, "and she is really popular in school. Brandon spent a lot of time with her at the prom." After that, Hannah wanted to talk about her dad, and that was the way we spent our afternoon.

I saw someone from a distance looking at Hannah and me, but it was probably just some old man wanting money for a coffee. We were at the park for goodness' sake, and that is what bums do at the park. He didn't look long; he quickly continued on his journey, and Hannah and I scurried home.

I used my journal that evening to write to James about Jasmine. I told him how Brandon was going after his learner's permit the next day, probably for the sake of Jasmine. That way he would be able to take her out on a date. How cute is that? I told him I wished he was there to see it, but the reality of it all was he wasn't.

Work was okay. Ms. Fable asked about my visit to the doctor, and I told her because she was my friend. She wanted to help, and I trusted her as my boss and as my friend. She told me that she had heard about people being depressed, and it was a tough road to be on. She told me that she hoped James would come back for the sake of me and the children, but if he didn't, she felt we would be just fine.

I could tell Brandon was nervous as I drove him and his sister to the DMV. I tried to take his mind off of it by telling him that I was planning a vacation to visit their Grandma Robertson. They both gave short answers when I asked questions and I wanted to laugh, but I would do that once they left the car. I guessed Hannah was nervous for her brother because she didn't talk much either. For her, that was unusual; it must be a twin thing, I thought.

When we arrived at the DMV, Brandon just sat there. Finally, out of the blue, Hannah said, "I guess I will take the test too. How hard could it be? I read some of the exam; it just seems like common sense to me. Can I take it too, Momma?" she asked.

"I don't see why not," I said, "if you want to. I guess it will be okay."

When I looked over at Brandon, he was the spitting image of James, and Hannah was the spitting image of me. He looked relieved that Hannah would be joining him. I knew she was going to support him. With that, they both got out of the car, and we went in for the exam. After I gave the clerk their information, I went back out to the car. I felt that my presence would only make them nervous. I just sat there in the car thinking how they were so mature and one day they would leave me so they could start their own lives. I imagined they would find love like their dad, and I once shared, and I could only hope that the ending was much better for them than ours had been.

It only took Hannah less than thirty minutes to come back to the car. Brandon was still in there, I knew, evaluating every question. He was the thinker, and Hannah was the one living on impulse. She came rushing out, "Momma, I passed! I passed! They need you in there. I passed! I passed!" I went in to sign for Hannah, and I tried to be quiet and not disturb Brandon.

When he came around the corner from the test machine, the look on his face was disappointing. It told me that he had failed the test. Hannah, for the love of her brother, didn't rub it in. She didn't even ask to drive home.

He got into the car and said, "Let's just go, Mom."

Well, I thought, he failed the test. I wanted to cry for him, but I wouldn't add to his frustration.

Once I was backing out, he said, "Where are we going, Momma?"

I said, "Home."

He said, "Not until you sign the paper and give me the wheel."

"I knew that" Hannah said.

"What?" I said.

"I got it, Momma. I got my learner's permit. You have to go sign." He was a jokester. I wanted to be mad at the awful joke he had just played, but I was so happy for him to be mad. I parked the car, went in, and paid for his learner's permit. I signed on the dotted line and cried, both at the same time.

"Since you are a crybaby and you are having a girl moment, can I drive us home?" he asked.

I didn't deny him, and the relief on Hannah's face and a wink of her eye let me know that she wasn't objecting. With her approval, I allowed him to drive us home, and he did pretty well actually.

Hannah was thrilled that her brother got his learner's permit too, and more thrilled with an envelope that she found in the mailbox.

"Look, Momma," she said as she handed me the envelope. "What is it?"

It didn't have a return address, nor did it have a stamp, and it was rather thick. I was hoping it was a letter from James, and I think that is what she thought too, but to my surprise, it was money—an envelope full, no check, no money order, but money. It was over five hundred dollars. Ms. Fable, I thought. She was only being a friend. What a friend she was.

Hannah was ecstatic. "Five hundred dollars, Momma. Are you kidding me? Somebody sent us five hundred dollars."

Brandon teasingly said, "Yeah, Jasmine sent it to me so that I could help with your trip."

"Yeah, sure," Hannah replied.

Their excitement spread to me, and my heart skipped a beat. It was a lot of money, and it was an overly kind gesture. Why is Ms. Fable being so secret about it? Why doesn't she just hand it to me? I thought.

Brandon and I helped Hannah pack for her camping trip. I had already paid for the trip in advance, but I still gave her a hundred dollars just in case she needed or wanted something; four hundred dollars was more than enough to go on vacation. I just didn't feel right, her being two hundred miles from home without money. She was excited, and Brandon was too. We knew that he was to start his paper route tomorrow, so that meant that I had to get up early and go with him. This was his first day, and even though he had his learner's permit, he needed a person with a license to tag along. I became excited too.

I wrote James a letter that night telling him about all that he was missing. I told him that it would be nice if he would get it together and come home.

Brandon and I woke early in the morning to see Hannah off. I cried, and Brandon held me. How sweet that was, I thought to myself. This is what your dad is supposed to be doing, but I wouldn't dare say it to him. We had to be there at five, and Brandon and I waved the bus away. I was happy for Hannah, yet afraid. This was her first trip away from me. I had told her to call every day. I bought her a prepaid phone and put a hundred minutes on it, because I wanted her to feel that she could call me whenever she wanted. I believe that is what James would have wanted me to do, and with her clothes packed, cell phone on her side, and money in her pocket, she was gone. Thank God for 2005, and the cell phone trend.

Brandon was excited to get to his paper route. He wouldn't allow me to help. Brandon said, "Mom, don't help me. You are only here because you are the only one with a license." I got out a time or two, but only if he had several boxes on both sides of the street. And I reminded him that I wanted my share for helping. "I know that" he said, "but how can I learn on my own if you keep helping me?"

"Fair enough," I replied. "I will just sit here and mind my own business."

We laughed and talked the whole way. It was good time spent, and I couldn't wait until the next day so we could do it all over again.

I dropped Brandon off at home, where I knew he would be on the phone all day with Jasmine. I headed off to work. My instincts told me to thank Ms. Fable for the money. But I decided against it, because if she wanted me to know it was from her, she would have handed it to me. I just decided to work extra hard for her to pay it back, and that was what I did.

First thing after I got home, I called Hannah. She didn't want to talk long; she had arrived at camp, and she was in the middle of a camping activity.

"Tell Brandon I love him. Got to go, Momma. Love you," and with that, she was gone.

Brandon was standing close by reaching for the phone, so I gave him the message from his sister and handed him the phone. I felt I would have no conversation with him now that he found a special friend, so I settled into a movie and then went to write James. I had to tell him about seeing Hannah off and about Brandon's first day on the job. I ended my letter with telling him that I needed him home and I wanted him to know that no matter what, I still loved him. With that, I went to sleep.

Brandon woke me the next morning by banging on the door. "Are you up, sleepyhead?" he called.

"I am now," I shouted back. "Give me a minute. I will be ready to go." Excitement filled me once more.

While Brandon was picking up his papers, I thought back to James when we were first married. How I would get up and see him off to work. But this wasn't my husband; this was my son. Where, oh God, where is my husband? I thought, bringing tears that I had to erase before Brandon saw them.

On the paper route, I continued to jump out from time to time to help, but this day was different. As I got out of the car to put the paper in the apartment complex boxes, I saw a figure that seemed to be on the sixth floor watching us. I didn't mean to stare, but my first reaction and thought was that it was James. The figure just stood there with the lights on, not moving. I thought that it was James wanting to cry out to us to rescue him. Brandon was ready to go, but I couldn't pull myself from that figure. When Brandon called out to me, he came to see what I was looking at, and the figure disappeared.

"Momma," he said, looking up with me, "is everything okay, what are you looking at?"

"Yes," I mumbled, and nothing and then I joined him in the car. I didn't dare tell him of my thoughts. Not only would he think I was crazy, but he might become angry because I knew he was angry with his dad. I carried those thoughts to work with me. Suppose it was James. Suppose the image I was seeing was his father. The words from Dr. Graves came rushing back, but I had to know. I wouldn't force him home, but I had to know.

I was only a figment in motion at work that day. I couldn't get the image out of my mind. Was it James? Was he wanting to come home and not knowing how to find his way back? Was he calling out to me, and I didn't understand the signs? I couldn't wait for the paper route the next day, so I could see the image again and make contact.

Hannah called me as soon as I got home. She said she had been trying all day, but I guessed Brandon was on the phone with Jasmine. She was doing fine, and she was having the time of her life. She missed us, and she asked if we had heard from her father. I told her no. That was all I could say, because I wasn't sure. With that, she said her I love you's and good-byes.

Brandon was in rare form. He had cooked on the grill. He made us hamburgers, and that was pleasing. He had something he wanted to tell me, and I knew he didn't know how. I kind of figured it was about this Jasmine girl, so I broke the ice for him. "How's Jasmine?" I said.

"Fine, fine. She wants to come for a visit."

"She does?" I said. "Well, imagine that! I would be delighted to meet her. When does she want to come?"

"Well," he said, "her momma could drop her off tomorrow around noon, but you would still be at work."

"Well," I said, "how about that?"

"Is that okay, Momma?" Brandon searched my face like his father once did.

"I suppose so, but I must ask, Brandon. No sex, right?"

"Right," he said. That was a question his father should have been asking, but I needed to know if they were sexually active because I didn't want a grandchild right yet. That was the last thing this family needed.

"Momma," Brandon said, "I want to be an engineer before I have sex, I want to have my future planned, I want to be able to take care of my family. When I have sex, I want it to be forever, and I want her to want me forever."

I was satisfied with that. I knew at that point that James was missing the best part of our children's lives. I thought I would write him that night and tell him.

I awoke before Brandon the next morning. I wanted to go back to that apartment complex. I wanted him to drop me off and pick me up after his route, but I knew not to say that. Brandon was in a world of his own, wanting Jasmine to visit. When we got to the complex, the light was on. I got out of the car, stood in the yard at the complex, and waved.

Brandon asked me who I was waving at. It was the familiar image, and it was on the sixth floor. When Brandon came to see who I was waving at, the lights went out. I just told him that I saw someone looking, so I just waved. I didn't dare tell him of my thoughts, but I couldn't shake the feeling that it was James.

When we finished the route, I told Brandon to straighten up for his guest and I would be home later, maybe even later than I had thought. I was going to the apartment complex, and I was going to see if James was there. I knew I shouldn't force him like Dr. Graves said, but I wanted him to know that we still needed him. I remembered the sixth floor, and if I had to knock on every door with a picture, I would. James needed to be home, and he was missing my children growing up; that was unacceptable to me, to us.

Work presented a challenge for me especially that day. The customers were as friendly as ever, and they wanted to get in my business. I told them we were fine, and James was okay, and they seemed satisfied with that.

There were times that I had customers that would be a little too nosy. They would ask questions that made me uncomfortable. Ms. Fable would come out of the back, and I could see by the look on her face that her claws were out. I knew if someone said anything out the way to me, she would be all over them. She made me a little more comfortable when it came to the busybodies. The questions would stop once her presence was known. I was so glad that she was my friend. I don't think I could have gone through this struggle without her. I knew ever since I came back to work that she was a little protective over me. She did more cleaning where I was working than she did in the whole store. One day after it was becoming too noticeable, I finally had to ask her, "Why are you watching me, Ms. Fable? Do you not think I can manage the nosy people on my own?"

"Victoria," she replied, "I am not watching you as you think. I just want to stay close, just in case someone strikes a nerve, and you lose it, that's all."

I could appreciate her help; I welcomed it, and she was right. Some of the customers were a bit too nosy and sometimes there would be hard conversations. Having said that I was glad that Ms. Fable was on my side I wouldn't want to fight my battles opposite of her. She knew too many people, and everybody respected her.

"But" she continued, "I am sure if you don't want me around, I can find something to do in the back. You can always scream out if you need me." We both laughed at the idea and decided it was break time. I put the break sign on the door, and we retired to the back for a rather extensive break.

"Coffee?" she said as I walked through the door.

"No, I brought tea," I replied. "It seems to relax me more than coffee. Ms. Fable," I said, trying not to sound like I was feeling, "do you think I failed my children?"

"Why?" she said. "Because you tried to keep your family together, and he decided to leave? No, you are not the one who failed, Victoria. If anything, you are the one that held everything together, even when it fell apart."

I sank down in the chair, letting her words soak in, before I asked, "Do you think he will ever come back, or do you think his mind is made up and he is where he wants to be?"

"Only God knows that answer, Victoria. You can't make yourself understand why he did what he did, and you definitely can't blame yourself. Everything is still new. He could be trying to get better without hurting his family, hoping that you will one day forgive him, or he could like the life he has and want to continue to waddle in his self-pity. No one knows but him and God, and whatever the case, it's not for our understanding. It's between him and God, and as long as you pray, God will help you and the children through."

"I worry about Brandon. He has a lot of hurt from his father's actions. I wanted so desperately for him and his father to have that special bond, and now all he has is Hannah and me, his anger, and his pain." Silence came over me as I relived the day that James had told the children that he was dying.

Ms. Fable cut into my thoughts with, "Just pray, Victoria. I can't imagine what you are going through, but you are a strong woman, and it is because God is keeping you in his arms. You may not see it, but a lot of women would have just given up. But I can see you are a fighter, and you will become stronger. One day, when you look back on this, you will see that it wasn't as bad as you felt at the time, and the outcome will be well worth what you are experiencing now."

With those words, we got up, cleared away our drinks, and returned to the front. It wasn't until after lunch that a customer came into the store that I hadn't thought about for years and at that point in my life was the last person I wanted to run into but just like that there was April. At first, I thought to go in the back and let Ms. Fable wait on her, but I am not a coward I thought I have raised two beautiful children and no matter what was on her mind or what she thought I had nothing to be ashamed of. I was sure she read the paper I was sure that she knew James left me. I tried not to look at her as she approached my counter but I knew she knew I saw her so I would just go with the flow.

"April how are you I haven't seen you in years." I said trying not to stare. I felt a little better once she was closer because I could tell by the bags under her eyes and the wrinkles that had formed that her life hadn't been peaches and cream. She still had pretty features, but they show signs of struggles. She wasn't the vibrant beautiful woman that was my biggest competition years ago. She looked more tired and stressed these days and even though I probably did too, I was glad that I wasn't alone.

"Victoria, I am doing ok how have you been doing? I saw the article about James in the paper a while back and I worried about the two of you, but I have since seen him and I know that he is ok, but ho------"What you seen him I asked before I thought where?"

"At the apartment complex in Abbs Valley, you know the one that is like a mile from the school. I have seen him several times." As if she felt the need to explain she then said, "I didn't talk to him very long I was over there taking care of a hospice patient and bumped into him, but that was a while back." As she continued to talk my mind trailed back to when I was on the paper route with Brandon. That was James I had seen because that is the apartment complex that she is speaking of but who was the man at the door.

"Victoria, Victoria" she said interrupting my thoughts "are you ok?"

"um yes, I managed to say I am fine. I knew he was at those apartments I said we had a little struggle, but we are better now." Wanting to know more but feeling the need to change the subject I said so what about you married, kids?"

"Yes, I have two kids but not yet married" she said, "good men are just hard to fine." "

There is some one for everyone" I said and with those words I felt Ms. Fables presence. I think she looked at that as her que because then she said, "well girl I guess I will leave you to it and I'll talk to you later, maybe lunch one day when you get the chance for catch up," she said with a smile as she turned and walked away. All I could do at that point considering my mind was in overdrive was say "We should" while nodding my head "take care" she hollered over her shoulder "you too" …. Then she was gone.

When April was out of my sight I turned to Ms. Fable and said "She saw and spoke to James" almost on the verge of tears.

"Who is she and where did she see him?" she asked

"April she's a girl that had a crush on James years ago she is a nurse and she said that she saw him while she was visiting one of her hospice patients at the apartment complex in Abbs Valley." She stood there as if she was soaking it all in then she asked,

"Who was he staying with?."

"I am not sure" I said, and I wasn't, but I would bet it was probably his father. "So, what now I asked eager to hear some promising words.

"Well," Ms. Fable said "Dr. Graves said he wouldn't be found if he didn't want to be. I say "it's good that we now know he's alive and don't want to be found. I know some people who know some people let me do a little digging to see what I can come up with. I'll do my research and get back with." She didn't wait around for another word just like that I knew she was on the prowl to find out all that she could that would help ease mine and the children's mind.

On my way home, I went on instinct and stopped at the complex, just wondering if I should enter. I let my curiosity get the best of me. I went to the door, and it was the kind of door that only the people of the building could let you in. I waited until someone, anyone, entered or left the building so I could gain entry.

There was one little lady who befriended me that day. She told me that if I helped her with her groceries, she would help me get into the building. I carried all of them. It was only four bags, and I was glad to see an elevator because, as desperate as I was, I wouldn't have been able to carry those bags up the stairs. Once inside, I could tell she was a nosy neighbor.

She had all the gossip from her floor. Some people she knew, and some she didn't. By the end of her gossip session, I was sure she would know everybody in the building before long. She got off on the fifth floor, and I was disappointed to find out that she didn't live on the sixth. She told me all about her floor: who was sleeping with whom, who was on drugs, what time they came home at night, and what time they left. I asked about the sixth floor, but the only one she knew on the sixth floor was a man named Ron. He hadn't been there long. Ron, I thought, could that be short for Ronald? Could that have been James's father's name? I was more eager to get into that apartment than I had any of the others. I tried to excuse myself as she continued to talk as if I was just the silent listener.

"He was a quiet man," she said. "He doesn't want company. I tried to give him a baked pie, but he didn't accept it. He is a man with many secrets," she told me. "He has a man living with him, but he doesn't talk much. Something must have happened when he was a youngster." With that, I put her groceries by the door, and I headed back to the elevator.

I went to the sixth floor and knocked on every door there was to knock on; there were only about seven.

At the sixth door, a man answered. "Can I help you?" he said. As he cracked open the door, I could smell a faint smell of alcohol as he spoke to me. He was not about to open the door all the way so I could get a peek inside. He wouldn't even look at me. As he spoke, he looked down at the floor. In spite of the small crack the strong smell of alcohol caught me a little off guard, but I continued on with the purpose for my intrusion.

I told him who I was, and I asked if he had seen James. I had a picture with me, but it was a picture of an old James, not the new. After a moment passed, he took the picture from my hand as if seeing this man for the first time. He had a certain expression on his face. I couldn't read this expression because I didn't know this man, or did I he had a familiar tone. He then returned the picture to me and said that he hadn't seen that man before. It was like he was unsure at first, but he told me that he was just an old man, and he didn't get out much. I wanted in to see if his window matched up with the tree outside, but I thought that was asking too much. I apologized for being inconvenient, and I left to knock again on the last door across the hall from him with no answer. While I was knocking, I felt that the man was watching me through his peephole, but maybe it was because I was a stranger. He was probably wondering how I had gotten into the building.

I felt like a fool when I left that building, and Dr. Graves's words came rushing back to me: "You can't find them if they don't want to be found." I almost felt defeated when I left the complex. Maybe if I had of told the man that I loved him and I only wanted to talk maybe he would have let me in. All I knew is that if James was hiding from me for whatever reason he didn't have to all I wanted to do was to talk to him. Once we talked, I just felt we could both better understand what happened and why. If closure is all that was needed to move forward, I would consider that as an option as well, but without knowing anything I just felt like I was going through life in limbo.

When I got home, I finally met Jasmine. She was as pretty as Hannah had described. I could see why Brandon wanted to be with her. She was a respectful girl, and she seemed to have a good head on her shoulders. I didn't tarry long when I met her. I talked for just a few minutes, and then I left them to themselves. Just to be on the safe side, I walked past Brandon's room to see if the bed was ruffled. It was made as Brandon had always made it, and with that, I went to my room and took a nap.

I awoke with a phone call from Hannah. "Hey, Momma, how are you?" she said.

"Good, girl, how are you?" I replied.

"I'm having a blast," she said. "I wish you were here, but I don't want to come back."

"Yeah, I wish I was there too, but you will come back?" I said, managing to get a laugh in.

"How's Brandon?" she asked.

"Good," I said. "Jasmine is here, so that is why he didn't want to come to camp. It wasn't because of his job."

"Tell him he's a loser," she said, laughing. Then we both laughed.

"Well, have you heard anything from Daddy?" she asked.

I replied, "No."

And with that I heard, "I love you; see you later. Bye."

"Love you too," I replied. "Good-bye."

I got up to check on Brandon and Jasmine and to see if they wanted dinner. They were in the living room watching a movie. They wanted to help cook, but only after the movie was over. We all cooked dinner together, and that was a fun evening. I saw how they looked at each other, and it sent me back to the way James used to look at me. I knew love was in the air, and it was a good feeling. I didn't dare tell Brandon about my evening. I just left well enough alone. He was having a good time, and I didn't want to spoil it.

Jasmine left around nine o'clock. I got a chance to meet her mother, and she was pleasant enough. She was a woman of business. She was an attractive woman, not a lot of makeup, just enough to highlight her age, which was around late thirties or early forties. She dressed in business attire, and she wore her hair shoulder-length. Her walk was of someone who was never late; she had a distinct stride to her, and her voice was of a calm businesswoman. I could tell by looking at her that she wasn't a mess like me. I thought to myself I wondered what she thought of me, in my faded blue jeans and T-shirt, hair in a ponytail, and wrinkles on my face that showed I had years of worry. Would the sight of actually seeing Brandon's dysfunctional family make her tell her daughter that she was making a big mistake?

Her mother knew, like I knew, that Jasmine and Brandon were happy in love. We both knew that it was their first love and that it wouldn't last.

She had a cup of tea with me, and we sat on the porch while Jasmine prepared to go home. I didn't tell her about James, and she didn't ask. I wanted her to think we were a functioning family; I certainly didn't want her to think otherwise. If Brandon wanted them to know, he would be the one to tell them, not me. I didn't want my troubles to interfere with Brandon's happiness. I felt a little nervous, and all the while, she was calm. I had hoped it didn't show to the point that she knew that we were a family with troubles. I had made a pot of tea and was sitting on the porch when she pulled into the driveway. She broke the ice, and I was glad. "Victoria, right? I'm Sophie, Jasmine's mom," she said, extending her hand. "She really seems to like Brandon." That put me at ease a little, knowing that Jasmine said good things about my son

"Good to meet you," I responded, extending my hand to meet hers. Um I made a pot of tea would you like some before Jasmine leaves trying to give Brandon a little more time with his friend. Sounds good she said retrieving my hand and hoping that she couldn't feel the dryness. As I led her in the kitchen I said, "That's good to hear,." "I'm glad Brandon has finally found a special friend" "She seems like a really nice girl," I said, trying to keep my conversation short but responsive.

"They are really into each other, aren't they," she said, looking around. I was thinking that she was comparing how we lived to how she lived. I quickly gave her the cup of tea and led her back to the porch.

"Yes," I said, trying to draw her eyes back to me. "Brandon really cares about her."

"Oh, I can remember my first boyfriend," she said. "I was a lot like Jasmine. His name was Harper, and I couldn't stay away from him. I tell her, though, to take her time."

I was still stuck on the words "my first boyfriend." Yeah, I thought, I remember mine too. He just left his family about six months ago.

"Well," she continued, "sometimes a first love lasts; sometimes it doesn't. We will just have to wait and see what happens. If nothing else, they can be lifelong friends. I am still friends with some of the guys that I dated. It's all in the maturity level."

Jasmines mom was a bit forward, I thought, but I just nodded. I was thankful that Jasmine and Brandon came to the porch.

"Good-bye, Mrs. Andrews," Jasmine said as she and Brandon went towards the car. We followed close behind, watching them as they walked hand in hand to the car.

Sophie turned to me and said, "Well, Victoria, looks like we could be spending some time together. Maybe lunch sometime or you can come to dinner. That would be a great way for us to get to know each other."

"That sounds nice," I said. "Lunch would be great. I will have to check my calendar and get back to you on that." I was thinking to myself, I don't know if I like you well enough to share a meal. Besides, maybe this is a passing thing with Jasmine and Brandon, so why bother getting to know you?

Sophie started up her car, and Brandon kissed Jasmine softly on her lips. Then Jasmine and her mother drove away.

Brandon grabbed hold of my hand as we walked to the door. "So, Momma, what do you think?"

"She seems nice, Brandon," I said, wanting to add "though her mom's a little forward," but I didn't. "Do you like her?" I asked.

Brandon surprised me with his words, as if he was reading my mind. "Yeah, I do. Jasmine's mom can be a little forward sometimes, but that is just her way."

"She invited me to lunch, and I told her that I had to check my calendar."

Brandon looked at me as though he knew my thoughts again, and we both just laughed and entered our home.

I wrote in my journal to James again, telling him about the happiness that Brandon had found, about my attempt to find him, and then I cursed him and went to bed. Shame on James, I thought, for bringing his family to shame, for hurting us. I hope he never returns. I didn't mean that; I was just angry. With that, I went to sleep.

Hannah was coming home in a few days, and Brandon would soon receive his first paycheck. I would take him to the bank so he could start an account. Get an ATM card, so he could make himself more important to the girl of his dreams. Not much longer, and the twins would have their driver's licenses. Then Brandon would be legal going out on real dates. He would feel better about himself and the situation that he was given.

Work didn't come easy anymore. I was a zombie going through the motions. I had a reality check at one point in my life I dreaded the grounds that April walked on but now a days I found myself watching the store door hoping she would come through, Even though Ms. Fable knew I wasn't as productive as I was before, she never said a word. She just told me that if I wanted to talk, then I could. If I needed to take days off, that would be okay too. I didn't want her to know that I was confused and a complete mess, so I continued to work and pray in spite of the fact that I wanted to go home and go to bed. I needed the money, and I didn't want charity.

James had destroyed his pride. I wouldn't let him take mine too. I had two beautiful children that I was raising, and that was just what I was going to do, even though sometimes I had to step outside myself and let this stranger that I felt I had become raise my children. I had to make myself available to them when they needed to talk. When they seemed to need me, I prepared myself by pretending this was all a dream and I would wake up. I would keep this dream to myself because it was too horrible to tell. I wouldn't want to upset them with the nonsense that I was going through. Pretending it was a dream helped me get through those long, dreadful days at work. I would have people who were generally concerned asking me how I was doing and if I needed anything. I would lie and say we were doing fine. Then I would go to the back and cry. When I returned to the front, I returned to my dream.

I called Momma from time to time, but I needn't worry her with my problems. Ms. Fable was a good friend; she wouldn't be affected like my momma would about all that was going on. I knew momma had wise words to guide me, and she was a straight shooter but sometimes I felt God wouldn't be upset if we bent the rules and bending the rules was something I knew my mother wouldn't do. With Momma and Ms. Fable, I had the best of both worlds both women were smart and strong. One solely depended on God which was momma and the other just took the bull by the horn to get the desired results by any means necessary and that was Ms. Fable. Approximated a week after I saw April, Ms. Fable called me to let me know that she had to make a few runs and she was coming in later.

I decided to go in a little early to get the store open and prepare for the day. About an hour after I got there in came Ms. Fable. To the back to the back its break time. Follow me she said. Anxious about her excitement I put the break sign on the door and headed towards the back. When I got to the back Ms. Fable was seated at her desk on the phone. She motioned with her hand for me to sit down. My mind was filled with curiosity to the point I thought my head was going to blow off, but I sat there listening. "Um hummm I see" she said well are there any other tenants"? I heard her say. Oh ok----oh I see----Well I guess if you got the money, you could do whatever you want to do-----no you have been more than enough help. If I can think of anything else, I will let you know thank you.... goodbye."

She laid down the phone slowly... then looked up at me and said "BAM...just like that" Looking at her with a burning inside I said, "Just like what" what are you talking about silly girl." As if she knew I was going to pop she said "hold on to your seat Victoria I found out some juicy stuff you see there is a tenant that lives there in that building that has paid his rent for 5 years he lives on the sixth floor and his Name is William Ronald Anderson, but you see where I am going with this? He undoubtedly has someone that stays with him from time to time or visits regularly. My source seems to think that it's his son. I bet you that it is James. None the less William is supposedly a well to do man. He had come into a lot of money and that is how he is able to pay his rent up. My source said with the money that he has that it's a surprise that he lives in an apartment. I know just about everybody in this town Victoria, and I have never I mean never have I heard of a William Ronald Anderson."

As my mind trailed off to its on space, I felt that she was able to confirm, what Mrs. Andrews told me about his father's name Ron, but could Willie also be short for William. The only thing that threw me off at this point was the name Anderson James last name was Andrews. Mr. Anderson couldn't be James dad because James last name was Andrews not Anderson and I thought I must call James's momma to see if she can help put together the missing pieces.

She must have felt that I was in la la land because she threw a ink pen cap at me " Laughing she said earth to Victoria come in Victoria" I had to laugh once tuned back in "That's not all, " she continued, "Okay so you can call me nosy later but so after I got a hold of my source I asked the question how hard it would be to get into one of the apartments and they told me they could do a check anytime they wanted to as long as they gave a 24 hour notice. I got the call yesterday that they were going to check a few apartments for water damage this morning and I could come along if I wanted to. Of course, I wanted to, so I met them there and we went into the Apartments. On the sixth floor the last apartment on the right side was the one in question. When we got there was no one home. While they looked for damage I did as much snooping as I could, and I found this picture. She handed me a picture that took my breath away. It was a picture of a boy and his father. The child favored Brandon and the man favored………James. Ron has to be his father. I knew I had to get this picture to Ms. Robertson she held the answers.

"Victoria", she continued, "we could stake the place out if you want to, I am in they have to go in and out at some point." I sat there for a moment in my thoughts before I said "true but if he was that close and didn't reach out to me, maybe he wasn't ready to fix what had been broken. Maybe if he saw me, he would look at me as a desperate woman then later criticize me for not letting him get the help as he saw fit. Would that push me back to square one Would he just come to appease me then get back to that old drunken state because he would figure out that he still can't cope and leave again this time going deeper in hiding? I had all kinds of questions bouncing away in my head that made me realize that I should find out all I can but not act until the time was right. "I think I will talk to his mother first. I don't want to rattle the cage to hard and after I see what she tells me we will take it from there, "how does that sound to you." I asked waiting for her approval "Hey" she said I don't have a dog in this fight its all about what you and the kids need and want not about me. I will and can do whatever."

"Fine then" I said feeling a blast of relief and excitement after I talk to his mother, I will have a better understanding of how to proceed. We then sat there for a few more minutes pondering on the what ifs and the possibilities before going back to work. I went through the rest of my day in a mass of confusion. I didn't know what was on James mind and now that I was that close to finding him if he didn't want to be found where that would leave me and the children.

When it was time to go home, I was torn between my next moves I definitely wanted to speak to his mom to see if she could make any sense out of all of this. I wasn't sure what I would do if she confirmed that this was James and his father. Maybe the reason Ms. Fable didn't see anybody at the apartment because maybe James decided to go on home. I was sure that the man at the door the day that I went to the apartment told James that I had come by. Maybe he finally came to his senses and went home. That is how I made it through my day and was able to drive home.

I kept telling myself when I got home, I would see James. He would have gotten hit on his head and lost his memory—that was why he left. It was not his free will, but because he had a head injury, and he didn't remember who he was and who we were. Then one day out of the blue, his memory would return, and he'd return to us. Then we would go on with our lives as before. He would find work, and we would pretend this never happened. I kept telling myself this, but every day when I got home, there was no call from the hospital or the police station, not even James. This day…..wasn't any different.

Chapter 28

I called Ms. Robertson and shared with her what Ms. Fable found out. She wanted to see the picture and I thought it was a good time that we paid her a visit. The kids and I decided on the following weekend to go for the visit. School had been out for over a month. I thought it would be nice to give the children a break from our small town and visit their grandma in North Carolina. It was only four hours from our home, and it would actually be our first road trip together. I thought it would be good for us to see her. Maybe after spending time with her in person versus over the phone she would see that we needed and missed James and she could help us figure out what to do. I called her, got her directions, and a few days later on Friday morning, July 8, we were headed down the highway.

Once we arrived and pulled up in her driveway, I saw her grass was neatly cut. She was outside in her flower bed on her knees cutting fresh flowers. She was aging now; she wasn't the feisty woman that I had met years earlier. She was thinner now, and it looked like her drinking had finally caught up with her. She was pleased to see us, and she greeted us with hugs and a warm welcome. "Just make yourselves at home. There is fresh tea in the fridge to take the heat off of the travel," she said as we entered her home. It was a small house, neatly kept. You could tell by her single items that she lived alone. She had one cup, one glass, and one plate in the sink. It was two bedrooms, but only one looked lived in. Her bedroom had pictures, and her bed was partially made up; there was also a TV and a little radio. The other bedroom was neatly modeled with only a bed and dresser, no pictures, TV, nor radio.

The children had their glass of tea and decided to take a walk to explore the neighborhood, and I finished helping her cut her flowers. She and I prepared dinner together that evening, and it was a joyful time. We had decided on the weekend versus the week because we wanted to take a few days to better get to know her then in time we would spend more time and she may even want to come visit us. It was a wonderful getaway. It had a lot of meaning.

My first thought was to come with the picture in hand because I wanted to know all she had to tell me, but once we arrived and I saw her frailness. I didn't want her to think that was the only reason I was there. I decided I would wait for the perfect time to bring up the picture and if she still wanted to see it, I would bring it out. If not, I would just wait for the perfect opportunity to bring him up and I didn't want it to be when the children were around. I knew Brandon was already feeling a certain type a way for his father and I figured it would just add more hurt and pain to how Hannah was feeling. For now, I would just enjoy the break and being away from Pocahontas.

The day before we were to leave Ms. Robertson still hadn't brought James up, I didn't know if she was waiting on me to or just the right time. She was more interested in spending time with the children and me. She had pictures to share, things I bet James didn't even know that she had. Her focus was getting to know us not so much as to what James had done or where he was. I was feeling a little anxious, but I still never brought up James. I felt that if she didn't say anything by the morning, we were to leave I would find a way to bring it up before we headed home. In the meantime, I would just let her focus be on what brought her joy and that was the children.

Sitting on her deck the night after the children retired to their room was the first time that she brought up James. The children had settled down for a movie, and she made a pot of tea. She asked if I had brought the picture, I told her I did then she just started talking about their passed life.

"You know, Victoria," she said, "James always blamed me for his father leaving. When we were a family, James loved his father, I felt a lot more than he loved me. I thought that his father and I would always be together and that having James would make our family complete. I didn't know that Ron had a different agenda. He wanted fast women and alcohol, not a family. I never seen it coming. We dated for over 4 years before we got married. Ron was then the perfect man. At first, he was a family man. He worked and took care of us. I thought that everything was okay."

"Everybody raved about what a good father he was. He was close to his mother, but his father was his heart. James was 2 years old when his grandfather passed away that is when Ron lost his way. He became angry at the world. That's when his drinking started. At first, he would sneak around, and do it then his mother questioned it and once it was out in the open, he didn't feel the need to hide it. His mother tried to stop him from drinking but that only angered Ron because he thought he was the man.

His father now gone he was the one in control. However, Mrs. Andrews wasn't having it. She scolded him about his drinking and that is what pushed him away."

"Ron forbade us to go around his mother. He also felt if his father didn't take such good care of his mom he would still be around. He wanted answers as to why his father had passed and when he didn't get what he was looking for he cast blame on everyone. The only way he could cope was his drinking. When he drank, he was unbearable and that is what caused our downfall. As his drinking got worse, his love started to fade, and it seemed like me and James was more of a burden than his family. He stayed gone more than he was home, and I was only allowed to eat and feed James when he bought food and sometimes, he would forget, and we would have to sneak over to his mothers to eat. Once his drinking was out of control, he left us, and we moved in with Mrs. Andrews."

"At first it was the perfect set up. When I wanted to go out and have my fun. I had a babysitter and sometimes I wouldn't come back for days on end, because I either partied to hard and was hung over or I was being entertained by the opposite sex, and I had no worries. Don't get me wrong in the beginning I looked for my husband tried to fix our family. When he found out that I was going out he came back to try to fix the problems because I belonged to him no matter what he done, and he didn't want me going out. For the sake of everyone involved I took him back we went back home, and things were working out I guess one could say for the good. He was still drinking but not as much. He would allow James to go visit his mother's, but then he stopped that completely."

"I will never forget this Victoria it is a day that was no fought of my own and I tried hard to fight for my family, I tried to forgive and forget but on this day my love died, I wasn't able to get it back and my life changed forever. …… On James's tenth birthday, a woman came to my house; She was carrying a baby, and she told me that the baby belonged to Ronald." I listened on as she continued, "I died inside that day, and my love for Ron did too. He never denied the child, and that was when our troubles started. He left me for that woman and child. At first, he would come by to see James, but the pain I felt was too much to bear and I eventually stopped his visits. That hurt James, and I know I was selfish, but knowing that he chose that woman and child over his family was too overwhelming. The thought of Ron loving another woman hurt me so bad that I turned to alcohol to cope with the hurt." I was sitting there trying to file that part of the conversation so I could replay it back was what I was trying to do as I listened for Mrs. Robertson to continue. "I also turned to the company of the streets." I sat there silently trying to soak it all in, feeling she had this bottled up inside of her for years and she finally had someone to talk to about why her life had its twists and turns.

"He was my first love, my first everything, and now I was a scorned woman at the age of thirty-three. I felt that I gave this man eleven years of my life, and this was my reward. From the beginning it was never perfect or great, but I didn't know what to do with a man or what was expected as a woman. To be honest, I didn't want a child without a husband; that was how James ended up with Ron's mother. I didn't know what it was to be a mother, because my mother died giving me life. I felt if Ron could live a carefree life, then why couldn't I?" Mrs. Andrews welcomed the fact that I gave James to her; she never counted me worthy to be Ron's wife. I blamed her for years after Ron and I broke up. I felt that she thought he could do no wrong and I was the bad one. I treated her badly after I gave James to her. I didn't care. I wanted to make her life as miserable as her son made mine. I would go on my drunken sprees, and when I ran out of money, I would threaten to take James from her unless she gave me money to continue my high. She gave me the money, because the thought of me taking James from her was unheard of. She treated James like he was a masterpiece, as if she was trying to recreate Ron through him."

"Did James ever tell you that he not only had one brother, but he has two. Ron was a busy man in those days. The look on her face was a mix between curiosity and anger. One died in a car accident, but he has another one named Justin Wilson he is the meanest man in Poky for sure. He was Rons first son by a girl that was underage and part of the agreement for Ron not to go to jail he had to take the child and never connect with the mother again. The girl was supposedly a preachers daughter, and they didn't believe in abortion, and she couldn't put it up for adoption because they feared one day the child would resurface so the only way it was fixed is they gave all rights to Ron. He was only eighteen at the time he had his first child. I met him after the child was put up for adoption some 9 years later. I think the boy's name was changed and I don't think Ron ever saw him again. The Wilsons had their own reputation. They of course came from dirty money, and they owned half of Poky. They had adopted Justin because Mr. Wilsons wife weren't able to have kids. Mrs. Wilson died about...." she thought for a moment maybe..........20 years ago let's see she started counting on her fingers before she continued "Mr. Wilson is still alive and barely kicking." I sat there soaking it all in as she continued "Rumor had it that he was horrible without her, and since her death he was angry and not to mention miserable. Justin was a young man when she passed, and rumor also says that Justin and his adopted dad didn't get along after Mrs. Wilson passed but the only reason is that Mr. Wilson couldn't cope with losing his wife and since his wife is the one who wanted the child ...well since she was now gone the old goat wanted to forget he existed."

Wilson, Wilson my mind trailed off Mr. Boots real last name was Wilson. I wondered if that was James's brother adopted dad everything Mrs. Robertson had said matched Mr. Boots. I quickly re-gave her my full attention because I wanted to know more.

She stopped long enough to take a sip of tea before she continued. I continued to sit there in silence because I wanted to know what, if any, of this would have led James to make the decision that he had made. "His grandmother, Mrs. Andrews, saw the life I was living, she saw the road that I was on, so she finally got smart. She got a lawyer, took me to court, proved me to be unfit, and she took him as her own. I felt betrayed and the real reason I think that she took James was she was hurt because of Justin getting adopted that she didn't want another one of her grandchildren in the system. I still feel that is why she took to James so much. She wasn't hurt by what her son had done to us. I thought at the time she just wanted James, but above all, after getting my sense back I had to come to the realization that it wasn't just the fact that she didn't want James in the system. She was hurt by what both of us had done to James. To be honest she said with sniffles added, I wish I could have one last chance to ask for her forgiveness and to thank her for taking my son as her own. She did a fine Job with James and neither one of them deserved the treatment that me and Ron put on them."

"Ron on the other hand left his momma and never looked back I think it was because he knew his parents values and Mr. Clarence was rolling around in his grave with anger. He was ashamed although Mrs. Andrews would have welcomed him with open arms had he returned but the Andrews pride is unheard of now adays. If it can't be done by them then it won't be done. They don't believe in asking anybody for anything, I mean nothing." At that point all I could do was nod because I knew of the Andrews pride all too well. I continued to listen in as she continued.

"When I found out she had cancer the first time I was glad to say the least I felt God was punishing her for what they had done to me. It was what she deserved I would think and soon I would have my son back as well as the check that the state provided. At that point in my life with the hurt that I felt I didn't care about being a mother I just cared about where my next high would come from. The last time I spoke to her I told her my feelings and I wished death upon her. Looking back after I got sober, I said things that I shouldn't have said. I wasn't in any shape to care for James and If she had of died, with her first bout of Cancer James would have went to the state not back to me. I thank God that he allowed her to live those extra years so James could be a man before she passed on."

She paused long enough to take a drink of tea and wipe a tear from her eye then she continued. "Thinking that death was upon her I continued on with my drunken ways, hating Ron and wishing the same on him. "Five years later, the woman and child that he had left me for were killed in a car accident, and it took its toll on Ron. They were both drinking, and she was driving with the child in the backseat. It was late at night, and from what I heard, the child wasn't strapped in and was killed instantly. She was hospitalized for a few weeks before she died in the hospital, and that really took its toll on Ron. I knew the reason for the accident, but it was eventually blamed on a faulty air bag and Ron was paid off of both the deaths. He had enough money that if he wanted to buy Pocahontas and kick everybody out, he very well could. I say had because he has spent a lot of the money on the weekends finest but he's a tight one to say the least. I know all too well but he still has a pretty penny. He might be paying for favors…. she said with a chuckle…but, he's paying clearance prices."

"Getting back to the subject" she said as she took another sip of tea. "Believe it or not, I felt bad for him. I hurt for him because I knew how it felt to lose someone you really loved. Even though Ron and I were not together, I could still see him. He would never see her again. He was seen walking the streets drunk, and I even bumped into him a few times because yes of course if I'm honest and I want to prove to be, I was drunk too. We had little conversation because by then, I was so self-involved that I had troubles of my own. I had turned into the woman that he once desired. I had turned into a party girl, a woman who had many men. I hated my life, and I blamed my troubles on him. We even at one point talked about getting back together. Picture that one, I declined that idea because we were both too far gone and by then there was too much pain, and I had many men. I thought about it because he had a lot of money, and I had a lot of habits, but I couldn't deal with what all he had put me through to give it another try. The money wasn't enough."

"He had his bottle, and I had mine. He never, as far as I know, ever dated again. He just drank. We had been separated for years before I divorced him and married a man who drank just as much as I did. It wasn't until my husband died that I realized that drinking wasn't for me anymore. I wanted to get James back, but by then he was old enough to make his own choices, and I wasn't one of them. I guess he figured Mrs. Andrews was the only one who loved him. I reckon he didn't want to be with me because he thought I would go back to my drunken ways, and I did. It took years and James growing up to become a man before I got the help I needed, and it was the help that made me realize that I had to find him and make up for the time I lost."

"You can't imagine the hurt I felt when I realized that James didn't want me in his life. On a happier note, you can't imagine that when I called that day and he allowed me to visit, how my heart was filled to see that he had you and the children. For that, I want to thank you. I had searched everywhere for James, especially when I found out Mrs. Andrews had passed away."

"How did you find James?" I asked, cutting into her spill of reminiscing.

"The way I found him was I traced the person who bought the house, and he had given your apartment address as a contact. Then when you moved, I was able to trace the house that he bought and then his number. I hurt for you, Victoria, and I wish that James had come to me. I feel that he was trying to tell me of his troubles on the porch at your house the night before I left, but I was so happy to finally see him that my focus while he talked was his hurt and how I hurt him."

"I didn't really think about our conversation until you called me and told me that he had left. My guess is that he is with his father, wherever he is. I can't see him with another woman, but I can see him with his father. They are probably drinking together. I would even bet Ron has found Justin too. Shoot Victoria for all we know they are all together. With all the money they have between them they could be anywhere doing God knows what. Justin has all the Wilsons money and Ron has all that money from the car wreck. "I wouldn't look--------she paused long enough to say, "speaking of looking where is that picture you were talking about let me see if I can see something familiar." I didn't give it a second thought I practically ran in the house to get my purse. I was careful once inside not to disturb the children. I felt this conversation may be too much for them, but I didn't want Ms. Robertson to stop. I wanted to get all I could get before my trip home.

My hands nervously explored my wallet for the picture. Once I had it in hand I was back on the porch. I immediately handed Ms. Robertson the photo and she instantly produced tears. "This is Ron and James during our happier days. If this picture was on a mantle at someone's house, then its somebody that Ron is connected to or he lives there, I guarantee it. My advice to you is to not go back or go up against them. James may have love for you and the children, but he very well could be up under his brother or fathers influence. I see you have only two choices unfortunately. Either wait patiently for his return or file for divorce. He shouldn't expect you to wait forever and if you throw those divorce papers at him, he will either wake up and fight for his family or its not in his plans and he will sign the papers without trouble. Either way it's known that you're a good mom and a good wife and if he throws that away then shame on him and I mean that. If his father calls me again, I am going to try and have a talk with him so he can guide James back to his senses."

Listening to her words took me back to my promise to James. I promised I would never divorce him and that I would always love him maybe that is what he's leaning on. Maybe I should file for divorce if he broke his promise then why can't I. I sat there numb from the thought of divorce as she continued on.

"I am so glad that you came down here to see me, Victoria, and I want to continue to be in your lives because you are a part of him, and I miss being a part of a family. Don't give up on him, Victoria; he will come back. I know he will because he loves you and the children. Just be strong and stay focused on your children."

It was on that trip that allowed me to feel close to her. I hurt for her because she made some mistakes, but she had paid for them. The wrinkles in her face and the crinkle in her forehead showed me that she kept her pain and her regrets close to her heart.

Leaving Ms. Robertson's was hard for me. She cried, and I did too. I felt that she felt that she would remain alone and that would be the final time that she would see us. I made a promise that I would continue to visit and remain in her life. The children said their good-byes, and it was Brandon who ended the visit with a happy note. He went over, hugged her, and told her that he loved her, and he too would keep in touch. She pulled the Kleenex out her pocket, dabbed her eyes, and stood waving until we were out of sight.

The children slept on the way home, and I thought of my conversation with Ms. Robertson. It was my thoughts of her that kept me company on the journey home. I couldn't help but feel sorry for her, and it was her choices in life that caused her the pain. I was glad that the children didn't blame me for James leaving, and I couldn't help but think of how James must have felt when his daddy left him. I couldn't imagine the real impact of his leaving had on Brandon. I couldn't help but wonder if James thought that I would end up like his mother did, a woman of the streets, with many men.

I got home and called both Ms. Fable and momma. I had to share the whole spill of what Ms. Robertson told me and after careful consideration and discussions with my two confidants We came to the conclusion that he was probably with his father and brother and that I should wait it out to see if he came back. We have made it this far and the children were doing well enough that I didn't need to force the issue of their father coming home. The fear was if I forced him to come home and he decided to leave again this time may not be so forgiving.

I missed him and as a woman I felt I needed my husband but making sure the kids grew up in a functional family was important to not only me but to them. I wouldn't be able to live with myself if I failed the children. Having their daddy fail them was enough and all I knew at that point is I had to keep moving forward giving the best I could so it would outweigh the dysfunction. The kids were growing and maturing at a fast pace now so I could wait a little longer. I missed him but the balance that we have had since he's been gone has been heavenly and I didn't desire another man at this point. I was satisfied with spending time with Ms. Fable and momma. I would give the kids time to settle away in college before I decided how I would move forward no need to bring on any hiccups that could cause a setback. I would have plenty of time to figure out what to do about their father once I knew they were where they needed to be in life. It would be better if when he came home, we fixed Us, before he fixed it with the kids. I don't think I have the energy to finish raising the kids and work on my marriage all at the same time. One day, one hurdle at a time lord is all I am asking from you at this point. One day at a time.

We were on our seventh month now without James. The kids were adjusting, but they were sometimes withdrawn. I gave them their space and waited patiently for them to call me for my advice or my thoughts, but they didn't do that often. If I know them, they didn't want to bother me, and I didn't bother them. I sometimes asked for their help outside—to cut the grass or to help in the flower garden—just so they wouldn't have time to think about their father.

School would start back soon, and the children would be seniors. Another envelope full of money came in the mailbox. We would be able to do school shopping. I wanted this to be the best year since it would be their last. Schools were already contacting them for college, and it was fun to discuss which one they would choose.

Brandon would continue on his paper route so he could have extra money. I was a little concerned with his decision to keep the route. I thought it would interfere with his schooling. He assured me that it wouldn't, and I told him that I would let him try it but if the paper route affected his grades, he would have to stop. He was satisfied with that, and Hannah decided to help him three days a week so they could get it done faster. That was the week that they had gotten their licenses, so they both could work together.

Jasmine came around a lot these days. She was at my house more than she was home. She and Brandon were getting closer and closer. She even went with Brandon when they went to get their licenses, and Brandon wasn't nervous at all this time. I guess he felt she was his security blanket, and with her by his side, he could do anything. I remembered feeling that way, years ago.

The children asked me to come along for my final ride on the paper route since they had their licenses. I went, and the whole time, I sat in the backseat of the car. I had to let them do it on their own, and that was my way of doing just that. That old familiar image that I had seen so many times before was standing in the window of the apartment. The light was on, and as we drove off, the light went out. I wondered why he never came outside, why he never made himself known to us. I felt in my heart that Ms. Robertson was right: James had finally found his father, and they were probably drinking together, I would bet that Ronald was short for Ron. If my thinking was right, then he was better off with his father. I didn't want those troubles around the children again. Yet I couldn't help thinking, what was it that took him to the window all the time? Was he lonely? Could he just not sleep? Why would he stand there? That thought entertained my mind for the duration of the paper route.

The children did a fine job, so my mind would be at ease when they were alone. Brandon let Hannah drive home, and she had somewhat of a lead foot, but she did a good job also. I let them keep the car because I didn't have to work that day. I was glad they were out and about because I wouldn't have been much company that day. I couldn't get that image of that person standing in the window out of my mind. Was that person looking for that certain loved one to return? Was he trying to find the strength he needed to find his way home? Did standing in that window watching us give him assurance that we were, okay, Was it a silent cry for help did he want me to come back and tell him it was ok to come home? I would drive out to the apartment building to see if that person was still standing there.

When the children came home, it was after ten at night. I had already bedded down, so I thought I would check on the image another day. The children would start school in a couple of days, so I wanted to get it checked out before I talked to the children about it. I needed to know that it was really him and that he was okay despite of the reason why he hasn't come home yet. I didn't want to get their hopes up or give them any confusion in their lives. Their senior year was so important to them and to me. I wanted them to go through this last year with the least worries possible.

The children were up and gone when I woke the next morning. It was a beautiful day. The birds were singing like it was their last days, and it was. Fall would be here before you knew it, and then our first Thanksgiving without James. I just wished God would give me the strength to get over that man or change him and bring him back to me. I didn't know how to go on. This was too much for anybody to bear. Why had God forsaken me? I was not the one who abandoned his family, I thought.

I let the children take the car to school on the first day. I wished they had a car of their own, but I knew I couldn't afford it. I was barely making ends meet, so I decided that we would have to share. I would make the car available to them whenever they needed it. Brandon would be the one needing the car more than Hannah because I was sure he would want to take Jasmine out. Even though I knew the children spent some of their teenage years at the park with their friends I must tell him about the park, even though we took the kids to the park in their younger years. I must tell him how special that tree in the park really is, and I could only hope that it would be as special for him as it had been for me and his father.

Things were really going along in a hurry. The kids were doing great in school, and the first real holiday was set to come in about a week. Thanksgiving had to be special this year. It was up to me to make the children forget about the last one. I would invite Ms. Fable and Momma; they would be the only two that could pull me through it. We would all cook together, and we would have to make it a Thanksgiving worth remembering. I made a pot of tea, sat on the porch, and thought about the holidays. I got kind of depressed, and for some strange reason, tears started, just like they did when James had left. I didn't understand what brought them on because I was rather happy; I knew that the children had finally gotten over their father's leaving. It must have been some deep inner hurt that surfaced when I thought about the holidays and the special times that we missed when we were so wrapped up in James. Instead of fighting the tears, I decided to let them go. No one was around but me; the children were out with Jasmine and some other friends, so if someone heard me, so be it. I was a scorned woman, and I felt I had the right to express my hurt any way I felt necessary to get through these days without my family, without James.

I saw an image through the trees. It was somebody who had stopped as if he or she heard my sobs. The image stood there for what seemed like minutes, and then it continued on its journey without a word. How foolish

I must have sounded to that person. He or she probably thought that I should have the decency to cry in the house.

I managed to scoop myself up off the porch and go in the house to continue with my pity party. It wasn't anyone's business, but I should keep my hurt private. It felt good, though, releasing my hurt into the wind so it could carry it away from me. It carried my hurt away from the home that I once was so thrilled about getting. That thought took me back to the day when James and Daddy surprised me with the key. I thought this would be the home that would be filled with happiness, not the sorrow that it had shared with me these past four years.

I had invited Momma and Ms. Fable to spend the night on Thanksgiving Eve to help cook and just have a good time to take away the sadness that was lingering about. Cooking Thanksgiving dinner with me and the children would be a happy time for us, and we would make it the best Thanksgiving ever. Even though I didn't have my husband I had my children and that is all that really mattered not to mention mommas love and Ms. Fables friendship., I knew that I was blessed. I had a lot to be thankful for.

"Count me in," Ms. Fable had said. "I will be there with bells on. It will be fun, and I can't wait to meet this, Jasmine. Doesn't Brandon know that I am a part of the family, and I am the bodyguard? No one gets through you until they get through me," she said.

I knew she was serious, and I felt secure because she was my friend. Brandon had his security blanket with Jasmine; I had mine with Momma,

Ms. Fable—and Dr. Graves for that matter. Those three women had carried me through in their own way, and without their guidance I knew I couldn't make it. I wouldn't be able to. It's the truth when people say that God allows for certain people to enter your life. Some just stay for a little while to teach lessons and others are lifers. Momma and Ms. Fable are lifers. James well…. the Jury is still out.

Ms. Fable and Momma did spend the night Thanksgiving Eve. I was glad about that. Momma and Ms. Fable had the opportunity to meet Jasmine. She offered small talk while Brandon went and got dressed for their evening out. Most of the conversation was about Jasmine and Brandon. After the children left for the evening, Ms. Fable said, "She's a keeper. She is very respectful, and she is pretty too."

Momma and I both laughed.

"She is a girl with principles," Momma said.

"And I can tell her values are of good people," Ms. Fable said.

I already knew she was a keeper, but it was good hearing it from them.

"Just tell him to take it slow," Ms. Fable said. "He has a bright future, and he has a good head on his shoulders. Tell him to take it slow."

The children returned around eleven o'clock, staying up long enough to get a snack before entering their rooms.

"Don't forget church is tomorrow, ladies," Hannah said as she went off to bed. I knew she was talking directly to me, so I nodded as if I understood her statement.

Momma, Ms. Fable, and I talked and cooked until the wee hours of the morning. Neither one of them mentioned James, which made me glad; I was glad they had stayed.

Momma reminded us again that church was in the morning and that we shouldn't be late because God had a blessing for us. I was a little ashamed to go because it took this loneliness to make me want to go, I told her I would. The last thing I needed was to anger God anymore.

We all got up Thanksgiving morning with just a couple of hours of sleep. The turkey was still slowly baking in the oven, and it smelled so good. Brandon came into the kitchen, and he confirmed what I had previously said but it was his news that threw me.

"Momma," he said, "that bird smells like the best thing since apple butter. It will be good eating," sounding like a true country boy. "It's a good thing I invited Jasmines parents. Now they can see exactly how we celebrate the holidays."

"What?" I said. "It's a good time to tell me. Why would you tell me only hours before they are to eat that they have been invited? You know we are going to church this morning, and you know that we have had little sleep. Why would you wait until today to tell me that you had invited them?"

"Because you are the best momma there is and your food is always the best," he said with a sly grin on his face. Besides they invited us, and I knew you wanted to be home for Thanksgiving that's why I invited them I killed two birds with one stone. Furthermore, you cook better than Jasmines mom. So, stop scolding me and appreciate this young man for making his own conscious decisions." I was taken back by his uninformed invitation, but he was right I wouldn't want to go there for Thanksgiving, and he wanted me to get to know them. I remembered at first, they never wanted their friends to come here but now even without their father we were functioning again and instead of getting upset I should embrace the fact that he was no longer embarrassed to bring company to our house.

Now I had to make an impression on Jasmines parents that I wasn't prepared for. It was good that he had trusted me but having both her parents here without James would be a challenge. This would be the first Thanksgiving that we would have without James. Even though he sometimes wasn't really here when he was here, at least we knew where he was. Now I was faced with entertaining Jasmines parents without my husband, not to mention no sleep and a morning at church. On the other hand, I thought, wouldn't it be better not to have him here rather than have him here and he was not in his right state of mind? How embarrassing would that be for Brandon—and me for that matter? Hannah would just go with the flow as usual.

We all planned on being at church by the time the singing started, but the devil was all on me that morning. I thought of a thousand reasons why I shouldn't go. One good reason was that evening I was to entertain Jasmines parents at dinner. Yet I knew that if I wanted answers or help in my life, I needed God. I was much more content in my own setting by myself with him. I knew that I needed the fellowship of the church, but I hadn't been to that church in years. I felt I was more embarrassed about staying away too long than I was about going. I knew the church people knew all that I had been through, and I didn't want them to feel sorry for me. I guess I was reading too much into it.

As badly as I wanted my family back and as badly as I wanted to turn back the hands of time, the one who could bring it all together was God, and I wasn't willing to give him three hours of my day. Maybe that was why things had gotten as bad as they had. The one person I should have been pleasing, the one person who could turn it all around, was the one that I was choosing to ignore. I had to get past the feelings of why I shouldn't go and focus more on the reasons as to why I should go. Better yet, why I needed to go.

I was sitting on my bed contemplating whether or not to make an excuse to not go to church when Hannah came into my room wrapped in a towel.

"Momma," she said, "you are going to make us late. Get dressed." She looked at me as if she knew that I was going to try and get out of it. She went to the closet and pulled out my blue suit. "Here," she said, "you look good in this," laying the suit beside me. "I will wear my red one. If Jasmine wears her white one, we will look like a flag," she said, teasing.

I did as she asked even though I didn't want to go; I got up, got dressed, and went into the living room. I was glad to see that Jasmine wore a brown skirt with a white blouse instead of the white suit. I didn't want the attention. It was bad enough that I hadn't been there in years, but the thought of walking in looking like a representation of the flag and giving the congregation something to talk about after the service was something that I really didn't want. The less attention, the better. We could sit in the back, and no one would know that I was there.

As we walked into the church, I could feel God was there. As I entered the room filled with people singing, chill bumps jumped up on my skin. People were standing there rocking to the music. Some had their hands in the air as if they were saying, "Here I am, Lord." The tears streaming down their faces let me know that what they were feeling was real. A few of the people started shouting to the song, saying, "Thank you, Jesus. Hallelujah." No one looked around to see who was coming through the doors. They were too busy appreciating the singing.

After the choir had sung their selection of songs, the deacon stood up and asked if there was anyone who would like to stand and give a testimony of how good God had been to them. I will never forget the way my heart started pounding as I looked across the room. What I saw next would change my heart forever.

A little old lady who could barely stand stood up and sang a testimonial song, her weak little voice cracking. Even with her frail, cracking voice missing just about every note that came out of her mouth, her song was from her heart, and it brought chills so heavy on my skin that I had to clutch my body with my arms so it would not show.

I want to go home; I want to go home. I want to lay my burdens down, while my knees are on the ground. I will do your will; just allow me to come home. I'm tired now, please guide my steps and I will say, it's not my will for me to stay. When you find me worthy, when your will is done for me, Lord, please let me come home. I want to touch your garment; I want to be made whole. I want to feel your grace and live in the new place. Please let me come home. Your work I will do because you are the one that has brought me through. When you find me worthy, Lord, please let me come home. I want to go home.

As she sang, it didn't seem to matter that her little voice was shaking, because she was singing to the Lord. As she sang her song, it was clear to me that she wanted to go be with the Lord. Tears filled my eyes like an unbalanced hourglass, and the tears fell without a second thought. After her song, she talked about how good the Lord was to her.

"I'm eighty-seven years old," she said, "and I can't imagine a day going by that I don't give the Lord some kind of praise. He sent out a divine invitation to my soul so I could be here today, and for that I am thankful. There is none greater than my Lord and Savior, even though there are many who walk this old earth thinking that they have just as much power."

The church sat in silence as they listened to this God-fearing woman give her testimony.

"The Lord knows I'm thankful that he woke me up this morning, and I'm so thankful that he keeps on blessing me. I should have been dead," she said, "and it was the Lord's grace that gave me the opportunity to get things right with him before he shut my eyes." She paused, tears running down her face. "His mercy," she managed to say, "carried me through. I used to get angry when I went through things, thinking that the Lord had left me to fight life's battles on my own, but just when I thought it couldn't get any worse, the Lord spoke and told me, 'Dorethia,' he said, 'this is not your battle but mine. Why don't you let go and let me fight this battle for you? All you do is get in my way. Let me carry you through. Look beyond your eye level and search for me with your heart.'"

"When the devil stepped into my life to try and make me sway and lose my faith, the Lord stepped in and said, 'No, no, devil, she's mine. Let her go,' and it was his mercy that kept me for all these years. God has a plan for all of y'all," she said, looking around the congregation, "so if you aren't ready, you better get ready. If you are going through a storm," she stopped, her eyes catching mine before she went on, "let go and let God. He is the only one that can carry you through. He is the only one that can fight your battles. No matter what the problem is, it is not hard for God. He has a will and a purpose for everyone, so instead of praying for your wants and needs, pray for his will to be done and pray for him to give you the grace and patience to endure it. Pray for him to have mercy on you to strengthen you. If it is God's will, all things, I say all things, will work together for the good. Patience is what you need; strength should be your desire to endure. Persevere, children of the Lord; walk the walk with Jesus. I encourage you to Pick up that ole cross and walk with the lord. Let him take your hand and guide your steps."

"You can't do it on your own." After looking around the room and catching my eyes again, she continued, "So don't try. He may not come when you're ready, but he will be there right on time. He is the only one that makes no mistakes, and I'm living proof. Continue to pray that I will continue to grow stronger in his word and continue to do his will, so I can go home and sit at my master's feet."

With tears running down my face, I felt she was the sign that I had needed all this time. God was working it out, and I had to give it all to him. It was as if that woman knew that I was going through troubles, and it was as if God had chosen her to deliver a message to me. I cried the whole service.

After the service, the little old lady wobbled up to me and said, "God is good, girl. Just believe in him, and he will carry you through. Your storm is about over. Just keep thanking God for the work he has already done and for what's to come. In the end, you will look back and see it wasn't all bad and he was with you the whole time. Everyone has to go through a season. It may get worse before it gets better. Just keep your eyes on the Lord, and it will be him to carry you through. When you take your eyes off of God, it gives the devil room to come in. Don't glorify the devil and give him satisfaction. Glorify the light that is in you, and that is the spirit of Jesus. Give your burdens to God, child, and watch how the devil moves out of the way." With that, she wobbled out the door.

After church, I felt good spirits surround me. One challenge down, I thought, and one to go. We rushed home to prepare for Jasmine's parents to arrive.

Around five o'clock, Jasmine's parents were knocking at the door. Dinner was perfect. Momma's rolls were screaming to be released from the oven, and the table was set. Jasmine gave the introductions, and a sense of peace covered my home. We chatted for a few minutes, and then we were joined at the table.

Momma and Ms. Fable were well appreciated. Ms. Fable led most of our conversations, and the children talked and laughed all throughout dinner. I was glad to find out that Mr. Davis, Jasmine's dad, was a big football fan; that helped bring back pleasant memories. Brandon and Mr. Davis watched the football game like he used to do with his daddy, and that was a good thing.

No one brought up James, but Mr. Davis told me that if we needed anything done around the house, he would be glad to help Brandon. I could tell Jasmines parents liked Brandon, and I liked Jasmine. I saw a future in the making. Everybody stayed until about nine o'clock that evening. While the guys watched the game, the girls straightened up the kitchen. That was something that was done throughout my childhood, as well as when James was around. Some things didn't change. The only difference was we had momma, Ms. Fable, and Jasmine, and it was a good Thanksgiving. I found myself peeking into the living room and watching Brandon and Jasmine father watching the game. Secretly I wished James was among them, but I shook that thought and finished up the dishes.

The whole time, the Davises raved about the meal that was prepared. It had been a great evening, and I was glad we had this time to meet and get to know each other better. Once again, a good memory that James was not a part of.

After everyone left it was then that I realized that I had sprinted through Thanksgiving dinner. I couldn't get my mind off that woman at church. It wasn't long after the children had retired to their rooms that I sat alone. It was on my heart to read the book of Job, and I did. That gave me my answers. Job lost everything. The devil tried to do all he could to make Job turn his back on God. In spite of what was put in his path, he kept his faith; and in the end, God rewarded him with much, much more. The devil took James away from me. Was that a test for me to turn my back on God? Did I fail the test? Was this woman sent to give me a sign that something was about to happen? I knew that God did have a plan, a plan that I didn't have the answer to, but it was coming so I must prepare myself.

My heart was filled, and I thought of that woman throughout the days and weeks that came and went. She knew that I was in a struggle and God had a plan. No one spoke of that woman directly to me, but I heard not long after her testimony that, she had passed away. She had done God's will, and he was ready to take her home. If I hadn't gone to church that day, I wonder what would have happened. Would she still be alive waiting on me so she could give me God's message and go to her homecoming? Was I the reason she was left on the earth, and once her work was done, God allowed her to come home? Was it I who had kept her here when she had been ready to go?

After finding out about the old woman's passing, I still couldn't get that woman off my mind, and in the following days, I often found myself sitting in my room with my tea and the Bible.

Christmas was right around the corner. I could only hope it would be as joyous as Thanksgiving was. The children, who were still doing their paper route, were able to do their own Christmas shopping this year, and I thought that was exciting. In the mailbox once again, there was an envelope full of money, another five hundred dollars. That was well needed. I had to step back and wonder if it was really Ms. Fable sending this kind of money. Since it came so often and always just at the right time, I was beginning to have my doubts as to where the money was really coming from. I vowed that the next time a special event or holiday came, I would watch the mailbox closely to see exactly who this generous person was. The money was much needed; without the extra money coming in every so often, I would fall behind on my bills.

Brandon insisted on decorating the outside of the house, and we made it a family affair. Hannah, Jasmine, and I separated the lights while sipping on hot chocolate, and Brandon put the lights outside. When he was done putting the lights out, Jasmine rushed to the door to help him take off his coat and had his hot chocolate ready for him to take the chill off. That was a bittersweet moment. I was pleased that he was growing up to be a responsible man, but at the same time, I hated the fact that he didn't have a father to help him.

After the lights were done outside, Brandon put the angel on top of the tree, and everybody went to their own corner of the house to secretly wrap the gifts that they had bought. Instead of putting my gifts in the closet like I had done for many years before, I put my presents underneath the tree like the children did. I could see a turning point in our family in spite of the fact a family member was missing.

Several days after we decorated for the holidays, a box came in the mail full of gifts from Ms. Robertson. Thoughts of calling her became vivid. The children and I sent her a box of her own. This wasn't a sad time, but a growing time. The children had been growing, and I felt as hard as it would be, it was time to put James aside so I wouldn't miss a thing.

Christmas Eve quickly came this year. It was a welcome time. The children and I cooked the dinner, and we stayed up until the wee hours on Christmas Day. This was the first-year anniversary of James leaving us. I kept that in the back of my mind. Even though I could tell that the children thought the same thing, they didn't mention it and neither did I.

Maybe this was going to be his return, since this was the day, he left. I wondered if he did, would the children be as accepting as I would? Oh, I knew I would have a lot of questions, and I knew I would be mad. But I also knew that, after his searching and seeing the longing in his eyes, it would only take a matter of minutes, and I would be completely wrapped up in him all over again. Maybe this was what he waited for to return—Christmas. What a present for our family that would be!

Brandon spent his time entertaining Jasmine, Hannah had some last-minute wrapping to do, and I watched the Christmas movies on the television. After all the wrapping was done, Brandon took Jasmine home. I didn't want to go to sleep, and with every sound, I looked at the door only to find it was the wind or the cat from across the street. Hannah came and sat with me on the couch until we both fell asleep.

I didn't get much sleep at all. I was up and about all through the night, despite being exhausted from all the cooking and last-minute shopping. I would have thought that I would fall asleep as soon as my feet left the floor, but I was up pacing and looking out the window. I was hoping that the present that I had hoped for this past year would be at my front door waiting to be invited in. Needless to say, it didn't happen.

Momma and Ms. Fable came over around noon on Christmas, and I called Ms. Robertson to wish her a merry Christmas.

"Hello, Victoria," she said. "It's so good of you to call."

"Thank you for all the wonderful gifts that you sent us," I said.

"I love mine too. Can I speak to the children?" She took her turn with each of the children, and then they handed the phone back to me.

"Are you doing, okay?" I asked.

"I am as well as to be expected," she said. "Have you heard anything from James?"

"No, I haven't, but we are adjusting." I didn't want to hear that name, but I guess that should have been expected.

"Just hang in there, dear," she said. "Things will get easier."

I couldn't see how, but I agreed anyway; it was Christmas. It was supposed to be a happy time. With that, we hung up. As I went back into the living room, the children were tearing into more gifts that Momma and Ms. Fable had bought. It was a happy day for them, even though last year it had been the most devastating. After we all exchanged gifts, Brandon went and picked up Jasmine. We ate dinner and just sat around admiring our gifts.

After everybody went home, I decided to let the children have their time, and I went into my room and took a nap. I must have had thoughts of James glued in my mind because I had a dream that he was knocking on the door. It sounded so real that I actually got out of bed and went to the door. It was just a dream, though. Looking at the children with their eyes glued on me, I just told them that I thought I heard someone knocking. Then I returned to my room. I wrote in my journal, wishing James a happy one-year anniversary, without us, hoping he was happy.

I got on my knees New Year's Eve just to let God know that I was thankful for his help in allowing us to get through the past year as painlessly as possible. Looking back, we actually had a pretty good year compared to the previous years with James.

"Jesus, my rock," I said, starting my prayer, "your will is your will and not my own. I thank you for the past year and all that came with it. I know a lot of things are not to my understanding, yet my trust lies with you. I don't think I could have made it without you carrying me, and I can see my strength grow. I have a lot. I want to do for you this year, but I don't want to make promises that I can't keep for fear that you will slow down your will for my family. Bless us this year with wisdom and courage for what is in store for us and be patient with me. Although I know you're real, some of the everyday struggles of this life on earth get challenging to the point I may seem to forget your capabilities. Thank you for our health, and I pray that my children may grow and have a closer walk with you. Also, whatever your will is, let it be. Let it be. Just give me understanding and guidance so I may endure."

"The ball's about to drop, Momma. Come on before you miss it!" I heard Hannah call from the living room. I hurried into the living room to hear them counting.

"10, 9, 8, 7, 6, 5, 4, 3, 2, 1. Happy New Year." We gave each other our new year's hugs as we had so many times before. We drank our nonalcoholic bubbly, and that ended our night. Yes, 2005 was a good year, I thought, and 2006 would be even better.

Chapter 29

After the new year came in, the winter months seemed to be in a race to leave and rest for another year. The birds were singing, the flowers were budding, and my tree was calling. I wasn't ready for that old tree; it seemed to have lost its meaning. I would share my memories with the children, and maybe they could pick up where we left off. Maybe they could plan their future under that old tree better, and yet use our own willow trees as their safe haven. Maybe they could find that true love, I thought, and not focus so much on a dream, but reality.

I did go to the tree, and I did put down the new flowers, but I had nothing to talk about. I sat under that tree for just a few minutes, and then I went to the cemetery to visit with Daddy. I told him about my holidays and that the children would turn eighteen this year— "adults finally," I told Daddy. I told him that I missed him and that I would return later in the year. I just figured he was up there with God, and he would keep him informed of what a mess my life was. I was sure Daddy—and Mrs. Andrews for that matter—knew of God's plans for me. I just wished he would tell me so I would know what to expect. I was sure it was a secret, but I could only hope they would send me a sign, a bird to land on my shoulder or a flower changing to a color that wasn't expected—something, anything to let me know that this thing we were going through would be ending soon.

The kids were waiting for me when I got home. They wanted to go to the movies. What was I supposed to tell them? "No, sit home and grieve with me"? I just handed over the keys, made a pot of tea, and went to my familiar spot on the porch. Tears started running down my face unexpectedly. I wasn't going to scream out like I had before, but I was going to let them run. What had I done so terrible in my past that I deserved to be lonely, hurt, and sad all the time? Why couldn't God have given me a sign that this was how it was going to turn out? Had I overlooked James's troubles to the point that God thought I got what I deserved? What did I do, and how could I change it so I could go on with my life? Life, now that was a strange word. When James left me, he took life with him.

May had jumped into place, and the prom was coming up again. The children decided this year they wanted to do it all on their own—the dress, the tux, the limo. They were good with their money, and they had earned it, so I just said, "Have at it."

I knew Brandon would take Jasmine, so where would that leave Hannah? I thought I might ask before it was too late.

"Hannah, are you going to the prom alone this year? I mean, Brandon has Jasmine now. How are you going to work that out?"

"She could have a date if she wanted one, Momma," Brandon said. "Boys like her. She's just a chicken."

"Shut up, Brandon," Hannah said, almost getting angry.

"Hey, hey," I chimed in. "Don't tease your sister, Brandon. What, Hannah? You are not interested? Do they have acne problems? Why don't you want to date?" I asked, but in my heart, I knew she didn't want to wind up like me—old and alone. James's and my troubles had made our daughter afraid to have a male companion. Why hadn't I seen that before?

"No, Momma," she said, interrupting my thoughts, "I just want to go to school and do good with that first; then I will date." My heart told me that she was lying to me, but I went along with it.

"Well, going to the prom doesn't constitute marriage," I said. "It will only be for one night. I think it will be fun for you to double-date." I said those words and went into the house. I wanted to burst into tears, but I had no escape. I didn't want them to hear me because she would know I knew the real reason. Why hadn't I seen this before? She never talked of boys, and she never went on a date. My and James's troubles had caused her to build a wall around her heart because she didn't want to go through what I was going through. How fair was that to such a beautiful young woman? God, please let her lift that wall so she too can experience love.

At work, I told Ms. Fable about the situation with Hannah.

"This too shall pass," she said. "I tell you what. Maybe I can talk to her and ask her if she would go with my nephew. He's a good-looking young man, and he has a good head on his shoulders. Maybe I will ask him if he would take her, and then I will ask her as if it is a favor for me."

Ms. Fable always had all the answers. That was a great idea. Hannah was very fond of Ms. Fable, and I knew that she wouldn't let her down. I would give her a chance to put her plan in motion, and then I would sit back and watch the wall fall.

It took Ms. Fable about two weeks to set things in motion, and I wasn't getting even a little worried. I knew that even though Brandon loved his sister, he would prefer that she had her own date. His time was wrapped up in Jasmine now, and I was sure he wanted to go alone with Jasmine, without Hannah hanging around.

The favor came in the form of a phone conversation. Hannah answered, and the whole time she looked at me as if I had put Ms. Fable up to it. I walked into my room when I heard Hannah say, "Sure, Ms. Fable, I think I could do that. Will I be able to meet him first?" I clutched my hands together and secretly thanked the Lord.

I was sitting on my bed reading when Hannah came into my room.

"Momma," she said, "what are you and Ms. Fable up to?"

"What are you talking about?" I replied.

"So, you don't know about the nephew who doesn't have a date for the prom?" she asked.

"What are you talking about?" I said, trying to convince myself that I didn't know what was going on.

"Now suppose he's ugly or has some kind of hidden problem? I know you told Ms. Fable about me not having a date for the prom. It isn't because I wasn't asked," she said, on the defense. "I wish now I had taken one of the offers. At least I knew what they looked like. Who they were for that matter. Sometimes, Momma, I just wish you would let me make my own decisions," she said as she left my room.

She's angry, I thought, and maybe I should have minded my own business. I only hope that he is good-looking and doesn't have some kind of problem. As a matter of fact, why didn't he have a date for the prom? If he was that good-looking, then he would have had a date. Oh Lord, I thought. What had I done? Had I ruined her last prom? I didn't know how to fix it.

The next day at work I didn't tell Ms. Fable the conversation that Hannah and I had. She was too good to me for me to hurt her feelings.

She broke my thoughts with, "I will bring Lewis over this evening after he gets off work so he and Hannah can meet." She was a smart woman, so she read my face. "Don't worry, Victoria, he's everything I said he was—and maybe a little more."

I could only hope.

"I know everybody always says, 'Isn't my son handsome?' or 'Isn't my daughter pretty?' and they look like the dogs dragged them in. You are left saying 'yeah' while lying through your teeth. If he wasn't good-looking, I never would have put her in the situation. Just trust me. It will be fine," she said.

I did trust her, and she was right. It would have to be fine; what's done was done.

I was still nervous all the way up until they pulled up into the driveway. Hannah was in her room, and I had to get a look first. That way, I knew what I was in for after he left. Ms. Fable was right about one thing: he was a very handsome young man. I ran to Hannah's room to secretly tell her he was there.

"How many zits does he have?" she said.

"Be nice, girl. He's gorgeous. I mean gorgeous." We made it back to the living room to find them standing right before us. Hannah stuttered a little when she introduced herself.

"Hello, I'm H-Hannah," she said.

"I'm Lewis," he replied. "You are beautiful, just like Aunt Teresa said. How come I have never seen you before now?"

I looked at Ms. Fable as if to say, "tea on the porch," and she nodded her head. I figured that was better than the both of us standing there with our mouths hung open. I put the pot of tea on and went to the porch to wait for it to be ready. We both went back in the house to get the tea, and Hannah and Lewis were sitting there in the living room chatting and talking away. What a good day this turned out to be, I thought. We took the tea back on the porch and sat there together.

When Brandon pulled up, I motioned for him to come to us. I didn't want him to go in teasing them or, worse yet, to scare Lewis off. He was mighty protective of Hannah.

"What's going on?" he asked as he approached us.

"There's a boy in there with Hannah," I said, excited to get the words out.

"Who is he?" Brandon said.

"Ms. Fable's nephew. He's going to take Hannah to the prom."

"Oh really?" Brandon said, anxious to see the boy that was taking Hannah to the prom. He started for the living room.

"Brandon," I said, stopping him, "don't you dare mess this up. Don't tease her; none of that."

"I got it, Momma," he said, and with that, he turned and went in the house. My nerves started all over again, and it wasn't until Brandon returned to the porch and gave his approval that I was able to carry on with the rest of my conversation with Ms. Fable. They stayed about three hours before she had to get him back home; he lived across town, and there was school in the morning.

"How can I ever thank you?" I said to her when she got up to leave.

"You thank me every day that you are my friend, Victoria, and that is enough for me."

Hannah and I walked them out to the car, and Lewis gave her a hug and told her that he would see her soon.

"I will be calling," he said, and Hannah smiled as he got in the car.

"Well?" I said, not making it into the house before I had to know what she was thinking.

"He's nice, Momma, and he's cute and we have a lot in common. But I'm telling you, right now I don't want a boyfriend. We can be friends, but that is as far as I want it to go."

"Fair enough," I said, not wanting to push it.

Lewis and Hannah talked a few times on the phone before the prom. It wasn't like Brandon and Jasmine, but I knew they were at least friends and maybe the prom would make something more.

The children didn't want me to go shopping with them, but they wanted my approval. They looked like a prince and princess all over again. Hannah had a maroon dress that flared out and came above her ankle. It had one sleeve on the shoulder and was off the shoulder on the other side. Brandon dressed in a white suit that fishtailed in the back, and he had a turquoise tie. Jasmine, of course, had a turquoise dress; it was slanted on one side and had the back out. Now we were waiting for Lewis. I was wondering when the limo would arrive, and Brandon kept looking out the window as if he was nervous about something. When Lewis arrived, he had a surprise of his own. He came to the house in a horse and carriage, with a chauffeur and four seats. He and Brandon had planned the whole thing, and it was amazing.

Lewis was dressed in a white suit similar to Brandon's fishtail in the back, but he had a maroon shirt no tie. The Girls shrieked when they saw the carriage. Thinking back to the limo ride last year was nothing compared to the attention the horse and carriage brought. There were neighbors taking pictures this time. A few even stood close enough to touch the horses as they trotted down the street. Ms. Fable and Momma were there, and we took enough pictures to fill a photo album. There wasn't a dry eye in our home as the rode out of sight. It was just too beautiful and romantic for words. There wasn't a cloud in the sky, and Lewis and Brandon each had a dozen roses for the ladies. How romantic was that!

My eyes seemed to be failing me. Glasses, even though needed, didn't seem like a priority at forty-four years old; I thought it was getting time that my body parts started to tire. I saw that same person walking down the street as the children were leaving. If I didn't know better, I would have thought it was James. He wore a hat that shadowed his face, and his walk was a walk that was familiar to me. Yet I couldn't really tell if it was a man or a woman, but I knew I had seen that person before. I followed the image with my eyes, and it got into a blue truck and left. I had thought for an instant that it could have been James, but he didn't have a blue truck, or did he?

The children had their stories to tell when they came home. They had an amazing time. They had danced all night, and then they went out to eat with the other children—and they had the only horse and carriage there.

Hannah went to Lewis's prom with him, but that romance was exactly what she said. It was a friendship. He would call or come by. Even though I knew Lewis liked Hannah, she didn't have the same spark in her eye as he did. Eventually his visits became fewer and fewer, and then he just didn't return. Hannah didn't seem to care, so I left it alone. What a wall she had built up!

The following week for their birthdays Brandon insisted on taking Jasmine, Hannah, and I to dinner. I tried to order light I knew the dinner would be expensive considering he was paying for it all. I was so proud of him when he whipped out his debit card to pay. I could see that he was proud, and he felt important. Jasmine excused herself from the table we thought she was going to the ladies room moments later she returned with several waitresses one was carrying a cake and they sung happy birthday to my two beautiful young adults. Considering that we had to plan for the graduation party and getting them off to school I had explained to them that the present from me had to wait for just a little while and as always, they understood, and that was about the extent of their eighteenth birthday celebration.

The year was in fast-forward mode. Graduation was coming up. Looking back, I wondered where the year had gone. The twins were graduating from high school, and it was sad that their father wouldn't be there to see it. I had a lot of tears and reminiscing going on in my mind. I looked back, and then I would come to the present time, ending in what their future held. Where would our New Year's see us? The last thing we expected ten years prior to the children graduating was that their father would not be present for their graduation. They were the top seniors in their graduating class. If James had stuck around, he would have known that. I had to make this day as positive for the children as possible.

The children were making decisions about their future. Brandon decided to be an engineer, and Hannah a lawyer. Those were grand ideas, I thought. Despite the fact that my children had to depend on my little income and Brandon's paper route for their class ring and their cap and gown, and despite the struggles they had to face, they seemed to understand and focus on their future, not their past. Without their dad being there, they turned out to be fine young adults. I hated their dad for doing this to them. I never thought I would say that, but I hated him.

A couple weeks after the prom, I took some time out to visit the cemetery. I took fresh flowers and talked to my father about my troubles. Even though I was mad at James, I asked my dad to forgive him because it wasn't his fault that he was sick; I said that one day he would return to fix his problem. I told my daddy that he was a troubled man and that he really loved us.

I didn't even go to the willow tree to visit Mrs. Andrews because my heart showed anger to her too. It was her who had brought us back together, and it was her leaving that took him away. I was angry that she hadn't gotten the chance to finish telling me what she wanted to before she passed on. I drove home thinking of how she was lying in her bed holding onto her last breath, wanting to be with Mr. Andrews but not wanting to leave James without someone to love him. Was she going to tell me of his past troubles? Could it have been a warning for me? Would I have listened? Had I wanted him so badly that nothing she could have told me would have changed things? Was that why God allowed death to interrupt her words to me?

I decided I could not let my anger get in between what we had, because she must have gone through her own things with James. She knew that he needed love, and she passed the duty of giving that love to James on to me. Thinking how I wished I had of run back then yet I gracefully excepted that duty on my own free will and I remember telling God after mommas warning that I would except him just the way that he was so with that, I stopped by the park, cleaned off the dead flowers, put fresh flowers under the tree, and went home. I had nothing to say at this time. I would come at a later date to tell her about the prom and graduation.

I found myself spending my evenings at the mailbox waiting to see who was going to drop off the infamous envelope full of money, but none came. Maybe the generous person felt that he or she had given enough through the years, and it was time we fended for ourselves.

Ms. Fable asked "Victoria, what do the children want for graduation?" I wanted to tell her "not too much," because if it was, she who had provided the envelopes, she had done enough. "They haven't really said," I replied. It really wasn't her responsibility to get the children big gifts, so I was as secretive as I could be without offending her. The children knew our financial situation so they didn't expect much, although secretly I was hoping that another money windfall would come through, if only for one last time.

Two weeks before their graduation on June 1, if my memory serves me well, I worked late to make extra money for their graduation. To my surprise, I received a phone call from Hannah.

"Momma," she said on the other end, "you are not going to believe this." Her excitement made me a little nervous, yet curious. "In the mailbox there were two envelopes, each one with one of our names on them. You won't believe how much money was in them this time. It was one thousand dollars, not together but for each of us."

Tears came rushing down my face. I was glad that it had come, but I wished I knew who was sending it. I became angry that I chose this day to work overtime; the mystery would have been solved if I had been home. The mystery now was that it couldn't have been Ms. Fable; she was at the pharmacy all day. I wished I knew where the envelopes were coming from. Right now, I would just thank God for the money. Without the extra surprise money coming in, we would not have made it. We could worry later about who was sending it. That money was enough to get them started into college, and with me working overtime, I had money to give them a surprise party.

Graduation for the children was incredible. Ms. Fable insisted on taking care of everything. When she put her name on the invitation, just about all the kids from school showed up and brought gifts. She threw them a party that neither James nor I would have thought about doing, even in our glory days.

I had to thank her because, without her being so popular with the people of our small town, I wouldn't have known who to invite. The children didn't speak a lot about the kids they socialized with at school. My heart was heavy because I felt that our troubles were the reason. Jasmine and Lewis were the only other teenagers that has ever darkened our doors. They never invited other children to our home. I often wondered if it was because their father was absent. I knew they wanted as much of that past to disappear as I did, but it was real. It was still there, lingering over our heads.

Brandon was going to engineering school, and Hannah wanted to study law. They were both accepted to prominent schools. I just wished their daddy was there to see it so he could share in the joy of our children, the children that we dreamed of the children that we had once wanted so badly. I couldn't help but cry thinking about all the pain their daddy—and I for that matter—had caused them, and through it all, they turned out to be at the top of their class. Not surprisingly, my tears fell as they were handed their diplomas. They each smiled and waved at me as they walked across the stage. Momma and Ms. Fable filmed and took pictures of their every step. I just sat there in my own thoughts of how proud I was at that moment at that time in their lives. Now I knew why God didn't allow me another child. He knew that troubles were coming, and he didn't want another child brought into this. I felt he gave me the twins because he knew I would need someone of my very own to get through this.

Neither James nor I deserved such wonderful children, but there they were standing within the crowd. They were all grown up, wanting to start their future. I remembered my last day of school, and I was thankful that Hannah didn't follow in my footsteps. I feared that she wanted to share my dreams of being a well-kept woman. But, I guess, after she saw me struggling, she wanted no part of that. I was glad that she wanted to have her own identity and live her life however she wanted. As the final speech was given, the class of 2006 threw up their hats and their tassels, and I made my way through the crowd to the children. We had to hurry home and prepare for the party. It would celebrate the ending to their success at high school.

Momma, Ms. Fable, and I rushed on ahead. I knew at any moment; the children would be arriving with their guests. I went to turn on the radio to find music for the mood, and several songs played as we saw the crowd forming. Once the children got there and their friends gathered around, I went into my own memories of how the last year and a half of my life had gone from total sadness to bittersweet joy.

Momma and Ms. Fable were taking out the rest of the platters of food when a particular song started to play. As the song by Faith Hill, "Just Breathe," came on, I felt that was exactly what I could do. I watched as the children gathered. Hannah was sitting with her college papers in hand, watching the crowd. She always was one step ahead. I knew she was nervous, yet excited about her new adventure. I saw a young man walk over to her as if he was going to ask her to dance, and she motioned at her book, and he walked away. I hoped the hurt that was caused by our family situation hadn't affected her decision about dating.

Brandon and Jasmine, on the other hand, were dancing as if they were just discovering one another. I saw them gaze into each other's eyes, and I was thankful that he had found her, wondering if he was determined not to let his father's actions interfere with his happiness with a woman.

That was the perfect song for the moment because school was over and new beginnings were headed our way. The sad part was I had waited all their lives for this moment, and that their lives were really just starting, where did that leave me?

I was proud that Brandon turned out to be the man that he did, with only me to guide him through his challenges. I was sad that James didn't keep the promises that he made my daddy. To me, the man that I once knew and the man who stood before my father and announced to the world that he would love me forever was short-lived and no more. I guess different people have their own thoughts of what forever is. To some it could mean for the moment, and to others it could mean a lifetime—or just however long they want it to be, no more.

Hannah wanted to be a lawyer, and that made the difference. I was so thankful that she had her own identity and didn't rely on my footsteps to guide her way. God works in mysterious ways, this is true. If James had been there and I never started working, always being dependent, I wonder if Hannah would have wanted to be a well-kept woman like I did years ago. I broke a lot of James's rules since he'd been gone and with that my heart was pleased.

I think the children were silently wishing that their father was there. But since the party was so overwhelming, his not being a part of our lives was now turning into a faded memory. I thought of James a lot, too much, because while I was in my deep thought, I could have sworn I saw him walking at a distance, looking on at the party. Looking out my kitchen window, I saw him just as clearly as I could see the crowd. I decided to go outside and get a better look, and when I did, he wasn't there. I would try as hard as I could to put that man out of my mind. I had to keep reminding myself that this day was for the children, not James.

Second only to the reality of James leaving, the children going off to school would be the saddest day of my life. Ms. Fable offered Hannah a summer job to have extra money for the necessities. Brandon still had his paper route, so I knew they would be fine.

It was mid-August two weeks before the children were to go off to school. The sun had faded. I was staring out the window from my porch, enjoying a cup of tea and thinking about the children and what my life held once they went to school. I noticed a car driving down my street. I couldn't make it out distinctly, and it didn't seem that important at the time. It drove out of sight and then returned, only to park close to my driveway. I watched what seemed to be an old man stick his hand out of his window and place something in my mailbox.

As I stared watching him, I decided to run outside and stop him, or at least see who he was. I ran to the door, but by the time I made it to the driveway, he had driven away. I made my way down to the mailbox, and inside were two envelopes, one for each of the children. Mesmerized by what had just happened and regretting not being able to get a better look at the driver, not to mention not being able to stop him, I headed back to the house with the envelopes in hand. Even though my name wasn't on them, curiosity got the best of me, and I tore into them. I was glad that I was beside the couch because I lost my balance and ended up sitting on the couch. In each of the envelopes was four-thousand dollars. That was enough money to get each of the children a good used car. I had been praying to God to make a way that they could come back and forth from school to home when they wanted, but I never expected this.

Looking for a car was pretty exciting. Hannah settled on a 1998 Honda Accord, and Brandon decided on a 1997 Toyota pickup truck. With Ms. Fable's wheeling and dealing, she talked the car salesmen down, so they got a really good deal.

I wrote James a letter that night, letting him know that he missed out on the most important time thus far in our children's lives. I hoped he was happy wherever he was, because my mind was now made up; this had to be for the better. While the children were away at school, I had to find hobbies to pass my time away. I decided to continue Brandon's paper route, at least until Christmas. After that, I would let that go; and from then on, I would just have to take it one day at a time. I knew that one thing I would do was go back to church. God had kept me and blessed me enough to raise my children, so the least I could do was show him I appreciated it by fellowshipping in a church.

Hannah and Brandon kept the roads hot since they both had cars. I barely ever saw them, with both of them working and all. They had a curfew of midnight. They didn't disobey the curfew, but I could barely stay awake long enough to hear them come home, let alone sit up and chat. I knew they both had their own lives, but I felt that I had lost them. I tended to write them letters too. I would just let them know that I loved them, and I wanted them to always be safe. I usually started my letters around nine o'clock, and I wrote all three of them—James, Brandon, and Hannah.

I would sit on my bed Indian style, with tea on the nightstand and paper in my lap. I would first start by looking up to the ceiling, as if God was watching me write, and then I would put my thoughts on paper. Not for God, of course, because he already knew my words, but for the memories I wanted to share at a later time. By twelve o'clock, I was usually cross-eyed. I would just bed down and hope I didn't fall asleep before the children got home.

Chapter 30

The days were winding down for the children to leave for college. Hannah would be the first to leave; Brandon insisted that he had to go with me to see her off. He was a leader, not a follower, and that was evident. He acted like he was the father sometimes, and I knew it got on Hannah's nerves. But I also knew that she felt safe with Brandon.

Brandon also wanted to spend a few more days with Jasmine. She and he had gotten close, and I liked her too. She and Brandon would be in different schools, but I silently thought that he wanted a well-kept woman. If Jasmine would agree to that, I thought Brandon would ask her to marry him. I just put that in God's hands. I knew for sure that Brandon would not let another woman suffer like I did; he would be a good man because he loves me. I remembered my momma saying, "If you can find a man who loves his momma, then he is a good man." I never knew what that meant until I met James. He never knew his momma, so he didn't love her like a boy should. Again, I should have listened to Momma, I thought.

Hannah and I spent the evening after work shopping for her wardrobe that she would take with her to school. It was a good time

Brandon met us for dinner at the old diner, and he brought Jasmine. She was part of the family now, so I didn't mind. I even invited Ms. Fable for this going-away dinner for Hannah, because without her and her generosity, I wouldn't have made it. We laughed and talked until late evening, but Momma would arrive the next day, so I had to get everybody rested. I knew she would come wanting to do something with Hannah before she left. I wasn't sure if she wanted to include us or not, but I wanted to be rested and prepared. Momma had insisted on seeing Hannah off. She and Hannah should ride together, me, and Ms. Fable would ride together and Brandon, and Jasmine would ride together.

I looked out the diner window, and there stood James; he was standing as pretty as he pleased. Not to interrupt the meal but I excused myself, hoping I could catch him and tell him to at least have the balls to say something to his daughter, but after I excused myself and went outside, he was gone. I was going to talk to Dr. Graves once the kids were settled; this seeing thing was making me crazy.

I wrote the children's notes first tonight because after that, I had to concentrate on James's hate letter. When I finally bedded down, sleeping was hard. I found myself tiptoeing into Hannah's room watching her sleep. I did it about three times before I realized that she wasn't asleep at all. As I was leaving her room for the third time, she spoke.

"Momma, go to bed. I'm okay."

"If you're okay, then why are you awake?"

"Because you keep waking me," she said with a chuckle. "Come on, sit down; let's talk."

I felt like the child, and she was the momma.

"What's on your mind, chick?" I said, joking back, trying to act like I wasn't sad that she was leaving me.

"Momma," she said, "I just want you to know that I love you and you are my best friend. If you ever get sad, then you call me. I know that this is hard for you, and I wish I could make it better. You have been through so much, missing Daddy and raising us, but it never went unappreciated. I miss Daddy too, and I wish he was here to be a father to me and Brandon and a husband to you, but he's not. He made his choice, and it wasn't us. At first it hurt, but it got better, and we still had you and we are still a family."

"I don't want a man, Momma. I want to be like most women nowadays. I want to keep my career and make something of myself so I will never have to depend on a man. I don't want to leave you, but I will be fine. One day we will look back on this and laugh. One day, after I have worked for fifteen years or so, maybe I might want a family. I don't know." She paused, looking at me with tears streaming down my face. It wasn't tears of sadness, but tears of realizing that my daughter was more mature than I was at her age.

She was a woman now, and she had proven that she was smarter than I ever was. I thought I had life figured out. I had my mind made up, but she was different; she had plans that could actually come true. Here I was, a middle-aged woman alone. It took me back to the bleachers at graduation. How I knew how I would plan my life, save myself for my husband, have this wonderful life, while the others dealt their hand in life quickly, only to make big mistakes. Some of the girls were pregnant, but I was going to save myself for my husband. I really showed my classmates, didn't I? That was my thought. They were probably reading my mind and making fun of me because they knew that planning on being a well-kept woman was a joke. It had its downfalls, and for those I didn't plan.

Tuning Hannah back in, I heard her say, "I will come home once a month to spend the weekend with you, and we will do big-girl things," she said, smiling, causing me to chuckle.

"What big-girl things?" I said with a laugh.

Ignoring my remark, Hannah looked deep into my eyes and said, "Don't think you failed me, Momma, because you are my hero. I want to be as strong as you, but I need a career to fall back on." Her gaze brought tears to my eyes. I was almost afraid to hear what was coming next. I sat still, trying to hold back the tears. "That is the only thing you didn't plan for, but you did what you could and that was all that mattered."

"Hannah, I don't know how to explain how good it feels to hear you say that you understood. I did do the best I could, and I only wanted you and Brandon to have a normal life. I can't tell you how proud I am of the way you and Brandon turned out. I know the help came from God, and for that I am thankful." With my tears finally flowing—and they were happy tears—I continued. "The switching gears on me was something that I wasn't prepared for." I will never forget Hannah's response.

"I love my daddy, Momma, and I still wish he would come home, but he's not and I have learned to accept that. I pray that God keeps him safe, and

I pray that one day, I can find out why he really left, and I don't mean from you or some doctor, but from him. One day when I get rich, I will look for him; and if he is dead, I will give him a proper burial. If he is alive, I want to be in his life. He is still my daddy, and everybody goes through something. I think about him often, but I know that thinking is all I can do for now. One day, I will have the resources to find my daddy, and I will. I owe him that, Momma, and I need answers too."

I could tell she knew I couldn't find words to respond, so she said, "Now, we will talk more later. Go to bed, silly girl, enough of this mushy stuff. Get some rest. Granny will be here tomorrow, and we all need our strength."

I thought for a minute, got up, and pulled her blanket snug upon her. I left the room thinking that my little girl was now a woman, a woman that I should have been, a woman who was actually sure of what she wanted.

Walking through my house to my room, I thought I heard footsteps on the porch. I stopped, trying to figure out if it was only my imagination, and I heard nothing. I went to the window to peek out to see if I saw anything. I saw nothing, so I just turned the light out and went to my room.

Sleeping was still hard. I had thought that I had slept for hours, but I would wake to see that only minutes had passed. Then I would do it over and over throughout the night. I guess in my mind, I didn't want to go to sleep because, when I would awake, it would be only one more day before Hannah would be gone. I just thought about her growing up and the woman she had become and prayed that the future held better for her than it had for me.

Music filled my home at about seven thirty the next morning. The children were roaming about, laughing and fixing breakfast. They made French toast and sausage, their favorite meal.

"Hey!" I yelled. "Can we get the music just a little louder?"

Watching them from across the room, I could see they didn't hear me because of the volume. I thought once to go turn the music down myself, but it was Hannah's day, so I might as well join in.

I decided to dance across the room over to where they were standing and take a bite of the freshly prepared French toast. The song that was playing was a favorite of the family, and we started singing it as loudly as humanly possible. When it was done, we hit rewind and did it all over again. We did it two or three times until we realized that Momma was standing in the living room.

"Helllooooo, helllooooo," she said, until we actually stopped singing. "Good day! It's a wonder you all got eardrums left," she said. "Can Granny get some kind of hug or something?" The children immediately stopped performing and ran to her, about knocking her down, and swallowed her up with kisses and hugs.

"You're here early, Ms. Adams," I said, laughing at her trying to keep her balance. "We weren't expecting you until about noon."

"I wanted to spend as much time with Hannah as I could before she left, so sleeping the day away wasn't a possibility. I brought a little something for both Hannah and Brandon. It's in the car," she said, holding out the keys to her Blazer.

Without another sound, the kids raced to get their shoes on and headed for the outside.

"How are you holding up, Victoria?" Momma said while fixing herself a cup of coffee. "This must be hard for you, seeing her all grown-up."

"Yeah, Momma, it is," I said, "but life hasn't been really good to me, so I have learned to adjust accordingly."

Moments later, the children returned, holding a mountain of bags.

"A little something'? Momma, you shouldn't go overboard for the children," I said.

"I wanted them to be the best-dressed kids in school," she said. "They deserve it."

Momma wasn't like me, even though she was a well-kept woman. She kept up with the times, and what she didn't know, she asked about. I, on the other hand, I didn't have time to keep up with the times. It was all I could do keeping up with life. She had brought them several outfits with the shoes to match, and she gave each of them a check for two hundred dollars. They were all set now, and time was winding down.

We cooked out, and of course, the usual family members came: Jasmine and Ms. Fable. Dark caught us before we were ready. While putting the dishes away, I drifted off to our past again. From the birth of the twins to the day James left us. I couldn't get past those feelings. Some were angry, and some were happy, all mixed up together. Ms. Fable came into the kitchen to check on me. She said, "I will be here bright and early in the morning, Victoria, and I expect a smile on your face. Are the riding arrangements still the same? You and me and your momma with Hannah. I'm sure Brandon will take his car, so he can have Jasmine ride with him to settle Hannah in her new home away from home." She must have known I was beside myself because she walked straight over to me and gave me a hug.

"Victoria, I know you are sad, but look at your accomplishment. That is the way you have to look at this. It's not like she will be gone forever. She is a little woman now. Let her grow. She doesn't need to see you sad because it might hinder her from leaving. Let her know that this is the best possible thing that she can do. Save your tears for when they are both gone, and you are home alone. Now is not the time."

With that, she picked up her jacket and purse and said, "I will see you around seven in the morning." And she was gone.

The last dish was washed, and everybody but me had gathered in the living room. I looked at Momma, sitting there with the children, laughing, and talking; I wanted to join in, but it was hard for me to laugh and talk. But I kept what Ms. Fable said in my head: remember to laugh, and cry later.

Even with that, I still couldn't go into the room, so I started for Hannah's room to check off her list and to place her letter carefully in her already-packed luggage. I was just going to make sure she had all she needed.

It was Brandon who came to my rescue. I was surprised, because he had been involved with Jasmine all evening it was as if he was the one that was leaving. I knew he was sad that his sister was leaving, but he and Jasmine never left each other's side until now.

"Momma," he said, "are you okay?" He startled me as he spoke, standing in Hannah's bedroom doorway. "Why don't you come into the living room with us?"

"I will be there in a minute," I replied. "I just want to make sure that Hannah is all set to go."

"Do you wish Daddy was here?" His question surprised me.

"In a way, I do, Brandon. But he isn't. We have made it this far. We will continue on with the memories, the good ones that is," I said. I tried to smile so he wouldn't think his words had upset me like they really had.

"Well, one day, Momma, he will look back and see what he missed; and that is when we can say that he got what he deserved. To be honest momma I am glad he's not here because if he was, I would not only give him a piece of my mind, but I will toss him out on his a—head I'm sorry momma. He missed out on his family we didn't push him away he made the choice of removing us from his life we didn't do it and I hope I never see that loser again I mean it. I am nothing like him and I never want to be and if he ever comes around talking about daddy's home, I am going to ask him whose daddy and why did he come back. That's before I toss him out."

With that he left the room, and he was justified in how he was feeling. Missing all the things that he had missed would be memories that he would need, and not having those was punishment enough. I knew Brandon was bitter towards his father and he's not a kid anymore he was now a young man. I wonder how many conversations Brandon and Hannah had of me. I wonder with his words if he had any ill feelings the way I handled things or if he thought I should have handled things differently. I couldn't focus my energy on that at the moment. I knew Brandon was angry at his father and I wouldn't do anything to change his mind. James did this I didn't, and they are now young adults with their own minds and thoughts, I didn't have to make excuses for James anymore. With that thought, I put the letter into Hannah's bag; then I went back into the living room and turned on the cd with our favorite song and danced across the room. The children at once got up and joined in, and that was basically how we ended our night.

Chapter 31

Brrrrrring, brrrrrrrrrring, the alarm sounded. I reached over and hit the snooze button. I wasn't ready for morning, so I thought if I hit that dreadful button, time would stand still long enough for me to get ready.

Ten minutes later, brrrring, brrrrring.

"Please. Please stop," I said aloud, "just a few more minutes." I could hear in the other room feet stirring around, so I thought I had better get up and face the day head-on. I jumped in the shower before going into the living room. I didn't want the children to see dread all over my face, so I thought if I left the room dressed, they would think I was excited about this dreadful day.

The first to arrive was Ms. Fable. She came into the house carrying her to-go cup of coffee. Shortly behind her was Jasmine.

"Hail, hail, the gang's all here," I said, trying to fake joy. "We better get this party started." Brandon packed the cars with all of the things Hannah wanted to take, and it was a good thing we were taking three vehicles because one or two wouldn't have held her things.

I must have fallen asleep when the alarm went off. I had tossed and turned all night long. My body was screaming for rest, but I knew I had to get up and make a way to push my mind and body to get through this day. Momma spent the night so we wouldn't have to go out of our way; she spent most of the time with Hannah. I was writing in my little notes to my family. I then joined them, trying to hold back the tears while Hannah gathered the rest of her things.

Before I could say my loneliness was getting ready to begin, we were on the road. Ms. Fable insisted on driving. I remembered her arrangements from the night before, but I needed something to take my mind off of what was getting ready to happen. I knew that driving would take away some of the sting, but I eventually gave in to Ms. Fable and let her drive. I guess she knew I wasn't in any shape—either that, or she did it for her safety. Hannah drove her car with Momma, Brandon and Jasmine wanted to ride alone, and it was me and Ms. Fable in the other vehicle. I didn't talk much on the way, and Ms. Fable didn't pressure me. I had a lot that I needed to sort out on my own. I felt like I was attending a funeral instead of seeing my daughter off to college, and I couldn't hold back the tears.

Ms. Fable said "are you ready Victoria we got to make this pleasant for her. We will follow her down and get her settled in, and the following week she will start her journey." We will follow her down, I thought to myself, and then I will be alone again.

I couldn't help but get mad at James, a man whom I said I would forget because this was the time that we should be enjoying life. We should be together doing things together. Here I am, a forty-four-year-old woman, seeing her daughter off to college alone. My life shouldn't be this way. I should have been with James doing things like yard sales, visiting relatives, bragging about the children and their accomplishments. Instead, I was in our home alone, thinking about what could have been, what should have been.

Ms. Fable let me cry until we were about fifteen minutes away, and then she said, "Okay, Victoria, you need to dry it up. The last thing Hannah needs right now is for you to be a mess. Wipe those tears and make yourself prepared for her. She will want to know that you are okay with her decision. If she sees you crying, it just might make her change her mind; so, wipe those tears, and put on your happy face."

Even though it was hard to do, I did as she requested because, again, she was right. I didn't need to let Hannah know that I was scared, and I had only my lonely fears on my mind. She needed to see me happy so she would know that I was okay with her decision.

Hannah's dorm was huge. It looked like a hospital. There were windows every few feet. I was glad that her room was on the bottom level. I had read how college kids fell from their dorm windows.

When we arrived at her room, her roommate was already there. She introduced herself as Madison Rhea and seemed like a really nice girl. Her parents were there, and she had a mother and a father; I felt bad that I was the only parent present for Hannah. Her mom looked worse than I did, and I was glad that Ms. Fable had given me that pep talk because Madison Rhea was sad for her momma, who wouldn't stop crying.

We all walked around the campus and got to meet the dean of the school. He assured me that Hannah would be well taken care of. With that news, we had to say our good-byes, and we were back in our cars headed for home. I decided to sit in the backseat and let Momma sit up front with Ms. Fable. I didn't want them to see me cry, and cry was what I did all the way home.

On the ride back, Momma spoke about things I never thought she felt. "Victoria," she said, "I am so proud of you and your accomplishments, you know. After all that you have had to endure, I think you did a fantastic job. Most women would have given up or had several men under their belt by now, hoping to find the love that they thought they had. Look at you. You have finished raising two beautiful, well-respecting children all by yourself. Not thinking about a man. You have done something that even at my age, I don't know if I could have done. I will let you in on a little something that I thought about on the way to your house last night. Your father would have been so, so proud of you. You were our only hope, the only child. You could have chosen a different road, a different path. When you got with James, the last time I thought oh lord here we go she has to be watched over Lord because she's head strong and if she fails me and her daddy will fail too because she doesn't have a sister or brother to pick up her pieces and be successful, but I tell you Victoria Andrews you did not I mean it you did not disappoint. You have made me so proud, and you have done a fine job raising such fine children and I am so glad God saw fit for me to be your mother."

"Momma, thank you that means a lot but what is that Mother?" What have I done that you don't think you could have done?" Momma's, word did my heart good. I am glad to know that my daddy would have been proud and that she was also proud of me at least I have done some things right.

"Momma said, "as in love as me and your daddy were, as God-fearing as I am, I am not so sure if he did to me what James did to you that I would not have sought out another man to take his place. Raising a child alone in this day and time is hard enough; I can't imagine raising two. That James with all his troubles really didn't know the love you had for him; he couldn't have. If he did, I don't think he would have left. Sometimes troubles come hard and unexpected, and it takes strong souls to be able to endure. That is why they say never judge anyone's struggles because everybody's walk with the lord isn't the same. What you can do some woman couldn't and vice versa. Even though all trials and tribulations seem hard God knows who to give what battle too. You are proof Victoria; God doesn't put more on us than what we can bare and even though you have had a hard walk with the lord. You have beautifully sustained most women can't say that and that is something to be very proud of."

"The kids were what kept me going," I said to Momma as she turned to look at my tearstained face. "It's hard to let them go," I continued, "because they have been my purpose for so long."

"I can understand that Victoria because after your daddy passed and I was along for those months it was you and the kids that gave me my life back."

It's funny, I thought to myself. All this time, I thought that she thought I had done something to chase James away. We had gotten distant for a while. I let our closeness go because she always wanted to talk to me about

God; I was praying enough for both me and James, so I didn't want to hear that. I thought she thought I had failed at being a well-kept woman because I chose to work and help take care of my family, instead of staying home and doing volunteer work like she had.

"I wish I had worked to get paid," she said, as if she was reading my mind. "Even though your daddy left me not worrying about anything, I still wish I had learned my independence like you did before I was forced to live on my own."

"I never had children," Ms. Fable chimed in. "I never had a chance to find out what I would do in either of your situations. I guess that is why I never took the plunge—because I knew that I could never provide a family for a man. I thank you, Victoria, because you gave me something that I would have missed out on. I am thankful that you let me share the lives of your children; now I don't feel so bad. The children have grown up to be such respectful adults, and you, my dear, should take praise for that," Ms. Fable said.

Hearing my accomplishments from others brought joy and tears. I knew I did a decent job with the children, but I never thought anybody else knew it because until now, no one had ever spoken about it. I couldn't talk, and I don't think Momma expected me to. I just kept the tears coming while she and Ms. Fable carried on a conversation.

A week after we saw Hannah off to college, it was Brandon's turn. I did manage to slip his letter into his bag. We didn't have time to talk anymore about his father or just things about the way Hannah and I did. I knew he didn't want to discuss his father anymore and I understood. He was one that I didn't want to see my tears. He was already angry with his father and me crying about anything would only make his regret his father more. With him the tears I needed to shed would be better served during our phone conversations from laughter and his trips home. He didn't want the fuss that we gave Hannah; he wanted to spend his free time with Jasmine. Yet seeing Brandon off was bittersweet. Momma and Ms. Fable rode with me while we followed Brandon to his destination. Jasmine, of course, rode with him, and I knew they would have conversation of their own. This was a sad time for them, and yet a new beginning. How wonderful that sounds: a new beginning. My children were starting their lives, while my life had stood still.

James had been gone for over a year. The children, both eighteen, were making waves for their future. I, at forty-four, was wishing I could turn back the hands of time. I was wishing I had someone to grow old with. I guessed I could date, but the promise I made to God and everyone that I would love James till death did we part kept ringing in the back of my mind. Hadn't I disappointed God enough? Even though the love for James kept fading as the days went by, I still loved him in a way that no one would understand or even care to know for that matter.

We walked into Brandon's new home, and we sat in his room. We met his roommate like we had with Hannah. We didn't want to interrupt his and Jasmine's good-bye, so we left them alone while we went and got a bite to eat.

On the way home, I couldn't help but feel sorrow for Jasmine. She was a young girl in love like I had been. The only difference was, she was leaving him, he hadn't left her. Silence filled the car, and it seemed like an eternity before we got back to our house. Jasmine was going to a school that she had decided on right in the community where she wanted to become a registered nurse, and her future with Brandon was a bright one.

When we pulled up in our driveway, I noticed that she had silently been crying. I gave her a hug and told her that whenever she wanted, she could call or come by. I felt that was what Brandon would have wanted me to do. With that, she hugged me back. Momma and Ms. Fable followed suit; they each gave Jasmine a hug and told her not to be a stranger, that she was part of their family too. We stood there and waved as Jasmine pulled out of the driveway.

"I feel like a hot cup of tea," Ms. Fable said.

"Sounds good to me," Momma replied.

"I'll put on the water," I said, heading into the house. I knew they were tired from the trip, but I guess they knew that I didn't want to be alone. Momma and Ms. Fable joined me in the kitchen. Momma reached in the cabinet to get out a box of cookies to go with our tea.

"The porch, living room, or counter?" Ms. Fable asked.

"Hmm," I said, "why not the porch? That seems like a nice spot for a cup of tea," I said, laughing. The porch it was. After the water told us that it was ready to join the tea bags, we each grabbed our cups, Momma took the cookies, and we headed to the porch for our evening's end.

We sat there until the sun went down. The air became cooler, so we decided to call it a night. Neither Momma nor Ms. Fable stayed at my house, even though I wanted them to. As they put on their jackets, I felt a sense of loneliness. I felt that I couldn't face the lonely house alone, but I knew they were tired too, so I didn't protest. I knew I had to get used to the fact that the kids were gone, and there was no time like the present.

The fact that they went with me was more than anyone could have asked, so I said my good-byes and went back into the lonely house. I turned the lights out, went to my room, wrote in my journal about my feelings, and then went to bed. I had to start Brandon's route tomorrow, and even though it wouldn't be the same without him, I was looking forward to it. I needed all I could to take my mind off of the children, off of James.

I was dreaming of James when the alarm woke me in the morning. I didn't want to wake up because the dream was too real. He was back home, and we were sitting on the porch, talking about what a good job we had done raising the kids. Brandon had told us he was marrying Jasmine, and we went to our old familiar tree to have a picnic like we had when James proposed. It was just a silly dream, I thought as I got out of bed to start the route.

Going down the lonely streets, I knew that somewhere in this lonely town was my husband. He was sleeping soundly, not having a care in the world, his family forgotten; and it was I who kept the good memories. I guessed

James had forgotten them. As I passed by the park, an image caught my attention. It looked as though someone was sitting under my tree. I thought once to go see who it was that would be up at the crack of dawn under my tree, but it was just a passing thought; it was probably some teenagers having sex or doing something that they had no business doing. Above all, it was none of my business. I could only see one person, but I was sure another person was close by.

It would be best if I continued on with my paper route and got ready for my shift at the pharmacy store. I finished with the paper route right on time. I had enough time to read the paper and have a cup of tea before I went to work at the pharmacy store.

Work was refreshing; it took my mind off of things, and that was a good thing. I didn't want time to think because I would only worry about the children or feel sorry for myself because I didn't have James. I thought of him often, and they were memories of both the good and the bad. I would sometimes get angry with him; other times, I would just feel sorry for all that he had missed. Fate dealt him a bad hand, and his sorrow and pain melted through our family. Even though he was gone now, that hurtful pain lingered on.

The days went by faster when I was working, and when I got home, I would think of the children and write in my journal before going to bed. Ms. Fable, Mother, and I would sometimes go out to eat, and sometimes we would just take a walk in the park. I didn't dare sit under my tree—it brought back too many memories—so we would just walk and talk about things, nothing in particular, just things. If it wasn't for Ms. Fable and Momma spending time with me, I don't think I would have made it through the changes that had been presented to my life. It was hard not seeing the children when I came home from work or going on Brandon's paper route without him. When it was time to prepare a meal, if Ms. Fable or Mother didn't come by to help me eat it, then the next day it would retire in the trash.

The children called every other day or sometimes every day, depending on what was going on in their school at that time. I could tell that they were growing up now because what started out as being calls asking what they should do about this or that were now calls about what they did or how they made a certain decision. I was definitely experiencing the empty-nest syndrome. There were times while they were growing up when I was going through my own struggles, and I wished that they didn't need me as much as they had; now I wished that they needed me more than they really did.

When they had an exam, I wouldn't hear from them until the test had been taken. The weeks turned into months. They were adults now, both of them nineteen years old, carefully following the paths that they had chosen.

Ms. Robertson would call from time to time and ask about me and the children, but her drinking in her early years had finally taken a toll on her health. She sounded much weaker than usual. She had to pause so her breath could catch up with her words. This was hurtful because I knew that I wouldn't have her around much longer. Sometimes after we spoke, I would sit for hours replaying our conversation, picturing her trying to catch her breath as she spoke. I could sense when she talked that her body was tiring. She blamed herself and James's father for the way James turned out; and sometimes I did too. Silently, of course; I would have never told her my thoughts. I often thought of how his life would have been if he had had a momma and daddy who loved him. I would listen to her sorrowful words and the way she regretted not being the mother she could have been.

"Oh Victoria, if I could have the slightest chance to change things," she would say, "I would be a mother more like you. James would have come first in my life. I can barely get around these days, and if I had raised James like I should have, then he would want to be here to help me. There are days that I'm too weak to fix myself food, and I say maybe I would be better off in a nursing home, where I won't be such a bother, but then there is just that little ray of hope that something will change, and things will get better for me. Sometimes I have good days sometimes not so good."

I would sometimes become a little angry at her words and think should have, could have, or would have. But you didn't. Then I would have to erase those thoughts, because I didn't know a thing about James's grandparents. All I knew was Ms. Robertson didn't have a mother. There were times it was easy to blame her for my failed marriage, but after I would think about it, James could have worked it out. His leaving was his own choice, so I could blame no one but him. Whatever they as parents were not able to give him growing up, the children and I tried hard to give it to him as a father and a husband, so the fault lay with him. Even though I knew nothing about James's father's past, it could have been a pattern. I hoped my children would break that pattern even though they had years of growing up without a father. I could only hope the good years with him instilled good in them.

Talking on the phone didn't do our relationship justice, so I decided it was time again to go visit Ms. Robertson. She would be glad for the company, I was sure. I told Ms. Fable about my plans, and she approved; she thought it would do me good to get away.

"Take all the time you need," she said. "This old store will be here when you get back."

I knew that Ms. Fable could handle the store on her own and I was just company for her, but I would only take a week and then I would return.

I will just surprise Ms. Robertson, I thought; I will not call her. I will stay for a week and help her do the things that she isn't able to do. Then I will return back to my life, which is now filled with God, and I will keep the thoughts of James in the back of my mind … not the front.

My ride to Ms. Robertson's house was a peaceful one. I took the time to stop on the side of the road and enjoy life. I saw the different flowers and the different parks that children were playing in. I had time to think about my life, about the children, about James. I was feeling better about myself, and I wanted to share my joy with Ms. Robertson.

When I pulled up to the old house, it looked as though she had moved. The grass had grown up, and the house looked like it needed some attention. It looked like no one had cut her grass all year, and the paint on her house was fading out. I started to turn back, but something told me that she was there in this lonely house that used to bring her joy.

I walked up the driveway onto the steps and knocked on the door. I could hear the television going, and I knew someone was there. Moments later, she came to the door.

"Victoria," she said, "what a pleasant surprise! What brings you here?" she said, motioning for me to come in.

"I decided to take a little vacation to visit you," I said, enjoying her smile.

"Well, thank God," she said, "I'm so glad that you are here." She was walking with a walker now, and she looked feeble. I could tell that her life was fading away, and I knew that it was God who brought me here to help her.

"Come sit down," she said. "Don't you dare mind the shape the house is in I have to find me another little helper."

I moved over the papers that she had been reading and sat down beside her.

"How are you, Victoria? Is everything okay with you and the children?" she asked with concern on her face.

"Everything is fine," I said. "The children are in school, doing well. I had a little extra time on my hands, so I decided to come for a visit. To see if you need anything."

"Oh dear," she said, "I let everything go. I am just not able to keep house like I used to. These old bones have a mind of their own. I was having this young man cut my grass, but he found a full-time job and he isn't able to do it anymore, so it just grows and grows. I'm not the most social person, you know, so I don't have anybody else."

I cleaned her house and cut her grass, and by evening we were sitting on her porch drinking tea.

"I'm so glad you thought enough of me to come for a visit," she said. "After what James did to you and the children, I'm surprised that you even talk to me, let alone come to help me," she said, with tears forming in her eyes.

"What James did has nothing to do with you," I told her. "That is between me, him, and God. Anyway, I have given him to God, and I decided to let God do it." I told her about the woman in the church and how I had come to peace with what James had done.

"Oh, I wish I could have helped you in some way, Victoria. I wish he would come to his senses and be the man that his daddy never was. I just wish I could reach out to him and show him the mistakes I made, let him know that I don't want him to follow in my footsteps. But I don't even know where to look. Don't you know that his father has never called me again, neither has James that's proof that they are together somewhere."

"And you," she continued, "even more I wish that I had given my troubles to God instead of drinking and turning to the streets. I wish I was more like you. If I had just let God take my troubles, maybe Ron and I would still be together. I have since forgiven him, because when you look at it, I was no better than he was. If I had been, maybe by now God would have changed him and sent him back to me in his new form. I have been praying that God speak to James and as they say sometimes God answered prayers in his time even if its after death. The prayer will be answered you can trust and believe."

"You are a wonderful woman, Victoria. If you still have love in your heart for James, God can fix it; he can fix everything. I'm so glad that he chose a woman like you. Even with the hurt that you bear, you still keep pressing on. God does have a plan; we just don't know what it is. When we do know, it will be well worth the wait. One way or the other, it will be well worth the wait."

I sat there listening to her words. They were wise words, words that I didn't expect to hear. I knew I still loved James, but I knew that I wasn't in love with him. If he came back today, I didn't know if I could love him the way I once had. I knew that I could love him for the troubled man that he was, and maybe that is what the plan was. For me to love him for the troubled man that he was, but not to be in love with him. Maybe God wanted to use me to bring James closer to him. I didn't know the reason, but I knew I had no choice but to wait on whatever was going to be.

I spent the rest of my time with Ms. Robertson looking for people who could come clean her house and cut her grass until I returned. I would return. I would make it a point to be in her life until she laid her burdens down and went home.

Chapter 32

Days were flying by. The fall leaves were turning, and a hint of winter was in the air. I hadn't seen the children since I took them to school in early September. This would be our first Thanksgiving since they left. Even though we talked on the phone, it didn't feel quite the same. This lonely old house that had only memories would feel like home again once the children were back.

I made a pot of tea and sat on the porch and planned their homecoming. I sat there thinking of the last Thanksgiving and how it was spent in church and how that woman's words changed my life, and I rejoined the church. I spent a lot of my free time with Momma and Ms. Fable when I wasn't visiting Ms. Robertson, whose signs of failing health had magnified. My children, now eighteen years old, were turning nineteen next year. This Christmas would mark two years since they had last seen their father.

Momma and Ms. Fable were beside themselves helping me prepare for the children's visit. Once again, I was counting on this Thanksgiving to be a happy time for us, This Thanksgiving will have to be better than the great Thanksgiving that we had the previous year. It would be a happy time for us, We would have could conversations I would be able to see how much they have grown. not only was my children coming home I felt that we were now friends too. What a homecoming this is going to be.

The children arrived home, and yes, Jasmine came too. She had only called a few times since the children left. I knew that Jasmine was focusing on her schooling, and the extra time she had was spent talking to Brandon on the phone. Brandon picked her up before he even came home, so I knew where this was heading. Seeing the children now was a pleasant surprise, even though they had only been gone for less than three months. They all looked like they had matured. Brandon and Jasmine were in their own little world, and Hannah and I talked about the experiences that she had during her months at school.

"They have a curfew, Mother," she said. "Sometimes when I go out with my friends, I lose track of time, but I have never been late. I even learned how to budget. When I first got my loan from school and I had all that money, I went out and splurged a couple of times, and before you knew it, I was out of money. I was eating soup and crackers for at least a month," she said, laughing. "I didn't want to tell you because I didn't want to worry you."

I felt a little cringe come over me; to think that my daughter was starving made me feel a little dizzy. "You could have called," I said, never wanting her to feel like she couldn't.

"I knew you were having bills of your own, Momma, and I had to learn, even if that was the hard way," she said with a giggle. "I even went on a date with a boy," she said, with her eyes opening wider. "Little did he know it was only because I was tired of soup, but to my surprise, Momma, I liked him."

Really now, I thought to myself, the Lord works in mysterious ways.

Hannah continued, "His name is Jerry, and he is going to law school too. There were other boys who liked me, but what isn't there to like?" she said, standing. "I'm gorgeous," she said, laughing again.

"Who told you that?" I said, teasing her.

"Jerry," she said matter-of-factly. "He is cute too, Momma. I'll give him some time." She paused and looked at me, then repeated, "some time," and then she laughed again.

Was my little girl falling in love? I thought. Jerry was right. She was truly a gorgeous young woman. She had long, almost black hair that hung down past her shoulders. She had her father's eyes, deep, deep brown, and she carried my smile, with perfectly straight teeth and olive skin tone that would make any girl envy her. She also had a shape that I only dreamed of having at her age. Looking at Hannah, I could see she was just about perfect. Personality and heart to match. I'm sure there were a lot of young guys who were attracted to her, but I could tell Jerry was the one who actually caught her interest. I didn't know if it was because he fed her when she was hungry, or just because. The reason didn't seem to matter; the thought of her dating made my heart smile. She didn't want to elaborate on him. I felt she was hiding something, but in her own time, I knew she would tell me.

Thoughts of Hannah finding love gave me little sleep that first night. I got up early to put the turkey in the oven, awaiting Momma's and Ms. Fable's arrival. We were going to spend the day before Thanksgiving cooking versus the night before like we had the year before. We made it a party. Both my children were there, and yes, Jasmine too, and we laughed and joked and cooked all day. By evening time, we were feeling our activities from our day. "Church is tomorrow Hannah" said and "we won't be late." Momma looked at Hannah approving and then she turned and winked at me "I know we are going to church tomorrow." That made us turn our attention to reminiscing about the year before, We had stayed up late church then that woman that gave me her testimony. Jasmine and Brandon took that time to put up the Christmas lights, they decided to do it the day before Thanksgiving this year. I had to laugh thinking that if the football game didn't go as well as Brandon expected he and Jasmine might have a tough time putting up the lights. Every now and again, Hannah would disappear to go talk on the phone. I wanted to know everything there was to know about Jerry, but in time, I thought. I was sure if he caught her interest, he would be around for a while, and there would be plenty of time to get to know him. After the exhaustion took over Brandon took Jasmine home and I went to my room to get prepared for church in the morning. I didn't want to be late, and I would let nothing stand in my way looking back I knew that God was the one that was carrying through this hurt and pain and I knew that I had rested in his arms on the nights that I was actually able to sleep after James left so yes, I was going to church and yes, I was thankful. After getting my clothes I took a long bath, and I said my prayers thanking God for all that he had done and then I without writing in my journal fell fast asleep.

The following morning, I was awaken by the phone ringing. Although I didn't feel too tired, I could have used a few more minutes of sleep. Making my way to the bathroom to wash my face a feeling came over me at first it was a feeling to get back in the bed, but I knew that I wasn't going to do that, so I shook that feeling off and hurried into the kitchen. There I saw Hannah sitting at the counter with the phone plastered to her ear. At first, I thought she might have been talking to momma or Ms. Fable but when I heard her say I have to go get ready for church I miss you too I knew it must have been Jerry. I waited until I knew she had hung up the phone before I started teasing. "Was that momma, or Ms. Fable that you are missing I said laughing. "Whatever momma she said accepting my tease, that was Jerry. He said he missed me first what was I supposed to say okay I talk to you later remember momma this is a man that fed your daughter when she was hungry. We both laughed. Out of curiosity Hannah does he know that story?"

"No momma I never told him, but I am sure the way I devoured the food from the restaurant that he must have knew. I remember the second date he wanted to take me to dinner and a movie. It was the new movie with the seven dwarfs and snow white. I hadn't eaten well that week so by the time I finally got a satisfying meal I was full not to mention sleepy. I fell asleep in the movie theater. He woke me up, I was snoring she said laughing so hard that tears were falling. Even though my heart was sad to think my daughter was starving I had to laugh too. "Could you imagine momma my embarrassment he thought it was the cutest thing. "He gave me the nick name snow white, which considering the movie, that we were supposed to be watching was about snow white." Our laughter was interrupted by Brandon "could you ladies keep it down a man needs his rest."

"Speaking of the seven dwarfs and in comes grumpy" Hannah said, and we laughed again.

"Ha Ha" Brandon said what's so funny anyways?'

"You" Hannah said still laughing "nobody told you to stay up daydreaming about Jasmine last night."

Brandon replied "What else could I do; I couldn't sleep with you cackling all night with Jerry.

"I wasn't dreaming about Jasmine he said teasing his sister. How could I sleep with you cackling all night talking to the loser Jerry?"

Hannah instantly got serious and said, "he's not a loser Brother, he's a feeder" and then she and I being the only two that knew about her hunger situation started laughing again but this time Brandon joined in.

After the laughter stopped Brandon said, "whose cooking breakfast this morning, I am hungry." "We could call Jerry" I said with more laughter added.

"I will cook" Hannah said. "What shall we have." "What's on the menu" Brandon said "cereal, cereal and cereal with milk" Hannah said. "Then I guess it will be cereal he said laughing.

"Get your showers I will cook breakfast" while my children were taking there showers happiness was my feeling. I loved the closeness they shared, and I loved the fact that laughter wasn't a stranger in our home any longer. We were the Andrews, and we did share love.

After breakfast was over and we were dressed for church momma and Ms. Fable arrived. Brandon left to pick up Jasmine and Hannah, Ms. Fable, and I road with momma. Church was packed I was glad we got there when we did, or we would have had to stand. The preacher preached on thanks and giving and the joy of both. It was a beautiful sermon, and no one brought attention to me I was happy all the same God was showing me happy things now so I guess he figured I was smart enough that he could show me own his own that he didn't need anybody to tell me.

Once home momma fixed her rolls and we prepared the table for Thanksgiving dinner once we sat down for the feast it was Brandon that surprised us all. He said the blessing, he carved the turkey and before we started to eat, he said. "Before we start this wonderful meal that was prepared for us to share, I want to bring back a tradition that I feel is important right now at this moment and I will start it. All eyes glued on Brandon he said. "I Brandon Andrews is first and foremost thankful for my momma he said looking at me. The strongest most caring woman I know. I think God for watching over her and for the love she has shown me through the years. I thank God for My grandmother and Ms. Fable too for being in our lives believing in us as a family in spite of" Clearing his throat he continued. I thank God for Jasmine who is a particularly important part of my life and I hope that she always will be and last but not least looking at Hannah, my sister my friend I couldn't imagine God giving me a different better half. I love you and in spite of he said again clearing his throat you are a strong amazing young lady, and I am proud that you are my sister. With those words he looked at me and he said Momma your turn."

"After that being said where do I begin, I said trying to catch my tears from falling. I Victoria Andrews thank god for my two wonderful children who have blossomed into two beautiful adults. I thank you for believing in me, never giving up persevering. For your strength and your love. I thank my momma for her guidance and her wisdom and her love. Ms. Fable, I thank you for just being the friend that you are and not only for being a part of my family but for loving my family. Jasmine, I thank you for bringing joy and happiness to the best son any mother can have." Then I looked at Hannah.

"I Hannah Andrews thank God for showing my family that there is love in the midst of everything that we have been through. I thank God for a mother that all girls dream of. I think you for your strength and guidance and love the most precious love momma. I thank you for all that you have done for this family and the fact that you keep pressing on. Jasmine, I thank you for being in my brother's life I know that he has found happiness with you. I thank you for your friendship. Grandmother I thank you for introducing me to God allowing me to understand his power and glory. I thank you for helping us through our good times and challenging times. I love you Grandma. Ms. fable I thank you for being a friend to my mother and a family member to us. I thank you for giving my mother the opportunity years ago when she started working for you to have some kind of peace and happiness for all that she was going through. Brother" she said I love you and I love your strength. I love everything about you, and I am glad that you are my brother and that I had, and always will have you to share my ups and downs. Jasmine."

"I Jasmine Davis am thankful for Brandon. My knight and shining armor. He's my strength, he's, my breath. Without him in my life I don't know where I would be. I think him for being there through our secrets that we share and the tears that we have shed. I am thankful for being a part of such a loving family all of you. Hannah, I thank you for your friendship as well for the secrets we have shared for the tears that we have cried together. I thank you for listening and for giving me an opportunity to crowd yours and Brandon's circle. I am thankful for my parents their understanding and there strength for all that I have been through in my life. Ms. Fable. "I don't know what to say I have never felt so much love in all my life. Clearing her throat, she said I Teresa Fable have so much to share with this family which will explain how I came about. I love you all and I know there has been pain and sorrow, but you've all overcome, and I thank God for that. I am thankful for being considered a part of your family everybody has a story to tell and one day you will all know mine. I love you all she said as she sniffed back tears. I love you all so much. Rebecca?"

"I Rebecca Adams am speechless I first give the honor and Glory to my lord and Savior Jesus Christ for giving the peace and tranquility that this family needed in their time of need I thank God for the strongest daughter any mother could ask for I thank God for giving her strength. My grandchildren I thank God for them and for showing them his love and guidance. I thank Jasmine for being there for Brandon and I thank Teresa Fable for being there for everyone including me. The love that we have all shared the closeness we share God proves with every breath that we take that he is able, and he proves faithful. I think him for all of you."

Everybody at the table had tears forming or formed over that was the best few minutes of our year. I don't know or understand what everyone was talking about I felt there were things in our lives left unsaid but at that time at that moment it didn't matter because there was love at that table there was a family at that table and there was a closeness that was well deserved at that table. It was Hannah that brought the humor back so we could get past or words and eat our dinner.

Hannah said, "Oh silly me I almost forgot" I thank God for my friend Jerry for be so caring and sharing such good food" She and I laughed the loudest which not knowing what we were laughing about made everyone else laugh and before we could say Happy Thanksgiving there were spoons and forks slapping in dishes all around the table..

After we had our Thanksgiving dinner, Brandon and Jasmine watched the game while the rest of us cleared away the dishes. It was fun watching Jasmine try and stand up to Brandon's accusations of cheating the Dallas team during the football game. Hannah disappeared yet again to go talk on the phone, and then we all gathered around the Christmas tree taking turns putting ornaments on the tree. After the tree was decorated, I made hot chocolate, and we sat around watching the lights glisten on the tree.

Momma looked at me as if for the first time in months, she saw me happy. Not long after that, she and Ms. Fable left, and I went into my own thoughts of how my last two holidays had been, hoping that Christmas would prove to be just as rewarding, if not more so.

The next morning the children returned to school, and it was a bittersweet moment. I knew they were growing up, and I was glad that Hannah had a friend, whom I was sure she couldn't wait to get back to see. Brandon was a little saddened. I didn't know if it was because he was leaving me or Jasmine. I was proud of my children, but a part of me wanted to rewind the times when they were home again. The house seemed empty, and it just didn't seem like home when they were away. After seeing them pull out of the driveway, I too got into my car and headed to work.

I felt myself just going through the motions, and Ms. Fable kept her distance. I thought she knew that the children were on my mind.

After a few days had passed and I still felt myself in almost a slumber, with the kids constantly racing through my mind, Momma came into the store. When she'd made her way to the register, she looked at me and said, "Victoria, what on earth is wrong with you? You look a mess. Haven't you been getting any sleep? Are you sick? What is wrong with you?"

I just responded, "I miss the children."

"Won't they be back for Christmas?" she asked as if she thought I'd forgotten.

"Yes," I replied, "but it's hard seeing them for just a little while before they are gone again."

"Well, I've got just the thing you need to pull you out of the slumber." By now Ms. Fable was at our side. "Our church is having a revival this week, and the two of you should join me."

Ms. Fable said, "I'm in."

Even though I was going to church regularly, I had since missed several Sundays, and I didn't feel up to it. Somehow, I was enjoying my self-pity. Before I could make an excuse, Momma said, "Good. I will meet you at Victoria's house at six thirty."

She didn't give me time to protest before she was out the door. Ms. Fable just looked at me. With a shy grin, she patted me on my back and went back to doing whatever she was doing before Momma came. I continued on with my day, dreading my evening.

I made it home around five thirty that evening, went to the closet, and pulled out the skirt and blouse that I was going to wear. Then I went and sat down on my bed, tired from not getting any sleep. Thoughts of a nap raced across my mind. Then the phone rang; it was Momma.

After I said hello, she said, "Are you getting ready?"

"Yes, Momma," I said. "I'm getting ready."

"Well, I will be there within the hour, so get prepared for your blessing."

With that she hung up the phone.

I pulled myself off my bed and headed for my shower.

Ms. Fable pulled up about six twenty, and Momma was right on time at six thirty. Then we were on our way to church.

As we pulled up in the church's parking lot, I began to feel God's presence. The people inside the church gave us a warm welcome as we took our seats. The choir took the stand, and we all stood and sang the selection with the choir. As the pastor started his sermon—which by chance was on "Letting Go"—I sat there focusing on his words as if he was speaking directly to me.

"Focus on your future," he said. "Don't focus on your past because it's gone. Don't spend another second focusing your time on what could have happened, because whatever happened was the will of God. If your past had been any other way, you wouldn't be who you are right now. We are under construction. Nobody here is God's finished product. We are in the making if you will. Tomorrow is the future." He paused before he went on to say, "Today is tomorrow's past. We need to quit pondering on what could have been and start focusing on what could be. Nothing happens by chance, and yet everything happens through the will of God."

"Life isn't for us to understand, so stop wasting time trying to figure it out. We need to put our energy toward enduring God's plan, not putting our energy to the whys and how's of his plan. We spend too much time regretting when we should be accepting and moving forward. Persevere, everyone. I came to tell you that is what you need to be doing—persevering; understanding will come later."

As he kept speaking, my mind faded away to the words accepting and moving forward. Those words kept replaying in my mind. I am who God thought I would be, so I need to accept it and move on.

While my thoughts completely took over my mind and drowned out the rest of his sermon, I realized that my life was what it was, and I had to focus on my future. By the time I snapped back into his sermon, the members of the church were gathering on their feet for prayer. I did the same, and I felt that a rainbow had encircled my heart and it was time I bounced back on track.

The preacher didn't let us get out the door before speaking to us.

"Good message again, Pastor," Momma said as she held out her hand.

He took hold of Momma's hand and said, "The spirit moved me to speak on this message." Taking his attention off of Momma, he turned to me, and as he looked in my eyes, he said, "God sent this message to someone who is special to him." With that he shook my hand and said, "Please come back, Victoria. God's not done with you yet."

The colleges had shut down for the Christmas break, and the children were coming home for Christmas. I knew that they would have only two weeks to spend with me—they had to get back for exams—so I decided to wrap the few presents that I had gotten so they would be sitting under neath the tree. Even though I wasn't in a rush to get things done, I was still scrambling around to get things done because I wanted things to be as perfect this Christmas as they had been the previous year. I decided that I would go visit Daddy's graveside before they got here. I had to get it ready for the winter months and put on fresh flowers for Christmas. I didn't want to wait until they got here because it would take up too much time; and after they left, Christmas would be over. I felt a need to talk to him anyway, so this day seemed to be the right day. Even though winter was obvious, the air was still; it wasn't as cold as what was ahead. I could spend some time without worrying about a storm coming, or worse, getting frostbitten.

I was baking cookies when Hannah arrived around eleven o'clock in the morning three days before Christmas. Brandon had to make the stop to pick up Jasmine, and he followed shortly behind. By a little after noon, the house was filled with the usual gang. I thought we needed Christmas music, so I stepped away to turn on the stereo. I noticed out the window that the snow had begun to fall. A white Christmas, how perfect would that be?

I was thankful that the children made it home before the layers of snow started to form. Brandon and Jasmine were baking their own cookies. Ms. Fable and Momma were not coming until Christmas Eve, and Hannah had slipped away to her room before returning to the cookie-baking contest. I decided to step into Hannah's room to see what she was doing. She was sprawled across the bed talking on the phone. When she saw me, she smiled. I went to shut the door, not wanting to interrupt, and she motioned for me to come in. I went in and sat on the edge of her bed.

To the person on the other end of the phone, she said, "Jerry, would you like to say hello to my mother?" Seconds later, she handed me the phone.

"Hello, Jerry," I said. "How are you? Hannah has told me wonderful things about you. You must come for a visit soon.... Oh, you're in town now? Good, good," I said, looking at Hannah. "Well then, you must come over for the holidays. We would love to meet you.... That would be fine," I said. "Um, whenever is fine ... okay. I look forward to seeing you. Here's Hannah."

Handing the phone back to Hannah, I was feeling happy for her and excited that she wanted Jerry to come over. She was smiling from ear to ear. That let me know that she really liked this Jerry guy.

I got up and found my way back to the kitchen. Feeling more in the Christmas spirit, I began to sing and dance around the children as they were baking their cookies.

After Hannah got off the phone, she came into the kitchen and said, "Doesn't he sound sweet, Momma?"

Sweet? I thought. I only talked to him for seconds, but not wanting to burst her bubble, I said, "He sounds dreamy. Well, he will come over Christmas Eve and help us cook, and everyone will meet him."

"I've already met him," Brandon said.

Hannah looked over at him, still smiling. "Isn't he cute, Brandon?"

"I don't look at men, Hannah, but he is nice. I wouldn't call him cute, but he is decent."

"Well, then, it's settled," Hannah said.

After baking cookies and eating just as many as we baked, we sat around talking and trying to guess what everybody got for Christmas. It was friendly conversation. While Brandon went to wrap the rest of his presents daring Jasmine to come in, she sat in the kitchen with Hannah and I talking about how much she loved Brandon. I couldn't help but reminisce how much I wanted love at her age much less having it. It wasn't long that the phone rang, and Hannah was off to herself. Listening to Jasmine speak I realized it was the very first time that she and I actually had a conversation without Brandon. "My life hasn't been all peaches and cream she said I have had my struggles and just as much as I have been there for Brandon, he has been there for me too. His love for you is so strong and believe it or not my mother and I aren't as close as I would like to be. I try Mrs. Andrews but she is so wrapped up in her work and daddy that she has very little time for me. I can't tell you how many times I started to call you to see if you would just go out and have dinner with me or if you wanted to go shopping while Brandon was away, but I didn't want to bother you and I just never made the time. I know Brandon is angry with his father" she said now my mind glued to her every word. "I have anger too but mine is towards my mother. Look at the way your family has pulled through all that you have been through."

I at this point didn't know what to say to her I had no idea that Ms. Professional had neglected her sweet daughter. "Brandon told me that there were times that he and Hannah felt that they were alone and by themselves but you found a way to make something happen that made him realize that there was still love and listening to him on Thanksgiving Day let me know that he is just about passed his hurt me on the other hand my parents especially my mother never tried to make me feel loved as long as she bought me something that was her way but sometimes all I wanted was a conversation."

"Have you told her I said looking at this young girl almost in tears. Have you talked to her the way you are talking to me"

"I have tried Mrs. Andrews but she doesn't care. Daddy has his life she has hers and I have mine that is the way it's always been. I am an only child and sometimes growing up I thought that they wished they hadn't had any children most time I felt I was in the way."

Oh my God in Heaven I thought its true everybody has a story if I wasn't hearing this for myself, I would have never believed it.

"Jasmine don't and I say this because you are a young lady too okay so don't take this wrong. Don't marry Brandon just to get away from your family life because there is going to come a time that they may snap out of whatever they are going through, and you will want to make up for lost time that wouldn't be fair to Brandon or you. I think that you have turned out to be a wonderful young lady and if your momma can't understand that then shame on her one day and I say this from experience. One day she will regret the years that she missed."

"I know I love Brandon Mrs. Andrews I know rather or not that my parents want to start a relationship with me that is well missed I will never ever put them before Brandon. There are times I have wanted to die she said but please don't tell Brandon I told you this, but I have, and I have went to him while at college and he has taken care of me. I love him Mrs. Andrews I mean I truly love him. I only want to make him happy. I'm eighteen years old and I can't remember the last time I heard either one of my parents tell me that they love me. It hurts I see you with Hannah and knowing that the years that you and Hannah missed because of what you were going through you have tried to get those years back and you succeeded my parents don't try."

"If my father left my mother, she couldn't go on I know that my father has a girlfriend but what can I do tell mother so he can deny it and then she dislike me even more. My mother has put her career before her family and that has hurt us more than it has helped."

"Your daddy has cheated on your momma." I heard my mouth say without thinking.

"Several times but she is so wrapped up in her job to even know to even care. When he buys her things, I know it's only for apology, but she thinks that it's because he misses her. I have seen him, and I am caught in the middle, and I have hurt all my life, so this is the Jasmine that is wanting to marry your son. Nobody knows my life better than Brandon and I want nothing better than to be his wife. I want to call you mom and share the love that you show them."

Speechless is the word that came to my mind how sad was that after all this time her mom's life was ten times worse than mine could have ever been. What makes it worst is she doesn't even know. Money was something we didn't have, and money is all that they did have "WOW" was all that I could think but I knew I had to give this girl some kind of assurance that God would work things out.

"Jasmine anytime you need to talk or feel alone I am here. My shoulders are strong I can hold up three children instead of two. I know that you love Brandon, and I would gladly accept you as a daughter. I am not perfect far from it, but I love my children. I love you too Jasmine.

"What is all the whispering?" Brandon said as he entered the kitchen "Whose whispering?" I said all that paper rattling was all we heard.

At first Brandon was joking but as he turned his attention to Jasmine noticing her tear-stained face and then back to me. With a look of concern on his face, like I had seen on his dad so many times before his forehead was crinkled as he asked, "You been crying Jasmine?"

"Brandon lighten up Jasmine is fine "We just had a mother daughter conversation that's all I said winking at Jasmine. Brandon just stood there as if he was waiting on a sign from Jasmine that she was ok. After figuring that Brandon was about to be upset, she gave a nod to let him know she was okay. Brandon then just said, "Well then, I guess I should understand how silly girls are" to lighten the mood but he then looked at me as if to ask what just happen, I winked back at him trying to let him know that it's truly okay.

As if to change the mood back to pleasant, Jasmine sat there for a moment then she jumped up and said "My turn I have presents to wrap no peeking Brandon" she said as she went outside to the car to get her gifts. Once she had shut the door Brandon asked momma "what's wrong with Jasmine'.

"Jasmine is okay" I managed to say without letting all the conversation out "she loves you Brandon and sometimes she just miss having a momma." Giving and understanding nod I said, "now please don't ask me anything else I want her trust too." "Enough said I probably know already but A I am glad that she had you to talk to momma you are the best."

"Now go see what your sister is doing she has been on that phone for an hour" I said smiling knowing that Brandon was going in her room to tease her.

Moments later Jasmine returned carrying several bags "Where is he" she asked, "Give me a minute I will keep him in Hannahs room until you get to his room" She nodded as if she was holding the biggest surprise ever.

I was right Brandon was teasing Hannah. "Kissy, Kissy Jerry, I love you" I heard him say as I entered the room. "Momma get him" she said motioning for Brandon to leave the room. "Come on" I said to Brandon as he laughed and poked his fun. I led him out the room and into the kitchen I made a pot of tea and he sat down across from me.

"Pretty messed up huh momma"

"What?" I said not knowing what he was talking about.

"Jasmines family" Well Brandon everybody goes through something. I said trying not to let on that I knew what she had told me. I knew he would one day marry her and the last thing I needed to do was take away her trusting me.

"Brandon, do you love her?" I asked wanting to know that his feelings were real not just sympathy. He looked at me for a moment and said Yeah momma I do. I am sure we will get married one day because outside of all that she has been through she is amazing I am not waiting on her I am actually waiting on me to make sure I am good enough we don't need any repeats he said catching me off guard.

My turn he said "do you still love daddy. "WHEW talking about a blow that is the last thing I thought he would ask me, but he is a young man now and Hannah and I have shared our conversations about her father, so I guess now it's time for Brandon to have his time.

"Love" I said "Brandon I guess I always will love him you know that I have tried to let God guide my steps since all of this has happened. In love now that is different. I won't lie to you I am afraid of growing old alone and since your father left, I think that is the way I will end up but I am stronger I am wiser so whatever will be will be."

"My turn do you ever think that you will forgive your father and try and have a relationship with him?"

Looking at my son as a young man and not a pitiful young teenager I waited for his answer.

"I seriously doubt it momma. I am still angry, and I don't understand why you of all people could still love him. He hurt us he didn't want us he embarrassed us. He could have confided in me. I would have helped him but instead he chose to leave us. No matter what he was going through momma he could have taken the high road and stayed with us instead he chose the low road and I know this is a strong word but momma I literally hate him."

"Brandon He was sick honey don't blame him for all that he did blame his sickness. I don't expect you to welcome him with open arms like Hannah would but at least let him explain if your paths ever crossed again."

"I serious doubt our paths would ever cross again momma because when I graduate from college I won't live here to many memories for Jasmine and me for that matter. I won't say never but he would have to try harder than I ever would I didn't leave him he left me. Having said that if by some strange coincidence you decided to go back to him before we had our chance to talk Know that I am not ready for a happy reunion. Know that I won't come around pretending that nothing ever happen."

I got up to get another cup of tea trying to think of the right words to say stalling if you will. As I was pouring my cup of tea, I told Brandon "I don't know what tomorrow holds Brandon I don't know if I ever would fall in love with him like you have with Jasmine, but I too want an explanation I too want to understand. Everybody goes through something and remember Gods will, will be his will no matter what we want but having said that I will say I understand how you feel but pray and ask God for guidance. I don't know what the future holds I may marry again…"

"Not while I am living Brandon cut in to say, "well then, I will live with you and Jasmine" "That's fine Whatever."

"I have done the best I could with the two of you now it's my time I guess you and Hannah have your lives ahead of you whatever you decide to do I have no choice but to except it because I love you, I expect the same from you and Hannah. Fair enough"

"Fair enough" he said, "but I don't want you with another man."

"But you don't want me with your father either come on give me some kind of leave way. I will pray about it and let you know by the time I get married to Jasmine."

"How fair is that I said laughing." "I don't know what my future holds and the last thing I need is some young adult guiding my future."

"Fair enough" he said laughing but this time Hannahs door flung open, and she was in the kitchen with us.

"Finished with Mr. Romeo I see" Brandon said probably going out for his next victim tonight while you sit here all starry-eyed waiting for his call" Brandon added.

"As long as he don't feed her." Hannah said which once again brought laughter that Brandon didn't understand. Not long after that Jasmine came through the kitchen carrying a mountain of gifts. After that we sat in the living room turned on our tree and settled in for some Christmas stories.

Although I didn't want the evening to end, After about my third Christmas story I knew I had a long day at the pharmacy store the next day, so I told the children that I was turning in for the night. "We have a lot to do to get prepared for Santa," I said as I left them in the living room in front of the television As I reached my room, I looked back at them, and they had gone back to their watching television. What a wonderful Christmas this is going to be, I thought as I closed the bedroom door behind me.

As I woke up the day before Christmas Eve, I was excited, but yet dreading my day. It would be a long day. Everybody would be running around trying to do the last-minute shopping and pick up prescriptions. I got up still having a happy spirit, made my tea, took my shower, and without waking the children, I headed off to work.

The snow had stopped falling, but the ground was white, with not a patch of dirt or grass anywhere. Please stay, snow, I thought as I moved through the streets to work. Passing by the park, I noticed my willow tree. It was also covered with snow and looking lonely as its limbs were frozen by the cold. "I promise I will visit soon," I said, knowing that since I had my own willow trees, I had neglected the one that started it all.

Turning into the parking lot of the store, I saw Ms. Fable's car was there. She was placing the open sign on the door. As she saw me approach her, she opened the door and said, "It's a chilly day, isn't it, Victoria? I came in a little early this morning to get the heat circulating. I hope the shoppers decide to come early."

"Me too," I said in agreement. I got us tea from the back; Ms. Fable already had it brewing.

"How are the children?" she asked as I was taking off my coat.

"Well, Brandon and Jasmine are the same, still joined at the hip, but you won't believe this," I said, filled with excitement. "Hannah's friend Jerry will come over Christmas Eve. We will finally get to meet the mystery man."

"Well, it's about time somebody has caught that girl's eye. Wonder what he's like," she asked, now filled with curiosity.

"I talked to him briefly on the phone last night, and from what I can tell, he is very well-mannered. We will just have to wait and see, but she stays on the phone with him constantly. Brandon says he's met him, and he doesn't have anything bad to say, so that is always a plus."

"Well, should we buy him a gift?" she asked.

That had never crossed my mind, but if he was going to be there, it did seem appropriate; we didn't want him to be the only one without a gift. "What should we get him? We don't even know what he likes."

"Well, how about a scarf and hat. That seems appropriate. And some cologne; all young men want to smell good."

"That seems like a clever idea, and we will get him something else as we learn just who he is and what he likes. Oh, this is going to be the best Christmas ever," I said as I prepared myself for the day of work ahead.

I found myself saying to the customers Merry Christmas as I rang them up. Being consumed with spending time with the children, Momma, and Ms. Fable, my day flew by. On my lunch break, I ran over to the pharmacy and picked up a gift set of cologne for Jerry. I chose carefully by the smell, and I was sure he would like it. When I returned, I told Ms. Fable to go on home and that I would close the store and make the deposit. I knew she was tired. She had to have her energy because we were going to celebrate Christmas like we had never done before.

I was closing down the store when I saw a man across the street. He made me kind of nervous, so I hurried to my car; I knew that people were robbed this time of year, and I had the store's money on my person. When I turned out of the parking lot and tried to shine my light on this man, he was gone. I hurried to the bank, dropped off the deposit, and headed home to start my Christmas. "Let It Snow" was playing on the radio, and I sang that song and "Jingle Bells" all the way home. When I got home, Jasmine and Brandon were there, and Hannah was on the phone. I decided to call Momma and Ms. Fable to find out what time they would be arriving tomorrow.

Momma answered on the second ring. "Hello," she said.

"Hello," I said back. "How are you?"

"I'm good. How are you and the children?"

"Filled with the Christmas spirit," I said.

"Me too, she said. "I am happier than I have been in years. I woke up with you and the children on my mind, and I have been so excited about coming over for Christmas Eve tomorrow."

"Well, then, I have got more news that is going to raise your spirits just a little higher."

"What is that?" she said.

"Well, Momma, we get to meet Jerry tomorrow."

"Jerry?" she asked. "Jerry who?"

"Hannah's friend, praise God."

She said, "Is he going to be around for Christmas? We didn't buy him anything, and it's hard to find him something on such short notice."

Laughing, I said, "That is exactly what Ms. Fable said, and that's all taken care of."

"I can't wait," she said. "I will be there early in the day."

"I know. Come as early as you like. It's going to be a great Christmas. Just plan on spending the night. We will make room for everyone. I've got to call Ms. Fable and tell her I deposited the money and have closed the store down. I will see you tomorrow. Love you. Bye."

I knew we all wanted to make a good impression on Jerry. We wanted him to like us because Hannah liked him, and we wanted her to find what Jasmine and Brandon had. With those thoughts, I dialed up Ms. Fable.

"Hello," she said.

"Hey, well, the store is closed, and the deposit is at the bank. Now it's time for our Christmas."

"When I left the store, I ran by the mall, and I got the best scarf and that they had. I even got a jacket to match, and I got a gift receipt so he can exchange it for his right size."

"Oh good," I said. "How much do I owe you?"

"We will split the difference later," she said.

"I got him a gift set of cologne from the pharmacy. I chose carefully and it smells good, so for now that will have to do. What time are you arriving tomorrow?" I asked.

"I would say around noon, no later than one," she said.

"That's perfect. Get some rest," I said. "See you tomorrow."

"I'll be rested and raring to go," she said as we hung up the phone.

I went to see what the children were doing. Brandon and Jasmine were playing checkers and Hannah was on the phone, so I decided to settle down with my usual cup of tea and watch Christmas specials. After the first two shows, the children were by my side joining me. That is how we spent the rest of our evening.

The sun woke me up on Christmas Eve shining through my window. Oh no, I thought, I want a white Christmas. Please don't melt until after tomorrow. With the smell of bacon frying, I made my way to the kitchen to find Hannah and Brandon fixing breakfast.

As I approached Brandon, he looked at me with a strange look and asked, "Momma, do you mind if Jasmine spends the night tonight?"

I must have showed a funny facial expression because he quickly clarified, "She can sleep in Hannah's room."

As if she was siding with her brother, Hannah took a bite of bacon and added, "That's fine with me, Momma. It's Christmas."

My mind went back to the Christmas that I wanted James to spend the night, and yet I was too afraid to ask. They were young responsible adults now.

"All right," I said. "If her parents don't mind, then neither do I, as long as no hanky-panky stuff goes on," I said with a wink to Brandon.

"It won't," he said, winking back. "We've waited this long. One more night can't hurt us," he said, adding another wink.

I left them to the rest of their conversation. I made my tea and stood by the window. As if Mother Nature had heard me, the sun had been removed, and the snow was trying to return.

As I looked out at the streets where the cars were moving slowly, I noticed that my mailbox was open. "Did anybody get the mail yesterday?" I asked the children, thinking that they might have forgotten to close it.

"No" was their response.

"Brandon, would you put your shoes on and go check it, because the door is open on it, and I don't need my mail blown all over the place."

"Sure," he said.

Moments later he came through the door with a bundle of bills. I thought, what a way to start my Christmas Eve day. As I fumbled through the mail, a card fell to the floor. No stamp, no return address, just the name Hannah.

Without saying a word to the children, I searched the stack that was in my hand, and there were two more cards, one with Brandon's name and the other one had my name on it. That instant, I called over the children. "Here," I said, "a card for each of you."

Without even caring who the cards were from, the children tore into them. It was one thousand dollars for each of them. I knew that they had already done Christmas shopping, but I knew that in their mind they wanted to get more.

Who had this come from? I was thinking when I opened my card. "Merry Christmas. I hope it is everything you ever wanted and more. My card had fifteen hundred dollars."

James, I thought. But where could he be getting all this money if it was James? Even the money through the years. The plant never reopened, and jobs were few. If it was James, how? Was he getting money from his father and brother so he could help support us? Did he leave to support us? Was his brother and father keeping him close and was not letting him come back and using the money to keep him there?" So many questions and not enough answers.

The children, on the other hand, didn't question the money; the only thing on their minds was Christmas shopping. I didn't expect any money and I had spent way too much on Christmas this year, so the only thing on my mind other than the sender was catching up on bills.

Without another thought, the children were prepping themselves for some shopping. Within the hour, they were leaving.

Hannah said, "The mall, Momma. See you soon."

"Hey, it's calling for more snow. Be careful," I yelled at them as they closed the door.

I got my shower and prepared to start the rest of my day. By noon the children still weren't back, and Ms. Fable and Momma arrived, each carrying a mountain of gifts. "Where is everybody at?" Momma asked as she put her gifts under the tree.

"Christmas shopping," I said.

"Well, I don't smell the ham cooking," Ms. Fable said as she followed behind Momma.

"It's in the sink," I said, "waiting for the two of you."

"Let's get started. I have had my energy restored, and now I am in it for the long haul," Ms. Fable said.

With her words, I turned the Christmas music back on and looked out the window for the children. The snow was coming down heavier now, and I became a little concerned. "It's snowing hard," I said.

Momma said, "The weatherman said we are expecting six to eight inches by tomorrow."

"The children need to hurry and come home," I added. "They don't need to be out in that type of weather."

As we started to prepare to fix Christmas dinner, the door was flung open, and in came Jasmine and Brandon, each carrying bags and wrapping paper. Heading to his room, he said, "Don't peek."

"I won't peek, but where is Hannah?" I said.

"She's coming," he said. She met up with Jerry. They will be here soon."

About an hour later, the door was flung open again, and in came Hannah, carrying her bags, knowing that Jerry was close behind. We stopped long enough to see him come through the door.

"Just set them there for now," Hannah said, pointing to the floor beside the door. "Momma," she said as they came toward us, "Grandma, and Ms. Fable, this is Jerry."

"Oh Lord," Ms. Fable said.

"Good heavens," Momma replied.

I couldn't say anything. There before us stood the most handsome man that we had seen in a long time. He was built like James used to be. He had deep brown hair, and he wore a goatee, just like James used to. He was around six foot one, and he had a smile that would melt butter straight from the fridge."

Trying to break the silence, I extended my hand, and almost stuttering, I said, "Jerry, it's nice to meet you. Sorry for the silence; we just didn't know what to expect."

Ms. Fable said, "I'm Teresa Fable. Pleasure, pleasure indeed."

Momma was next. "I am Hannah's grandmother, and it's good to meet you."

"The pleasure is all mine. Hannah has told me so much about all of you, and it's good to finally meet you." His voice was a lot deeper than over the phone.

"Well," Hannah said, probably a little embarrassed by our staring, "he's going to help me wrap Christmas gifts. If you need me, I will be in my room."

Jerry went back to the door to pick up the packages that he had laid there before, and we watched him as he walked to the door. Hannah caught us staring, and she said, "Ladies, he's just a man, and he's taken by me. So please stop gawking. It's rather annoying," she said as she smiled and led Jerry to her room.

"Oh Lord," Ms. Fable said, "if that thing isn't pretty. No wonder she wanted to take her time and choose a man for herself. She did a superb job."

"He favors her father," I said, thinking back to the way James looked when he was in his early twenties.

"Whew," Ms. Fable added, "let's refocus. We've got a lot of cooking to do."

Changing the subject, Momma said, "I can't remember the last time we had a white Christmas."

"No, but this Christmas seems different in a lot of ways. A lot of beginnings are forming, and I am so glad I am a part of them," I said. Trying to take my mind off of Jerry and the way he looked like James, I added, "This is going to be an amazing Christmas."

We baked and baked, cooked, and cooked, tasted, and tasted all the way up until late evening. I went to check on the children, and now Hannah and Jasmine were together, and Brandon and Jerry were together I assumed they were now wrapping each other's presents.

By ten thirty that night, the children emerged from their rooms with their gifts. Each was smiling as if they had secrets. The snow continued to fall, and after they put the gifts under the tree, they sat down to watch more Christmas specials. I watched Jerry and how he interacted with Hannah. There were times when I would see him just gaze at her if she laughed at something on the television, and then he would smile at the thought of her happiness.

By 1:00 a.m., all the food was finished except Momma's infamous rolls, and she would fix those on Christmas day. Jerry said his good-byes, and Hannah walked him outside. Once they were outside, I ran to the window to see if she was going to kiss him, thankful that I had a porch light. It was Brandon who caught me off guard. "Nosy," he said. "Now I know what you did the night you met Jasmine."

"Shh," I said, still peeking out the window. They stood in the falling snow. He brushed the snow from her hair, and they stood holding hands; then he kissed her. It was a longing kiss, and then he stood there for just a moment, as if they were silent, and then he kissed her again. Then he got in his car and left. She watched him back out of the driveway, and she started back toward the house. I ran back into the kitchen so she wouldn't see me snooping. It didn't matter if she saw me or not, because as soon as she came through the door, Brandon told on me.

"Momma saw you kissing Jerry," he said, "and there wasn't even mistletoe out there." Jasmine nudged him as if she wanted him to stop, but he continued on. "Hannah's found love; Hannah's found love."

"Shut up, Brandon," Hannah said as she made her way past him into the kitchen. "Momma, you didn't snoop, did you?" she asked with a smile.

"Okay, okay, a little. He's just so handsome," I said, not wanting her to know the real reason for my snooping.

"Yes, Momma, and he treats me with so much patience and respect. I like his parents too."

"You have met his parents?" I asked, shocked at her words.

"Yes, Momma," she said, still smiling.

"Are you getting serious about Jerry, Hannah?" I asked.

"I don't know about all that serious, but yeah, I like him." She paused and looked at the three of us standing there like three lost sheep. "A lot," she added. "Now let's taste some of this tasty food you have the whole neighborhood smelling."

We continued to talk and dance to the Christmas music. Every now and again, we would join in and sing a Christmas carol. It was a great night. By 3:00 a.m., we all were exhausted, yet we refused to let our bodies tell our minds what to do. I don't think any of us wanted that night to end. We continued on with the singing and dancing, and by five thirty, we were opening gifts.

The children had everything that they could have wanted, and they raved about their clothes. Jasmine even had several gifts under the tree. She was now a part of our family, and it was like she belonged there. Brandon and Hannah decided that they would give Jerry and Jasmine the gifts they had bought for them later in the day. Hannah wanted Jerry to be a part of it.

While the children were admiring the gifts that they had opened, Ms. Fable, Momma, and I decided to bed down. Momma and Ms. Fable slept in Brandon's room, and the children, who were once sleepy but were now wide-awake, stayed in the living room. As I retired to my room, I thought, What a wonderful day. Thank you, Lord, for an amazing Christmas. I guess this is your way of making up for the past, and what a fantastic job you're doing.

When we woke up Christmas day, the children had left. It was around noon, and it was evident that they had made breakfast. The weatherman had been correct: we had at least eight inches on the ground. The roads looked to be clear. I guess they worked around the clock for the families who would be traveling for Christmas. Momma and Ms. Fable were tidying up the kitchen while I tidied up the living room, and by two o'clock, the children had returned, Jasmine and Jerry included.

Jerry was the only one that looked rested. The other three looked to be a little tired, but their excitement returned when they went to open up their gifts. Not wanting to bother them, I thought I would ask if we could join in.

"Sure," Brandon said.

Without losing a moment, Momma, Ms. Fable, and I joined in from a distance. We stood behind the couch as the children opened their gifts to each other.

Jerry bought Hannah a beautiful diamond necklace, with a tennis bracelet to match. Hannah bought Jerry a watch and a key chain that matched hers that said "gether." Her key chain, of course, had the "to" written on it. Which when the words came together it read together. Brandon bought Jasmine a promise ring, and chills ran down my spine because I thought it was an engagement ring. It had diamonds surrounding a stone that represented the month of June. She, of course, was beside herself. He also bought her perfume and a couple of outfits. She bought him a ring, also with the stone in the middle that represented June. Could that have been a secret that only the two of them knew? She also bought him a jacket and a couple of outfits as well as cologne.

Jerry, as well as Jasmine, liked our gifts. Then the children turned to look at me and said, "Oh, Momma, we almost forgot. There's one more under the tree for you."

"For me?" I said. "From whom?"

"Just come open it. It was Jerry and Hannah's idea, but we all pitched in to get it for you," Brandon said.

It was an oil painting of me at the park underneath the willow tree, writing in my journal. They had put a picture with me, and the willow tree together had had it made into an oil painting, and in the background, it had the writing magnified that said, "The Andrews Tree of Love."

Tears formed in my eyes. "Wherever did you find this picture?" I asked. In the picture I had to be in my early twenties. The kids were not yet here. "Wherever did you find this picture?" I repeated.

"We've got our ways, Momma."

How beautiful that gift was, I thought. What a way to spend Christmas! We were the Andrews, and that tree was where it all started.

I looked back at Momma and Ms. Fable, who both stood in amazement; they had a tear or two of their own.

"I will hang it over the mantle," I said, wiping my tears. This was the perfect thing to replace the urns that James had taken.

"I'm going to start fixing the rolls," Momma added with a smile.

"I'll help," Ms. Fable said. "You must teach me how to make them."

"My pleasure," Momma said.

I gave my children a tight hug and told them that this was the best Christmas ever. As they started to clean up the wrapping paper, I took my painting, and Jerry helped me hang it over the mantle.

While dinner was reheating, the children sat admiring their gifts. I couldn't get my mind past the painting, but I helped heat dinner. Momma and Ms. Fable put the rolls in the oven, and Jasmine and Hannah set the table. By five o'clock, we were sitting at the dinner table enjoying Christmas dinner; and by seven, the dishes were done, and the children were leaving again. Ms. Fable and Momma stuck around for another hour or so before they left. By nine o'clock I was alone, standing in front of the painting, admiring the detail. I don't remember a picture like this, I thought. Nonetheless, it was truly a piece of art. The tree was exactly how I remembered it years ago. It has lost some of its spunk, but it's still a beautiful tree to me.

As I went to bed down, I thought, What an amazing Christmas this has been. I will write about it in my journal tomorrow. I'm just too tired to write tonight. Throughout this entire day. I remember thinking that James never crossed my mind.

I still had the Christmas spirit and a sense of peace. I found myself looking at my painting as it hung carefully over the mantle. It would be only days before the children would be gone again. The new year was approaching, and I thought it was time for a new beginning and for whatever God had in store for my life. I hoped I was ready.

The children didn't spend much time at home for the rest of their vacation. I returned to work to finish out the year, and they were about doing whatever kids their age did these days. We would only see each other in the mornings or late in the evenings. I sprinted through the days, knowing that the children were home, still thinking about the great Christmas. By the time I stopped and took a breath, it was New Year's Eve.

I decided to cook the traditional black-eyed peas and cabbage. The gang showed up around seven, and yes, Jerry was there too. We were waiting to bring in the new year before they went out on the town. By nine o'clock, the children each took their turns getting ready for the night out. Ms. Fable, Momma, and I sat enjoying our tea. We had the television tuned into New York preparing for the ball to drop. By eleven thirty, the children were all dressed waiting for the ball to drop. By eleven forty-five, I was in the kitchen getting the nonalcoholic champagne. At five minutes to twelve, I was pouring it into glasses. At 11:59, we stood together in the living room waiting for the countdown: "10, 9, 8, 7, 6, 5, 4, 3, 2, 1. Happy New Year," we shouted. "Group hug." We all gathered around for our group hug.

"Bring on 2007," I shouted.

"Here, here," Ms. Fable said.

"Let God's will be done," Momma added.

Within minutes the children were getting their coats on and heading out for their night's celebration.

"Be careful," I said as they left us.

Momma and Ms. Fable gathered up their bowls of black-eyed peas and cabbage, and within the hour, the two had left. Not wanting this wonderful holiday to end, I went to the Christmas tree, turned on the lights, and stared at the glimmer for the last time that year. I sat there thinking about our holidays and wondering just what the new year held for me.

Chapter 33

The year 2007 quickly came and went. Brandon and Hannah were in their second year of college. I was now used to the fact that the children came home for visits and left again. Thanksgiving and Christmas were a good tradition, even though Hannah now had a boyfriend to call her own. Brandon and Jasmine were still going strong. They were set to graduate from college in a couple more years with their degrees, but they were getting ready to start some intern work, so they were really excited about getting a taste of their future and their lives were good. Each had a plan of where they would start their career, and even though they didn't want to start them here in our hometown, I knew they would be the best wherever they were.

I went to visit Ms. Robertson twice a year for the last two years, and I actually saw her life dwindling every time I went. I went to church every Sunday with Momma and worked at the pharmacy store for Ms. Fable like I always had. I continued to put flowers on the gravesides of Daddy and Mrs. Andrews. Life was as good as it could get for me.

Even though I was lonely, I occupied my time with church, writing in my journal, and helping out around the community. James, well, I never heard from him. Those images of the man in the apartment seemed to disappear; memories of him seemed to fade away. I wrote about him sometimes in my journal, but my energy was now focused on God, Ms. Robertson, Momma, and the children. Those were the ones I would most write about.

I didn't hate James; I felt nothing, and maybe, I thought, that was God's plan. I still cared for him, but it was a care for a troubled man, not a care for a man that I loved. I guess you could even say it was a God-caring love that, if not already, maybe one day he could experience the love of God like I had. My tears dried up, and my trust was now in God. I had peace, and things were going as well as to be expected.

Winter 2007 had closed its eyes for yet another season, and Spring 2008 was on its way. The air was warm, and any other time, I would have been filled with joy by the blooms that were forming and the thoughts that the children might be home in another few months or so, but Momma weighed heavily on my mind to the point that I decided to call her once I had gotten off of work.

That Friday afternoon, Momma fell on my heart, and sadness took over my mind. I had been missing the children, although they called on a regular basis, but Momma took thoughts of them away. It had been three days since I had heard from her, and that wasn't like her. She would usually call in the evenings after she knew I was home from work, and I just thought that she was doing something with the church. We did attend church on a regular basis, and I knew they were all the time doing something for the community, but I didn't remember anyone mentioning doing anything this week.

I allowed Momma to fill my thoughts until I got off work. It was about five thirty in the evening. She usually called by at least six fifteen. I waited for her call, and when it didn't come by six thirty-five, I was dialing her number. Her phone rang about four times before she answered.

"Hello," she said as she picked up the phone; she spoke in a tone that I had not heard from her before.

"Hey, were you asleep?" I asked.

"No," she responded, "I was praying."

"Oh, I'm sorry for interrupting your prayers, Momma. I just hadn't heard from you in a few days. Is everything okay?"

"Yes. I'm sorry I haven't called, Victoria. I have just had your father on my mind. How are you?" she said as if she wanted to change the subject.

"Just missing my children," I said, "but other than that, I'm good."

"Are you off tomorrow?" she asked.

"Yes, I am. Why? What's up? Did you have something in mind?"

"Well," she said, "if the weather permits, I was thinking about visiting your father's grave site."

Silence took over the phone. Knowing that Momma had never been to Daddy's grave site, I asked, "Would you like for me to take you?"

"Yes, I was hoping you would go with me."

"I can stop off and get some fresh flowers, and be there around noon, if that's not too early."

"No, that will be fine," she said. "I went today and got some flowers just in case you wanted to go with me, but if you would like to get more, that's fine too."

"I will get just a few more," I said. "After that, if you're up to it, we can spend the rest of the day together."

"That would be nice," she said.

Not liking the depression in her voice, I added, "If you like, I can spend the night with you tonight."

"No, honey," she said, "that isn't necessary. I will be all right; God's got me."

"Yes, he does, Momma," I said. "Okay, then, noon it is. See you then."

"I love you, Victoria."

"I love you too, Momma," I said as we hung up the phone.

That's unusual, I thought. After all these years, why now? She never wanted to visit his grave site before. Chills ran across my body as I sat there worrying about my momma, wishing I could take the pain that she was feeling away.

The next morning, as planned, I stopped by the flower shop and picked up a bouquet of flowers. By noon as promised, I was pulling up in Momma's driveway. As if she was waiting for my arrival, she came out the door. What she had on was a bit alarming. She had on daddy's dress and shoes the last ones I could remember daddy buying for her and she carried a card and the flowers that she had picked up the day before. I was trying not to let the sight of her bother me. Besides, I was more concerned about her visit with him more than anything else.

The sky was clear, with a few clouds forming, but there was no call for rain. As she got into my car, I looked at her, and she had a look of sadness that I hadn't seen since Daddy passed. Trying to get past her look, I asked, "Momma, are you sure you want to do this?"

"Let's go," she said, "while I've still got my nerve up."

I slowly backed out the driveway, giving her a moment to change her mind. Since she didn't change her mind, we were on our way to Daddy's grave site. Except for a few sniffles from Momma, silence filled the car as I drove the streets to where my father was buried. As I approached the cemetery, before going through the gates, I looked at her as she wiped away a tear. I asked, "Momma, are you sure this is what you want to do?"

Clearing her throat, she said, "Not what I want to do, but it's something that I have to do."

Not completely understanding her words, I put the car in drive and moved forward. I took the bouquet that I had bought out of the backseat of the car and opened my car door. Not wanting to put any pressure on her, I headed to Daddy's resting place alone. Once I got to his grave, I heard the car door shut. Moments later, Momma was standing next to me.

"So, this is where he lies?" Momma asked.

"Yes," I said as I looked at the tears rolling down her cheeks.

Momma then knelt down on the grass. As she settled on the grass, she said, "Oh what a good man your father was, Victoria."

"Yes, Momma, I know," I said, now kneeling beside her.

"God's will was done, and as hard as it was for me to accept the fact that he was taken from me, I still have those wonderful memories. I guess the kind of love that me and your father had doesn't come around very often, so I guess God felt that his will on earth was done and he had done what God's plan for him was, and that was to show me a love that I had never known. I have to thank God for that."

Looking down at the grass that covered my daddy's body, Momma said, "Bless the Lord. I know your soul is gone; that is why I haven't been here until now. There wasn't a need," she said. "You're with our master. I miss you dearly. I wish that I could hear your voice one more time. I wish I could feel your touch just one more time. I wish I could smell your breath after you had gone to the shed to steal a nip."

She caught me off guard, and I said, You knew at the same time I said, "You knew."

That brought laughter. We both laughed at the fact that Daddy's secret wasn't really a secret after all. After moments of laughter and wiping away tears, Momma said, "Of course I knew, Victoria. I've never tasted alcohol, but I smelled it plenty of times on my father, and I knew when your father came into the house that he had been nipping. Oh, I didn't like it, but he was never violent, and he never raised his voice. The only way I knew was the faint smell and the way he shied away after his nipping. Honestly, he didn't have to hide it. His father took nips, and his father's father. I'm sure it went on for generations that had gone by. I would laugh at him sometimes, wondering if I had ever let on, would he have been so secretive about it?

"When we were younger, your father would drink beer every once in a while, but when I knew, I scolded him. I remember the day your father proposed to me. I told him that I would marry him, but no more beer. He looked at me with this coy kind of look and said, 'If you marry me, you will never see me take another drink.'" With a laugh, she said, "He didn't lie either. I never saw him take another drink, but I did smell it and that wasn't part of his promise."

Turning her attention back to him, she said, "Oh, how I miss this man, Victoria. I miss his chuckles. I miss cooking for him." Wiping a tear from her eye, she said, "but he's in a better place. I feel in spite of his nipping, God made a place for him in heaven. He's with the master now, waiting patiently for my arrival. I know your father was ready, and I know that he's happy now, happier than I ever could have made him. I desire that happiness for you, Victoria. I desire you to have the love that your father and I once shared. I desire for you to have a closer walk with the Lord. Right now, I can see your father standing at the gates of the kingdom, saying, 'Is it time, Lord? Is she here yet?' The Lord is saying back to him, 'She's not yet here. Her work is not yet done, son.'"

The air seemed cooler now, as if it was shooting a breeze, letting us know rain was on its way. The sky now clouded over, and a few sprinkles fell here and there. Momma started cleaning off Daddy's grave site so she could place her flowers in the leaves' place. She then gathered up some rocks to secure the card so that the rain wouldn't ruin it. It was as if her actions sorrowed Daddy, and more raindrops fell.

"Is that rain, Victoria?" she said, as if she hadn't noticed the clouds forming over.

"Yes, it is."

"I didn't know it was calling for rain today," she said.

"It wasn't," I told her, "but you know how that goes."

Looking back at the ground, she said, as if she was speaking to Daddy, "Wait for me; I love you." Then she got up and said, "I will wait for you in the car."

I sat there for a few moments. Now the rain was coming down more consistently. I said to Daddy, "You weren't as coy as you thought with your nipping, were you?" As I went to lay my flowers down, a bolt of lightning covered the sky, followed by a jolt of thunder. It was so loud, I took it as Daddy belting out laughter, knowing that Momma knew about his nipping. As I touched his grave, I immediately felt as if some force was holding me there. The tiny drops of rain were now a misty shower, and yet I couldn't move. It was as if Daddy was trying to tell me something. A chill rushed through my body, not because of rain, but I felt sadness overcome me. It was like it took over my soul. "Daddy," I whispered, "what is it? Show me a sign. If this is of you, show me something."

It took Momma blowing the horn to make me realize I was sitting in a downpour. I gathered my senses and headed toward my car. Still, I had this feeling that I couldn't shake. Thunder and lightning were now controlling the sky and earth. I continued to have this presence, this feeling I couldn't shake.

"Good grief, Victoria, you're going to catch pneumonia. You're soaking wet. Do you have anything in this car to dry off with?"

"No," I said, trying to focus my thoughts on Momma.

As I started up the car and was getting ready to leave, she said, "It's a mess out there."

I looked at Daddy's graveside one last time before I left the cemetery, and what I had just experienced clouded my thoughts.

Momma said, "I can't get over this sudden cloudburst, the sky being as blue as it was. The weatherman must be on vacation."

Trying not to show that I was troubled, I turned up the heat, and I turned on the radio. As Momma's words faded out, the music filled the car, and I went back to my own thoughts once again. Daddy, I kept playing in my mind—was he reading Momma's thoughts? Was he angry because I had taken her there? Had the heavens showed him something, and now he was trying to show me? I had visited Daddy's grave many times before now, and I had never had this feeling.

Thinking that maybe he knew Momma's thoughts and was saddened by them, I felt I should do something to make things better, if for no reason other than to cheer up my momma. As I pulled into her driveway, I said, "Momma, go in and pack a bag. Let's go back to my house, find us some movies, order in a pizza, and pop some popcorn." Using Hannah's words, I said, "Let's just have a big girl night. I'll call Ms. Fable to see if she will join us, and we can have a little slumber party."

"Okay, Victoria," was all she said, and she got out the car.

I got you, I thought, talking to my daddy. I will take Momma's mind off of things. You can go back to resting now.

About ten minutes later, the sun returned and so did Momma. As she entered the car, I said, "Comedy or love?"

"What?" she asked, as if she was confused.

"Are we going to watch comedy or love tonight you silly girl?

"Well," Momma said, "I was thinking more on the passion of Jesus Christ, but I guess a good laugh never hurt anybody."

"Then a love story it is," I said as we both started laughing again.

When we made it to my house, it was around two thirty. I knew Ms. Fable was still at work, so I called the store. "Fable's Grocery," she said as she answered the phone.

"Me and Momma are waiting," I said.

"Waiting for?" she asked, not knowing what was coming next.

"We are having a slumber party, and we are waiting for our best girl to arrive so we can get this party started."

"Woo-hoo," she said. "I get off at six. If it slows down any, I will be there sooner. I'll grab the pizza and a few snacks. I'll be there as soon as I can. Don't start without me."

"The clock is ticking," I said, laughing at her excitement. After we hung up the phone, I joined Momma in the kitchen.

"Coffee or tea?" she asked.

"It's your choice," I said.

"Then tea it is. I have grown accustomed to the taste," she said, laughing. Hearing her laugh did my heart good. Knowing that Momma was laughing again, I felt that Daddy was back to resting, so I was looking forward to a night with the girls.

Momma and I sat in the kitchen while waiting for Ms. Fable, enjoying a glass of tea. She started a conversation off with, "Victoria, I am glad you took me there." I knew "there" meant the cemetery.

"No problem, Momma. Anytime you want to go, just let me know. I will go with you."

"I doubt I will be going back. Just one more time, but it will be then that I won't be leaving. It's just so depressing," she said, "knowing that he is there, and I can't touch him or hear him. And the worst part is knowing that he can't leave with me."

"I understand, Momma, but he's not suffering any longer. This is a cruel world we live in, and he has no worries. I am glad he is with God."

She nodded her head in agreement. After pausing for a moment, she said, "I knew you and your father were close, Victoria, and watching you there let me understand that you miss him too. If something were to happen to me, by you being the only child, do you think you would be okay?"

Watching her words fall hard out of her mouth, I knew the last thing I wanted to think about was something happening to her, but I tried to think of the best answer for her question as she looked curiously at me, waiting for an answer.

I said, "Momma, first of all, the way my life's been going, you will probably outlive me." I was trying to get a smile from her, but it wasn't a smile but a look of worry, so I continued on, trying to smooth out the words that just came from my mouth. "God has blessed me; he has kept me thus far. I have no doubts that whatever comes our way that God will watch over us. God has blessed me with two beautiful children. No, I don't have a wonderful husband who could help me with the pain if something were to happen to you, but I've got my kids. I won't lie to you. I will hurt, and I can't even imagine something happening to you; but until I healed, I would feel that hurt, I would even feel alone. Sure, I've got Ms. Fable, but she is not you. But I guess I would have to be okay. You have no health threats, but if God saw that your will on this earth was done and he saw fit to take you, I guess I could only hope that he would carry me through. I hope that he would find me strong enough to deal with something like that before he took you from me.

"I had James when Daddy passed. Now that my children are grown and James is gone, losing you is the least of my worries, but if it happened, I have made it this far. It would be a shame if God left me now," I said, trying to capture a bit of humor. Not getting any laughter, I continued, "My children would be my strength. I would have to keep moving for them, even though they are strong. Look at all they have been through and look at where they are now. I have watched them stand when I have fallen before. I'm sure they would help me through if something like that was to happen. Why do you ask?" I said, now feeling a little uneasy about this conversation.

"Victoria, God has a will for everybody. I don't know what tomorrow holds. I'm glad you have the children, and you're right—I know they will be strong. If God decides to take me, I'm ready. I don't know if I have fulfilled his purpose or when his purpose for me will be fulfilled. All I know is that I am ready whenever he sees fit. I just want to make sure you are. I only desire your happiness. You were taught well, and I know that everything works together for the good. God has a plan for you, and even though we really don't understand his work, he doesn't make mistakes. I feel it's not over with you and James. I started having that feeling when the children gave you the painting for Christmas. James was put in your life for a reason, whether it was for love or trials. So far, you've had both, but I just don't feel God is through with the two of you. It could be just to bring you closer to God. He knows what you've been through—and are still going through for that matter. It's not over, no matter what your heart feels, until God says it's over; everything comes together for the good.

"From the first moment I held you in my arms, my desires have been for your happiness. I couldn't have been happier than when you were born. You are a strong woman, Victoria, and my desires haven't changed from then until now. One reason I feel that God's not done with you is because, after all the years that I have served him and prayed to him, you're not where I want you to be with love. The love of a child is different from a man's love, and I don't feel God has allowed my prayers about you to go unnoticed. You have great children, Victoria, but you are lacking a man's love. Maybe that's not for everybody. Maybe the love that your father and I shared isn't for everyone but know this: the trials that have come upon your life are just disguised blessings. Everything works together for the goodness of the Lord.

"God is trying to prime you for his will. Trust and lean on him. He has a purpose, and it's for the good. I could live to be a hundred, but when his will for me is over, he will take me up and I will be ready, so you won't have to wonder where I went. I love the Lord, and he knows my heart. Just know that your father loved you, I love you, and the Lord loves you too. Lean on him when you feel there is nowhere else to turn, and he will take care of you. Honestly, Victoria, that is where our true love comes from. It comes from God. Let him have his way."

I was looking at my mother's stress-filled face that now had turned to peace, a peace that came from her heart.

"I love you, Momma, and if something happens to you, know that I will be with you and Daddy one day. I can picture you both standing at that gate saying, 'Is she here yet, Lord? Has Victoria arrived?'" Smiling I said, "If I lost you, Momma, I would lean on the Lord. Really, what choice would I have?

"Just know, whatever happens in your life, there is a reason, so continue to praise him through the good times and the bad. He loves you more than your father or I ever could."

Watching my momma get up to pour herself another cup of tea made me silently pray, "Please, God, don't take her until you know I am ready, until you know that I can handle it."

As if she heard my prayer, Momma said, "Victoria, you can make it without me, you can make it without your children for that matter, but you can't make it without Jesus."

All I could think to say was, "I love you, Momma," and she responded, "I love you too, Victoria."

The rain returned as we sat there a little longer, sipping on tea and talking. I looked down at my watch and it was five o'clock. Ms. Fable would be there shortly, I thought, so I got up, went into Brandon's room, got his box of movies, and said, "Let's pick out something to watch. This was a friendly conversation," I said to Momma, "but let's shake this mood and get ready for our girls' night in."

Within the next hour, we heard Ms. Fable enter the house. "Fable's pizza delivery," she said as she made her way to the kitchen. She stood there in the kitchen drenched from the rain that had started again, holding two boxes of pizza. "Tip please. Let's get this party started," she said as she took off her wet raincoat.

Momma and I could only smile at the presence of our friend as she stood there soaked by the rain. Somehow, she had managed to get the pizza in the house without a trace of rain on them. With Ms. Fable came the good mood. We laughed, we watched movies, we talked, and we cried. At four in the morning, not wanting the fun to stop, I went into Hannah's room and brought out her curling iron, makeup, and nail polish. "Oh girls, look what I have."

As they turned to me, Momma said, "Oh no, you're not putting that devil's paint on me."

"Mommmma," I said, "only for a few minutes; it will wash off."

"Put it on me," Ms. Fable said. "I always wanted a makeover. Probably can't change me much, but it's worth a heck of a try."

Once I did Ms. Fable's hair, nails, and makeup, she looked years younger. I ran into Brandon's room for the digital camera and Hannah's room for her vanity mirror. "Ready?" I said, hiding the mirror behind my back.

"If it won't scare me," Ms. Fable said with a chuckle.

"See what a little makeup can do?" Oh, my stars and garters she said where did I go. This woman is a movie star. She turned her head all around as she looked in the mirror, girl you got skills. I look 20 years younger maybe I can get me a boyfriend now that I don't look like a haint. We all laughed at Ms. Fables words and even though she was making jokes, she actually looked years younger.

Momma must have thought the same thing, because she said, "Okay, Victoria, you can do my hair and just a little makeup; then I am washing it off."

By five thirtyish we were all dressed up with nowhere to go. We posed for pictures, but that was about the extent of our girls' night in. Momma quickly washed off her makeup, and by six o'clock we were ready to bed down. Momma slept in Hannah's room, and Ms. Fable went into Brandon's room. I went to my room. I felt I had pleased my dad, and I'm sure God excused Momma for the few minutes she had on the devil's paint.

After our big girls' night, Ms. Fable and I joined Momma at church every Sunday. I guess she was feeling guilty about putting on the devil's paint, but the sermons were relaxing, and it helped us get through the year. The months were rolling on through, and June was approaching faster than expected. I knew the children wouldn't be home because they were going to go on through the summer months so they could finish their schooling faster. They were both making good grades and I was anxious for them to get started with their careers, so I let them make their own decisions about school.

My time was occupied with talking to Ms. Robertson on the phone and spending free time with Ms. Fable and Momma. I spent some of my time helping out with the church functions, and even though I wanted to see the children, I was satisfied with my time with Momma and Ms. Fable. We made a vow after our big girls' night that we would do the girls' night in thing once a month. Momma made me promise no more devil's paint, yet we took turns at each other's house and whoever's house we ended up at had the plans for the evening. This had proven to be a good year, and James never crossed my mind; I was adjusting to the kids' phone calls only.

One evening I was getting ready to prepare for my girls night in with Momma and Ms. Fable when I got a surprise phone call from Jasmine.

"Hey," she said as I answered the phone. "What are you doing?"

"Nothing much," I responded, "just preparing to go spend the night with my mother and Ms. Fable. We have decided to have another girls' night in. Want to join us?" I asked, wondering why she called. She is probably just missing Brandon, I thought. Then my mind went back to our conversation at Christmas. "Are you ok Jasmine"? I asked, "do you need me"? I just felt the need to make sure she was ok and didn't need a mother figure. The last thing I needed was for something to happen to her that I could have prevented.

"No," she said. "I have made other plans. So are you going to spend the night at Grandma's," she said, referring to my mother's.

"Yes, honey," I said, "but I will be home in the morning or midafternoon. Do you want to come over?"

"Yes," she said, "that is a wonderful idea. I have something for you, and if I feel it can't wait until tomorrow, do you mind if I drop it off at Grandma's house?"

A surprise for me? I thought. How thoughtful. "Sure, honey," I said. That will be fine. I am sure we will probably be reading scriptures all night since this is Momma's house and her turn for the girls' night in, but sure, you are always welcome."

"Okay," she said. "I will probably see you tomorrow, but if not, I might just drop on by."

"That's fine, honey," I said. "Talk to you soon." As I hung up the phone, I thought, That is strange. I knew Jasmine was hard into her studies, like my children, but that was a strange phone call. Not giving it a second thought, I packed my bag, along with my Bible, and headed to Momma's house.

When I got there, Ms. Fable was already there, and Momma had already put in the movie of choice for the night.

"I brought my Bible," I said, letting Momma know that I was prepared.

"Bible?" she asked. "Whatever for?"

"I just thought we would be preaching and shouting for your girls' night in," I said, teasing.

"Lord, Victoria, I can't force the Lord on you. I just got two movies that I thought would be appropriate."

Ms. Fable was in the kitchen popping popcorn, and as I joined her, she gave me the look to let me know she didn't know what to expect either.

"Okay, girls," Momma said. "It's about to start. Hurry up with the popcorn. I don't want you to miss a thing."

We hurried into the living room, where Momma was sitting on the couch. Ms. Fable held the bowl of popcorn in her hand, and the movie started. It was The Book of Ruth.

Close enough to the Bible, I thought, but it was Momma's night, so we sat there and watched, and it was actually an incredibly good movie. It kept our attention, and no one spoke a word until it was over.

"Now then, if you liked that one, you would love this one." By now we were looking forward to the next selection that Momma had in store for us. While she was putting the movie in, there was a knock at her door. "Who on earth could this be?" she said as she went to the door.

"Jasmine," I said. "She said she might stop by this evening."

"Boy, is she in for a surprise," Ms. Fable said. "She won't stay long," she added with a chuckle. I had to laugh at her words because I knew that spending the evening watching Christian movies would not be Jasmine's idea of a fun evening.

"Oh, my Lord," I heard Momma say. "What a surprise!"

First Jasmine walked in, empty-handed. "It couldn't wait," she said as I was wondering what she was referring to.

Within seconds, in walked Brandon, Hannah, and Jerry. With shock on my face, I couldn't move.

"Surprise!" Brandon said as he came over to hug me. Hannah and Jerry followed, and what a surprise it was. "Oh, my Lord," was all I could say.

"Now don't get too excited, Momma. We are only here until Monday."

"Two weeks, two days, what does it matter?" I said. "You are here now," looking over at Jasmine, I said. "Shame on you for not telling me."

"I was sworn to secrecy," she said, smiling at Brandon. Little was it known at that point but, there was surprises for everyone.

As they made it into the living room, Brandon said, "Well, there is a reason for the visit, Momma, and we have to wait just a little bit longer. And just so you know," he whispered in my ear, "the surprise is really on Jasmine, not you."

Moments later, there was another knock on the door, and in walked Jasmines parents. Each came in with a smile on their face. Jasmine was now looking a bit confused as they took their coats off and joined us in the living room.

Brandon turned to Jasmine and said, "I am glad that you were sworn to secrecy, but the surprise isn't for them. It's for you."

"Me?" Jasmine said.

"I knew you were coming, but you didn't know why I was coming." With a look of surprise on Jasmine's face, my son knelt down on one knee and said, "I love you, Jasmine. I have for a few years now. Everybody that means something to me is here right now, and I love you so much that I want you to know in front of everybody that I love, that I love you and I have chosen you to wear this ring and be my wife. I promise you that I will do everything in my power to make you happy. I am sure we will have difficulties, but once you take this ring, you must understand that whatever this marriage holds for us, you will stand behind me because whatever I do, it will be for love of you."

We all looked at Jasmine as she took the ring from Brandon, with tears streaming down her face. What she did next surprised all of us. She knelt down in front of him, barely making out her words, and said, "Never above you, Brandon; never below you. Always beside you, I promise. I have loved you since high school, and no matter what the future holds, I would like nothing more than to go through my future with you by my side. I may not always agree with you, but know that through our disagreements, I will always hold our love true." She removed the promise ring she had on her ring finger and replaced it with the engagement ring. "Yes, Brandon Andrews, I will." She slid the ring on her finger, and then she said, "I will wear this ring proudly."

There wasn't a dry eye in the house. Oh, my Lord, I thought, my son never ceases to amaze me. Looking at Hannah and Jerry, I knew that one day they would feel the same.

Jerry, looking a little nervous, said, "Maybe one day, Hannah, we will feel the same way."

About ten minutes later, there was yet another knock on my mother's door.

"Um," the woman said as I opened the door, "is Jerry here?"

"Why yes," I said. I called into the room, "Jerry, someone is here to see you."

While everyone stood by admiring Jasmine ring, Jerry returned to the room, catching us all by surprise. He said, "Um, everybody, I have a surprise of my own." He then walked over to Hannah and got down on one knee; she shrieked.

"Jerry," she said.

He said as we all looked on, "Hannah, I have only known you for a year, but this has been the happiest I have been in my life. At first, I thought about a promise ring or just a keepsake ring, but as I talked over this special occasion with your brother," he said, looking over at Brandon, "and realizing that twins can only be different for a little while, I decided. I know our careers are in the same field and there are going to be trying times, but I can't think of a single soul that I would rather take my challenges with. You are the stars for me at night, and you are the sun that brightens my day. Though there will be trials in our life, and we haven't had the first argument, I am sure we will disagree; but know that I will only have your best interest in mind. I want to be your eyes, your shoulder, and your ears. I want you to know that whatever comes our way, if there isn't a plan, I will make one before we go through whatever God has in store for us.

"I know you wanted to take it slow, and I have been slow because the very moment I laid eyes on you, I knew in my heart that I wanted you to be my wife. Now I am not asking for a date, but I am asking that you take my ring and promise that one day, when you are ready, you will become my wife. I love you, Hannah, with every fiber in my being, and I can't imagine my life any other way than with you by my side, so here." He handed her the ring, and we all watched in suspense. We knew that Brandon and Jasmine was a given, but we were a little concerned with Hannah.

"Well," she said as she pulled him up to where their eyes were meeting, "Marriage was never in my plans, and when I met you, I just wanted us to be friends. But now," she said, looking over to me and seeing my tearstained face, "I only think of you. I dream about you. I can't wait to be near you. I don't know what my future holds, but whatever God's will, I hope he has included you. Jerry, I don't know when or where, but I do know that I would like nothing more than to be your wife, so my answer is yes."

Tears and hugs followed. The rings were absolutely beautiful, and our big girls' night turned into a family night, and it was a night to remember. No one slept that night. It was the first time that I had met Jerry's parents, and they were amazing people. Jasmine's family was now going to be part of our family, so we spent the rest of the night bonding. What a wonderful surprise, and for an instant, James flashed through my mind. In the early morning hours, everyone left.

Ms. Fable, Momma, and I bedded down. Although there was only happiness left, we wouldn't have had it any other way.

The next morning, I felt I had no time to waste. I got up and left Ms. Fable and Momma having tea at the counter. I had to spend the day with the children. I had to know all the details, and I knew they would be gone soon. Momma and Ms. Fable would have to make up our time later.

I was sure they understood as I said my good-byes. "I will call you later," I said.

Momma spoke up and said, "Don't you want more tea before you leave?"

"I'll grab some at home," I said as I got my coat and headed toward the door.

My mind was racing as I hurried through the streets to my house. My children, I thought, married—how exciting that was. I had known it was only a matter of time for Jasmine and Brandon, but Hannah—oh my God, how great you really are. Happiness was always my desire for my children. Oh, and grandchildren—oh joy, joy, joy. Although I secretly wanted James to be a part of this, I was beside myself with joy for the children.

Daylight had taken its place as I made it home, and Brandon's car was there but not Hannah's. Not wanting to wake them, I still had not a moment to lose. Wondering where Hannah was, I went to Brandon's room. As expected, he was sleeping. I peeked into Hannah's room just hoping she was there, and she was. I decided to make a pot of tea. Sleep wouldn't come, and I wanted to be up when they awakened.

Moments later, as if someone else other than me couldn't sleep, the phone rang. I answered, thinking it was Momma.

"Victoria," the voice that wasn't Momma's, said, "I didn't expect you to answer the phone, but I can't sleep." It was Jasmine's momma. "I am so happy," she said. "I don't know what else to say. Jasmine just now went to bed. Her excitement is overwhelming. She genuinely loves Brandon."

"I know," I said. "He loves her too. I am just waiting for a date. Brandon is sleeping soundly. I guess his weight is lifted from his mind; I know her saying yes meant more to him than anything in this world."

"I want to help with Hannah's wedding too," she said. "What joy this is. I am beside myself."

"Me too," I answered. "I am just waiting for them to wake up so I can get more details. I will call you later, so try and get some rest. I know it won't come easy for me."

"I know," she responded. "I will." With that we hung up.

After the children awakened, I was still beside myself. I knew they could see the joy all over my face.

"Brandon," I asked, not giving him time to grab some juice from the fridge, "have you and Jasmine set a date yet? Are we going to have a double wedding for my twins? Are you going to wait until after you graduate? Tell me something. You can't spring something like that on me and then leave me hanging. We have to prepare."

"We haven't decided on a date yet, Mom. I had to get an answer first. There is a lot to think about and there is a lot of planning, but you, ole girl, will be involved every step of the way." I had to laugh to myself because that is what James used to refer to when he was talking about his grandma and the truth just rehashed, I was indeed now an ole girl.

Then Hannah came into the kitchen. "No questions please, Mom. I am just as surprised as you are. I had no idea marriage was on his mind. I can't believe Brandon knew before I did," she said, looking over at Brandon.

Brandon said, "You should have asked; I probably would have told you."

Unperturbed, Hannah continued, "We probably won't start planning anything until next year. He has to graduate, and I still have a couple more years to go, so right now everything is just floating in the air. Oh, and by the way, Brandon," Hannah said, "my ring is bigger than Jasmines's."

"For now," he just said. "For now."

Floating was the right word. I was if no one else was. Such excitement to hear, such a surprise. The children grabbed a quick bite of breakfast, and they headed out for the day. It's funny, I thought. I have no one to call. Everybody who is in my heart was there. Ms. Robertson, I thought; I will call and give her the wonderful news.

When the phone finally picked up, it was not Ms. Robertson but another woman who answered the phone. "This is the Robertsons' residence," she said.

"Yes, this is Victoria. Is Ms. Robertson around?" I said, feeling a little uneasy about her not answering her own phone.

"She's resting," the lady said. "Shall I take a message."

"Well, is she all, right?" I asked.

"She's fine," the woman said. "She just had a spell, and I am here just to help her out. I am her neighbor from across the street."

"Oh, okay," I said, now feeling a little relieved.

"We just moved here a few months back, and when we were meeting our neighbors, we just sort of took to her."

"I'm glad." That was all I could say. "I am glad she has someone close to her now."

"You did say Victoria, right?" the woman said. "I have heard so much about you and your twins. I look forward to meeting you next time you're down this way."

"Same here, I said. "Well, I didn't really want anything; just checking in," I said, not wanting the news about the children to come from anybody else but me. "Just tell her I called, and I will check back at a later time."

"Will do," the woman said. "Good-bye."

"Good-bye," and I hung up the phone.

I had the rest of the day by myself. I was surprised with the lack of sleep that came the night before, I still didn't feel tired. I decided to go outside and sit under my willow tree. The air was calm, and the children would be with their future mates probably way up into the day. I made a pot of tea, and I sat there with my journal, writing about the girls' night and the proposals.

The children's visit was about a month ago, and the summer was changing over to fall. One Sunday Momma, Ms. Fable, and I went to church. The deacon asked if there were any testimonies before the service began, and Momma stood up.

She said, "I'd like to stand and give honor to my Lord and Savior this morning and thank him for giving me another day. I've been in this church all my adult life, and the Lord continues to bless me. I have a wonderful daughter, good friends, and two beautiful grandchildren. I think sometimes that even though I try to live worthy and serve a gracious God, there is something else on this earth that he wants me to do before he calls me home. So many people take life for granted. Through my years, I have watched a whole lot of blessings come forth, and there is nobody—I mean nobody—who could have done them but God. It amazes me how, knowing the goodness of the Lord, how easy it is to forget him when things are going well, but as soon as things get to going bad, he is the first person we call on. We all need to live our lives like it's our last day, because it very well could be. We should count it a blessing that our Savior is giving us another breath. When we stand before the great throne of judgment, we will stand alone, not with the people whom we have shared our lives with on earth. We will each be held accountable for what we have or have not done. Get ready, church people. If you are not ready, get prepared for the day that the Lord decides to take you up. Say the kind words, give a helping hand, be ready," she said. "That is what I want for my life. I want to be ready, and I one day want to hear my Savior say those words to me, knowing that I have done all that I could have done to be pleasing in his sight. Continue to praise God for the work he has for me to do for the upbuilding of his kingdom." Then she sat down. She grabbed hold of my hand and said, "Get ready, Victoria. God's got a plan. Get ready."

I sat through the sermon trying to understand why after all the years that I had been going to that church, it was today that Momma decided to testify. She was the Sunday school teacher, and she would say her amen, but I had never heard her testify. There were several Sundays that I had missed, so she could have just felt the need to say a few words on the Lord's behalf, and with that all, I could say was amen.

After church, Ms. Fable and I l went to Momma's for Sunday dinner. We talked about the children and the proposals. We talked about the upcoming holidays, and just out of the blue, Momma said, "Ladies, I have decided that I am going to take a road trip."

"Road trip?" I asked. "To where?"

"Oh, not too far," she said. "I have just had some people on my mind, and I want to pay them a visit before the weather breaks. I think I will only be gone for a week or so, but it's something that I feel I need to do."

"We're not invited?" I asked.

"Now, if you come along, I would feel that I wasn't doing it on my own. I haven't traveled since your father passed, so this is something I just want to do."

Understanding, I said, "I take road trips, and you're right. Sometimes you need to do it by yourself. You won't have to rush; you can take your time and enjoy things. Sometimes it's the best thing a person can do. Sort of gives you a new meaning to life sometimes."

"Well, I personally think it's a wonderful idea," Ms. Fable said, "and if you enjoy it, then maybe I will take me one next year."

"Then it's settled," Momma said. "Now don't have too much fun without me. I am thinking about leaving on Tuesday. I should return by Sunday, just in time for Sunday dinner. By the way, whose turn is it to cook?"

"I believe it's my turn," Ms. Fable said. "Now, what shall we have?"

We spent the rest of the evening talking about church and Momma's road trip. We planned our menu for the next Sunday, and before you could say another enjoyable time with the girls, it was time to start the workweek.

Monday, I started my Monday workweek with my children in my heart and my mother on my mind I made it through my first day at work, but I felt something was about to happen good or bad something was in the making. When I got home that evening, I called momma to make sure she was ready for her week of travel. After finding out she was all set to go I then felt the need to pray for ever the reason I felt the need and that is just what I did. Momma was all set to go the children was well in school was it

James that I was praying for I had no idea, but prayer was on my heart, and I pray for all just in case God had something in store for me that I wasn't aware of. After praying I wrote in my journal, and I bedded down only to wake up in the middle of the night with my mother on my mind, but I just said a quick prayer again and then off to sleep I went.

Tuesday morning, I called Momma first thing to wish her well on her road trip.

"I love you, Victoria," she said before we hung up the phone.

"I love you too, Momma," I said. I knew I would worry about Momma traveling the highways alone, but I knew that going away and collecting her thoughts would do her good. Getting ready for work, I had a feeling come over me. I didn't know if it was sadness or joy, so I shook it off because I knew I had to get through this workweek and starting your workweek in a bad mood makes for a long week. I decided I would visit Daddy's grave site after work that evening and tell him about Momma's road trip—as if he didn't already know, but I had to change his flowers so now seemed like the perfect time to do it.

My day went pretty quickly. The sky was a bit cloudy, but I figured if I hurried, I could get the flowers set on Daddy's grave site before the storm came. It called for rain all week, so if I didn't do it now, then I guessed I would have to prolong it another week.

I rushed to the flower shop and grabbed a nice plastic bouquet of flowers to put on his grave for the winter and hurried to his grave site. It was around five o'clock. It had sprinkled all day, and I knew that the storm was coming. As I pulled up to his grave site, I noticed that someone had put fresh flowers down. Momma, I thought. Could she have brought them here on her own? I went over to where my father was lying, and someone had cleaned off his grave site. Momma's flowers were gone, but the card that she had put there, although it had lost its color, was still neatly placed under the rocks. As I knelt down, that same force that took over when I had brought Momma there returned.

"Daddy," I said, "what's wrong?" I just sat there, not being able to move, wondering what he was trying to tell me. "I love you, Daddy," I said. "Can you show me a sign, show me what the heavens have shown you?" It was as though I felt a hand go across my shoulder; it was such a real feeling that I turned to see if someone was there. "Please, God," I said, "allow Daddy to show me a sign, or could you show me a sign on his behalf?"

Sitting there feeling as though I was lost in the wind, I laid his flowers down. As I touched his grave, a warm sensation took hold of my body. It was as if Daddy was touching my hands. "Was Momma here?" I asked Daddy, as if he could hear me. "Was it Momma that brought those fresh flowers?"

Thunder bounced off the walls of the earth, and lightning followed. "So that is what you're trying to tell me. It was Momma who was here." As if that wasn't exactly what he was trying to tell me, the warm sensation suddenly left my body. The rain and wind started, and the thunder and lightning followed. I quickly said good-bye and told him that I would return soon.

I ran to my car. Taking the short way home, I passed by the park, and something caught my eye. lightening must have hit my tree, because some of its limbs were now lying on the ground. The sadness took over again. I had never in the years that had passed known of a time that lightning had struck my tree. I had seen where lightning had struck the surrounding trees, but never my tree. I started to stop and get a closer look, but the wind and rain were so strong that I decided to head home and wait until the next day to find out what damage was done.

As I made it home and put on a pot of tea to warm me, I couldn't shake the sadness. I couldn't get the feeling from the grave site or the tree out of my head. What was Daddy trying to tell me? Did he tell me something that I just didn't understand?

Sleep was not easy that night. I tossed and turned all night long. My tree, I thought, Daddy, the thunder, the lightning. l couldn't shake the feeling. Before I knew it, the sun was out, and I had to get up and start my day.

Taking my shower, I decided to just drink one cup of tea and leave a little early so I could go by the park and see the damage that was done to my tree. As I rode through the streets, I decided that I would wait until sometime the following week to visit Daddy's grave again. I didn't know why I had those feelings, and I didn't want to again experience the uneasy way they made me feel.

As I pulled into the parking lot of the park, I noticed that the only tree that was affected by the storm was my tree. It was like the lightning split it in half. Limbs and brush from my tree were scattered about the ground. The lightning probably killed my tree, I thought as I looked in amazement at the damage that it had done. I went to touch the tree, and a shocking sensation went through my body. Feeling numb for a moment, I was wondering if Daddy was trying to tell me something about this tree. I shook the thought off and tried to get about my day. Three more days, I thought, and then I would be able to concentrate more on my feelings. I had to get to work today and try and get through the next three days.

When Friday came, I welcomed it with gladness. I only had to get through this day, and tomorrow or Sunday, Momma would be home. I could tell her about my experience. She could explain things better, especially if it was a sign from Daddy and God.

Just two more hours, I thought as I looked at the clock.

Ms. Fable came by and asked me if I was okay. "You have been noticeably quiet this week, Victoria. Is something on your mind, or are you just missing your momma?"

"A little of both," I responded, and without saying another word, she went on to doing whatever she had been doing.

Going home from work that day, it was on my heart to go back to that old willow tree. I didn't want to stop going completely, and maybe it was time that I started going back on a regular basis. Maybe I could help bring its life back. I had good memories of that old willow tree, They didn't all come from James either, so if I started going back, I could continue to write and watch the children play like I had so many times before. Watching them play is what gave me pleasure years ago. One day my grandchildren would be tramping on the grass, so I needed to get back in the habit of going there. Maybe Mother Nature felt that since I had my own willow trees, this one was not as important to me anymore. I must prove her wrong, I thought. I decided to stop for a few moments before the storm struck again. Someone had cleaned up the brush and limbs from the previous storm, and now my tree stood there looking broken and lonely.

I sat under the old tree watching the clouds move in and the sun move out. It was around five o'clock when darkness filled the sky, proving that a storm was headed my way. I envisioned Brandon's and Hannah's weddings. It would be beautiful; it would be the most memorial time at this old willow tree. It had to survive if only for that special time. I could also envision my grandkids running through the grass like Brandon and Hannah once had. I had to laugh remembering when the children, barely able to walk, came to the park and played with their daddy. Those were good times, and even though James was gone, I would keep those memories close to my heart.

As the wind started to bring forth its introduction of the storm, I made my way to my car, wanting to get home before the storm settled in. I pulled up in my driveway with sadness in my heart, a feeling I couldn't shake. The rain was pouring down hard, piercing my thin jacket with cold drops of wetness; and as thunderbolts danced across the sky, I made my way into the house. Feeling a sense of loneliness, I could clearly hear Ms. Robertson say, "A change is going to come." With her words playing in my head, I decided to spend my evening with the usual pot of tea and a good movie.

The tea would relax me, and the movie would take my mind off of my worries. I would choose a comedy versus the same ole love stories. Love stories always sent my heart into turmoil. I got my bath, put on my favorite pajamas, boiled my tea, and settled in for the night.

I was taken away from my movie with a pounding on the door. It was around nine thirty at night, the rain steadily pouring down. As I rushed to the door to see what all the noise was about, my heart skipped several beats as I saw Ms. Fable standing there, coat drenched from the downpour.

"Victoria," she said, almost screaming with fear in her voice, "I have been trying to reach you."

"Is something wrong?" I asked, not really wanting to know the answer.

"Your phone must be down. The hospital called. They have been trying to reach you for over an hour. It's your mother," she said before I could even absorb the word "hospital." "There has been a terrible car accident. We must get to the hospital right away."

I tried to call the children, but I got no answer.

As we raced through the darkened streets, my only thoughts came in the form of prayer. "Please, Momma, be all right. Daddy, please don't let this be what you were trying to tell me. Lord, please watch over my momma. Please, Lord, spare me. I can't bear any more pain and sorrow. Please, Lord, step in and change the change that you are presenting to me. I don't want to deal with any more hurt, any more pain." Tears formed in my eyes to the point that I could barely see the roads as Ms. Fable drove through the semi-busy streets in route to the hospital. "Hold on," I said to my mother. "Please, God, step in and take it all away."

As Ms. Fable pulled into the parking lot of the hospital, an uneasy feeling came over me to the point that I felt weak and nauseated. I tried one more time to call the children, with no answer. As we ran into the ER, Ms. Fable led me to the woman at the window of registration. "This is Victoria Andrews," she said. "We are here to see Ms. Adams."

The woman at the desk said, "She is in room 1022. Once you reach her room, the nurses' station is right outside her door. They will be able to help you."

Ms. Fable guided my numb body to the elevator, and before I could realize what floor we were on, the doors flew open, and we were headed to Mother's room.

As we approached the door to the room, we saw a nurse standing inside with her clipboard. When she saw us, she hurried out of the room. "Can I help you?" she asked.

"Yes." Ms. Fable said. "This is Victoria, and that is her mother in that room. How is she?"

"Well, she's stable at the moment, but it's not looking too good. There is internal bleeding and head trauma. Several broken bones, including her ribs."

My mind got to swirling around, and dizziness filled my body as she spoke the words. I tried to focus on what she was saying, but the words "not looking too good" kept rewinding and playing back inside my head. The thought of losing my momma was more than I could bear.

As I tried to focus in, I heard the nurse say something about signing for her to have more surgery. "We are waiting for some tests to get back, and the surgeon to arrive before we continue. Mrs. Andrews," the nurse said, bringing the reality of all this back in, "is your mother on any medications?"

Trying to think, I said, "Yes. Blood pressure medication and medication to regulate her sugar."

"Is that all of her medication?" she asked.

"Yes, that is all," I responded, looking into my mother's still room, hoping for some reaction.

"She is medicated," the nurse said, "but she can hear you. You may go in, but I must warn you: you need to be prepared for what you are about to see. There is a lot of bruising and discoloration to her skin, and she is hooked to a ventilator to help with her breathing. We should have the tests back and the surgeon should be here soon."

"We've got to get in touch with the children," I told Ms. Fable. "They need to be here."

"I will give the numbers to the nurse. She can try calling them," Ms. Fable said as she left my side.

I just stood at the door to Mother's room, not wanting to see her in the condition that the nurse had described. In a matter of seconds, Ms. Fable joined me. I felt her hands on my waist as if to guide me. As we entered the room and I saw Momma lying there as if lifeless, it took my breath away.

I made my way to her bed and said, "Mother, I am here. Hold on. We are trying to get the kids here too. I love you, Momma," I said, tears streaming down my cheeks. I felt her give my hand a squeeze, as if she heard the words that I was speaking. As I sat there holding her hand, I could hear the beeps of the heart monitor counting the beats of her heart. I said, "Pray, Momma. Tell God to help you get through this."

I was thinking this is not the way things should be. I shouldn't be here sitting by this bed holding my mother's hand, praying for the best, fearing the worst. She lay there, a sixty-seven-year-old woman, her body weak from the trauma she had experienced. I didn't know how the accident happened. I must have tuned that part out when the nurse was speaking. That didn't seem that important at the moment. The fact was she was here fighting for her life, and it seemed so unfair. She didn't even look like my mother, but a frail, weak woman. The machines and the wires that surrounded her body only made her appearance worse.

The nurse came back into the room with the news that she had reached Hannah and she was on her way, but she couldn't get hold of Brandon. Just knowing that Hannah was on her way gave me a wave of comfort. I knew she would get hold of Brandon, and then we could all go through this together.

Later the nurse returned. This time she held a consent form. "Mrs. Andrews, we need for you to sign this, giving the surgeon consent to do the surgery. They are going to go in and try to stop the bleeding before it gets worse."

I didn't want them cutting on my mother at her age, but I knew I had no choice at this point. I gave them the go-ahead to do whatever was necessary to save my mother. I couldn't lose her. I wasn't ready. I didn't think I would ever be ready.

"How long before they start the surgery?" I asked, wanting them to hurry. I knew time was of the essence.

"They are getting prepared to take her down now," she said.

Moments passed, and they arrived to take Momma down for her surgery. I gave her a kiss on her forehead and told her that I loved her, and they wheeled her out. Ms. Fable and I went into the waiting room to wait for the results, and while we were sitting there in silence, Hannah arrived, her eyes swollen from crying.

"What happened?" she asked while she stood there, her arms around my waist.

It was Ms. Fable who gave the saga of events that had brought Mother to the hospital. Even though I knew the nurse had given us the information, I sat there hearing the words for the first time. There had been an accident.

She was at a red light. As your grandmother was about to turn on her street, a carful of college kids ran the light. They had been drinking, and the driver of the car being inexperienced, no doubt, lost control of the vehicle and hit Momma head-on. They say Momma tried to move out of the way, but the car came with such a force that it wasn't any use. I thought to myself, she was on her way back home from her road trip. Three of the four children had died, and now we were waiting on the fate of Mother.

Brandon showed up shortly after Hannah; Jasmine came with him. We all sat there in a numb state. Silence filled the air as we sat waiting. Even though I knew he was hurting, he didn't cry as much as the rest of us. I knew he was trying to be the stronghold that we so desperately needed at that time.

Hours went by, and it was hard waiting for the doctor to come out. It felt like we had been there for days when he finally came around the corner.

"Mrs. Andrews," he said as he walked up to us, "I can't tell you how sorry I am." Those words that you knew were coming but were never prepared to hear. "We did all we could do to save your momma, but she had lost too much blood before and during the operation. We couldn't stop the internal bleeding, so we didn't make any progress …"

His voice trailed off, and it was replaced with crying, pain-stricken crying.

"No, no, no, no, no," I heard Brandon yell. He gripped his head and walked away, with Jasmine close behind.

I was grabbed up by my own pain after that, and nobody else's pain seemed to register. I felt that something was draining the life out of me. I felt something grip my heart and secretly stole my breath. The thought of not hearing my momma's words, not having her there for her advice was unthinkable. Me leaving her in that hospital, never hearing her laugh or her voice for that matter, was unheard of, unthought of.

"Victoria," Ms. Fable said, "would you like to go see her before we leave? I will help you through this." She was a good friend, but right now I wanted my momma. I wanted to go somewhere and sleep. I knew she meant well, but she had no idea what I was feeling. I didn't want her to comfort me; I wanted my momma.

I couldn't be mad at her. She wasn't the one that took my momma's life from me. She was only there trying to help, but I still didn't want her to comfort me. I didn't want to be around even the children. I wanted to be alone. I wanted to understand what had happened. I wanted to know what I had done this time to anger God. I wanted my momma back.

The days that followed were hard. Eating and sleeping weren't part of my life's agenda. I felt as though I had lost my will to live. My thoughts were not of the children; there were times that I didn't even realize they were there. I didn't want to talk; I only wanted to think of the memories that I had with my mother and try to prepare myself for the future without her. I wanted to stay in bed and forget this whole situation had ever occurred.

There were times that my anger would rise up against God, wanting him to make haste to give me the explanation as to why he felt the need to take my mother from me. If there was a good reason, I felt he could have shared it with me so that I could understand why this was happening. I wanted to know if he was just that busy that he didn't feel the need to tell me why. Then my mother's words would flash in my head: "What God does, Victoria, is not always meant for us to understand, but he is perfect in every way. He makes no mistakes."

"Well," I thought, saying it aloud, "he got it wrong this time. You were not supposed to leave me, Momma, not now."

While lying in bed, I felt the need to cover my face with the pillow and scream as loud as I could, not so the children would hear me (for I knew they were in their own little world), but just hoping I would burst my lungs and my last breath would be taken from me. I knew the children were hurting and I couldn't comfort them. I couldn't do anything. It took everything in me to breathe, let alone supply the comfort that they needed.

Ms. Fable helped me make the arrangements. More money had been placed in the mailbox; it had to have been sometime in the early morning hours. It came in the form of hundreds and fifties, and I was glad it did.

Hannah brought the package in to me, and she said, trying to force a smile, "Momma, God has supplied again. Now I may be wrong, Momma, but I don't think Ms. Fable is the one who has been giving us the money. It's funny how just when we have needed it, every time it has come. Just in time. I know she is our friend, family even, but I think this money is coming from a church. You have been going regularly, and Grandma was a favorite there. I just don't think, even though she might want to, but I just don't think it's coming from Ms. Fable."

Hannah brought up a good point, and she was probably right. It may have been the church. I knew with each situation we had faced, Momma would put us on the prayer list, and I also knew that when the church did for one of its members, it was an unspeakable act, so she was probably right. I knew that they loved Momma and they would want the homecoming of one of their own to be as perfect as possible, so Hannah's assumption was likely. Besides, I was a member too, and for years Momma and now I had paid our tithes, so maybe this was their way of giving us blessings. Just for a moment, I thought our church focused on needs, not wants, and through the years, the money had come when we wanted something, not necessarily needed something. Neither here nor there, it didn't matter how, who, or when. I was only glad that I could give Momma the burial that she deserved.

Ms. Fable confirmed my thoughts by saying it was just enough to give my momma a proper burial, and that was just what I did.

Life had been taken from my momma. I knew she was with my daddy, and she was pleased. I still wanted her here. The children and I went to pick out the casket, and I gave Momma the flowers that I knew were her favorites: lilies. I added an array of white roses because I knew now in God's eyes, she was pure.

The newspaper seemed magnified today because Momma's obituary was there in black and white. I was taken back to the time that James and I had to prepare Mrs. Andrews's obituary, but Momma's was much longer; I had a lot to say.

The funeral would be in two days, and I had to prepare myself. How could I prepare myself to say good-bye to the person who gave me life? How could I stand there and watch them close her up, later putting her in a cold and dry, dark place? How could I get back the time that I didn't spend with her? How could I move forward, knowing her life was over? Why had God allowed such pain to be cast over my family yet again?

Sleep didn't come easy for me. Now I knew how James must have felt when he lost Mrs. Andrews. I hurt badly for Daddy, but this was a different kind of hurt. It was a hurt that James must have felt, knowing that the last person on earth who genuinely loved him was gone. It could have been different if Momma had died before Daddy, but now this was my feelings, my thoughts.

This time when we gathered together as a family, everyone was called to join but Momma. We would be going to see her for the last time. Somehow that seemed like a bad dream. Every time we came together, she would be the first one I called. I found myself picking up the phone to call her to let her know that we would be meeting this afternoon.

Tears formed all over again once I realized that she wouldn't be joining us, because we would be going to see her. The children kept to themselves. I didn't know if they felt they would upset me, or if they were just in the first stages of their own grieving process.

Ms. Fable came by early; I wasn't even ready to go. I didn't think I would ever be ready to go.

"Victoria," she said in a soft voice as she came into my room, "everyone is waiting. You must get ready to go." I knew she knew I didn't want to go, but somehow, I had to find the strength to do this.

I wanted to be strong for the children, but how was that possible? My first thought was to pray, but to whom? I thought angrily. Should I pray to God, a God that continually punished me even though I had tried hard to please him? Would he next take my children, leaving me to face this world alone, making me live way beyond my years? Should I pray to a God that had seen each of my troubles before they came and didn't feel the need to prepare me? Pray to whom? What else was there to say?

I stumbled around going through motions, trying to get myself together long enough to make sure that my momma looked as good as she possibly could for her grand finale—even though I felt there was nothing grand about it. Even though I was now a God-fearing woman, and I knew that God had carried me up until this point, anger took over my sadness, and I allowed the devil to come into my heart. I felt anger toward God. I felt that he did leave me and forsake me. I felt that he had handed me the cross yet once again to pick it up and carry it. I just didn't feel I had the strength or energy to fulfill his request.

As I sat on my bed, I couldn't shake the anger of losing my momma. Feeling selfish, I thought, Why not Ms. Robertson instead? She said she was ready to go. I knew Momma was ready also; I just wasn't ready to let her go. With a surge of anger and confusion, I found myself kneeling beside my bed. God had to give me some type of understanding as to why this had to happen.

"I need strength," I said, starting my prayer. "I need some kind of divine power to help me get through this. Although my heart is angry, I need some type of help from you. You know my life's story; you know my heart. Tell me what my purpose is. My marriage has failed; you took my daddy; my children are now grown; and now you have taken my momma. What else is there? I feel like I have had struggles the biggest part of my life, so tell me," I said, fists clutched together, tears streaming down my face, "what is my purpose? I have no fight left in me. If there is a purpose for me to continue living, you have to make haste and show me. I can't do this on my own, and I can't continue to live without a meaning. Please, I beg of you, please raise up your wrath that has fallen on my life and find me worthy enough to at least spend the rest of my days on earth with some type of happiness. Carry me through this era of pain. I need some type of understanding, please. Please."

Hannah interrupted my prayer with a knock on my door. "Momma," she said as she opened my door, barely giving me time to scramble to my feet, "I'm sorry, she said. "I didn't know that you were praying."

Feeling a little disoriented, I regained my focus on her words and said, "That's okay, honey. I was done anyway."

"Are you ready?" she asked, concern in her voice.

"As ready as God will allow me to be," I replied, wiping the tears that were slowly trickling down my cheeks.

Reaching over to give me a hug, she said, "God heard your prayer. It's going to be okay, Momma."

I didn't reply because I was thinking on her words. I just nodded my head. I needed God to hear my prayer, because if he didn't, I wouldn't make it.

It would be hard, but all I could hope for was for God to somehow let down his grudge against me long enough to give me the strength to get through this.

Ms. Fable drove me and the children to the funeral home. At times she would pull a tissue from her pocket and dab at her eyes, careful not to let me see her crying. She loved Momma too, and this was hard for everyone. How selfish I was to think that right now it was all about my hurt and pain, when everyone was hurting!

Arriving at the funeral home, I could feel rocks in the pit of my stomach. The funeral home was a dark place, a lonely place. I felt we were being watched as we entered that lonely place, but I shook off that thought because there wasn't any need to focus on anything but Momma and the children. Approaching her casket, tears came back, and the pit in my stomach rose to my heart. We were all holding each other at this point. She was beautiful; she looked so peaceful, as if she was resting. I rubbed her face, thinking how lonely I would be without her. I tried to stop the tears, but I couldn't. They were coming, and nothing was going to stop them.

We stood there for at least an hour before the director came to seek our approval. Ms. Fable did all the talking. Hannah just said, "She's beautiful, Momma." I knew in my heart that Momma was where she wanted to be, and that was with Daddy. That was with the Lord. I knew that she expected me to be the strong woman that she thought I was, but my strength was now gone. Like my momma's life.

The director told us if there was anything else he could do, to let him know. Then he left us to our grieving.

I believe Ms. Fable would have let me stay the night if I chose to, but I knew we had to leave. The next day would be the worst day, and we all had to try and get some rest. The children would talk at the funeral, and it would be a sad day. Strength was all I was looking for from God at this point.

We turned to walk toward the door. I saw the director standing as if he was blocking the opening. We moved closer to the door, and it was the children who made me realize that it wasn't the director at all. Brandon stood there as if he had seen a ghost. Hannah lit up as if she was seeing life for the first time. Ms. Fable just stopped and shook her head. Looking at their reactions put more fear and confusion in my heart. As I looked to see what had startled them, I too had to stop, not being able to move. In the doorway of the funeral home stood their father. There, with his own tears, stood James.

There are two sides to every story. You just heard from Victoria. You had the opportunity to step in her life and experience her pain first-hand. Now there is James stay tuned he wants to give his accounts on where and why he allowed for her struggles. Never judge anyone or anything based on one side. We have to have an open mind when our friends and family share their struggles. A lot of times we in the physical form tend to side with whose closer to us, not knowing the whole story. Before you judge James, I want you to step into his life and feel his struggles then you can decide. Stay blessed and Prayed up and as always find the strength to PERSEVERE.

Printed by Libri Plureos GmbH in Hamburg, Germany